I0675460

LOGAN

Innerworld Affairs Series

Book Five

Marilyn Campbell

Cover and Book design by eBook Prep
www.ebookprep.com

September, 2014
ISBN: 978-1-61417-657-2

ePublishing Works!
www.epublishingworks.com

CHAPTER 1

Earth, 2058 A.D.

Ex-Sergeant Logan McKay used the toe of his right combat boot to lift the weight of the iron shackle off his left ankle. A few minutes later he reversed the procedure. It was tedious, but effectively kept the blood circulating through his icy feet. Knowing that once the aircraft reached its assigned flying altitude the cabin temperature would be more comfortably regulated also helped. He only had to be patient, but after months of being half-frozen on the Manchurian border, the anticipation of warmth seeping into his bones was more enticing than a good meal.

Warmth was definitely the first thing he could appreciate about his current state. A sound sleep would come second—the kind of sleep that can't be had in a war zone where bombs interrupted any moment of silence and the enemy could be ten feet away, just waiting for you to doze off so he can slit your throat.

After he was warm and rested, he might even give some thought to the shackles on his ankles, the handcuffs on his wrists and the sentence he'd been given of life imprisonment at Leavenworth. But at least for the next nine hours, while he was in the air over the Pacific Ocean, his dismal future was on hold.

Logan's eyes drifted shut in spite of his numb fingers and toes, but before he could enjoy the peace, a voice came over the loudspeaker.

"Good morning. This is your pilot, Lieutenant Nathan Boswell. We've been cleared for take-off. Make sure all seatbelts are fastened and loose items stowed away. There's an ugly storm hovering out there, so we're going to be taking the scenic route today. If there are any tourists on board who want to follow our progress, we'll be heading south off Hokkaido, past what used to be Tokyo, toward Iwo Jima, then east to San Francisco. We don't expect the detour to add more than an hour to our arrival time but we'll keep you posted."

As the aircraft began taxiing down the runway, the military police officer sitting in the aisle seat next to Logan uttered an obscenity. Intent on sleeping, Logan pretended not to hear his armed escort but the MP sitting in the opposite aisle seat couldn't ignore it as easily.

"What's the problem now, Higgs?" Corporal Gianni asked. "Forget to say goodbye to one of your sweetie-pies?"

"Didn't you hear what he just said?" Higgs asked then went on before his superior officer made any comment. "A southern heading takes us right into the Dragon's Triangle. We'd be better off flying directly over China."

"For God's sake! You and your stupid superstitions again. Throw some salt over your shoulder or whatever you normally do and grab some sleep like McKay's doing."

Higgs's voice raised a pitch. "Sleep? I'd just as soon

spend my last hour awake. And this is not superstition! I read a book about it. Hundreds of planes and ships and thousands of people have disappeared in the area between the Philippine Sea and the Pacific Ocean. It's like a triangle that runs from Yokohama to Guam to the Mariana Islands and back to Japan."

Gianni laughed. "You've got your triangles confused, kid. The *Bermuda* Triangle is where vessels supposedly disappear, and it's clear on the other side of the world."

"Oh yeah? What would you say if I told you the Dragon's Triangle is on the *exact* other side of the world and that there's a magnetic field that runs straight through the planet from one triangle to the other?"

"I'd say you spend too much time reading fiction. If you aren't going to sleep, make yourself useful. Go find out if they put coffee on board."

Logan heard Higgs huff then unfasten his seat belt. He hoped the kid wasn't the kind that had to hear himself talking all the time but he had a sinking feeling he was. As the plane leveled out and he felt the first waft of heat, he decided he could even put up with a nutcase like Higgs if his toes got thawed out in the meantime.

Suddenly he heard a woman's voice out of a dream, yet he knew he wasn't sleeping.

"Corporal Gianni? I'm Captain Yan. Private Higgs said you asked about coffee. There are meals and beverages on board, but I don't think self-service is a good idea with the possibility of turbulence from the storm. Since your prisoners aren't going anywhere and my nurses are busy with patients, I would like to enlist the private's help."

"Sure. In fact, if you could keep him busy for about

nine or ten hours, I'd appreciate it."

Logan raised one eyelid a fraction of an inch to see just how accurate his memory was. *Bullseye.* The voice did indeed belong to the Captain Yan who occasionally crept into his dreams despite his wish to forget she existed. She looked exactly the way he remembered—exotic, secretive...*untouchable.* Her body was compact and toned yet clearly female. Her very straight, nearly black hair was tied at the base of her neck and her thick bangs framed her slightly slanted dark eyes...exactly as he remembered.

But it was her voice rather than her appearance that first bewitched him. It was unlike any voice he had heard before or since. Somehow she made the most ordinary statement sound like a lover's whisper— husky and intimate, as if she were physically stroking him with her words.

Eight months ago, he had been wounded during a shelling and, although it wasn't anything to be sent home over, he had spent four weeks in a mobile hospital unit. It was her voice that had made him want to return from the concussion-induced darkness he was hovering in. When he finally opened his eyes, the dark angel watching over him made him wonder if he'd been sent to heaven or hell.

Her eyes had been filled with compassion, tenderness and sincere concern. They flashed images in his mind of a loving wife, a cozy home and children. Since he knew none of those things were for the likes of him, he'd come to the conclusion that she was merely a hallucination.

He told himself that her being on the same flight back to the States was pure coincidence. She would never remember him out of all the wounded men she'd cared for in the past years. All he had to do was ignore her existence for a few more hours then they'd be going their separate ways—her to the safe and simple life she'd enjoyed before the war, him to a men-only prison cell.

Tarla Yan took one more glance at the sleeping prisoner then led Private Higgs to the galley. She had considered passing out the food and beverages herself just to keep occupied...until she saw *him*. His presence, with or without shackles, was enough to convince her to stay in the front of the plane with the patients and nurses. Not that he'd remember her, but she certainly remembered him and knew enough to steer clear.

How could she not remember Sergeant Logan McKay? She remembered all the men who had hurt or disappointed her. He was merely the most recent.

Though the manifest for this flight showed only names and ranks, she was aware of a little more than that. Of the one hundred seventeen on board, three were crew, forty-five were critically wounded—mostly burn victims—with seven nurses to care for them, and thirty-one others were healthy male and female soldiers whose stints were up.

One of those was her friend, Robin Pascal, a tall green-eyed redhead with a body that attracted every man within a mile, but a sharp wit that kept them at arm's length...unless *she* chose to let them come near. Though their military assignments differed drastically—Robin's specialty was aircraft mech and tech—she and Tarla had enlisted at the same time and survived boot camp together. Now, three years later, treaties and agreements had finally been signed and they were headed home together.

The rest of the passengers—two military police and their twenty-nine convicts—were corralled in the rear of the plane.

When she'd heard the make-up of the passengers, she should have realized there was a possibility of Logan McKay being one of the prisoners. After all, everyone had been talking about his court martial for weeks.

The sight of the shackles and armed escorts relieved her mind somewhat about spending a day in close proximity with that many criminals. From what she'd been able to learn, they were guilty of such charges as embezzling, assault and battery, rape and smuggling.

Logan McKay had the dubious distinction of having single-handedly committed an entire list of crimes including operating a drug ring, consorting with the enemy and killing his captain.

How could she have been so wrong about him?

She recalled the first time she'd seen him being brought in on a stretcher. She had guessed he was well past forty, twice the age of most of the wounded she had attended. Also, his dark hair was barely trimmed around the ears and neck and left even longer on top instead of shaved off as most of the younger soldiers kept theirs.

The next thing she'd noticed were the scars—a wide one over his left brow that his hair probably covered most of the time, a straight, thin one on his jawbone which was almost hidden by the dark shadow of new beard growth, and several circular ones along his right shoulder and arm that she recognized as wounds caused by an automatic weapon. Now he would have another, much larger scar on the outside of his right thigh. When she learned he was only thirty-four, she'd deduced he was a career soldier or had had one hell of a tough life.

Even unconscious, he had looked hard, not just the body, which was formidable, but the man himself.

She had been checking on him when he first came

to and what she'd seen in his eyes had totally belied his appearance. He had looked up at her with such open adoration and need, she'd been about to tell him that whatever he needed she'd be there for him, when he laughed. Grinning from ear to ear, his rugged face looked boyish and quite handsome as he enjoyed some private joke then nodded off again.

During her time on the front, she'd encountered plenty of soldiers with tough-guy exteriors and baby-soft centers. Usually it only took her a day or two to peel the crust away. Logan McKay, however, wasn't like those men at all.

His initial reactions to her *had* been baby-soft and he had seemed instantly enamored with her. Though other patients had developed temporary crushes while in her care, she had the feeling there was something different about Logan, something very special, and that there might be a chance for a true affection to develop between them. Her usually trustworthy intuition had assured her it would be safe to open her heart to him.

Circumstances prevented him from wining and dining her, but their time together had felt like a courtship nonetheless. Whenever he was awake during the first few days after surgery, she sat by his side and held his hand. They talked or she read to him, and by the end of the second week, they shared their first kiss. It was innocent and tender but held a promise of passion in the future.

Then he said the three words that let her know what a mistake she'd made. "I love you," he told her, much too soon to really mean it. True, it sounded more sincere coming from him than the hundreds of other patients who had said the same words to her, but she reasoned that was only because he was more mature.

Unfortunately, she had already let herself hope,

desperately wanting to believe what he felt for her went deeper than the usual patient/nurse gratitude. So when she gave him her standard reply to professions of love from patients, she held onto the hope that his feelings for her would last beyond his release from the hospital.

Thus, it had hurt that much worse when his infatuation wore off so easily. Overnight his demeanor went from welcoming to totally closed off. The more effort she made to comfort him, the nastier he acted and the more lewd his comments became. He never gave an inch throughout the remaining time he was in the hospital, nor did he give an explanation for his change of heart other than "he had finally sobered up."

It was only recently, when she heard about the crimes he'd committed, that she understood that the gentle man she had fallen for had existed only because of the drugs that had temporarily altered his personality. He had never been the usual tough-guy with a soft center for her to uncover. The truth was, he was hard through and through...and she'd been a fool to believe otherwise.

Fortunately, she had discovered his truth before she told him *her secret*. Despite the friendships that had developed between her and some of the others on board, none of them knew the truth of who she really was, where she had come from or the fact that she had a completely separate, covert life.

Logan's toes were finally warm. Higgs was being kept occupied. His seat was a damn sight more comfortable than the ground or the cot in the brig. All conditions were perfect for him to catch some z's. Instead he was wrestling with old memories.

Why couldn't he let it go? Eight months had passed,

most of which he'd spent in one nightmare after another, and still he was more haunted by images of Tarla Yan than anything else he'd run up against.

When he was being honest with himself however, he admitted that he didn't always resent the memories. In the last few months, whenever things got too tense and he thought he couldn't take another minute of the insanity around him, she would slip into his mind, and he would embrace her. Eventually, fantasies about her became his mental lifeline, though he never completely forgot that they *were* only fantasies. In reality, he knew he and Tarla Yan had always been, and always would be, of different worlds.

The plane took a sudden dip that almost made Tarla lose her balance. Private Higgs wasn't so surefooted. He and two cups of coffee landed in one poor soldier's lap.

"Sorry about that," the pilot said over the loudspeaker. "We've found the edge of that storm we heard about, so I'd recommend you stay belted in until we can get clear of it."

As Tarla and Higgs returned to their seats, the powerful air turbulence had the aircraft vibrating like an old washing machine with a lopsided load. Tarla frowned at the dark clouds churning outside the window next to her and prayed that the "edge" the pilot mentioned would be behind them soon. She'd never cared for air travel but what was going on outside was as foreign and frightening to her as the first time she heard bombs exploding outside the field hospital.

A moan of pain distracted her from her fears and she quickly sought the source. The sound had come from one of the young men who'd suffered severe chemical burns over most of his body. He would have massive scarring, but it was a miracle he had survived at all. He was heavily drugged and special padded straps had been used to hold him immobile on the stretcher which was bolted to the floor, but the turbulence was so strong, his body was still being shifted just enough to cause him excruciating pain.

Tarla unbuckled her belt and staggered to the injured soldier. Sitting on the floor next to him, she held onto the side of the stretcher and leaned close to his ear. "Willie? It's Tarla. I know it hurts, hon, but it will only be for a few minutes, and I'm going to stay right here with you the whole time. Okay?" She paused to softly touch his bandaged hand and his body seemed to relax ever so slightly.

"Did I ever tell you about the time my friend, Connie—you remember my talking about her, don't you? She was the one who always got me in trouble—well, anyway, she accepted a dare from these other girls for us to spend a whole night in a cemetery."

A streak of lightning flashed outside, instantly followed by an explosion of thunder that rocked the plane for several seconds. Tarla pressed her hand against her chest as if that might slow down her stampeding heartbeat.

It took no more than a slight head nod at one of her nurses to remind them of their duty. If there was one thing they had all learned on the battlefield, the comfort of the patients came before their own needs or fears. Tarla took a deep breath and forced herself to keep talking to Willie. She wasn't sure which one of them needed her fabricated story more, but it didn't matter.

A second explosion of light and sound seemed greater than the first and this time, the plane made another sudden drop in altitude as well. Voices raised throughout the cabin, some with worry, others in anger over the crew's ineptitude. She heard one man question why the pilot wasn't taking them above the storm if he couldn't get around it and she began wondering the same thing.

"I have to go check on something, Willie. I'll be right back, so don't you go wandering off anywhere."

Struggling against the vibrating and pitching of the plane, she made her way to the cockpit and yanked open the door. The frantic dialogue of the crew and the way the pilot was straining at the control wheel increased her anxiety. Pulling the door closed and bracing herself against its frame, she tried to guess what was going on without disturbing anyone.

The sky before them appeared to be an ocean of rolling, pewter-colored clouds, sporadically illuminated by jagged streaks of light. The continuous rumble of thunder no longer seemed to have a beginning or end.

"Can't you take us above this?" Tarla shouted.

Without turning around to her, the pilot yelled back. "What the hell do you think we're trying to do? Just get back there and buckle yourself in! Damn!" He pounded his fist against the altimeter.

Tarla's gaze fell to the control panel and she saw the reason the pilot was swearing. Some of the indicator hands were spinning madly while other controls seemed to have stopped functioning completely. What in God's name was happening?

She was about to obey the pilot's order when the thunderous rumble around them rose to a deafening roar and the vibration became so violent, she was positive the plane would be pulled apart any moment. Sheer terror now kept her standing there, clinging to the back of the navigator's seat.

All of a sudden the clouds began to part and roll to the sides as if an unseen hand was opening a pathway for the plane. There was light beyond the clouds and, the wider the gap grew, the brighter the light became, until there was a hole in the sky big enough for the aircraft to fly through, but the light was nearly blinding in intensity.

As if someone flipped a switch, the vibrating abruptly stopped and the plane picked up speed with a tremendous jerk.

"Full flaps!" The pilot shouted. "Reduce power! We've got to slow this mother down."

Nothing the crew did seemed to make any difference. Tarla found herself pinned against the cockpit door and comprehended that the increased gravitational pull meant they were going faster and faster toward the light.

She watched the navigator fight the g-force to bring his hand up to his forehead then make the sign of the cross. A hundred different thoughts tried to form at once in her mind but only one was coherent.

After surviving the third world war, they were all going to die anyway.

CHAPTER 2

Innerworld, Planet Terra (Earth)

"Governor Romulus here." It felt like he'd been waiting for this call from Outerworld Monitor Control for days instead of hours.

"The team has completed all scans. There is not a single trace of evidence remaining. The aircraft and all its passengers were being tracked one second and gone the next. It definitely was not a result of the conflict. No country involved has the technology to accomplish such a total erasure."

"Were the coordinates confirmed?"

"Yes, sir. Directly above our tunnel off the coast of China but nothing took place on our end to cause it."

Twelve powerful magnetic fields had been used to create tunnels in and out of Innerworld, the Noronian colony in the center of Terra. Occasionally an Outerworld vessel was in the path when the doorway opened, but apparently that had not been the case this time.

"I was able to find a few vague historical references suggesting that other, much smaller craft may have mysteriously disappeared from that precise spot in the past, but there is nothing in our records to support those assumptions."

"And the passenger list?"

The OMC agent cleared his throat. "I am sorry, sir. It's been verified. One of the passengers was an Innerworld emissary. Tarla Yan was on board when the aircraft vanished."

"Oh Rom, I am so sorry."

Rom felt Aster's empathy as clearly as he heard his mate's words in his mind.

Aloud, Aster said, "She may be perfectly fine somewhere, just like I was when I went for a cruise off the Bahamas and ended up here."

By remembering that long ago day, he was able to force a half-smile. When the yacht she'd been on was accidentally pulled into Innerworld, he had already known something major was about to change in his life. He just hadn't realized *how* major it was going to be.

At that time, he had been a provincial chief administrator and Tarla had been his assistant and very close friend. She'd been exceptionally efficient and supportive but it was always obvious that administration wasn't giving her any sense of fulfillment. After he and Aster were formally joined and became the Co-Governors of Innerworld, Tarla had tried a committed relationship with one of the other transplanted Terrans, even moving out to a mining camp with him for a while, but that hadn't lasted either.

Tarla was one of the few people Rom had ever met who envied the Outerworld Terrans and the unstable, chaotic lives they led. She'd always wanted *less* control rather than more. With his endorsement and considerable training, she became an Outerworld emissary, living a "normal" Terran life as an emergency room nurse while secretly being an observer for Innerworld.

That was over two decades ago. At first, she'd made a point of paying him a visit whenever she returned to Innerworld but he now realized it had been at least three years since she'd been back.

When the current Outerworld war broke out, Tarla hadn't hesitated to accept the more dangerous assignment of observing the action from a front-line position since her cover as a trauma nurse more than qualified her to do so.

Many Outerworlders held the belief that the war could have been prevented, but after millennia of observing Terrans, politically-minded Noronians, like Romulus, knew there was nothing anyone could have done. By 2050, people of Asia and Eastern Europe were in dire economic straits and ripe for a takeover by a hungry, overcrowded country. China made its move so unexpectedly, it was weeks before the rest of the world realized that the sleeping dragon had truly awakened and no country on the planet could feel safe from its voracious appetite. While the United States government discussed whether to reinstate the draft, China simultaneously invaded Japan and Germany and there was no longer a question of non-involvement of any Outerworld country.

After three years of wasted lives and massive devastation, the dragon was somewhat caged but still very dangerous. Months of negotiating between China and the United Nations ended with a barely acceptable, yet absolutely imperative, compromise. China's borders were extended to encompass all of Asia, the Middle East and Africa and, in turn, the dragon would keep its claws off Europe, the Americas and Australia.

More than ever, Norona, and more importantly, Innerworld, needed courageous, highly-trained, emissaries throughout Outerworld, observing and reporting back from ground-level points of view.

Thus, for personal *and* political reasons, Romulus wanted Aster to be right, that Tarla truly was "perfectly fine somewhere."

CHAPTER 3

Tarla tried to block out the voices buzzing in her ears. She wasn't ready to wake up yet. Rather than fading away, however, the voices kept getting louder. After several more minutes of attempting to stay submerged in murky sleep, she reluctantly swam to the surface.

Even after opening her eyes though, she wasn't certain she was awake. There were vaguely familiar faces around her, but the structure they were in was totally unfamiliar. It was obviously an enormous wooden barn, complete with horses, cows, stalls, and straw covering the ground. She just couldn't remember why she and the others were there.

A second scan of the building brought another oddity to Tarla's foggy mind. Light was being provided by lanterns with burning candles in them, secured along the walls and on wooden posts. There wasn't a window or door in sight.

She forced aside the question of where she was and focused on the people. Some seemed very excited though she couldn't distinguish the words. Others, like her, were just rousing from sleep. Regardless of how conscious they were however, everyone seemed to bear an expression of confusion.

Tarla's eyes touched on a young man about twenty feet away, who was fretting more than most. *Private Higgs.* The name popped into her head along with an image of him losing his balance and spilling coffee from two paper cups in his hands.

But in that picture he was wearing a soldier's uniform and now he was dressed in light blue cotton pajamas, at least that's what his outfit appeared to be. Glancing at the others and checking her own attire, she noted they were all dressed similarly, in loose-fitting pants and short-sleeved, vee-necked shirts, like hospital scrubs. Although the colors differed, they were generally soft pastel shades. Hers was peach.

She sat up and rubbed her temples as she concentrated on the image of Private Higgs that had come to her. That image blurred into others. Patients, swathed in bandages like mummies. Rows of cots. Logan McKay lying on one of those cots with blatant need. Logan, asleep in a seat with metal cuffs on his wrists and ankles. An aircraft. Instruments going crazy. *The storm!*

As the pieces of her memory joined together, she rose unsteadily to her feet. Surely the plane they were on had crashed into the ocean. Hadn't they been hit by a series of lightning bolts? How had they all survived? How had they gotten into this barn? How—

The bewildered gaze of her friend, Robin, met her own from across the shelter and the two women rushed toward each other. The tight hug they shared said more of their fears and relief to see each other than words ever could.

"This is very weird," Robin said as they stepped apart. "Am I in your nightmare or are you in mine?"

Tarla shook her head. "Actually, I'm toying with the

theory that everyone on the plane died and this is some sort of transfer station before we're sent off to an after-life."

Robin expressed her disbelief by cocking one finely arched, auburn eyebrow.

"I just woke up," Tarla responded to the unspoken skepticism. "My brain's still only at half speed." She nodded at the large group around Private Higgs. "Let's see what they think." A man's voice stopped them before they took a step.

"Tarla? Captain Yan?"

Tarla turned around to see a slightly-built young man with dark brown skin and a shaved head. His eyes begged her for help in the same way a thousand wounded soldiers had in the past three years, but he didn't appear to be in physical pain.

"You are Tarla, aren't you?" he asked, a bit less certainly.

"Yes, I'm Tarla." She wondered why he didn't look at all familiar to her.

He gave her a shaky smile then reached out and shook her hand. "I recognized your voice. It would be pretty hard not to since it was the only thing that kept me from going crazy the last few weeks. I guess everyone tells you what a beautiful voice you have, but I just had to let you know how important it was to me."

Tarla gave a slight frown as she tried to remember him.

His grin broadened to reveal one crooked incisor. "I'm Willy."

She took a step back and scrutinized him from head to toe. "That's impossible." Looking at Robin, she explained, "Willy was one of the patients on the plane. He suffered severe chemical burns. He was barely alive, let alone able to walk and talk."

"That's right," Willy said excitedly. "I don't understand it, but I'm healed. And so are the others. At first I thought maybe I'd just been unconscious for a long time but that doesn't explain why there aren't any scars. Then I thought, maybe there was no war and I was never burned. You know, like it was all a bad dream. But everyone else remembers the same things I do."

"Did I say very weird?" Robin murmured to Tarla. "Let me change that to incredibly spooky."

With a wave of her hand, Tarla led Robin and Willy over to the group that now included most of the survivors. When she spotted three of her nurses, she moved next to them. Giving each a light pat on their shoulders, she tried to offer a semblance of reassurance. She didn't know any more about how they'd gotten here than they did but at least she had the advantage of knowing that a healing such as Willy experienced wasn't all that extraordinary in an advanced civilization.

She suddenly realized the possible explanation. Based on what Higgs' had said about The Devil's Triangle, they might have been on top of one of Innerworld's tunnels. They could have been accidentally pulled into her home! Tarla automatically reached for the ring she kept on a chain around her neck but it wasn't there.

Whoever changed her clothes must have taken it. And without her Innerworld ring, she couldn't transmigrate or even contact her handler.

Though residing on the surface of Terra had been her assignment for twenty-two years, she still thought of Innerworld as *home*. Life there had been extremely easy compared to that of most Outerworld natives. She'd never experienced illness, fear, hunger, poverty or even lack of comfort. Life in Innerworld was peaceful, safe, fairly predictable…and dreadfully dull. How very anxious she had been to experience passion, excitement and adventure, all the wondrous things she imagined would be hers as an Outerworlder.

And for a very long while it *was* fascinating and fulfilling and she loved the unpredictability of her second life…except for not being able to maintain any long-term relationships. Because of her secretive work for Innerworld and the fact that Noronians age at half the rate of Terrans, she had to relocate several times to avoid suspicion. Her current identification showed her age to be a completely believable thirty-four and she had a solid background story that she maintained to ensure she didn't forget which lie she'd told to whom.

Although her life as an Outerworlder had been filled with surprises and uncertainties, nothing had prepared her for the horrors of war or the frightening changes that were bound to occur as a result of the China Compromise. After three long years of unending hardship, she was actually looking forward to returning to Innerworld or perhaps even an extended visit to Norona.

The more she thought about it, the more she really, *really* hoped they had landed in Innerworld. But her intuition warned that was not the case. And her logic told her this was not like any recovery room she'd ever seen back home. Her spirits plummeted again as she realized that, if this *was* home, there would have been a medical team or at least android caretakers waiting for them to awaken. If this was home, anyone who saw the ring would have known she was one of them.

Separated from the group, on the opposite side of the barn, four men were huddled together. They appeared to be having an intense conversation while keeping an eye out for any eavesdroppers. Tarla was fairly sure all four were convicts.

Also standing apart, but quite alone, was Logan McKay. He looked bored, leaning negligently against the post of a horse stall, yet Tarla had the distinct feeling that he was absorbing everything and simply waiting for the dust to settle before committing to one group or another. She looked away for fear he might catch her staring, but then her gaze darted back to him as another realization came to her. He wasn't wearing cuffs or shackles! A glance back to the four convicts confirmed what she feared—the prisoners were just as free as she was.

Her concern escalated as she noted that the two military police officers were now unarmed.

"It doesn't matter where we are or how we got here!" Corporal Gianni shouted to be heard over the multitude of speculations being thrown back and forth. "Everyone just break off and try to find a way out."

"Hold it!" yelled a man from behind Tarla.

She turned to see that the small group of convicts had approached. Their spokesperson was a tall, muscular man with a blond buzz cut, who had a very threatening demeanor. He instantly commanded everyone's attention. The crowd parted as he pushed forward, followed by his three companions. Corporal Gianni stood his ground and tried to appear taller than his medium height.

"What do you want, Wilkes?" Gianni asked defensively.

"Nothin' much, 'cept I was wonderin' who the hell put you in charge?"

Tarla swore she could actually feel the tension gripping the people around her as everyone began inching away from the two men. No words were spoken for several seconds, during which the crowd seemed to divide into two distinct sides.

"The way I figger it," Wilkes said, "I outrank you."

"Like hell," Gianni countered. "You were stripped of your rank at the court martial, and everyone here knows it."

He looked from side to side at the people he referred to as if hoping for a show of support.

When he didn't get it, Tarla guessed that the corporal wasn't much more popular than Wilkes. Accustomed to being in a military environment, however, the soldiers were prepared to obey the orders of the superior officer whether they admired that person or not. They simply needed to know who was in charge.

It looked as though Wilkes and Gianni were about to resort to physical violence to answer the question of command, when another man spoke up.

"Excuse me, gentlemen."

The voice bore a British clip and belonged to a nice-looking man with short, ash blond hair. As he strode into the center of the ring of people, Tarla could see that he was nearly as tall as Wilkes but considerably leaner. She recalled seeing him on the plane mainly because Robin had made a comment about personally helping him relax before they reached the States.

"I believe this matter can be settled without fisticuffs," the Brit stated politely but with supreme authority. "I am *Major* Geoffrey Cookson...and I outrank you both."

Wilkes snorted. "That's easy to say while you ain't wearin' no bars to prove it. You ain't even American."

"Since we have no idea what country we're in, the matter of my birthplace is irrelevant. However, if it will ease your mind, I am a naturalized citizen of the United States as well as an officer of its armed forces.

Now unless someone outranks me, I—"

Wilkes gave the major's shoulder a shove. "Not so fast, limey. You may have the rank but I got somethin' more important...*strength*." His three friends took a step closer to his back to emphasize his point. "I'll be givin' the orders from now on."

Major Cookson had no intention of backing down or using violence to maintain his authority.

"This is really quite unnecessary under the circumstances. Until we determine the logistics of our situation, arguing over power is a waste of time and energy that could be better spent investigating our surroundings."

A subtle stir among the people behind him was followed by the four convicts easing back a bit. For a moment it appeared that they were giving in to the major's rationale but their attention was focused on someone behind him.

Tarla's breath caught in her throat as she watched Logan McKay position himself to Cookson's right. His additional inches of height and shoulder breadth might have been threatening enough to a bully like Wilkes, but the look of promised danger in McKay's dark eyes cinched the matter.

"I think you're right about wastin' time, Major," Wilkes said. "We'll let you do the orderin'...for the time bein'." His last words were accompanied by a narrow-eyed glare at McKay.

As Wilkes and his cohorts backed away, the major finished the sentence he'd begun earlier. "I suggest you all do what Corporal Gianni ordered. Check every inch of this building for the exit. That includes inside the animal stalls. If they got in, there has to be a way out. In the meantime, the flight crew should report to me for a debriefing."

Logan turned to walk away but the major

murmured, "Stay, please," so he stayed. Logan wondered how the man could look so damned dignified standing at attention in a pair of pajamas. Personally, he felt ridiculous.

The pilot, co-pilot and navigator walked up to Cookson and saluted.

"At ease," the major said, returning their salute without relaxing a muscle. "Name and rank, please."

An African American man about Logan's age responded first. "Nathan Boswell, Second Lieutenant. I was the pilot."

"Jeremy Fleischer, Second Lieutenant, co-pilot."

Logan thought he didn't look old enough to be weaned from his mother let alone be trusted with an aircraft.

The third, a young man with a glazed look in his eye, had to clear his throat twice before any sound would come out. Even when it did, it was barely audible.

"Edward Smith, Airman First Class, flight navigator."

"What do you remember?" Cookson asked Boswell.

The pilot delivered a concise report that ended with the plane being sucked through a hole in the clouds toward the sun.

"It was as though someone else was flying the plane. I had no control whatsoever at the end."

Fleischer and Smith confirmed his statements.

"Thank you," Cookson said with a nod at Boswell. "Let me know if anything else comes back to you."

As soon as they walked away, the major turned to Logan, with the same no-nonsense expression he had used with the men. "I hope a verbal thank you for your timely intervention will suffice. I believe prostrating myself at your feet in gratitude might diminish the troop's confidence in me."

Logan was caught off-guard by the man's admission and dry humor, and almost smiled before getting control over it. With a face as serious as Cookson's, he replied, "Let's just save that show for when morale gets really low...say, about an hour from now." Logan hesitated then asked the question on his mind. "Why the honesty with me, Major?"

"Please call me Geoffrey and, since I might need your support again in the future, I thought it best to be truthful with you. Mind you, I'm not a coward. I'm simply a realist. That man, Wilkes, would have attacked me and, given his greater size, undoubtedly would have caused me considerable pain. I'm an engineer, not a fighter, but my stepping forward seemed to be the best way of maintaining order until we find out what's going on. You apparently carry a lot of weight with Wilkes and his pals, yet you chose to support me. In case my leadership is required for more than the next hour, I hope you will consent to continuing to back me up."

Logan decided the man's honesty deserved the same in return. "I get the idea you don't know who I am, so let me introduce myself. The name's Logan McKay. I was a Chief Master Sergeant before they sentenced me to life at Leavenworth. Want to know why?"

Geoffrey met Logan's challenging stare. "Not particularly. For the moment I know as much about you as I need to."

Logan was about to tell him how wrong he was when Captain Yan walked up to the major and saluted. Logan's chest muscles immediately contracted but outwardly he controlled any reaction. He couldn't help but notice how she kept her eyes fixed on the major and hadn't even spared him a glance as she'd approached.

"Major Cookson, I'm Captain Tarla Yan, formerly

head nurse at the fifty third mobile hospital unit. It seems that I'm the second highest ranking officer here, so I wanted to put myself at your disposal. The nurses have spoken to each of the patients and I assume you want a status report."

"Of course, Captain. I welcome your assistance."

"It makes no sense," Tarla said less formally. "But every single patient has had a miraculous recovery. There's not even a scar to show that any of them were recently wounded or burned."

Logan automatically touched the scar over his eyebrow. It was still there, which proved once again that he couldn't come out ahead, even in Wonderland.

Geoffrey slowly rubbed his jaw. "I've heard a number of suppositions about what happened but they were all from men. Since I've always been a believer in feminine intuition, I'd like to hear your opinion, Captain."

Tarla had to smother a smirk as she wondered what he'd think if he knew just how strong her intuition was...*and why*. She shifted her balance from one foot to the other. "Well, sir, it sounds a bit crazy but when I first came to, I thought we might all be dead. After seeing the patients, that idea doesn't seem so far-fetched."

Logan had had the same thought but it wasn't until she said it aloud that he came up with a way to test it. He had been so relieved to be free of his restraints, how it had come about wasn't all that important to him.

While Tarla and Cookson discussed the possibilities, Logan walked over to a post, picked off a thin splinter of wood, and peeled away a few slivers until one end came to a sharp point. Squeezing the middle finger of his left hand with his thumb and ring finger, he brought blood to the surface of the fingertip then jabbed it with the splinter before he chickened out. He had been knifed and shot without a whimper, but needles had always made him queasy.

As blood oozed out of the tiny puncture, he swallowed hard and returned to the two officers. "Sorry to have to blow a hole in the death theory but I'm pretty sure people stop bleeding once they're dead." He held out his hand to show the fresh wound.

Though Tarla looked at his finger, she had yet to look at his face. Logan knew he should let it go but he just couldn't. "If you still have doubts, Captain Yan, I'd be happy to give you a prick." Her gaze lifted abruptly and he was treated to a rosy flush across her perfect cheekbones. "Then again, maybe you'd rather do it yourself." He held out his makeshift needle.

"No, thank you," she said, ice dripping from her words. "One *brave* soldier shedding blood for the cause is quite enough."

Logan raised one eyebrow, as his stomach twisted beneath her sarcasm. "Maybe you would have preferred me to slash an artery or two."

She raised her chin a notch. "Maybe I—"

"*Ahem.*" Geoffrey noisily cleared his throat. "Without jumping to any rash conclusions, can I assume you two are acquainted?"

"Barely," responded Logan.

"Hardly at all," answered Tarla.

"I see," Geoffrey said with a nod. "Then I don't need to worry about any personal conflicts getting in the way here. Until we get to the bottom of this situation, you are second in command, Captain Yan, but Sergeant McKay will act as my adjutant."

Logan was certain she wanted to protest but all she said was, "Yes, sir. If I may be excused now, sir?" As soon as Geoffrey nodded to her, she turned on her heel and strode away.

Tarla restrained the urge to feel her cheeks. She didn't really need to touch them to know they were warm. Nor did she need to check her pulse to know that it was racing. Logan McKay was not the first man to make a suggestive remark to her, but for some reason, he was the only one whose comments she couldn't ignore or laugh off.

Besides the fact that she had made the mistake of caring too much, there was another reason he managed to embarrass her. Where most men used sexual innuendo to make a safe pass, Logan used it like a sharp weapon, poking it at her to make sure she kept her distance. She had misinterpreted it to mean that he was actually needier than the average man she dealt with. Her caretaker skills automatically had her trying harder to get through to him in spite of the blows he repeatedly delivered.

She had thought he wouldn't remember her but it was quite clear that he did. And even though she had made a point of not speaking to him, he still found it necessary to provoke her. Before she could give it more thought, Robin walked up to her.

"Hey, what's with the face?" Robin asked quietly. "Did you find out we really are dead or is it something worse?"

Tarla smiled despite her dismal mood. "Something worse than death?"

Robin shrugged. "Sure. It could be that Private Higgs is right—that we were snatched from the plane by aliens and taken to their planet on a spaceship."

Tarla rolled her eyes as though she truly believed that explanation was even more ridiculous than their being dead. "How does Higgs explain the fact that there are Earth-type horses and cows in here with us? Did the aliens abduct them also?"

"Absolutely," Robin said with exaggerated

seriousness. "The aliens wanted to create an environment similar to what we humans were accustomed to. Apparently Higgs's aliens are a little fuzzy on certain details. Anyway, he says this barn is actually like a cage in a zoo and alien tourists are watching us through the one-way windows at this very moment."

"You're right," Tarla said with a grimace. "There are some things worse than death. Like being forced to spend time with men like Private Higgs or Wilkes. Can you just imagine what might happen if we were all stuck in here together for very long?"

"Yeah. World War Four. Except this time we don't even have the limited privacy of a latrine."

Tarla made another face at her friend. "I've been trying not to think about that. Or about food. Or water."

"You're not the only one, believe me. But something the darling major said stuck in my head."

Tarla smirked. "I think the darling major is just plain stuck in your head."

"True," Robin admitted with a wink. "I thought he was luscious the first time I saw him but when I heard that English accent, I almost wet my pants."

"How can you think about a man at a time like this?" Tarla knew her question was rhetorical. There was always room for thoughts of handsome men in Robin's mind.

Robin cocked her head as if giving Tarla's question real consideration. "It's hard but some things are worth the extra effort." She grinned and wiggled her eyebrows, then straightened her expression again. "Anyway, what I was going to bring up before you sidetracked me was what the major said about the animals. They look healthy. Somebody must be in charge of giving them food and water and letting them out. So I'm willing to bet that whoever, or whatever, put us in here, will take care of us too. It's just a matter of being patient until they show themselves."

Tarla nodded. "It sounds logical but I'm worried about how far some of these men's patience can be stretched." Her gaze sought out Wilkes to see what he was up to, but before she located him or any of his friends, all six of her nurses joined her and Robin. Their worried expressions mirrored her own.

Darcy, a young woman with blonde-on-blonde frosted hair and a courageous air that made her seem larger than her petite body, spoke first. "No one has been able to find a way out."

Kara, Darcy's closest friend, stood silently behind her, as usual, staring at the ground. She was as timid as her friend was brave. Kara was a good nurse though and that was what mattered to Tarla.

Sunny, a brunette whose nickname perfectly suited her bright personality, rather than her drab appearance, offered her information next. "There doesn't even seem to be a loose board anywhere that could be pried away to make an opening. It might be possible with a tool, but no one's found anything usable."

The "Three Mouseketeers", Trish, Mandy and Charlene, had nothing to add but Mandy gave voice to the words they were all thinking. "I'm scared, Captain. More scared than the time the sniper was taking potshots at us."

"At least then we knew where we were and who the enemy was," Trish said.

Just then the group was expanded as two more women walked up and saluted Tarla. She automatically returned the salute and waited for them to identify themselves. They obviously knew who she was, or at least they knew of her superior rank.

"Airman First Class, Alicia Samples, helicopter pilot," said the taller of the two. With her statuesque form and long blonde hair, she looked more like a model than a pilot.

"I thought you ought to know, someone just found a supply of tents, cots, and bedding in the tack room. Looks like someone's expecting us to make ourselves at home."

The other woman had distinctly oriental features. "I'm Lee Tang," she said. "Ninth Infantry. We hope you don't mind our joining you, but in case you haven't noticed, there are ten of us and over a hundred of them."

Tarla looked at her curiously for a moment before realizing that she was referring to the male-female ratio. It was a fact of life in the field, something each woman dealt with in her own way. She had told Robin she was concerned about physical needs such as food, water and latrines. She hadn't given a thought to the kind of physical needs that might drive a man like Wilkes.

Suddenly she was filled with that new concern but she knew better than to let the other women see it. After all, she was a captain, the second in command. They were expecting her to take care of them and, as always, she would do everything in her power to do that. She introduced herself, Robin and her nurses, suggesting they all use first names under the circumstances.

"There's no reason to worry about something that's not an immediate problem," Tarla stated firmly. "I agree that we should be aware of the situation, especially considering the fact that twenty-nine of them are convicted felons. However, I'm sure the rest of the men can be counted on to behave in a civilized fashion. Besides, we'll probably find out what's going on here any minute and—"

A creaking noise coming from one end of the barn caught everyone's attention. Very slowly, a large section of the wall opened at the bottom and rose upward like a giant door.

With each inch the door opened, sunlight filled more of the barn. Tarla was torn between racing for the opening and being afraid to find out what was beyond the barn. For several seconds, it looked as though the fear of the unknown was keeping everyone else from moving as well.

"Captain Yan, I believe our place should be on the front line."

Tarla turned to see Major Cookson and Logan waiting on her. To the women she said, "Stay back until we see what we're facing." She then posted herself on the major's left as they strode toward the opening. With each step, others fell in behind them until Tarla felt a bit like the Pied Piper. Cookson halted them at the edge of the barn and waited for the rising door to complete its journey.

Tarla's heart pounded in her chest as she prepared for the worst and hoped for the best. When the outside world finally came into view, it was not clearly one or the other. The warm air temperature suggested it was summer. The brightness seemed to make it midday. Although her first thought had been that they might have been rescued by a transport to Innerworld, her thought as the barn door began to open was that they were on a farm somewhere in Middle America. Now she knew neither was the correct answer.

Outside of the barn, the ground cover and tree leaves were deep shades of blue, the cloudless sky was celery green and there was a second, smaller orb of light to the left of the sun.

And the large gathering of oriental men waiting for

them to exit was evidence that they were not the only humans in this place...wherever in the universe *this place* was.

CHAPTER 4

Tarla, Logan and Geoffrey walked cautiously out into the yard. Scanning the group of men a second time, she noted some were not oriental, but they all bore the same expression of wonder. Within seconds, the rest of the soldiers and nurses filed into the yard. Their verbal reactions ranged from the spiritual to the obscene. As the two groups stared at one another, it was impossible to tell which looked more surprised.

"Hello," Geoffrey said to break the stalemate.

The group of men smiled slightly, bobbed their heads and replied with greetings in a variety of languages.

"Does anyone speak English?" Geoffrey asked.

A very old, bald-headed man limped forward, leaning heavily on a wooden cane. He offered a toothless grin. "I do. And a few others. Don't use it much though. Mostly learned to get our ideas across without words." His speech was slow and subdued, and his gaze wandered as if he were distracted.

"Please, sir," Tarla said, "could you tell us where we are?"

His eyes focused on hers, then widened with

gradual awareness. "A woman?" He squinted at the crowd behind her. "Never had women before. Never had so many newcomers arrive at once either. Not quite sure what to do about that." He frowned a little as he seemed to struggle with his thoughts for a moment, then his toothless smile was back in place. "But they will. They always take care of any little problems. Must get back to work now." He turned and motioned for his people to get moving.

"Wait!" Tarla cried and the old man stopped and looked back. It occurred to her that he could be senile but what about the rest of them? Standing there with passive smiles and vacant gazes, they reminded her of well-fed sheep—contented, slow-moving and almost mindless.

"Oh, yes," the old man said as he hobbled around again. "You asked me a question, didn't you?"

Tarla could tell he had no recollection of what she'd asked. "Where are we? How did we get here?"

"Wish I could tell you, my dear, but can't. Got here about ninety years ago myself, far as I can figure. People here then didn't know where they were either."

"What's the deal, Major?" A soldier shouted, then several others added their own questions.

"What kind of place has green sky?"

"How'd we get here?"

"How do we get back home?"

Logan turned around and, with no more than the slash of his narrow-eyed glare across the nervous crowd, silenced the voices.

Tarla didn't see Geoffrey acknowledge Logan's assistance, but she clearly sensed that he did.

"As you can hear," Geoffrey said to the old man, "we would appreciate any information you can offer. I am Major Geoffrey Cookson of the United States Army. We were all on an aircraft heading to the

United States from Japan, when a storm—"

"Yes, yes," the old man interrupted. "A storm. Always a storm. Thunder and lightning, then the bright light, then waking up in the barn. Sometimes a plane. Sometimes a boat. But always a storm…and the second sun."

"The second sun isn't always there?" Geoffrey asked.

The old man shrugged. "Now you see it, now you don't. Sometimes when you see it, there's a newcomer waiting in the barn. Was on a fishing boat off Guam myself. The rest are gone now." Again he appeared to mentally drift away, then return. "I am Duncan, the eldest of this lost tribe." He waved a frail hand toward the men behind him. "You'll have the rest of your lives to meet everyone else. Must go to work now." He started to move away once more.

Tarla's worried gaze darted to Geoffrey but Logan spoke up. "You said *they* take care of problems. Who are *they*?"

Duncan shook his head. "Don't know that either. Just know they're out there, past the invisible wall, and they take care of problems." He crooked his finger for Tarla to come closer. When she did, he whispered, "I think they're fairies."

The more Tarla was hearing, the less she understood.

"This is getting nowhere fast," Logan muttered to Geoffrey. "And the animals at your back are starting to show their teeth."

Tarla worried that decision-making was not one of the major's strong points. His decision to keep a man like McKay at his side was her first clue. She offered a suggestion when Duncan tried to leave again.

"Duncan, you said you have to get back to work. Perhaps we could help. There are an awful lot of us. If we broke up into groups, and you assigned an English-speaking person to each group, we could be shown what it is you do here and give you a hand."

Duncan smiled broadly. "That's a fine idea, young lady. Lots of strong backs. Must work to eat. Must eat to work." He called five men forward and repeated Tarla's suggestion.

"I'll take the women and go with Duncan," Tarla stated. "We nurses are known for our endless patience." Her remark won a smile from the major but Logan had an objection.

"You'll take ten men with you too," he said while his eyes scanned the crowd for candidates.

Tarla automatically bristled at his authoritative tone. He had no right to give her orders. "That won't be necessary."

Logan's gaze slid to hers and held. "I say it is."

Tarla lifted her chin, crossed her arms and pretended she wasn't a full head shorter than him. "Listen up, McKay. That evil-eye of yours may work on the men but it doesn't intimidate me one bit."

Geoffrey cleared his throat before Logan could counter. "I believe the sergeant made a valid suggestion, Captain. If what Duncan said is true, and these men haven't seen women for years, there's no telling what difficulties you might encounter. My recommendation would be to select ten of your patients. They would be most apt to be protective of you."

Tarla still didn't believe the women needed men with them, but at least the major explained his reasoning rather than just giving an order, and unlike McKay, he *was* a superior officer. Besides, Willy and some of the other patients would probably prefer to be with the nurses. "Yes sir. I'll select ten to take with us."

Before going their separate ways, Geoffrey had one last thing to say. "I want to assure you both that, although I have been a bit out of my element thus far, I am quite good at strategic planning. Once we gather sufficient information, I'm sure we will find a solution to this peculiar dilemma. In the meantime, I appreciate the assistance."

Tarla thought it took quite a man to admit his weakness and decided right then that she liked the major. As she gathered the women and chose the men to stay with them, she noted that Logan put Wilkes in his own group and split up the other troublemakers. Though she abhorred the macho tactics he'd used so far to maintain control, she could see that his methods had some merit under the circumstances. But she wondered just how long Wilkes would be held off by hostile glares before he tested McKay's strength. Then again, maybe Wilkes was intimidated so easily because he'd already tested McKay and learned what Tarla had—that his rough appearance went all the way to the bone.

"Now what?" Robin asked as soon as Tarla came near.

"We follow the leader and pry anything out of his fuzzy mind we possibly can." She led her group to Duncan. "We're all yours, Duncan. Where to?"

The elderly man beamed as he was surrounded by young ladies. "Used to work in the fields, but can't keep up any more. In the kitchen now, with the other old ones. Women's chores are all we're good for these days."

Robin raised an eyebrow but Tarla quickly touched a finger to her lips. Duncan would never have heard of women's equality and this was not the time to explain it.

A whinnying sound caught Tarla's attention and she

turned to see several of the other groups climbing into horse-drawn wagons. "Where will they be going?"

Duncan squinted at the wagons. "Could be the orchards. Plenty of ripe fruit needs picking. Corn's ready too. Could be either."

Since Tarla couldn't see any orchards or fields, she guessed the farm was very large. "And what's beyond the farm?"

Duncan started his slow hobble again. "Don't know. The farm land ends at the invisible wall."

Tarla and Robin shared a skeptical glance. "You mentioned that before," Robin said. "Can you describe it?"

"Can't describe something invisible. It's just there and you can't walk through it, dig under it or climb over it."

Robin leaned toward Tarla and murmured in her ear. "Sounds like one of those force fields in science fiction movies. I think we should bring Higgs in as a consultant. He's probably been right all along."

Tarla was more tempted than ever to tell Robin her secret. However, under the circumstances, she was afraid revealing her knowledge of alien worlds might make the situation even more stressful.

Matching their pace to Duncan's, they were only moving along an inch at a time, but Tarla could see they were headed toward another large wooden building similar to the barn. Four smoke-spewing chimneys protruded from the corners of the roof.

Beyond the large building were rows of smaller ones. Every structure, including the barn, was painted white with red doors and roofs. The area looked like a cross between an army unit and summer camp.

Duncan pointed to the smaller buildings. "Men sleep in those. New people have to build their own. No hurry though. Rainy season's over and colder weather's not due for months."

"You have regular seasons?" Alicia, the helicopter pilot, asked.

Duncan stopped and took a few breaths before answering. "After the big war, I lived in New York before I set off to see the world. We had seasons there. This place always reminded me of California. Never liked California."

After the big war? Tarla guessed he was referring to Terra's World War II and quickly did some arithmetic. If Duncan was remembering his timeline correctly, he had to be a hundred ten or fifteen years old. It was likely that whoever healed her wounded soldiers also had the ability to extend life spans. Naturally she was aware of a whole range of alien civilizations that had such technology, but she'd never heard of any humanoid supportive planets so similar to Terra with green sky and blue trees.

Duncan started moving toward the buildings again. "Kitchen's in the big house. Necessary room too. Don't have a separate room for women though. That might be a problem."

Robin snorted. "*Might* be a problem? I'll guarantee it. How many men live here?"

"Fifty-five...no fifty-four. Moishe passed on a few months ago."

Robin made a face at Tarla. "Fifty-four, plus one hundred seventeen more. All using the same bathroom? We've got to find a way out of here fast."

"Excuse me, sir?"

Tarla turned to see Willy coming up alongside her. Duncan paused again to listen to the young man.

"My name's Willy. Me and these other guys, well, we were half-dead on the plane and now we're walking around like nothing ever happened to us. We were hoping you could tell us how, or why, or something."

Duncan sighed and looked at each of the men. "Half-dead, eh? Knew they could fix a broken bone good as new or heal a bad cut. Guess they could have fixed you fellas up before putting you in the barn."

"Do you mean the ones you think are fairies healed these men?" Tarla asked.

Duncan nodded and gave her a wink. "Don't know the how or why of it but when someone here gets sick or hurt, they go into the tack room in the barn and close the door. A while later they come back out all better."

Robin voiced the question in everyone's mind. "What does the sick person say happened to them?"

"No one ever remembers," Duncan mumbled and got moving again.

"Here we are," he said as they reached the big house. Willy quickly opened the door and held it, while everyone entered.

Inside were a dozen elderly men performing a variety of chores but one thing was instantly noticeable. There were no appliances. A hearth was in each corner with large cauldrons hanging over the smoldering fires. The man doing dishes was working a hand pump to get water.

Not only had they been dropped into a strange world, the contradiction between advanced medical technology and a barely civilized farming community couldn't be ignored. Tarla suddenly recalled Higgs's theory that a superior race had put them all in a zoo of some sort suddenly seemed way too possible.

Robin murmured her similar conclusion close to Tarla's ear. "Okay, I hate to say it, but I'm starting to worry that Higgs nailed it with his zoo theory."

Once the elderly men heard how many more people would be eating with them, they welcomed the extra hands.

Before they were put to work, however, they were offered a snack of bread, cheese and some fruits that tasted like apples and pears, but had white and pink skins. Everyone agreed that it was possibly the best food they'd had since they entered the army. The water they were given was lightly carbonated and was so refreshing, they each had a second cup. Darcy declared that it had to be from a mountain spring but Duncan only knew that it came through the pump.

As soon as they had their fill, Tarla made sure each person had an assignment while she stuck by Duncan. She could tell he was tiring of all the questions but she prodded him a bit further.

"You said you'd been here about ninety years. What about the others?"

Duncan rubbed his ear lobe. "Hard to say. Some have been here as long as me. Some only a little while."

"You must have been very young when you arrived."

He considered her words a moment then shrugged. "Was twenty four. Never thought I'd see sixty let alone pass a hundred. But they don't let you die so easy here. Just keep fixing a body until it's too old to wake up one morning…like Moishe." He stared at a spot on the floor. "Going to sleep and not getting up. That's the only way to leave this place."

Tarla waited for him to say more on his own but after a few seconds, the placid expression returned to his wrinkled face.

"Must get to work now," he said and took her to the table where another man was shucking ears of corn.

As her fingers peeled away the husks, her mind tried to make sense of what she'd seen and heard so far, but she only came up with more questions. Besides the technology extremes, the general demeanor of the men in residence was most peculiar. She could understand how the older men might accept being in this strange place, especially when some of them, like Duncan, had been here for nearly a century.

But what about the others? Her first impression of them had been that they were like sheep. Or maybe robots. If they had been transported to an alien planet, these men could be machines instead of humans. Yet, she recalled Duncan's comment about the wall. At one time, someone must have tried to scale it or dig under it for him to say it couldn't be done. A robot wouldn't attempt to escape.

Another explanation could be that they were all tranquilized, but their pupils appeared normal and, though their movements seemed a bit slow, they were fairly smooth and coordinated. Rather than exhibiting symptoms of being drugged, she would describe them as being incredibly complacent.

Had they all given up? Or were they simply too afraid to face whatever power was out there?

Logan tipped the clay jug to pour another cup of the cool water. It wasn't that he was still thirsty, he just had never tasted anything so...clean. That word replayed itself in his head as he realized *clean* was the best description he could come up with for this whole weird place. The water, the air, the whitewashed buildings, even the animals and the men—everything looked too clean and fresh.

As a kid growing up in one of the lousier neighborhoods of Detroit, he hadn't believed there were places in the world where the sky was actually blue. As far as he knew, streets and sidewalks always had garbage and urine all over them. He had seen pictures of cleaner, more colorful places in books at school but he doubted they were real. For him, the world was dirty and gray, a place to survive rather than appreciate its beauty.

Thirty-some years later, his opinion of the world was still pretty much the same, which was why he knew this place—even without the green sky and blue grass—wasn't part of any world he was familiar with. He didn't belong anywhere this squeaky clean.

Exactly where he *did* belong was a question he'd stopped asking himself years ago. As a child he was constantly daydreaming about being somewhere else. He was always the good guy fighting the bad, righting wrongs and saving the world from dark forces. As he aged, his daydreams spilled into real life. Whenever some kid was getting picked on, he just happened to be there and could never resist lending a hand to the underdog.

For his efforts, he occasionally received mementos, like the scar on his jaw, when he had stopped some punks from beating a wino, and got razor-slashed in the process. Or the scar on his forehead when he interrupted a man trying to force himself on a woman and learned what it felt like to get hit in the head with a brick.

Despite numerous lessons however, he never seemed to learn to keep his nose out of other people's business. Fortunately, he grew big enough and became tough enough that his wins soon outnumbered his losses. Eventually he discovered how to cast an impression of danger without having to fight all the time. The strangest part was, the only time he felt right was when he was playing the hero. Otherwise, he always had the feeling he was in the wrong place and time…like he didn't belong anywhere.

The closest he'd ever gotten to belonging was in the military but, as it turned out, the politicians in control had no use for heroes either.

One of the oriental men came up beside him carrying a large basket filled with pink, pear-shaped fruit. He smiled at Logan and, with a movement of his eyes and head, requested his assistance in emptying the fruit into the back of the wagon. Logan gave him a hand then walked back with the man to help him pick some more. The men here didn't move very quickly or work all that strenuously but they did keep working…and looked rather happy about it.

Duncan had been right about there being little use for English or any other language for that matter. These men had barely spoken a dozen words aloud. Whatever thoughts they'd needed to express so far had been accomplished silently. Normally that would have been just fine with Logan but he needed to learn more from them than how to tell which fruit was ripe enough to be plucked. Only verbal questions and answers were going to explain what had happened to them.

Hans, this group's English-speaking guide, was a slightly built, middle-aged man from Frankfurt, Germany, who had arrived here when he was in his twenties. He knew very little and didn't particularly care.

That attitude would have seemed odd coming from anyone in this situation, but when Logan uncovered the fact that Hans had previously been a research marine biologist, it made even less sense. When had the man stopped questioning things around him and peacefully accepted a life of performing brainless tasks?

On the way to the orchard, Hans had politely answered every question Logan could think of about the layout of the farm, the residents and how they filled their days. The farm sounded as though it was about a mile square and the men worked it from sunrise to sunset. Besides their chores, they ate and slept. Nothing else. No entertainment, playing or distractions of any kind.

When asked if he or any of the others had ever tried to leave the farm, Hans said everyone tries at first, but they soon realize what a pleasant life they have here and how satisfying it is to put in a good day's work. His dumb-looking smile had stayed plastered on his face the whole time he was talking.

As Logan considered the bits of information he'd learned, another question came to him and he sought Hans out again.

"I'm curious about something, Hans," Logan said as he pulled a piece of fruit off a branch and dropped it in the basket at his feet. "I can see how important it is for you fellows to do your work. How is it so many of you were standing outside of the barn when we came out?"

Hans's smile broadened a bit. "Because it was locked."

Logan could tell that was supposed to explain everything and took a stab at what he meant. "And when the barn door's locked...new people arrive?"

Hans nodded. "Sometimes. Not often. Usually it just means Duncan's fairies are at work."

"At work doing what?"

"Trading."

Logan reined in his frustration and forced himself to use the same easy tone Hans used. "What is it they trade?"

"We give them some of the fruits and vegetables we grow, and they leave us things we need but can't make ourselves." Hans caught sight of some ripe fruit on another tree and started dragging his nearly full basket toward it.

Logan picked up the basket and carried it for him as he asked, "What sort of things?" Hans cocked his head at him with a totally vacant look in his eyes as if he had no idea what he was talking about. "You said the fairies leave you things you need. Like what?"

Hans's smile came back. "Tools, clothing, sugar. Things we need. Sometimes we put a drawing with the crops so they'll know what we'd like. Other times they surprise us."

Logan wanted to hear more about the fairies, but Higgs chose that moment to do some more fretting.

"Can I talk to you?" he asked, looking nervous enough to throw up.

Logan let Higgs lead him out of the others' hearing range.

"I just want to make sure there's no hard feelings," Higgs said, not quite meeting Logan's eyes. "You know, between us. I mean, I was just doing my job, you know. It's not like I had anything to do with your court martial."

"Forget it, Higgs. We were all just doing our job."

"Well, anyway, I just wanted you to know, you and the major have my support if you need it. My guess is, Wilkes and his pals aren't the only ones who might cause trouble."

Logan smirked. "Thanks for the news flash." He stopped himself from taking his frustration out on Higgs. "Just pass on anything you get wind of. This situation's bad enough without us fighting amongst ourselves." He was about to return to Hans when Higgs stopped him.

"Do you think they're androids?" he asked glancing at Hans. When Logan furrowed his brows, Higgs added, "You know, robots that are really close to being human but are still just computers? Or maybe they're aliens that have taken our shape to gain our confidence."

Logan didn't want to hear why Higgs thought the aliens needed to gain their confidence. "I don't know any more than you do, Higgs, but I'll tell you this much. I'd lay odds that these guys aren't the ones we need to worry about. They're just puppets. What we've got to do is find a way to reach the ones who pull their strings."

Higgs glanced from side to side as if expecting to see an eavesdropper. "If it's aliens we're dealing with, I should be able to help. I've read thousands of science fiction novels, you know."

"Thanks, Higgs," Logan said, giving him a pat on the back. "I'll keep that in mind."

As he made his way back to Hans, Logan rubbed his temples. *Damn!* He was getting a headache. Considering the tension he was holding inside, it wasn't surprising that one was coming on. All he needed now to make his day complete was a killer migraine—a blinding, five-day cluster type ought to about do it. Especially since there probably wasn't an aspirin in the whole friggin' place.

What the hell had possessed him to step forward and help the major? He knew when he did it, he'd regret it. The welfare of the men was no longer his concern. The army had spit him out of its womb and forgotten him, much like his own mother had. But he just hadn't been able to stand there and let an ass like Wilkes get the upper hand.

So here he was, back to being the one everybody was counting on to make the right decisions and keep them safe.

Well, almost everybody. Wilkes wasn't counting on him for anything but a hard time. Though even that was something he'd have to live up to.

Then there was Tarla. She certainly wouldn't count

on him for anything. Not if she could help it. In fact, he'd done such a good job of putting her off, she'd probably refuse to ask him for help, even if her life was threatened.

Logan was accustomed to life being one kick in the teeth after another, but this little turn of events sure beat the hell out of anything that had come before, including the court martial. It was the typical sort of trick fate always played on him. He had been spared from life in one prison, only to find himself being held captive in another in which his wardens were either fairies or aliens.

And the only woman in the entire universe capable of twisting him into knots with nothing more than the sound of her voice, was there to make sure he didn't have a moment's peace.

As he had a hundred times before, he drifted back to the moment when he first realized that Tarla was neither an angel nor a hallucination...

He squinted his eyes in an attempt to focus on the woman looking down on him. Either the concussion or whatever drug they'd used on him for the surgery still had him feeling disoriented and drowsy, but the throbbing pain in his thigh assured him he was very much alive.

"Welcome back, Logan."

Her voice sent a shiver up his spine in spite of the numbing narcotic. The way she said his name suggested they'd known each other forever and the way she smiled at him made it seem as though they really had.

Her fingers combed his hair back from his forehead. "I'm Tarla. How do you feel?"

He wanted her to touch him again, but he didn't dare ask aloud.

"Hurts, doesn't it?" She lightly stroked one of the scars on his shoulder. "But it looks like you've been through this before."

"Slovenia," he mumbled hoarsely.

Her fingertip traced the scar along his jaw, then his forehead.

"Detroit."

"Is that where you're from?" He nodded once. "Too bad about the Chevies, huh? I thought they were a shoe-in for the championship this year."

He wasn't much of a soccer fan but he was willing to discuss any topic that might keep her by his side. The drug in his system prevented him from intelligently holding up his side of the conversation, but she seemed to understand and did most of the talking.

He remembered fading in and out for a day or two. Each time he awakened, she was there, smiling, telling him little bits of news and gossip. Once the amount of narcotic he'd been prescribed was reduced, he was able to get her talking about what he really wanted to know, which was anything and everything about her.

She was from Baltimore, Maryland, thirty-four, had a large number of relatives and friends, each of whom she could relate a humorous story about. She liked children, rescued stray animals and, most important, had no husband, fiancé, or boyfriend waiting at home.

The strange part was she seemed to really like him. For some reason, she saw right past what everyone else saw when they looked at him. He even had the urge to tell her about his own life, thinking she might be the one woman who wouldn't judge him by his past, but he needed more confidence for that.

With each encounter, he grew more certain that she was feeling the same attraction to him as he was to her. And when he held her hand and she didn't pull it back, his hope rose.

His leg felt a little better by the end of the second week and her nearness was keeping him in a constant state of arousal. He could tell Tarla wasn't the type of woman he usually associated with, and normally, he wouldn't have even bothered talking to her, but everything about her had him believing his life could be different with her.

He wanted her, but he didn't want her to see him as an animal. He vowed to go slowly with her but he couldn't stand another day of only holding her hand.

That night, after it was dark and quiet and she came by to say goodnight, he shifted to one side of the cot and asked her to sit next to him.

"I know it's only been a couple weeks," he began, then stopped because her eyes were telling him he didn't have to explain. He reached up and, with his hand lightly stroking the back of her neck, he brought her head down to his. The moment her lips touched his, he *knew*, without a doubt, she could change his life—be the sweet woman who would lift his dark soul from the depths of hell and stand at his side through good times and bad.

Knowing they had no assurance of continued privacy, he controlled the desire to pull her down onto the cot and bury himself in her softness. Instead, he kept the kiss light and closed-mouth and his hands above her shoulders.

"I love you, Tarla," he whispered, and waited for her to return the sentiment. For several heartbeats, he was certain she wanted to do just that, then she sighed and slashed his exposed heart in two.

"Logan, I'm flattered. You're a wonderful man, and I'd be honored to have your love. But sometimes, a man thinks he feels something for a woman who's taken care of him when really it's only gratitude. A few weeks from now, after you've gone from here, you probably won't feel anything like you do right this minute."

"That's not true," he protested, unable to keep the hurt out of his voice. "I'm not some kid fresh out of high school who can't tell the difference between love, lust and gratitude."

She touched her fingers to his lips. "I know you're not. But I've been through this before with patients and, if I believed everyone who said he loved me truly did, I'd be perpetually heartbroken. Please don't misunderstand, I really care about you, but I can't afford to love you."

She dipped her head to kiss him again but he turned his face from hers. It had been so long since he'd allowed himself to feel, that to have it thrown back in his face hurt worse than any physical wound he'd ever received.

It made him remember the first and last time he'd been in love. He was fourteen and his raging hormones had clouded his mind enough to make him forget who he was and where he'd come from. When the prettiest girl in school was nice to him, he'd bragged that she was his girlfriend. As it turned out, she had only been treating him politely, as she had been taught by her upper-middle class parents. Behind his back, she told her friends what she really thought—that she'd rather kiss her dog than Dirty Logan McKay.

After that, he improved his personal grooming habits but remembered to keep his hormonal sights on girls who didn't mind being kissed by white trash.

The morning after Tarla's rejection, he wised up and started paying attention to what was going on around him. The pain in his leg was tolerable now without any narcotics, so his mind was no longer clouded by that either.

The first thing he noticed was the number of other patients in better and worse shape than he was and Tarla was sweet to every last one of them. He told himself that was her job, so it was stupid to be jealous. But when he saw her lean over one young soldier and brush his hair back from his forehead, he pounded the last nail into the lid of the coffin that usually housed his heart.

He had been a fool again.

At least she hadn't lied the night before. She just called it like she saw it...and she was probably right. He wasn't in love. He was grateful. His mind, temporarily confused by drugs and pain, had mistaken her simple kindness for what she was, rather than what she did for a living. He knew from personal experience how vastly different those two things could be.

By the time she came to visit him, he thought he had it all straightened out in his head, but he was still wrong. Just hearing her voice caused an ache inside him that no drug could fully numb. From that moment on, he did the only thing he knew to protect himself. He pushed her away. When ignoring her didn't work, he resorted to crudity to stop her from being so nice. Yet she kept coming back just as sweet and solid as hard candy, until he thought he'd go crazy before being sent back to his battalion.

And when discharge day finally came, he was sure he'd be able to forget her. As it turned out however, he had needed the fantasy far too often in the gruesome months that followed.

A tug on his sleeve yanked Logan's mind back to the present and the job at hand, but one thought lingered. Even a cell at Leavenworth was preferable to a lifetime of being within hearing range of Tarla Yan, yet knowing he could never touch her the way he did in his dreams.

There had to be a way out of this mess. If it meant taking charge of the whole damn bunch of misfits and puppet-people, he'd just have to do it.

Right after he got over the migraine.

CHAPTER 5

"Assimilation has begun," the elderly Domestic Affairs Advisor Iris of Mergany announced.

Imperial Prefect Parisia of Acameir nodded her approval. "Thank you, Iris. Keep a watch for the next few days until the antidote takes effect. I trust you'll advise me of anything problematical."

"I'm sure I won't need to bother you."

Parisia was not so optimistic. "I hope you're right, yet I can't help but be concerned. We've never had so many arrive at once, nor have any previous crossovers been in chains or carrying weapons. Speaking of which, have they been destroyed?"

"Of course," Iris replied. "Exactly as the law requires."

"Yes, yes, that's right." Parisia sighed. "Perhaps I'm worrying needlessly but I will feel better once the antidote has adequately adjusted them." The Prefect dismissed Iris and motioned to her daughter, Brianne, who had been standing quietly in the rear of the office awaiting instructions.

Brianne had not been her original choice for the post of First Aide, but Parisia was now glad her child had nagged her into giving her the chance to prove herself.

As Brianne gracefully moved to one of the chairs on the other side of the desk, her mother's heart filled with pride. She was reminded of herself two and a half decades ago, just before she conceived her twins, Brianne and Jason. The only genetic characteristic Brianne had inherited from her sire, Delbert, was the jade coloring of her eyes. Otherwise, she looked very much like herself—willowy, someone once said—tall and lean, with ivory skin and hair nearly as light. On the other hand, Jason was nearly a duplicate of Delbert, with his dark hair and angular features.

It had recently become apparent that Brianne had also inherited her mother's organizational skills and leadership tendencies. She was going to make a fine Prefect one day.

Parisia gave her daughter the necessary time to comfortably seat herself and arrange her long flowing caftan, then asked for her opinion of the new group of crossovers.

"I share your concern," Brianne answered without hesitation. "It's been eight years since any Earth people were drawn through the gateway to Heart, and over a century since any females arrived. But it's the physical appearance of the males that is most troubling to me. The ones who have come before never seemed so young...or so...*dangerous*."

Parisia angled her head curiously. "Perhaps they just seem so now that you are older and more aware of the differences between Earth men and men of Heart."

"Perhaps," Brianne conceded. "At any rate, their masculinity will be neutralized very shortly and the size of their bodies will no longer have import."

"Agreed. However, I am seriously considering bringing the ten women to us, or at least separating them from the men."

Brianne gave that some thought then shook her head. "I believe the cost and complications involved in creating a separate, secure environment for them would be harshly criticized by the opponents to your budget proposal. You know Nadia would never go along with such a radical idea."

Parisia gave a slight grimace. "Nadia will take the opposite stand from me no matter what I recommend. Everyone is aware of that."

"Hmmph. Everyone is also aware that she is power-hungry and hopes to unseat you one day, but that doesn't quiet her. Unfortunately, Nadia is not the only concern in this matter. Until we have a chance to observe the female crossovers' behavior to be certain they do not have the volatile personalities of Earth men, I wouldn't risk integrating them into our society. Our cultures are simply too different for them to make a smooth transition."

"I don't fully agree, but I will wait a few weeks before making a decision. In the meantime, I'd like to go over another matter that has been brought to my attention. Did you have a chance to see the report that came in this morning from Delegate Koballa?"

"Not yet," Brianne replied. "I spent most of the morning in the Observation Room, watching the crossovers awaken. Did you hear, not even one hour passed before a power struggle occurred?" Her eyes grew wide and she leaned forward in her chair. "One man actually *pushed* another and I believe they might have come to blows if another man hadn't interfered!" Realizing that she had become a bit too animated, she resumed her sedate pose. "I found it very interesting."

Parisia refrained from criticizing her daughter's momentary lapse of composure. She had been a very passionate, active child and, though she was now a mature woman, occasionally that child still broke through the adult veneer. There were times she feared Brianne would never fully overcome her excitable nature, but it didn't seem to interfere with her work, so there was really no reason to medicate her yet.

"It's fortunate that you had the chance to observe their primitive behavior firsthand," Parisia said. "Most of our people have only seen old visual recordings. However, I can assure you that in a few days, they will be quite normal and not at all *interesting*."

"That's good. They are just a little frightening in their natural state." Brianne frowned thoughtfully for a moment, then abruptly recalled her mother's earlier question. "I'm sorry. You mentioned a report from Delegate Koballa. She's been at the Interplanetary Health Symposium, correct?"

"Yes. She just returned. Here's her summary." Parisia picked up a folder and handed it to Brianne. "You can read the entire contents later but there was one notation I wanted to discuss with you before I spoke to any members of Parliament." She paused a moment to collect her thoughts. "It has nothing to do with the meetings Koballa went to attend. In fact, she clearly states that it is an unsubstantiated rumor."

Parisia watched the expression on her daughter's face change from curiosity to concern and got to the point.

"Do you recall the legend about the time when Heart had only men as rulers?"

Brianne smiled. "Of course. Mythology is a required subject in primary school."

"Tell me what you remember."

Brianne's expression altered to curiosity again but she began the tale she had memorized as a child. "Once upon a time, all of Heart was ruled by men. Women were assigned the menial chores such as home-caring, food preparation, wardrobe maintenance…the sort of functions our men perform for us. But the men of that time were barbarians. They fought with one another over the most trivial matters and abused the women's bodies for sport. One day they were visited by beings from another galaxy." She interrupted her narration and cocked her head. "I'm sorry, I can't seem to remember what they were called."

"Velids," Parisia said in a flat tone. "Go on."

"Yes, Velids. According to the legend, they looked like giant centipedes as they exited the ship, but once they saw the humans of Heart, they altered their physical appearance to copy them. Rather than attempt to communicate, the men killed all the alien visitors on sight. Apparently the men had never heard of metamorphs and automatically assumed they were evil. Before long, another ship of Velids arrived to avenge their people's deaths. Because Heart men believed women were helpless, they placed them and the children in protective shelters during the brief battle."

Brianne rose from her chair and slowly paced the office as she continued.

"When the fighting ended and the women left the shelters, they discovered that nearly half of the male populace was dead and the planet had been decimated. Without the men to restrain them, the women's natural superiority surfaced. They used their innate skills to rebuild the cities and reorganize Heart's culture, with the focus on peace and serenity." Reaching that point, Brianne stopped but her mother motioned for her to continue.

"It was clear that the men's violent instincts were solely responsible for the death and destruction. In the restructured society their behavior was controlled, first by physical restraints, later by medication."

"Something else was attempted," Parisia reminded her.

Brianne frowned thoughtfully then her eyes lit up with recollection. "Yes, genetic alteration was attempted, but the results were so disastrous, further attempts to permanently alter the men were outlawed. They used only the special antidote thereafter.

"As long as men were required for reproduction, they couldn't be eliminated, but the women soon learned how to accomplish conception without having to subject their bodies to invasion as if they were dumb animals."

She returned to the chair and folded her hands on her lap. "I remember asking you what an invasion was. Your explanation was so upsetting I didn't ask another question for days. Did Koballa learn something new about the reproductive process?"

Parisia hesitated a moment before answering. Someday she would have to have another discussion with Brianne about conception but not today. "No, dear. It's not that. Koballa's report includes information regarding the possible destruction of a humanoid planet in the Templar System."

"That's light-years away from here. The information, if it was factual, would be ancient by the time news reached us."

"Not necessarily. Koballa states that several cultures represented at the conference are developing faster-than-light travel. Soon no corner of the universe will be out of reach. If we accept that fact, then we must consider the possibility that the information from the Templar System could be current and accurate."

Brianne looked doubtful. She had to see something to believe it. "How was the planet supposedly destroyed?"

Parisia took a slow breath. "An army of giant wormlike beings, with the ability to morph their shape, attacked unexpectedly, killed every human and levelled the cities."

"Velids?" Brianne asked in a shocked whisper. "But they're mythical creatures."

"What if they're not? What if the legend is completely true, and those beings are still seeking revenge against the human race? With faster than light travel, might they return to Heart one day in the near future?"

"Oh, Mother, I hope you're wrong."

"So do I. But it brings up a serious question. What will we do if there really is a threat out there? If not today, tomorrow? We've lived in total peace for thousands of years, as have all the other life forms in this quadrant. We have no weapons, no defenses. There has never been a need for such."

"Surely we could request assistance from outside."

Parisia raised her eyebrows a notch. "Request assistance? From one of the more aggressive, male-dominated planets that we have always shunned? I wouldn't count on them hurrying to our rescue after we've consistently refused to deal with them. No, I believe we would be on our own. My question to you is this. Do you think an unsubstantiated rumor is sufficient for me to go before the Parliament and suggest we alter our constitution to permit the creation of a defense system and the manufacture of weaponry?"

Brianne needed to rise and pace again before answering. "If you go before Parliament with a rumor, you could be ridiculed. Worse, suggesting we change one of the basic laws of our people could get you impeached and Nadia would lead the move against you. However, if you do nothing and the threat is real, our world will come to an end and protecting your position will have been futile." She stopped and met Parisia's troubled gaze. "If I were the Imperial Prefect, I would have to argue for self-protection."

Parisia gave her a sad smile. "Good. Because that's precisely what I'm going to do. But I feel like I'm walking into a cage of hungry she-wolves."

"When do you plan to talk to Parliament?"

Parisia glanced at the calendar on the wall. "Three days. That should be sufficient time for the new crossovers to be fully assimilated before I introduce any new problems."

She didn't tell Brianne what was bothering her more than suggesting Heart develop a defense system. *If* Parliament could be convinced to change the law, who would design it? Who would implement it? She didn't believe a single female on Heart was capable of killing another being. Only men, in their natural state, had the aggressive traits necessary to wage war, and Heart men had been medicated for so many generations, no one knew if the neutralization could be completely reversed at all let alone in time to make a difference. In any event, Parisia was certain the women would never agree to expose themselves to male dominance, even if it meant survival of the race.

Nadia of Hinac pretended to listen to the inane gossip of the two women that had waylaid her. Her need to keep them as supporters forced her to be polite and feign interest, though her mind was on a drastically different track.

She had spent an hour that morning in the Observation Room watching the new crossovers awaken. Some of the observers with her were repulsed by the barbaric behavior of the Earth men. Others, like the Imperial Prefect's brat, were intrigued, in the way a child might study an ant colony.

Nadia's reaction was neither of those, though no one else could tell. Outwardly, she showed disgust and spoke of how relieved she would be once the antidote took effect. Inwardly, her pulse raced, her stomach fluttered and she had to clench her thighs to ease the itch between them.

It had begun when she received news of their arrival. So many of them at once. Some in chains. Some with weapons. The danger was so close she could practically taste it.

She had given in to the temptation to watch them being taken care of in the hospital, knowing that later she would be obsessed by visions of their large, masculine, nude bodies. Tortured by fantasies of how she could use them to satisfy her secret needs—needs that women weren't supposed to have. But the itch had already begun and she was never able to resist the dark pleasure that followed it.

At a very young age, Nadia had learned that the itch was not normal and shouldn't be mentioned, not even to one's own mother. The result of revealing an unhealthy interest in the male gender was medication. It only took a few doses for Nadia to realize she didn't like having her personal strength neutralized. After that, she kept her curiosity secret and became the perfect Heart woman…at least in public.

In private she experimented with different ways to appease the itch. Before long, she discovered that she could increase the intensity of the satisfaction by prolonging the build-up. Sometimes, she would make herself wait all day before giving in to it. She would ease the throbbing a little by crossing her legs or squirming in a chair, but she would hold off the final burst of sensation until she was nearly crazed with need. That way, the sweet darkness was often so powerful, it would last half the night.

There were times when the itch came on by itself but more often it followed thoughts about men. Like every school girl, she had learned the facts about the male species and why they had to be medicated. In their natural state, they posed a severe danger to women. Their strength, aggressive nature, and especially their male anatomy were all structured to dominate.

While the other girls were shivering with distaste, Nadia had trembled with excitement. The characteristics of men that Heart women were so adamant about controlling became the trigger for Nadia's secret fantasies.

Throughout Heart, men were forbidden by law to touch a woman without her permission and proper behavior dictated that such permission should be granted only under very specific circumstances. Thus, Nadia could only imagine feeling their forceful hands on her body, touching all her private, ticklish places.

The day she had learned how animals reproduced and equated the activity to humans, the itch had been so demanding, she had been forced to seek the privacy of the school lavatory to relieve it.

During one of her private experiments, she discovered the pleasure she could generate by pushing the hard, rounded handle of her hairbrush in and out of her womanpiece and her fantasies took on a new dimension.

While medicated, Heart men did not suffer from the malady that made their manpiece swell and harden while their minds emptied of everything except thoughts of relief. While medicated, a man was unable to invade a woman's body with his mighty weapon…even if he was given permission.

Nadia became so obsessed with the idea of using a man's body to stop the itch, one day she ordered her mother's personal servant to remove his clothing so that she could inspect his anatomy. Her examination clearly made him uncomfortable but his manpiece failed to enlarge, even when she pulled on it.

Since men were not permitted to attend school, he had never been taught the lessons Nadia had. He hadn't known what it was she had expected from him, but he could see he had somehow disappointed her and had been willing to accept whatever punishment she saw fit.

The rush of power she had experienced in response to his submissive attitude launched a whole new series of experiments for her. While the antidote tempered a man's masculinity, it also enhanced his need to provide useful service.

After that day, she'd spent long hours imagining unique ways a servant could be put to use and ingenious ways to punish him if his performance was less than satisfactory. Unfortunately, she was unable to enact any of her fantasies without risk of being medicated herself.

Though daughters normally remained in their mothers' homes all their lives, Nadia found the arrangement suffocating. By the time she'd reached her thirtieth year, she decided she needed a home of her own. With her freedom came privacy and she selected her personal servant with great care. Fulton was completely inexperienced but especially pleasing to her eye and anxious to be of service. She quickly guaranteed his loyalty to her by utilizing his sperm to fertilize her egg.

Following the birth of their daughter, Chloe, childcare was added to Fulton's responsibilities. Only after Nadia was certain of his attachment to the child, did she begin demanding more unusual services from him.

As politically ambitious as she was, she had to be very protective of her reputation, which meant she had to be certain Fulton would never speak to anyone about the special services she required of him. Technically, he was still her employee and, though he didn't have all the same privileges as a woman, he had the right to change employers if he was unhappy, or felt he was being mistreated. Another employer, particularly one who was a supporter of Parisia, might encourage him to gossip about her, and that could spell disaster.

Unwilling to give up her secret pleasures despite the risk of discovery, Nadia found ways to bind Fulton to her. Through trial and error, she learned that he thrived on words of praise about his work and would do absolutely anything for a few minutes of being petted by her. If she criticized his work or ignored him entirely, he would be desperate to make it up to her. Only a handful of times had she caused him physical pain, but the threat of it was always there.

Then, of course, she made sure he knew that if he ever left her, he would never be permitted to see Chloe again.

All things considered, their association had gone along rather smoothly for the last five years. But recently, she'd become bored with the predictability of his behavior and had begun thinking of hiring another young, trainable man.

If only there was a way she could acquire one of the Earth men.

Several of them had been especially appealing to her and the dark-skinned men were so different from any she'd seen before. Then there was that tall, dark-haired man with a scarred face and the larger than average manpiece. He would undoubtedly be the lead character in her fantasies for weeks to come.

For now, however, Fulton and his limited abilities were all she could count on to ease the itch that the Earth men had caused.

As soon as she entered her home, she let him know the mood she was in by her greeting. "Fulton! Where are you, you lazy creature?"

"In the kitchen," he replied. As she strode into that room, he gave her a hesitant smile. "I've made your favorite sweet to go with your tea."

"I don't want tea," she snapped. "I called to tell you I was coming home for a *bath*, not tea. If you don't start paying better attention when I give you instructions, I am going to replace you. Do you understand me?"

Fulton frowned and bowed his head. "I'm sorry, Nadia. You didn't say how long it would take for you to get home and I was worried that the bath water would cool if I prepared it too soon. I'll get it ready immediately." He took a step then paused and looked back at the tea kettle. "Shall I pour you some tea—"

"I said I don't want tea, you dolt! *Go,* before I lose my patience entirely." As Fulton hurried from the kitchen, Nadia's pulse quickened. He had been on the verge of tears. In fact, he was probably in her dressing room sniveling away while the water ran. He was primed to do anything she ordered and she was aching for much more than the usual bath. There probably wouldn't be a better time to try out her new creation.

As she considered how she could introduce it to Fulton, she broke off a chunk of the sweet he had baked for her and placed it in her mouth. Rich chocolate superbly blended with black raspberry melted on her tongue. Though Fulton was beginning to bore her in some ways, his culinary skills assured him a permanent position in her household no matter how often she threatened to get rid of him.

She finished the sweet and headed for her bath. She had designed the spacious dressing room with her unique needs in mind. The walls and closet doors were mirrored, and the floor was covered with plush black carpeting. On one side of the room was an oversized black tub with gold fixtures, and on the other side was a gold velvet chaise wide enough for two people to lay on at the same time. The few women who had seen the room questioned such extravagance for something so private. They preferred to show off their luxuries. But Nadia had always been a little different from the other women.

As she entered the dressing room, she smelled the perfumed oil rising with the steam. Fulton stood next to the tub, awaiting her. As usual, he had undressed, so that his clothing would not get wet while he assisted her. She gave his ample body a lingering look. He was taller, heavier, and broader across the shoulders than she, but he lacked the hardness that she noticed about the Earth men. Looking at his short dark hair, she decided to focus her attention on that feature and pretend he was the scarred crossover that had fascinated her.

"You may remove my robe," she stated in a harsh tone to remind him he had yet to make up for his earlier failure to please.

In the mirrors, she watched him move around her, carefully drawing back the hood of her robe and untying the bow at her throat without touching any part of her. With the same caution, he undid the fastenings down the front of the garment and slipped it off her body.

As he hung up the robe, she reminded herself that the longer she could put off the physical contact, the better the reward would be. "Now brush my hair out. Slowly."

One at a time, he removed the pins that kept her waist-length black hair wrapped in a braided crown around her head. With unhurried strokes, he brushed it out until it hung around her like a satin cape.

Nadia was always fascinated by her own transformation from civilized woman to primitive creature. "That's enough. You may take my slip and briefs. *Carefully*."

She hadn't needed to say that. She knew he would take the utmost care not to touch her flesh until she gave him the specific order to do so. As he removed her briefs, she wondered if he noticed how damp the crotch was today and whether his dull mind ever figured out what that meant. She doubted it.

"You may touch my hand to help me into the tub. And make sure my hair doesn't get wet."

As she submerged her body in the deep water, Fulton placed a pillow behind her head and draped her hair over the back of the tub. Normally the hot, perfumed water would instantly start relaxing her but today the itch was too strong to be calmed so easily. Fulton dipped a washcloth into the water and held it out to her.

"I'm quite worn out today. You do it." He pressed the cloth to one of her feet but she kicked it away. "Not with the cloth. Use your hands. The way I showed you before. Remember, the doctor said I have poor circulation and should be vigorously massaged to improve the condition." She closed her eyes and smothered a sigh as his fingers closed over the toes of her one foot and squeezed. It would take some time for him to get to her abdomen, but he had learned the routine well and it would be worth the wait.

One leg, up to the hip joint. The other leg. One arm, then the other. Her nipples were tightly puckered long before his palms pressed over them. He kneaded her breasts and rolled the nipples until her breath came in gasps. "Go on," she whispered, and his fingers slid down over her stomach and into her womanpiece.

Instantly she felt the first streak of pleasure and gripped the sides of the tub. "More," she said, spreading her thighs so that he could fit his whole hand over her. "Faster," she demanded, gyrating her hips in the opposite direction of his motions. When the explosion came, she bit her lip to keep from crying out. It would not do to let him know how very well he had served.

She rested in the tub awhile, but the itch was still nagging at her. This was definitely the day to teach Fulton a new trick.

She gave him permission to help her out of the tub and towel her off. While he was on his knees, drying her feet, she ran her fingers through his hair. His hopeful gaze leapt to hers. "Did I hurt your feelings before, Fulton?"

He lowered his eyes again. "I deserved your criticism. I wasn't attentive."

She stroked his cheek and neck and noticed how he angled his head for more. Continuing to pet his face, hair and shoulders, she softened her voice to complement the gentle touch. "But you usually are and I shouldn't have been so stern with you." She eased him forward just enough to tickle his nose with her pubic hair and he giggled in response.

"I tasted the sweet you made me. It was excellent. You really are very good most of the time. You can't help being slow about some things. I should be more patient." His lips parted, and she felt his hot puffs of breath against her womanpiece. A little more attention and he wouldn't question anything she ordered, no matter how outrageous it was.

"Would you like to rest on the chaise with me?" His

gaze darted to the golden lounge then back to her. She didn't know what he liked more, her petting or the feel of velvet against his skin. To give him both at once was the closest he could come to ecstasy.

She considered reminding him that this was a very special privilege that he would never be granted from another employer. But he knew well that, since it was so distasteful for a woman to touch or be touched by a man, her gift to him was extremely rare and should be cherished. His payment for the privilege would continue to be silent loyalty and total devotion.

"Before we rest though, there is another service I require…something you've never done before, but it was prescribed by the doctor to…stimulate my circulation from within. Remain on your knees while I get what I need."

She opened one of the closets and brought out a drawstring bag. As she withdrew her creation from the pouch and saw the bewildered expression on Fulton's face she nearly changed her mind. What she was intending was terribly daring. Then she felt the insistent beating at the base of her abdomen and decided again that the risk would be worth it.

She had no way of knowing what a swollen manpiece looked like, but having once seen a pair of horses copulating, she assumed it wasn't much different for humans. With a little ingenuity, some leather strips and her favorite ceramic hairbrush handle, she had made an artificial manpiece for Fulton.

As she knelt in front of him and strapped the invention around his hips, his expression turned fearful but she scraped a thumbnail over his nipple and glanced purposefully at the lounge, and he forgot any objection he might have had.

Positioning herself on her knees before him, she

thought to imitate what the horses had done. She guided the brush handle into her slick crevice and instructed Fulton to shift his hips back and forth, but the result brought her little satisfaction.

It was better when she made him lay on his back and mounted the piece from atop, yet she still required manual stimulation to feel the pleasure.

Certain there had to be a way to make her creation work properly, she tried several different positions before she found one that sent a tremor through her. Symbolically, his laying on top of her was completely unacceptable, but physically, his lower body rubbing so intimately against hers was extremely titillating. Fulton required more practice—that much was clear—but this new method of seeking pleasure was worth a little clumsiness.

She held off the mind-numbing release as long as possible, but eventually it overwhelmed her. She was so pleased with Fulton and her invention, she spent much longer than usual with him on the chaise. Her fingers tickled and scratched his flesh until he whimpered with a mixture of pain and pleasure. She even toyed with his private parts in ways she'd never thought to do before.

The expression on his face was one of excruciating pain, but the shivery bumps on his skin revealed an appreciation for his torment. Nadia wallowed in the raw power his torture stirred in her and the itch started up all over again.

Suddenly his entire body was racked with shudders and a tiny drop of clear fluid seeped from his manpiece. If she didn't know it was impossible, she might have thought he just had a sexual experience.

She was about to order him to massage her one more time when she noticed he had gotten teary-eyed again. His weepiness was really becoming quite tiresome. Waving him away, she didn't bother to conceal her annoyance. "Get up, you fool. Go fix my tea now. I'll have it in the sitting room."

The moment he left, she proceeded to take care of the itch herself. Visions of the Earth men filled her mind and she wondered how close Fulton and her invention had come to the real thing. As delicious waves of sensation flooded through her, she knew she would never be truly satisfied until she could make the comparison firsthand.

All she had to do was come up with a reason why she should be permitted to make contact with one of the crossovers...preferably the big, dangerous-looking man with the scars.

CHAPTER 6

Tarla stretched and wiggled her tired fingers. After two hours of husking corn, the boring task was finally completed. It might have been less tedious if she could have kept Duncan talking but he had nothing more to say. In fact, it was unnaturally quiet throughout the kitchen. Normally her nurses were so talkative, she had to hush them.

She got up and walked over to Robin and Sunny. They had been helping the dishwasher but that chore was finished as well.

"It's too quiet," Robin murmured the moment Tarla sat down with them.

"I know," Tarla replied. "Duncan said these men don't talk much, but what about our people?" She gave it some thought. "Maybe everyone's suffering from post-traumatic shock."

Sunny nodded, her usual smiling face clouded with worry. "I know I am. I keep thinking this must be a bad dream, but I can't make myself wake up. Nothing we've heard makes any sense."

Before Tarla could respond, Kara and Darcy joined them. As Darcy sat down beside Tarla, she asked,

"So, how do we get out of here?"

"I wish I knew. Duncan insists that no one has ever left here…unless they die of *really* old age."

"Swell," Robin said. "I can't accept that. If we were brought in, there has to be a way out. I absolutely refuse to live out my days like some hippie in a nineteen-sixty commune."

"At least the communal bathroom facilities aren't as antique as this kitchen," Sunny said, trying to find a bright side as usual.

Kara nudged Darcy and made a face that prompted Darcy to speak. "We want to go home, Captain. Our families are expecting to pick us all up at airports today and tomorrow. They're going to think we're dead."

Tarla patted Darcy's hand and put on her most reassuring face. "We'll find a way. These old men may have been cowed by whoever's pulling the strings here, but that doesn't mean we have to be. We're soldiers and trauma nurses. We're used to making instantaneous, life or death decisions under impossible conditions. And it definitely appears we have a lot more tech knowledge than most of the current residents. Surely that gives us an advantage even if we're being held by a superior alien race like Higgs believes."

Again Tarla fought the temptation to reveal how much knowledge she actually had and how she just might turn out to be their secret weapon. But she just couldn't take the chance of losing their trust at this stage.

As the women tried to console one another about their loved ones waiting for them at home, Tarla fell silent. She understood but couldn't really empathize. The last time she was in Innerworld was three years ago and the only person she'd met with was her handler. When she'd first relocated to Outerworld, she'd kept in contact with several men and women she called friends but, within a few years, those relationships faded. And because of her double life, she made a practice of never getting too close to her Outerworld neighbors or workmates. If it hadn't been for the war, she knew none of these women, including Robin, would consider her a close friend.

As to family, there was only her father and he had disavowed her when she'd openly shared a living space with her first Terran lover. That man's disapproval of Noronians and Terrans having equal rights was so great he had moved back to Norona when Romulus was given permission to join with Aster, even though Innerworld had been his home most of his life.

A rumble of wagon wheels outside alerted the kitchen staff that the field workers had returned. Tarla and the others pitched in to help fill plates of food while the incoming men lined up at the water pump to wash. Since there was a shortage of tables and chairs inside, a lot of people carried their dinners outside and sat on the grass. When Tarla saw Major Cookson heading out the door, she got her own dinner and followed him. Robin stayed right behind her.

"Would you mind if we joined you, Major?" Tarla asked once she caught up with him.

"Not at all, but please call me Geoffrey," he said pleasantly.

She smiled in return. "And I'm Tarla. This is my friend, Robin."

His hands being full, he simply nodded his head. "How do you do."

Robin smiled and held his gaze. "I do very well, thank you. And how do *you* do?"

Geoffrey's only response to her obvious flirtation

was to clear his throat and turn away. "Shall we sit over there?" he asked, looking at a spot under a tree. As they seated themselves, he caught sight of Logan coming out of the big house. "McKay!" he called. "Over here."

Tarla watched Logan sway and bump into the wall of the house. A moment later the glass he was carrying slipped from his grasp. Without hesitation, she rose from the ground and started toward him.

"Sergeant McKay?" When he continued staggering around the corner toward the back of the house, she picked up her pace. "Logan! What's wrong?"

Closing his eyes, he leaned back against the wall and slid to the ground.

"Are you ill?" Tarla asked, dropping to her knees beside him. His eyes were squinted shut and his upper lip was dotted with perspiration. She placed her palm on his forehead to check for fever but he jerked away from her hand.

That abrupt movement caused him to groan aloud and press his hands against his temples.

"Headache?" she asked softly.

"Migraine," he whispered. "Just leave me alone."

Tarla clucked her tongue and continued to speak in a gentle voice. "I will *not* leave you alone. Is there anything that helps?"

His voice remained a harsh whisper. "Medicine was in my bag...wherever that is. Aspirin helps a little. And ice."

"Hmmm. I'll go find Duncan and see what he's got. Will you be okay here for a few minutes?"

He didn't bother to answer. It was taking his entire concentration not to throw up all over himself. The setting of the dueling suns was drilling a hole through his eyelids, but the effort it would take to find shade was beyond him. He just crouched there, helpless as an infant.

It seemed like Tarla had been gone quite a while but he knew from previous experience, she'd be back. She couldn't resist fussing over a man incapacitated by pain.

"Logan?"

That voice. He covered his ears to shut her out.

"I need you to get up and walk a little ways with me." She grasped him by the arm and tried to lift, but he didn't budge. "Don't be stubborn. There's a tent set up for you with a cot and lots of soft pillows. It's *dark* in there. I couldn't get any ice, but Duncan gave me a powder that might help."

The pillows and darkness did it. Logan mustered sufficient strength to open his right eye and pull himself upright. She hadn't been completely honest about it being only a little ways. Despite his limited vision, he noted a number of soldiers erecting tents in the area. Each thud of a hammer forcing a stake into the ground was like a railroad spike being rammed into his brain but he was in no condition to stop them.

Tarla led him away from the construction and past the small wooden shelters to a tent that had been set up by itself. She held the flap open as he entered then closed it except for a sliver after she was inside.

The simple act of eliminating the brilliant sunset went a long way toward relief for Logan.

"Sit down on the cot but don't lie back yet," Tarla ordered. "There's a bucket there if you need it. I had a supervisor once who got migraines that made her nauseous, so don't try to be a tough guy if your stomach's queasy."

Whether it was her words or the sight of the bucket, his stomach overruled his mind. When he was finished, she handed him a glass of water to rinse his mouth then removed the bucket. Efficient as always.

He started to lie down but she stopped him again. "Wait. Take the powder first." As she mixed it with the water, she explained, "Duncan says this is all they have. It doesn't sound very strong but it tastes like ground aspirin. I figured it's worth a try."

While he drained the glass, she arranged the pile of pillows so his head and shoulders would stay elevated. "Okay, lie back now and try to focus on breathing."

He might have been able to do that if she hadn't sat down on the cot next to him and slipped her hands behind his neck.

Instantly his fingers clamped around her wrists and held. "What are you doing?" he asked through gritted teeth.

"There are pressure points in your head that will release your endorphins, which are natural painkillers. Would you rather suffer or let me touch you?"

He groaned and released her wrists. What he couldn't tell her was that tolerating her touch caused another kind of suffering. He groaned again as her fingers worked some kind of magic, pressing and rotating two spots at the base of his skull. From there she went to the points behind his ears, the sides of his head, then the top and started at the base again.

The pain was still there but the sharp edge had been slightly dulled, making room in his mind for more awareness of her. He didn't need to open his eyes to see her. She was a permanent fixture in his memory. He knew he should send her away but the migraine and her gentle treatment had sapped his willpower.

He relaxed a bit more as she massaged the tension out of his neck and shoulders. Now he felt her hip pressed against his, and how her forearms brushed lightly over his chest as her hands manipulated his muscles. His fingers curled into his palms to keep from stroking her back and urging her closer until he—

He reminded himself that he was only allowed to do that sort of thing in his fantasies. This was real life, and it wasn't personal. She was a nurse, caring for a patient, just like before. Nothing else.

Tarla could see by his clenched jaw that he was still in pain, though somewhat more comfortable. A wicked thought briefly crossed her mind that he probably deserved whatever pain he was in but she immediately banished it. Who he was or what he had done didn't matter at the moment—only that he was ill and needed her attention.

It occurred to her that she could massage his neck and shoulders better without his shirt in the way but she cancelled that idea. As unreasonable as it was, in spite of everything, she was still having a hard time ignoring the fact that Logan was a man. He was just so big, so hard-muscled...so incredibly masculine.

Of all the men she had treated, most of whom she had seen completely nude, he was the only one who had ever made her want to forget that he was a patient. For that reason, she had always been extra careful when she changed the dressing on the wound in his thigh and *never* helped him bathe. Somehow that would have been too intimate with him.

To distract herself from thoughts of his body, she moved her fingers to his face, spreading all ten fingers to evenly apply a web of pressure.

Instantly an avalanche of images and sounds filled her mind. She was curled protectively on the ground, vomiting up blood as she was kicked and pounded to within an inch of her life.

No, it wasn't her body being brutalized. It was Logan's.

And she was seeing the scene through his eyes.

She pulled her hands away from his face so abruptly, he jerked upright. As he grimaced in pain, she pressed his shoulders back down onto the cot. "I am so sorry, Logan. I…I thought I saw a spider on the pillow next to you and…anyway it was just a leaf. Nothing to worry about."

She moved her attention to his hands and he closed his eyes again. As she massaged the areas at the bases of his thumbs, she allowed herself to analyze what flashed in her mind.

Although many Noronians were capable of reading another's thoughts or watching a remembered scene by placing their fingers on that person's temples, she had never had that ability. And yet, she had just had a ton of random information instantly downloaded into her brain from Logan's mind.

Tarla kept massaging Logan's hands while desperately trying to untangle the mess of data in her head, but it was too new. Given time, she would probably be able to sort it all out but since Logan hadn't given her permission to invade his personal memories, she would do her utmost to forget it or at least keep all of it locked away.

However, the memories connected to the one image that rose out of the heap insisted on being looked at before being shelved.

Logan was being beaten by other soldiers…because he'd tried to turn them in.

Out of the hodgepodge of data, Tarla came away with one important fact.

Logan had been framed.

Robin picked up two pillows and a stack of linens and headed for where she had last seen Geoffrey.

When Tarla unexpectedly left her alone with him, she had thought it was a nice bit of luck. Then the oddest thing happened. She couldn't think of anything to say. Not even one funny joke to entertain him. And he hadn't helped the situation any, sitting there with his perfect posture, eating dinner with his perfect manners. As soon as his plate was clean, he excused himself, very politely, and set about organizing work details to get everyone settled for the night.

That was when she realized the only way she was going to get to know the major better was by working with him…and she *really* wanted to know him better.

After circling the big house, she finally spotted him helping Willy erect a tent.

"Hi, Willy," she said cheerfully. "Did you get linens yet?"

Willy grinned. "Sure did. But if you run into the guys distributing cots, I could use one here."

"You got it. Geoffrey, do you need anything for your tent? If you point it out, I'll be glad to make sure you're set up."

Geoffrey smiled…politely. "I haven't gotten to mine yet, but thank you for the offer." He returned his attention to the stake he was pounding into the ground.

Robin wasn't willing to give up that easily. "In that case, just point out where you'd like your tent to be and I'll see to it that it's set up. I have nothing else to do. The linens are all distributed."

He finished setting the stake and stood up. "All right then." He looked around the area a moment. "I think it would be best if I were in the midst of the men. Any place you pick will be fine."

Robin nodded and took a few steps away when he spoke again.

"Robin? A moment please."

She turned and faced him with a soft smile that she knew disarmed the average male.

Geoffrey's gaze darted away from hers and he cleared his throat. "I, uh, was wondering if we should check on Tarla and McKay."

Robin arched an eyebrow at him. "*Check* on them?"

He covered his mouth and coughed as if it would help him get his words out. "Yes, um, I mean he seemed ill and I sensed some antagonism between them, and—"

"And *nothing*, Major," Robin interrupted defensively. "Tarla is a dedicated nurse, who would take care of Attila the Hun if he was in pain. If anyone can get your bodyguard back at your side, it's her." She thought she saw Geoffrey's fair cheekbones darken and regretted her choice of words. "I'm sorry—"

"It's quite all right," he said quietly. "I didn't make myself clear. I was concerned about your friend's welfare...being alone with him for such a long time."

Now it was her turn to blush. "Oh. Well there's no need to worry. Tarla can handle the worst of them. And believe me, she has."

"She does seem very capable."

Robin laughed. "If the war had gone on any longer, she probably would have made general!" His smile seemed more genuine this time, so she hoped he had forgiven her rash comment. "Well, I guess I'll go see about your tent now." She walked away, but at least she had the satisfaction of knowing he was watching her for several long seconds before getting back to work.

"Geoffrey!"

He turned to see Tarla hurrying toward him. "What's wrong? Is McKay—"

"No, no," she said waving her hand quickly. "He'll be fine, eventually. He has a bad migraine though and, from what he told me, without his medicine, it could last for days."

"Days?"

Tarla nodded. "But it's not necessary. Duncan gave me some medicinal powder they use for minor discomfort. He said that in cases where the powder isn't enough, the injured or sick person is sent to the fairies for treatment."

"Yes. I was told the person goes into the barn and comes out cured, but with no recollection of how it happened."

"Right. It also sounds like the fastest route to whoever's in control here. So, why not test it ourselves...with Sergeant McKay? Who knows how long it might be before someone else legitimately falls sick? And if someone *is* observing us, they would know he's truly ill."

Geoffrey rubbed his chin. "If he was in good enough shape to defend himself, I wouldn't think twice about sending him into unknown territory, but under the circumstances..."

"McKay already volunteered," Tarla said, putting a quick end to Geoffrey's vacillation. "In fact, as soon as I mentioned Duncan's fairies to him, he came up with the suggestion himself. Not only does he want to find out what's going on here, he said he'd try anything that might get rid of the migraine."

The expression on Geoffrey's face made it clear that he hated having to make the decision but he did it anyway. "All right. I'll get McKay and help him to the barn while you find Duncan."

Ten minutes later the four of them were standing in the open doorway of the tack room at the back of the huge barn.

"How does it work?" Tarla asked Duncan.

"He just goes inside, closes the door and tells them

what's ailing him."

"Tells who?" Geoffrey asked.

Duncan almost looked exasperated. "The fairies, of course."

"You mean you can see them when you're in there?"

"No. They're invisible. Like the wall."

"What if—" Logan pressed his temples to shut out the excruciating pain uttering those two words had caused. Taking a slow breath and maintaining the pressure, he tried again. "What if someone goes in with me?"

Duncan shook his head. "They don't help the sick person unless he's alone and the door's locked tight from the inside." His smile faded as an old memory came to him. "Tried that myself once…a very long time ago."

"Okay," Logan said, stepping into the room. "Let's get on with it."

As Geoffrey and Tarla backed away, Duncan said, "Just throw the bolt on the door and say your problem out loud."

"We'll wait for you right here," Geoffrey added.

Although Logan thought the idea of telling a bunch of farm equipment that he had a migraine was completely ridiculous, he locked the door, turned around and voiced his complaint. When nothing happened immediately, he sat down on the floor to wait. It was all he could do to keep from closing his eyes but he didn't want to miss whatever was coming despite the pain.

Several minutes later, a hissing sound, like the air being let out of a tire, drew his attention upward but it stopped before he could discern what had caused it.

The ping of the transmitter next to Nadia's bed

surprised her. It was rare for her to receive a call in the evening. She touched the red button on the top of the small white box. "Hello?"

"This is Simone in Observation."

Nadia's attention perked up. "Yes?"

"By coincidence, not long after you called, something occurred."

Though she was tapping her fingernails impatiently on the table beside her, Nadia replied with only slight interest. "Can you tell me about it?"

After a slight hesitation, Simone spoke again. "Not really. Too many ears, if you know what I mean. I get off in half an hour. Why don't you come by for a visit?"

"That sounds fine. See you shortly." Nadia touched the red button again then bounded from the bed to her closet. She didn't bother to call Fulton to help her dress. She needed to hurry and he didn't know the meaning of the word.

What could possibly have happened to prompt Simone's call so soon? She had called the woman earlier and requested that she be kept up to date regarding the new crossovers. Nadia had insinuated that there could be a problem that might reflect badly on Parisia and any small occurrence could be important. Fortunately, Simone was one of the women who believed that Nadia would eventually be in a position of great power, which could personally benefit her later, if she proved ingratiating enough in the meantime.

Unfortunately, Simone was nearly as ambitious as Nadia herself, which could eventually become a problem, especially when Simone had a natural advantage. Nadia was tall, large-boned, dark-haired and mocha-skinned, with a prominent nose that openly proclaimed her hawk-like disposition. Simone was petite and fair with tiny ringlets of honey-colored hair framing an ivory, innocent face. She was femininity and grace personified, the ideal of every Heart woman.

Nadia managed to reach the Observation Room as Simone was signing out for her break, but she still had to wait a few more minutes until they walked out of earshot of the relief operator.

"One of the crossovers came in for medical treatment," Simone said in a conspiratorial tone even though no one was around.

"Male or female?" Nadia asked in the same voice.

"Male. Rather dangerous looking too."

"Oh?" Nadia's interest increased another notch. "Can you describe him?" As soon as Simone began, Nadia was positive it was the same man she had been intrigued by that morning. "What was the problem?"

"He said, 'migraine' and was holding his head. He did look uncomfortable."

"Were normal procedures followed?"

Simone nodded. "He was anesthetized and taken to the sanatorium. I happen to have a friend who's on duty there tonight. If you're interested, I'm sure she wouldn't mind filling us in on his condition and treatment."

Nadia managed to conceal her excitement beneath an indifferent façade. "I have nothing better to do this evening."

At the sanatorium, Simone's friend, Olympia, informed them that the man had a headache caused by a severe chemical imbalance in his brain and, though there was no way of determining what had caused it, the medic was able to correct the problem. She could not be certain however that the imbalance would not reoccur. As a precaution, vital signs and brain activity were being monitored for two more hours before returning him to the commune.

"He is unconscious, isn't he?" Nadia asked.

"Of course," Olympia replied.

"Would it be possible for me to get a look at him?" Nadia asked as casually as possible.

The woman pressed a key on the numerical board in front of her then turned the monitor toward Nadia and Simone.

Nadia inhaled sharply as she stared at the screen. It *was* him, just as she suspected. "You were right, Simone. He does appear to be extremely dangerous."

"There's no need to worry," Olympia said. "His room is completely secure."

"Thank the suns for that," Nadia said, pretending to be greatly relieved. Actually she was racking her brain to come up with an excuse to get into that room. After her experiment with Fulton that afternoon, her curiosity about the Earth men was increasing by the hour. But no reasonable explanation came to her. After a few more seconds studying the shape of the man's body beneath the sheet, she had no choice but to leave unsatisfied.

"Thank you for your help, Olympia. Perhaps I'll be able to return a favor one day in the future. Simone, I'll speak to you later." With a formal nod to each of the women, she headed back home.

Somehow, she was going to gain possession of that man. Regardless of the danger he posed, she wanted him before the antidote completely stripped his masculine qualities. Based on his size and the dosage he should be consuming daily, she estimated she had two days at the most to come up with a viable scheme and implement it.

After that, the scarred man would be as mellow and impotent as Fulton.

CHAPTER 7

The click of the bolt being pulled back on the tack room door instantly drew Tarla and Geoffrey to their feet. Robin, who had brought Tarla's uneaten dinner then stayed for the vigil, remained on the floor until Logan actually appeared.

Tarla could see he felt better even before he spoke. His usual bored expression was back.

"Headache's gone," Logan said as he walked up to them. "But I have no idea what happened to me."

"Think, man," Geoffrey prompted. "There has to be something. You were in there for four hours."

Logan shook his head. "I was awake and miserable one minute then I was waking up without a headache the next. I don't even remember falling asleep but I obviously did."

"Any aftereffects?" Tarla asked.

"No," Logan answered. "In fact, I feel like I just had a great night's sleep."

Robin glanced at Tarla. "Maybe it's some kind of mind control."

"Whatever it is," Geoffrey said, "we don't know anything more than we did before—that someone with advanced technology is in control here and this tack room is some sort of way-station between them and the farm."

Logan frowned. "I think we can assume they're keeping tabs on us too. I'd say the first step should be to tear this room apart."

"Right," Geoffrey responded. "Considering the number of mouths there are to feed, we'll have to continue to do a fair share of the work but a few less hands won't matter. In the morning, your team can concentrate on the barn. I'll put my team on examining the invisible wall."

"And keep the women in the kitchen all day?" Robin asked in a falsely sweet tone. "I don't think so."

Tarla spoke before Geoffrey could reply. "If I might make a suggestion, it might be best to rotate chores. Everyone's going to want to feel they're contributing to an escape plan."

"Quite right," Geoffrey said. "Preparing a rotation schedule will be the first order of business in the morning."

"With my help," Robin amended. "If that's okay with you, Tarla."

Tarla gave the major a chance to object but he only cleared his throat. "That will be fine. Two heads are always better than one. And now, if I don't get a little sleep, I won't be much good for any kind of chore when the suns come up."

The others agreed there was nothing more to be accomplished that night. As they walked out of the barn, a star-studded sky lit their path and the rustle of leaves was the only sound in the air. Everyone had apparently given in to fatigue. Just before they split up, Logan asked, "Could I have a word with you, Captain?"

Tarla gave Robin a sign to give her a minute.

"Come on, Geoffrey," Robin said with a smile. "I'll show you where I put your new home then I'll come back to guide Tarla to ours."

Tarla grew tense the moment they walked away, leaving her alone with Logan. He hadn't made her nervous as long as he was incapacitated. Even though she now felt certain he was neither a murderer nor traitor, he was still a very large, dangerous man…with the ability to crush her heart with a few words. It seemed as though he sensed her nervousness for he just stood there looking at her, as if daring her to run away. She made herself stay perfectly still and meet his gaze. And when he stepped closer, it took all her courage to stand her ground and not show the slightest trace of fear.

Slowly he extended his right hand toward her. "I just wanted to say thank you," he said in a low voice.

It took her another moment to realize that he was only trying to shake her hand. By the time she did, he had withdrawn his hand and walked away. She hadn't meant to be rude. His gesture had simply been a shock. It was completely out of character for him to say thank you for anything.

"Sergeant McKay?"

He stopped without looking back at her.

"You're very welcome."

His response was a casual salute.

"He's a strange one, isn't he?" Robin said coming up behind Tarla.

Tarla turned and shrugged. "I didn't understand him when he was my patient either."

For fear of disturbing anyone, they kept silent as Robin led the way to their tent. All of the women and most of the men were bunking two or three to a tent, partly for a sense of companionship and partly because there were only half as many tents as there were people. The caretakers must have assumed they would sleep in pairs. There was probably some sort of clue in that, but she was too tired to figure it out.

A candle lantern burning inside the tent allowed Tarla to see what Robin had accomplished while she was with Logan. Their cots were made up and a few changes of clothes were stowed beneath each. Since they were relatively close to several other tents, they kept their voices to a whisper.

After Tarla thanked Robin for setting them up, she said, "Considering the unreality of this whole situation, we're fairly well settled in."

"Yeah. When we get back we can all send thank you notes to the Pentagon for training us to adapt so well."

Tarla pulled off her shoes and examined one. It was stretchy, like a one-size-fits-all slipper sock, but the expandable sole was made of a harder, rubbery substance that was similar to the bottom of a sneaker. "Whoever our caretakers are, they're quite ingenious."

"About some things," Robin amended. "About others, they're practically prehistoric. If they can heal a man with severe burns, why do they need to barter for food? Why have a semi-modern lavatory but a kitchen from pioneer days?"

"Good questions. Now I have one for you. If the men we met today didn't have to work the farm or prepare food the old-fashioned way, what would they do all day?"

Robin gave it some thought then said, "I think we can rule out socializing. They barely talk to each other. Maybe they'd just sit and stare at the green sky like a bunch of zombies."

Tarla shook her head. "I don't know. They seem to take pride in working and no one I saw today tried to shirk their responsibilities. That in itself is odd."

Robin laughed. "Yeah. That many men and not even one goof-off. Back to Higgs's theory that they're all androids."

Tarla gave a sigh and sat down on her cot. "We'd better get some sleep while we can."

Robin blew out the candle and settled between the soft sheets. "Mmm. Maybe I'll get lucky and this will all turn out to be a weird dream."

Tarla was certain she'd be asleep in seconds but she couldn't let go of her sudden ability to touch Logan's mind. Since she'd never been able to do that before, she assumed the skill would only awaken when she joined with her soul's mate. And since she had given up ever meeting that man, she hadn't expected it to happen at all. Thoughts of soulmates and joining always made her a little melancholy but there was nothing she could do to change the reality of her solitary life.

She had never lacked for male companionship but none of the Noronian men she was attracted to ever triggered the mating fever. Time and time again, she would be hopeful only to be disappointed. Even her one, fairly long, committed relationship had ended in heartbreak. Since he wasn't Noronian, Nick Valentino could never have been her soulmate. But she had cared deeply about him and enjoyed his companionship for over a year...until he met the woman who captured his heart.

Once she had passed the usual mating age without ever having experienced even a hint of the fever that supposedly would strike when she met *the one*, she finally gave up hope of ever encountering her elusive soulmate. Letting go of that hope suddenly allowed her to imagine a very different life in Outerworld and she'd gone after it with all her heart.

Tarla had finally dozed off when several voices shouting obscenities broke the stillness outside. As she and Robin quickly pulled their shoes back on, she could tell both men and women were involved in a furious battle over something but the cause wasn't clear. They hurried outside at the same time everyone else did.

At the center of the commotion, Wilkes and Lee Tang circled each other—her in an offensive fighting stance, him clearly defensive. On the ground, one of Wilkes's pals lay holding his crotch and moaning in pain. Standing guard over him was the beautiful Alicia Samples, and she looked furious enough to do him more damage if he dared to rise.

"What goes on here?" Geoffrey shouted as he shoved his way through the crowd.

"Stay out of this, limey," Wilkes growled. "The bitch wants to play rough and I'm gonna oblige her." He swung a meaty fist toward her face but she instantly blocked it with her left forearm and followed with a powerful right jab to his diaphragm. As his body folded forward under that blow, she spun around, leapt in the air and delivered a kick to his jaw that sent him sprawling beside his friend.

Lee stood poised to continue the fight until she was certain he had given up. Leaning over his barely conscious, pain-contorted body, she said, "Thank you so much for obliging me, asshole. Let's do this again sometime." An angry flame still glowed in her eyes as she turned toward the major and defended her actions. "These two guys physically intercepted Airman Samples and me coming back from the lavatory. When we told them we weren't interested in spending our free time with them, they got nasty. We only defended ourselves from assault." Her narrow-eyed gaze scanned the circle around her. "And we'll do it again if we have to."

Logan cut the tense silence from the back of the crowd. "Show's over, everybody. Back to your tents. Except Gianni, Higgs and Yan." After a moment's hesitation, all but a handful of people drifted off. Robin remained despite his order.

Geoffrey grimaced at the two men on the ground then asked Tarla, "Would you mind seeing to them?"

"Wilkes's jaw cracked," Lee stated without remorse. "I felt it go. Other than that, they'll recover...physically."

A few seconds later, Tarla confirmed Lee's prognosis. "We should put Wilkes in the tack room and let our caretakers check on him."

"Good idea," Logan said. "That'll keep him out of trouble for a few hours. Who knows, maybe he'll remember something I couldn't."

Geoffrey explained the procedure to Higgs, Gianni and Wilkes, and the two MP's helped the patient to his feet. As they headed toward the barn, Lee and Alicia *assisted* Wilkes's cohort back to his tent.

"This problem isn't going to go away," Logan said to Geoffrey. "We may have to assign guards for the women."

"I beg your pardon?" Tarla demanded. "In case you missed it, Lee and Alicia did just fine without a man to protect them."

Logan looked down his nose at her. "That was one on one. What do you think will happen when Wilkes comes out of that tack room in one piece again? He's going to want blood. And he probably won't care if it's his attacker's. Any female will probably satisfy him. Only next time he'll make sure he's got better back up." To Geoffrey he said, "I'll move my tent next to the women's and tomorrow we'll split them up on two teams. You and Gianni take half, and I'll take

Higgs and the other half."

Tarla had the strongest urge to object just for the sake of opposing him but her common sense kept her quiet. She didn't resent the protective measures as much as the fact that *he* had given orders for them. As hard as it was for her to accept, the one person in this entire group most capable of leadership and commanding obedience seemed to be the last one she wanted to take orders from.

"Like I said before," Robin murmured, guessing at Tarla's thoughts. "He's a strange one."

"Don't tell me you're interested in him too?" Tarla smiled to hide the queasy sensation that touched her stomach as she thought of Robin going after Logan.

"Hell no!" Robin said with a laugh. "Even if he wasn't a murderer, he's the kind that never lets a woman push him around and I'm the kind that prefers the top." She wiggled her eyebrows at Tarla and made her laugh.

"Wait a sec," Tarla said. "Do you have doubts as to whether Logan's guilty?"

Robin shrugged. "I probably wouldn't if I'd never seen him close up. But if he was such a bad guy, wouldn't he have backed Wilkes instead of trying to keep the peace with Geoffrey? Don't get me wrong, there is something kinda scary dangerous about him but I feel like I can trust him not to hurt us. Okay, let's talk about Geoffrey."

"Seriously?" Tarla said with feigned shock. "You still find him attractive after an entire day? This sounds serious."

Robin made a face at her. "Very funny. I've met the man of my dreams and you develop a sense of humor." She looked out into the dark for a glimpse of him then sighed. "The truth is, he hasn't even noticed I'm alive."

"I doubt that! If anything, you might be *too* alive for him."

Robin's eyes opened wide. "Quiet, reserved little me? *Hmmm.* You could have a point there. I suppose I could tone down my aggressiveness just a bit. At least until I can get past his defenses."

Tarla knew better than to try to talk Robin out of something she'd decided to do but she secretly hoped Geoffrey didn't give in to Robin too easily. She might benefit from running up against a man who didn't instantly fall at her feet. Maybe she could even learn to appreciate him for something other than good looks and an English accent.

They returned to their tent but it took Tarla a while to fall back to sleep. During her time in the military, she'd discovered the darkest traits of men. Of course, she knew the textbook definitions of assault and rape but had never needed to put those words into a real-life context. It was very hard to comprehend, but she had no doubt that Wilkes would have raped Lee without a second thought, if she had been less skilled.

As a resident of Innerworld, she'd been accustomed to an orgasm being a simple physical release that could be shared with a friend or purchased at the Indulgence Center. Romance and love were not required for pleasure and coupling of any sort was only done with mutual consent.

Tarla had always enjoyed her fair share of pleasure, even on Outerworld. Although Terrans often made sex more complicated than necessary, she still had no trouble finding willing partners to play with when the urge struck her. Occasionally she'd found a man she wanted to spend more than a few hours with. But since her move to Outerworld, she'd never spent more than a month with any of them. When it was over, however good it had felt, it was completely over.

Even with Logan, the only one she'd even considered breaking her one-month rule for, there was no looking back.

So why did she care if Robin was interested in Logan?

Because he's dangerous and she feared for her friend's well-being.

She toyed with that explanation a moment and gave it some credence, but she knew it wasn't the whole answer. What she had felt earlier was closer to jealousy than fear.

Did that mean she still had an interest in Logan herself?

Absolutely not. If anything, she'd experienced a momentary pang of jealousy at the thought that Robin—with her sensual beauty, lush figure and quick wit—could get through Logan's shell and find the heart she'd been unable to locate with her vast experience at softening up tough guys.

Yes, that's all it was. A tiny pin prick in her professional pride.

Then why was she suddenly remembering what it felt like to be kissed by him?

There was nothing wrong with being a little curious about a man like Logan and the sort of woman he'd prefer. He had the kind of body any healthy woman might want to get to know better. It was a simple matter of feminine curiosity…and not having coupled with any man in over a year. She certainly didn't desire Logan McKay. She couldn't.

And if her body didn't agree…well, she simply wouldn't permit such disobedience.

Parisia maintained a show of calm control throughout Iris of Mergany's report. No other Imperial Prefect of Heart had ever been faced with so much turmoil at one time. The past twenty-four hours had been terribly upsetting for her, but her normally sedate Domestic Affairs Advisor was practically undone.

Parisia had not thought attending the monitors during the night would be necessary. A clear tactical error on her part. The barbaric Earth men apparently required continuous observation. She now realized that the men in chains may not have been slaves after all. They might have been bound because they were even more dangerous than usual. And she had been responsible for releasing them among the tranquilized innocents of the Earth commune. Another tactical error.

Should she take some decisive action immediately to correct her mistakes or wait the full three days for the antidote to take effect then re-evaluate?

"Despite the distance and lack of sound," Iris continued, "the visual scanner of the sky monitor provides evidence that two of the women were forced to defend themselves against the men and did so quite efficiently."

"Do you think we should bring the women here?" Parisia asked.

"Oh my, no," Iris instantly replied. "They would never fit in."

"Then you believe they should be left to fend for themselves against all those men?"

Iris hesitated a moment before giving her advice. "I don't believe we have a choice. We must be content in knowing that in a few days they will be as safe as we are among our own males."

Parisia sighed. "I suppose you're right but I don't feel good about it. After all, they are females and we must never forget our foremothers' oath to protect every member of our gender from male abuse."

"But that oath wasn't meant to include barbarian races," Iris protested.

"Are you sure they're as barbaric as the men? Or have they just learned how to deal with violence in the only way available to them? If you'll recall, our ancestors had to keep their men bound or imprisoned for centuries before the antidote was perfected. Throughout universal history, females have done what they have to do to survive in worlds dominated by males."

Frowning, Iris conceded a bit. "As always, you have managed to make me doubt my own convictions. Yet, I still believe you should leave those women be for now."

Parisia nodded. "And I agree…for now. But we will discuss this matter again before I speak to Parliament the day after tomorrow. Was there anything else?"

Iris's frown deepened. "It's about Nadia. An observation tech, Simone, informed me that Nadia is showing an unusual amount of interest in the new crossovers. She actually left her residence last evening and went to the sanatorium to get a look at the man with the headache. My guess is, the tech is playing both sides of the political field but she denied any knowledge of how Nadia learned about the patient. You might consider having Simone relocated to a less sensitive post."

Parisia shook her head. "No. Leave her where she is. As long as she believes we don't suspect her of duplicity, she might be of use to us at some later date."

That made Iris smile. "Very good. You never know when we might want to pass a little misinformation on to Nadia."

"McKay?" Tarla called from inside the tack room.

"Could you come here, please?"

His team had begun examining the barn, inch by inch, right after breakfast. In the two hours since, no one had been able to pry even a sliver of wood off the walls with any tool they tried. Nor had they discovered how the outside door had been sealed then automatically opened.

Logan stood in the doorway holding a cup of water. "Yes, Captain?"

She immediately noticed his relaxed posture then she saw his expression. He was almost smiling. "Are you all right?"

He drained his cup. "Never felt better. Just a little thirstier than usual but that happens to me after a migraine. What can I do for you, Captain?"

He had just said more words to her at one time than he had all together during the last weeks of his stay at the hospital unit and it flustered her. "I…I, uh…please call me Tarla. Everyone else seems to have dropped formality."

"Fine. Did you need something…*Tarla*?"

His unusual congeniality was playing havoc with her composure. "Yes. I…" She had to pull her gaze away from his before she could remember what had been on her mind when she called for him. "We have to be missing something in here. I thought if you acted out what you did when you came in with the migraine, you might recall something else."

He shrugged. "It's worth a try." Imitating his previous actions as closely as possible, he stepped inside the tack room, pulled the door shut and threw the bolt. "It's only a guess, but it's probable that locking the door works like an alarm to let them know someone needs medical attention, in which case, you might get to experience the miracle firsthand."

"No. Duncan said they never take anyone unless

they're alone, so that's out. But it also suggests they might be able to see into this room to know whether it's only one person." She scanned the solid walls and ceiling for the hundredth time. "I just don't see how though. Okay, so you bolted the door. Then what?"

"I turned around and said, 'I have a migraine, a very bad headache.' They must be able to hear what is said in here as well. Anyway, I stood here for several minutes but nothing happened, so I sat down." He lowered himself onto the straw, set down his cup and leaned against the bolted door. His gaze returned to her face and stayed there.

Tarla had seen plenty of male patients look at her that way before—as if she were some sort of angel. She knew enough not to take it seriously. But Logan shouldn't be looking at her that way. Not now. "Are you sure you're feeling all right?"

He laughed. "Of course. Why?"

"You...you don't seem...normal." It was the best explanation she could come up with. "Never mind. What happened after you sat down?"

"Some more time passed. The next thing I knew I was flat on my back, waking up like I'd had twelve hours of good sleep."

Tarla shook her head. "If nothing else, at least Wilkes's recollection is the same as yours."

Remaining on the floor, Logan closed his eyes. His brow furrowed as he struggled to remember when and how he was rendered unconscious. Suddenly his eyes opened and he stared at the ceiling.

"What is it?" Tarla asked, following his gaze to a wooden beam in the ceiling.

"I was gassed," Logan declared, rising to his feet, with his eyes still focused overhead. "I don't know why I forgot it but it just came back to me. I heard a hissing sound right before I blacked out. It seemed to have come from up there." He pulled her over to where he was standing. "Look up. See that dark knothole in the wood?"

She could see the impression he referred to but failed to see his point. She watched him pick up a long piece of straw and point it toward the knothole, but he was about two feet short. "Here," he said handing her the straw. "You try it."

She couldn't understand how he thought she could reach it if he hadn't, until he bent down, circled her thighs with his arms, and lifted her into the air. "McKay!" she scolded, quickly grasping his shoulders for balance.

"Now try it," he said with a grin.

She felt the strength of his arms beneath her bottom and knew he wouldn't drop her, but she felt his warm breath against her stomach and tightened her grip on his shoulders nonetheless.

"I won't drop you," he assured her in a husky voice. "See how deep you can make it go."

Her cheeks flushed hot and she felt his low chuckle all along her body.

"The straw, Tarla."

Despite his words, his eyes told her she hadn't misunderstood what he was really thinking about. Since a response would probably only further her embarrassment, she proceeded with his experiment. Without meeting any obstruction, she was able to feed the straw completely into the hole. "It appears to be a tube," she told him as she extracted the straw and dropped it on the floor. "Your assumption about being gassed is probably correct."

Rather than acknowledge her comment, he let her body slide a few inches lower and his mouth brushed back and forth over her taut nipple.

"*McKay.*" She meant to sound offended but his

name came out in a whisper that revealed too much of what he was making her feel. His mouth treated her other breast to the same light caress and she forced out the words her mind demanded she say. "Put me down, McKay." But her back arched into him instead of away.

He let her slide a few more inches down his body so that their eyes were now level. "Call me Logan."

She could feel his heart pounding hard against her own and told herself to run. His hold on her was supportive, but not so restraining that she couldn't escape…if she wanted to.

Her hesitation made him clarify his terms. "I'll put you down after you call me Logan. Say it the way you used to when I was your patient and you wanted me to believe you cared."

The intense longing in his voice accompanied by the need so visible in his eyes stripped her of what little sense she had left. "*Logan*."

His lips came to hers then left again with a tenderness that made her heart ache. Her fingers combed the lock of hair off his forehead, as she repeated, "*Logan*."

Once more his mouth met hers, softly, as though he feared her rejection. When she didn't retreat, he murmured something unintelligible and pressed a bit harder. She felt the muscles in his arms tremble slightly, so she wrapped her legs around his waist to keep from slipping away. Intent upon the depth of emotion he was pouring into the simple, closed-mouth kiss, she barely noticed when he descended to his knees with her on his lap.

His lips grazed her cheek and tickled her ear. When he spoke, she felt his words more than she heard them.

"You can't know how many times I've fantasized

about holding you like this." He continued planting butterfly kisses down her neck, up her throat and moved to her face. "I'd see your caring eyes and hear your sexy voice, and you never, ever left me to go take care of someone else."

His claims made no sense and yet pure honesty laced each kiss. The hand easing up and down her back, his fingers threading through her hair, every touch gave proof that having her in his arms filled him with innocent wonder. Though she knew she shouldn't believe him, her intuition insisted she should. "You fantasized about *me*? Like this?" She felt the vibration of his muffled laughter.

"Like this." He lowered her onto her back and stretched out beside her. "And *this*." His fingers explored her face as his dark eyes made seductive promises. "In my fantasies, you open your mouth for me. You stroke my tongue with yours and let me taste you for as long as I want."

She pulled his head down to hers and whispered against his lips, "Like this?" His groan of pleasure assured her that she was living up to his fantasy. For her, however, he surpassed any fantasy she had ever had of what the perfect kiss would be like. Time passed without either caring, while the kiss went on and on.

Finally Logan raised his head and said, "Like that."

He had her trembling with a need for more than deep kisses and, with a brazen smile, she asked, "And nothing more?"

His return smile was equally suggestive. "Sometimes that was enough."

"And other times?"

He took a deep breath and dragged his bent leg up across hers. "Sometimes I need more. You touch me. And you ask me to touch you."

Although Tarla felt his arousal throbbing insistently against her thigh, so far he had done nothing more aggressive than enticing her to make a choice that would please them both. "Like this?" Her fingertips caressed his cheek, trailed down and up his arm and settled on his chest.

His adoring gaze held hers and he whispered, "And more."

"Show me." She closed her eyes when he guided her hand down below his waist to confirm just how hard he was straining to control his desire for her. As she learned the width and length of him, she made the request he awaited. "I'd like you to touch me too, Logan."

Her breath caught in her throat until his hand slowly found its way to her breast. Cupping it in his palm, his thumb teased the hardened peak through her shirt as his mouth returned to hers for a kiss that could only be described as reverent.

He made her feel things she didn't know were possible. There was nothing in her considerable sexual experience that compared to this. And yet, she wasn't surprised. She had believed from the first that there was something special about Logan. She was torn between wanting this sweet torture to go on forever and the desire to rush headlong toward the magical burst of satisfaction she knew he could give her. To her immense relief, he made the decision for her by slipping his hand beneath the waistband of her slacks.

"I love you, Tarla."

His words brought back a painful memory but she couldn't hold on to it. As she tried to respond, he found the tiny bundle of nerves at her core and her only answer was a gasp of pleasure. She wanted to feel him in the same way but his experienced touch brought her to a peak so quickly, she could only lie there, melting, dying, feeding on kisses that had finally, thankfully, become demanding and urgent.

"*Logan*!" Geoffrey shouted through the door, then pounded on it for good measure. "Are you in there, man?"

CHAPTER 8

Logan's hand stilled as both his and Tarla's heads jerked toward the door in shock.

"*Sh-sh-sh*," Logan sounded. "He'll go away if we don't answer him." His mouth returned to hers and his fingers resumed their exciting play between her legs.

For several heartbeats, she was more than willing to complete what they had begun. Then she heard Geoffrey's voice talking to someone just outside and the sensual haze began to lift from her mind. Ending the kiss and moving his hand from her body, she whispered, "We have to answer him. If we don't, there's liable to be a whole crowd out there waiting for us to come out." He tried to pull her close again but she managed to resist this time. "*No*. Logan please. This shouldn't have happened…and…and they'll *know*."

That seemed to make an impression on him and he took a deep, calming breath. "I'm in here," Logan said loudly enough to be heard through the door. He and Tarla sat up and started extracting straw from each other's hair. "Just running an experiment."

"Have you seen Tarla?" Geoffrey asked. "She's

nowhere around."

"She's in here too," Logan replied, his eyes still making love to her. "We're almost finished. We'll be out in a minute."

"Right. I'll meet you outside. Lunch is on and I need to discuss something with the both of you."

Tarla made a move to rise but her legs weren't ready to support her. She closed her eyes and tried to regain control of her body.

Logan wrapped his arms around her and stroked her hair. "I'm sorry. This should have waited until we were assured of privacy. After lunch, we can—"

"*No*," Tarla protested, her head bobbing up from his shoulder. Sanity abruptly returned like an icy gust of wind. "This...this *really* shouldn't have happened. I don't even know how it did. Something is very wrong."

Logan eased back from her and frowned. "What do you mean?"

"You...I...I'm not sure what I mean," Tarla stuttered as her mind tried to form an excuse for her reckless behavior. "It must be this crazy situation. We're both under a lot of stress, and—"

"I'm not feeling any stress," he countered with an easy smile. "In fact, I don't remember ever feeling so relaxed."

"You're doing it again," she said rising to her feet and stepping back from him.

"What?"

"Smiling."

He stood up and kissed her nose. "Of course I'm smiling. I just had my own personal angel in my arms."

Her heart wanted to believe the look of utter devotion on his face but her intuition was insisting that something was off-kilter besides her balance.

"That's not why. You were smiling before. I wondered about it when you first came in but then..."

His smile turned sexy and he bent to kiss her mouth. She almost gave in but the moment his lips touched hers, she moved away. "I have to think. Please. Just give me some time to work this out."

Logan's fingers stroked her cheek. "I've waited this long for you. I guess a few more hours won't matter." His hand slid around to the back of her neck and urged her closer. "I'll give you the time you need but I need something from you to tide me over. Just one more kiss, angel. Please."

She knew she should deny him but her head angled beneath his and she couldn't resist one more quick flight to ecstasy. Much too easily, her body responded to him and the one kiss became several more. Only when both of them made an effort to remember that Geoffrey was waiting were they able to compose themselves enough to leave the tack room without clinging to each other.

Simone wasn't at all sure what she should do. The scene she had just witnessed on her monitor had her very confused. She had learned the facts of primitive male behavior long ago and thought they were quite clear. But the man in the tack room hadn't appeared cruel or violent. Nor had the woman looked repulsed or in pain. If anything, she seemed to be enjoying the way he was touching her and pressing his mouth to her face.

Watching them had caused the most peculiar feelings, a discomfort of sorts, especially in her womanpiece, yet it wasn't entirely unpleasant, either.

Should she tell Nadia or should she simply make a note of the incident in her report to Advisor Iris? Nadia would be furious if she wasn't informed of such an unusual occurrence. But if Iris learned that Nadia was aware of it, she would know that Simone had to be the one who had given out the information. Simone was the only one on duty at the monitors.

After a few minutes consideration, she decided it was a situation in which she could only come out a loser. The only way around it was to edit out the scene, as if it never happened. Before she erased it, however, she played the recording twice more to get a better understanding of what the pair had been doing. Nothing in her education explained it and yet she was certain their actions and dialogue had some importance.

"I can't put my finger on it," Geoffrey told Logan, Tarla and Robin as they ate lunch. "But something is going on. I expected Wilkes to cause trouble this morning. Instead, he was pleasant and worked as hard as everyone else. And when Lee Tang passed right by him in the kitchen just now, the look on his face was practically contrite."

"He's not the only one who's acting different," Robin interjected. "Now don't get me wrong here, but some of our men were giving me the eye yesterday. You know, like they were ready whenever I was."

Tarla noted the way Geoffrey grimaced at Robin's comment then kept his eyes glued to his plate as she went on.

"Today, though, those same men smiled nicely without any hint of sexual interest. I know it sounds egotistical but I'm a realist. I know what most men think when they look at me and those thoughts were noticeably missing today."

Tarla met Logan's gaze and knew his thoughts. Something strange had happened to them as well but neither was ready to discuss it with the others.

"How do *you* feel, Geoffrey?" Tarla asked. "Anything that you'd describe as unusual?"

"I feel fine," he answered with a smile. "If it's something in the air, I don't think it's affecting me."

She prompted him a little further. "Would you say you feel better than *fine*? Maybe more relaxed than you should under the circumstances?"

He chuckled. "Now that you mention it...I slept better last night than I have in years, even with all the excitement."

"Logan's very relaxed too," Tarla stated then glanced at him for confirmation. His smile said all that was necessary. "Robin? How about you?"

Robin pressed her forefingers to her temples, closed her eyes and hummed in a monotone for a few seconds. "All systems are A-OK," she said, imitating a computerized voice. Then with a thoughtful expression she amended her report. "Maybe I feel more relaxed than I should though."

Tarla nodded. "Same here." Mentally, she acknowledged that for her, it was more than being relaxed. What she had just done with Logan suggested her memories had been stifled and her entire defense system had broken down. "Now, I want you all to think about that. Is there any reason we should be at ease? Yesterday at this time we were nearing hysteria. Don't you think it's strange that no one—not a *single* person is fretting over our situation today?"

Logan's smile had faded as he realized how right Tarla was, and yet it still didn't worry him overmuch. "Did any of you see Higgs this morning? He was the worst yesterday."

"I did," Robin said. "I didn't give it a thought at the time, but he wasn't even trying to bend anyone's ear. He seemed perfectly content to quietly go about his work."

"Just like everyone else," Geoffrey said, his eyes narrowing with concern.

They were silent for a moment as they drew the same conclusion. Tarla said it aloud. "Whatever causes the residents here to act like androids must be affecting us as well."

"In another day or two," Robin said, "we could all be just like them. We might even give up the idea of getting out of here."

Logan forced himself to remember what his attitude had been twenty-four hours ago. As good as he felt at the moment, he knew that wasn't the case then. He would never have acted on his desire for Tarla yesterday and he definitely would not have spouted his private thoughts to her. It was as if all his personal barriers had been stripped, leaving him vulnerable...and mindless. Just like the puppet people around them.

"Okay," Logan said in a voice that was almost back to normal. "We're being relaxed in some way. How?"

"The food?" Robin offered.

"The water?" Logan asked, immediately thinking about how many gallons he had consumed already.

"I was being facetious about the air before but we shouldn't rule that possibility out," Geoffrey said. "Or sonic waves, either."

Tarla sighed. It could be anything. "Obviously, we can't stop breathing or absorbing sound. And we might be able to fast for a day or two, but eventually we'd have to eat and drink again. The only way we'll be able to avoid whatever it is, is to locate the source. And only our caretakers have the answer to that."

"True," Logan stated. "But at least we can fast as long as possible, while we step up our escape plan."

"We have an escape plan?" Robin asked in surprise.

Logan laughed. "That's Geoff's department. He

claimed he's a master of strategy."

Geoffrey made a face. "I believe I did say something along those lines." He rubbed his chin as he organized his thoughts. "All right. Let's start with what we know. The barn is a go-between but it's impregnable. An ill person can get out of here, but only if he's alone and then he's gassed first."

"We might be able to block the flow tube without them knowing it, so the patient could stay conscious," Logan suggested.

Geoffrey shook his head. "But that would still only be one person."

"Sometimes a single man can be more effective than a whole squad," Logan reminded him.

Again Geoffrey contradicted him. "Only when he knows what he's up against."

Robin brightened with an idea. "What if a whole squad was in the tack room, but hiding? You know, create an optical illusion for whoever is watching so they think there's only one man in there?"

"Excellent idea," Geoffrey said with a grin. "When all the candles are extinguished, it's completely black in there. We could set it up in darkness, during the night, then surprise them."

Tarla played devil's advocate. "At most, you could only hide a dozen people in there. Besides, we have no weapons. That's not much against an unknown power. I think we should hold off trying that until we're positive there's no break in the invisible wall where the whole company could get through at once."

Geoffrey nodded. "That would be preferable, but from what we've been told, I don't have much hope of our finding such a break. At any rate, the team examining the wall will be reporting back this evening. We should work on the tack room plan this afternoon and have it ready to go if the findings on the wall are negative. We could try it tonight. Agreed?" He met each of their eyes.

"Agreed," they replied in unison.

"Robin and I can spread the word about fasting," Tarla said.

Geoffrey gave another nod of agreement. "I'll start working on the optical illusion. Logan, are you willing to head up the squad?"

"Of course. Besides, I'm probably the best decoy we've got since they already treated me and shouldn't be suspicious if I claim to have another migraine."

"Good. Then I'll leave it up to you to select the others that will go with you."

Logan accepted with a thumbs-up sign. To Tarla he said, "Don't worry about our being unarmed. There are plenty of things in the tack room and elsewhere around the farm that could be used as weapons. It won't be the first time I've had to improvise."

"That's it then," Geoffrey said and everyone nodded their agreement.

"I have a different question," Robin said. "Has anyone else noticed that only one sun rose this morning?"

Although they looked skyward with some bemusement, only Geoffrey responded. "I suppose if there were still any question of whether or not we've been drugged, not noticing the absence of a ball of fire in the sky would seem to prove it. Perhaps it's more of a moon orbiting the sun than a secondary sun. It will be interesting to see how long it takes to reappear."

"Duncan mentioned something about that," Tarla recalled, trying to pull the memory out of her foggy brain. "I think he said, when a new person arrived, there was always a storm and the second sun. Could that be important?"

Geoffrey shrugged. "Maybe, maybe not. Either way, we can't afford to ignore anything here. Thank you, Robin."

She made a face. "Noticing that an entire sun has vanished from the sky doesn't take a brainiac. Maybe I'm immune to the drug."

"That could be important also," Geoffrey said seriously. When no one had anything else to discuss at the moment, he ended their meeting.

As they each got up and threw out the remains of their lunch, Logan motioned Tarla aside, but she spoke before he could. "Before you start apologizing, I want you to know that what happened was obviously a result of whatever is being done to all of us. I don't blame you, nor do I hold you responsible for anything said. And I hope that you will forget my behavior as well."

Logan gazed down into her eyes for several heartbeats before speaking. "You took the words right out of my mouth." Without another word, he turned and went about his assignment.

Tarla had to fight the temptation to call him back. The way he had looked at her made her think she had hurt his feelings. But she knew his expression was no more genuine than the tender, respectful way he had treated her, or the beautiful romantic words he had spoken. He had been manipulated to behave that way by some unseen force. It was very similar to the way the narcotics in the hospital had altered his personality. Only this time, she had been affected as well.

How else could she have forgotten how he really felt? Now that she was aware of the cause though, she could make certain nothing like that ever happened again.

What a terrible shame, the little voice in her head

whispered, for nothing quite like that had ever happened to her before.

As she struggled to dismiss the entire episode, another unsettling realization sunk in. More than likely, a caretaker had observed her moment of weakness. How could she have so completely forgotten the probability that they were being observed from the instant Logan had bolted the door? It wasn't logical but the thought of the love scene being enacted for another being's amusement was terribly upsetting.

Throughout the rest of the day they each performed the tasks agreed upon. At one point, Tarla felt as though someone were watching her. She turned around and met Logan's gaze. Again she read something so vulnerable in his eyes that she had to stop herself from going to him. When he realized she was looking back, he had hardened his expression and turned away. She fortified herself with the hope that their plan would be a success and things would soon be back to normal.

All of the soldiers and nurses were cautioned about the food and water before dinner. The fast caused some half-hearted grumbling but everyone was too relaxed to make a serious fuss.

When the team that had been examining the wall came in, their report was a confirmation of Duncan's statements. The invisible barrier began at one rear corner of the barn and ended at the other. The back wall of the structure was apparently part of the barrier. There was no interruption or detectable weakness around the entire perimeter. It couldn't be scaled and went far higher than anything they could construct to climb over it. They had dug a twenty-foot deep hole, but the wall appeared to be bottomless.

They now had no choice but to attempt an escape

through the tack room.

Geoffrey had selected five men and women to assist him in preparing the hiding places within the room. In case they were being observed, one person at a time went into the tack room to fetch or return an item and did their best to make their actions appear innocuous.

When everything was in place, Geoffrey met with Logan's team, which consisted of nine other men, Lee and Alicia. Logan and Geoffrey had decided that the major should stay behind. Each was given a diagram of the tack room and an assigned spot so they would be able to find it in the dark. The tube would be blocked only when the maneuvers began.

Taking advantage of what was available on the farm, each member of Logan's team had at least two weapons. Knives, cleavers, pitchforks, hammers and a variety of other implements had been scavenged by sundown.

As any good leader would, Logan warned them of the risks involved. For all he knew, they could be about to face an army of alien beings whose minds were all the weapons they needed. They could be charging into a situation more dangerous than anything they'd faced in the Orient. Their escape attempt could result in retaliation that would make their future even bleaker than it already was.

He gave each person the option to back out. No one did.

Since they had no way of knowing if activities outside the tack room were observed, it was decided that everyone else should retire to their tents as they had the night before. If anyone was watching, everything should appear to be normal.

Tension mounted throughout the evening as the time for action approached. Tarla knew part of the reason was coming from anticipation but she hoped it also meant that whatever had been relaxing everyone was losing strength. She asked one person after another if they could tell any difference since they had stopped eating and drinking but no one could be positive. Finally she sought out the one individual who seemed to have been the most drastically altered. Standing outside the circle of men and women around Logan, she waited for him to notice her then asked, "Could I speak to you for a moment?"

He excused himself from his team and walked away with her.

When she was certain no one could overhear, she stopped and looked up at him. "I want to wish you good luck."

He accepted her wish with a stiff nod. "You could have said that in front of everyone else."

She flinched at the harsh edge in his voice. "You're back to normal, I see."

With a negligent shrug, he said, "More or less. At least I'm in control of what I'm doing. Adrenaline alone has been known to counteract some pretty strong drugs, but it's been ten hours of no food or water and everyone seems to be getting back to being tense. So I'm fairly sure that's the delivery system."

"That's what I was thinking also." There was more she had wanted to say, but it no longer seemed necessary. They were back to being hostile acquaintances. "Good luck, then," she said and held out her hand.

He hesitated a second before taking it and, when he did, he held it considerably longer than necessary. She tried not to think about how the simple contact caused her heart to pick up its pace or how warm and strong his hand felt enveloping her own, or what she saw in his eyes. He had claimed he was in *better* control. Now she understood what he had not said. He still wanted her.

What she didn't understand at all was how hard she had to fight the urge to drag him to her tent and finish what they'd started in the tack room.

Immediately after Iris of Mergany had received the report of the unusual amount of activity in and out of the tack room that afternoon, she assigned a second technician to the monitors. It could be nothing but she didn't want to take any chances. They were both instructed to keep her posted and take no decisive actions regardless of how routine or peculiar it seemed to be.

Now it appeared that her precautions were warranted. The visual showed the first man who had been brought over the day before. He was again claiming to have a terrible headache. Had she not ordered the techs otherwise, they would have automatically opened the door to bring him over.

"Do a slow scan of the entire room," Iris said. The one candle lantern he had carried in with him didn't provide much light, but it was sufficient to confirm he was alone. "Fine. Transmit the anesthesia."

The first tech flipped the proper switch and almost instantly a red warning light appeared on the panel. She directed the computer to run a check on the system.

Iris watched the man on the screen slump over as he should have and thought the light was a false alarm. A few seconds later the system check was complete and a message flashed across the screen announcing a blockage in the pipe. But if it was blocked, the man should still be conscious.

"Bring up a life signs report."

The tech pressed a series of keys and the visual of the man blacked out. Instantly a white rectangle was drawn on the screen, in which the letters A through L were printed along the inside edges.

SPECIFY LIFE FORM OR PRESS ENTER
FOR ALL

Iris stared at the words on the monitor and counted the letters. There were eleven other people inside that room! Neither she nor the techs had seen them. How very ingenious of these Earth men. She could hardly wait to share this information with Parisia.

"It appears that our new crossovers had thought to surprise us, ladies," Iris declared. "But due to your diligence, we have a surprise for them. Do nothing. Eventually they'll tire of their cramped quarters and give up. We will have to be even more observant for the next twenty-four hours in case they have any more ideas for escaping the commune. After that though, we should be able to return to our normal routines. Just continue to keep me advised, as you have, and pass the instructions on to your relief in the morning."

By midnight, Nadia's frustration level had reached an all-time high. Knowing Fulton was merely a weak imitation of a man prevented her from seeking any relief with him. What she wanted was the real thing and there were over a hundred of them practically at her fingertips. *Practically.*

Therein lay the problem. Two different men had been taken to the sanatorium and neither time could she gain access to them. With each hour that slid by, her chances of experiencing the ultimate pleasure decreased a little more.

Nor had she come up with a single plausible reason why she should be allowed to make personal contact with any of the new crossovers.

There was only one thing she could do, but the risk

of discovery was extremely high. If she were caught, her career, possibly her life, could be ended.

On the other hand, if she didn't try it, there might never again be such an opportunity. She could die of old age and always regret having passed up her one chance to reach nirvana.

From what Simone had told her that evening, they had doubled the observation staff but they were concentrating primarily on the tack room. There was a good possibility that she could quickly pass through the barrier at a point far from the barn and the momentary disruption in the force field would go undetected. She rationalized that the chances of being recognized after that would be greatly hindered by a concealing shroud and the minimal moonshine that night.

After all, who in their right mind would purposely enter the commune? Perhaps if she were in a different frame of mind, she wouldn't either. But frustration, curiosity and anticipation had control of every bit of reason she possessed.

Exchanging her nightgown for a black, hooded, floor-length caftan, she became a figure that could slip into the night and walk through walls.

Higgs was so frustrated, he wanted to scream. He burned up a little nervous energy by kicking at the loose stones on the ground.

It just wasn't fair! He was a military police officer. He should have been chosen to serve on McKay's advance team, like Gianni. Instead, he'd been assigned to patrol the area outside the barn and around the tents to make sure everyone stayed put. He figured this was McKay's way of getting back at him for being his guard, but dammit, that wasn't his fault. He'd tried to explain his position but no-o-o, McKay had to be the kind to hold a grudge.

On top of that, Higgs was hungry and thirsty. He knew the orders to fast were justified since he was back to feeling as jumpy as always. It was just so hard to ignore an empty stomach and dry throat. Hopefully it would all be over any minute and—

He thought he saw something in the distance. The stars and crescent moon were partially clouded over, yet it was bright enough for him to detect a shape moving across the open field. His duty may not have been on the front line but he did have a job to do nonetheless. Picking up his pace, he headed for whoever it was who dared to disobey the major's order.

"Halt," he shouted when he was about fifty feet from the shrouded figure. "Who goes there?" Rather than stop or identify himself, the person kept walking toward him.

Higgs's empty stomach did a somersault and he took a step backward. It only just occurred to him that this might not be one of his kind, but one of *them*, and he didn't even have a weapon to defend himself. "Who...who are you?" he asked, nearly strangling on the words.

The figure stopped a few feet away and pushed back the hood, allowing Higgs to see what appeared to be a woman. She was at least six inches taller than he, with a plain face except for a rather large nose. With a slight shake of her head, black hair cascaded loose and settled down past her waist. He was momentarily distracted by all that beautiful hair, but he quickly regained his fear. "You're not one of us," he stated unnecessarily.

"No, I am not," Nadia replied in a velvety voice. "I am from beyond the barrier. You may call me Parisia. I have come to copulate with you."

CHAPTER 9

Higgs almost swallowed his tongue. "Co-co-copulate? W-w-with me?"

"Are you not an adult male from Earth?"

"Yeah, sure, but—"

"Then we will copulate." She unfastened the caftan and let it drop to the ground at her feet.

Higgs gaped at the voluptuous body being offered to him but he was too frightened to respond in a normal manner. "Uh, Parisia? Couldn't we, uh, get to know each other a little first?"

She took a loud, exasperated breath that caused her large breasts to jiggle. He couldn't help but notice, but it struck him that maybe she was tricking him in some way. Like, maybe she could read his mind and make her body appear to be the kind that would normally drive him up a wall with lust, when really she looked like a lizard or something equally gross.

The woman slipped her fingers into the dark patch of hair between her legs and his lower body gave a hint of response regardless of what she truly was.

"What is it you wish to know before you proceed?" she asked, while readying herself for the act.

Higgs racked his brain for a coherent question. "Uh, you said your name's Parisia. Mine's Higgs. Ray Higgs. Where are we? How'd we get here? Why are we confined to this farm? How many of you are there beyond the wall? Are you human or—"

"Enough! I have no patience for this 'getting to know each other.' I will answer one question only, then we will copulate...or you will be punished."

Higgs gulped as he imagined all sorts of horrible punishments that she might subject him to. If he was going to have sex forced on him by an alien, only one question was really important. "Uh, are you, uh, human, like me?"

"Yes," she hissed impatiently. "I am as human as you, perhaps more so. Now remove your clothes before you anger me further!"

Higgs's hands shook as he shed his clothing as quickly as possible. He always knew this was going to happen to him someday. How many hundreds of stories had he read about alien abductions and their abusive treatment of the humans they chose to study? Almost every report referred to experimentation involving the sex organs. *Good God*. He was about to become a sex slave to an alien, possibly even father a baby mutant for her.

As the cool night air shriveled his manhood even more than her threats had already, he wondered what sort of punishment she would deliver if he tried, but *couldn't*.

The woman scowled at the useless appendage drooping between his thighs. "You are not engorged. Are you not stricken with madness at the sight of me?" She lifted her heavy breasts. "Do these parts not interest you enough to make your manpiece grow?"

Higgs watched her toy with her own nipples, pinching and twisting them between her fingers and felt another twitch of interest. "You have a beautiful body, Parisia, really. It's just that you, uh, caught me by surprise, and I, uh, never had to do this under orders before."

"Oh?" she asked with a curious expression. "How *would* you usually become ready?"

He couldn't believe this was happening. Not only was she planning to take advantage of him, she needed lessons in how to do it!

For the umpteenth time in his young life, he thanked God for his mother's best friend, Celia, who, upon accidentally glimpsing his excessive endowment, had taken it upon herself to tutor him in subjects never covered in the classroom. Thinking of "Aunt" Celia helped calm his fears enough to say, "Well, uh, gentle persuasion goes a lot further than orders in this kind of situation."

"Explain how this *gentle persuasion* works."

"Well, uh, first there's usually some kissing, then some touching, and, uh, it helps if you use your mouth too."

She reached down and squeezed his genitals.

"*Ouch*! Easy does it." He took her hand and demonstrated what he meant. "Gently." His shaft extended an inch. "You see? That works better."

"Yes. I understand the touching. Show me these other actions you require."

He pulled her head down to his and closed his eyes. If he could just block out what she was for a few minutes, his body would take over after that. She was momentarily shocked when he pushed his tongue into her mouth but she caught on quickly enough. And she moaned with pleasure when he moved his mouth to her breast and used his tongue and teeth on her there. He *could* do this after all. She tasted and felt like a human woman to him and that was the only thing that mattered at the moment.

When his fingers slipped into her thatch of tight curls, he was the one shocked by how damp she already was. He inserted one, two, three then all four fingers as far as he could and her only response was a frustrated cry. At least he was assured that she could take all he had to give, which he had often been told was more than the average man could boast of.

Handling him the way he'd shown her, she brought him to a respectable size but he knew he could do even better. "Now your mouth," he told her, and explained exactly what he needed her to do. He anticipated her surprise but her hesitation was brief. A minute later he gave her points for being the fastest learner in the universe.

And a few minutes after that, he was able to deliver what she had come to him for. As she squealed and bucked beneath him, he forgot what she was and enjoyed the free ride. But once they were both satisfied, he felt cocky enough to demand answers to the questions he'd asked before.

"I do not wish to converse," she declared in her authoritarian manner. "We will copulate again."

"That's easy for you to say," Higgs replied. "You sure don't know much about this. If you're human, how come you don't know about men's bodies?"

She made a growling sound of irritation. "Our men are not capable of performing this function." She examined the softening flesh of his genitals. "What is required for you to become engorged again?"

He was fairly sure he could manage it again, but he was now clearheaded enough to bargain for his service. "It takes a little time and a lot of the kind of attention you gave me before. But in exchange, I want some answers."

Her eyes opened wide. She was clearly not

accustomed to making deals. "Do not forget that I can punish you for your insolence at any time. However, you pleased me well enough. I will answer another question after we copulate again."

Higgs had only needed a reminder of punishment to weaken his flash of confidence. "Okay. But understand, it won't be so fast this time and there's no way I'll be able to go a third time, no matter how much you threaten me."

"Understood. Proceed."

She needed no further instructions this time and even improvised a bit, much to Higgs's surprise. Her enthusiastic efforts had him ready for another bout much sooner than he'd thought possible but, when it was over, he insisted there was no way he could do it again that night.

She was openly annoyed to have her fun come to an end so quickly despite the fact that he had warned her in advance. "How long before you are able to function again?"

"A day," Higgs answered without thinking.

"Then I will return at this time tomorrow. You will be here when I arrive and you will teach me more about this."

"More?"

"Don't think to hide anything from me. I will know if you do. I wish to study every position of copulation and method of inducing pleasure."

It hadn't occurred to Higgs that she would demand a rematch. Then he recalled that some abductees swore that their alien captors came for them more than once. If he was to be studied, however, he wanted to get something in return. "What about my questions?"

As she rose and picked up her caftan, she said, "One more question tonight. You may ask another tomorrow if I am satisfied with your performance."

Higgs figured one question was better than none. He knew her name was Parisia, she claimed to be human and there were men among her people but they were impotent. "Okay, one question. Uh, where are we?"

Fastening her gown, she answered, "This is Heart, a mirror planet to your Earth."

"A parallel universe?" Higgs exclaimed. "But how did we get here? Did the storm create a gateway of some sort and our plane—"

"Cease. I have answered your one question. If you wish more information, you will be here tomorrow night…prepared to please me in some new fashion."

He watched her remove what looked like a cigar from her pocket and point it at him. Before he could avoid it, she sprayed a mist in his face.

Instantly his eyes blurred and he tried to wipe them, only to discover that his hands didn't respond. In fact, his entire body was paralyzed where he stood.

She had one final order for him before she departed. "Until I tell you otherwise, do not drink any of the water or eat any food cooked in it."

Nadia ran as fast as she could toward the barrier. At the medium setting she had used, the paralyzer spray only immobilized a large creature for a few minutes. She had kept the canister of deterrent after her last safari into the wilderness, though at the time, she hadn't any idea that she would be using it on a very different sort of beast. Hopefully, it wouldn't harm the man in any permanent way.

Her lungs burned from the unusual exertion but she didn't dare slow down until she reached the barrier. Barely pausing to extract a thin, rectangular box from her pocket, she created a narrow opening, hurried through and closed it again. That box was another object she had kept without reason, except as a souvenir of her stint with Protective Services. The tool's main function was to detect, repair and reinforce any weakness in the barrier, but it could also work in reverse to cause a flaw just as well.

Now that she was safe, Nadia stopped to catch her breath. She couldn't believe how perfectly splendid the adventure had gone. Closing her eyes and hugging her body, she wallowed in the remnants of pleasure still skipping through her. What was most exciting about what she just experienced was knowing she could have more whenever she liked. It simply required a certain boldness and relying on her intuition to hone in on the Earth male's fears as well as his natural urges.

She hadn't found the scarred man as she had hoped but Ray Higgs was quite adequate for her purposes…at least until she tired of him.

She recalled how she had called herself Parisia and laughed aloud at how mortified the Imperial Prefect would be if she learned how her name had been used. Nadia thought it made a delightful private joke, but it was also a slight precaution against being correctly identified if Ray Higgs ever managed to reveal her activities to anyone.

As she neared her residence, she considered taking a long, hot bath to soothe her strained muscles and cleanse the man's leavings from her body. She could wake Fulton and—No. She didn't want that half-man's hands on her tonight. Not after having the real thing. She would see to her own bath, and her need, which was already creeping back to life.

Tomorrow night couldn't come soon enough for her.

Higgs slowly regained control of his muscles along with his vision. He was so anxious to tell someone about what just happened, he'd taken several steps before realizing he was still nude. Between his nerves and natural lack of coordination, it took him longer than usual to get himself clothed and headed toward Major Cookson's tent.

Geoffrey heard someone approaching and got up from his cot. He was disappointed to see that it was only Higgs.

"I'm sorry to disturb you, Major, but this is of urgent importance."

"Come in," Geoffrey said, immediately wondering how long it would take to get the man out again. He was tense enough waiting for news of Logan's team without having to deal with Higgs. He lit his candle lantern and made himself ask, "What's the problem?"

"It's the water. There's something in it."

"That possibility occurred to us. That's why you were ordered not to eat or drink anything all day."

"It's not the food. She only told me not to drink the water."

Geoffrey could see Higgs was upset over something but he was making less sense than usual. "She who?"

Higgs waved his arms in the air and tried to pace within the small tent. "A female alien…from beyond the invisible wall. I was just with her out in the field."

Geoffrey turned away so Higgs wouldn't see his look of disbelief.

"I'm telling you, she came for me. She…she wanted to…she forced me to…to *copulate* with her…that's what she called it…right out there."

Geoffrey couldn't hold back the chuckle at that one. "Are you trying to tell me you were just raped by an alien woman?"

"*Twice!*" When he only got another laugh at that, he tried harder to be convincing. "She was *huge*, and strong, and she tortured me first, and she had a weapon that paralyzed me."

Geoffrey nodded with feigned comprehension. "An amazon used a stun gun on you then took advantage of you while you were helpless."

"No, no," Higgs said, getting more frustrated by the second. "She used me first *then* paralyzed me while she ran off."

"Just out of curiosity, Higgs, how did you happen to be in the condition necessary to be used?"

"She...she must have used some sort of mind control. I couldn't resist."

Higgs clearly believed what he was saying but Geoffrey could hardly accept the truth of such an outrageous tale coming from a man who had been whining about aliens and androids from the moment they'd arrived. There was a strong possibility that this was just another attempt by Higgs to get others to accept his point of view.

"I'm not crazy, Major," Higgs insisted. "She said her name was Parisia, that there were humans on the other side of the wall, and that their men don't...*function* like Earth men. We landed in an alternate dimension. Actually, she said it's a mirror planet to Earth called Heart."

"Heart?" Geoffrey asked sarcastically. "I suppose it's a coincidence that Heart is an anagram of Earth."

"Maybe. Why not? Maybe it's not an *identical* twin. It could be like Earth, but twisted—like the green sky and blue grass, and men that can't have sex. But you don't have to believe me. You can see her for yourself. She said she was coming back tomorrow night...for more. The last order she gave me was not to drink the water. I'm sure that had to be because there's something in the water that would relax me too much to be able to service her."

Geoffrey was no longer certain that Higgs was off

his nut. The more he talked, the more believable his story seemed. He needed another opinion. "Come with me," he said and led him to Tarla and Robin's tent.

The flap to their shelter was pulled back, but he didn't presume to enter unannounced. Standing to the side, he spoke in a hushed voice. "Tarla? It's Geoffrey. May I speak to you?"

"Of course," she replied, and a moment later, she and Robin stepped outside.

Geoffrey's gaze automatically slid from Robin's mussed hair to her long legs exposed below the large shirt she was wearing and, for a moment, he was rendered mute. Only by turning his full attention on Tarla, was he able to get back on track. "Higgs just came to me with a rather extraordinary story and I'd like you to hear it from him."

Higgs shifted from one foot to the other, looking extremely embarrassed, but he managed to relate his experience to the two women. Geoffrey noted that it came out in better order this time and with more colorful description. Also, the alien female had become more monstrous and terrifying with the second telling. Whatever truth there was to Higgs's claims would probably be completely obscured in exaggeration by the fourth or fifth time he told it.

Tarla noted the skeptical expressions on both Geoffrey's and Robin's face. Higgs had a tendency to let his imagination take over whatever logic he might have in his brain, but there was no question they were in a world alien to Earth. Under the circumstance she didn't think any story should be dismissed, no matter how crazy it sounded or who was telling it.

When Higgs finally ran out of details of his close encounter, Tarla asked, "Is there a possibility that you had a hallucination? If they could tranquilize us without our being aware of it, couldn't they also administer a hallucinogenic?"

Higgs shook his head. "No way. It happened. I'm positive."

Geoffrey had another thought. "Is there any way it could have been one of our women and you mistook her—"

"Geoffrey! That's ridiculous," Robin stated with annoyance. "There are only ten of us, two of whom are with Logan's team and another two of whom are standing here."

"Robin's right," Tarla said. "I'd vouch for the other six. None of them are thinking of fun and games right now."

Geoffrey shrugged. "I'm just trying to cover every possibility. No offense meant."

"None taken then," Robin said with a smile of forgiveness. "So what's the verdict?"

Tarla looked to Geoffrey but he was waiting for her to speak. "I think we have to assume it happened as Ray said. In which case, we can trust the food and fruit juice but not the water."

"Thank God!" Robin said with a laugh. "I'm starving! How much longer are we supposed to pretend everyone's tucked away for the night?"

Geoffrey glanced at his watch and made a face. "Logan's team went into the tack room nearly two hours ago. We agreed to give them until sunrise before taking any further action. But I have to admit, I'm worried."

Tarla wished he hadn't said that. It made her identify the queasiness she'd felt for the last hour—a combination of worry and guilt. Now she wished she had spoken kinder words to Logan before he left. It might not have meant anything to him, but it would have made her feel better now.

After Geoffrey and Higgs said good night a second time, Robin and Tarla went back inside their tent to wait for sunrise. Sleep was out of the question.

In spite of her support of Higgs's story, she still thought his mind may have been playing tricks on him. The drug, or whatever it was, obviously had the power to drastically alter one's personality. It had turned a cold-hearted soldier into a gentle Romeo, complete with a fabricated memory of sensual fantasies and delusions of unrequited love.

That considered, Higgs's eight-foot tall, sex-starved alien could have seemed completely real to him.

"I think he's attracted to you," Robin said, abruptly breaking into Tarla's thoughts.

With her mind on Logan, Tarla automatically thought that was who Robin was referring to. "It was just the drug. Nothing else."

"I don't think so. Right from the start, he kept his eyes on you. He barely *glanced* at me. The only time a man *doesn't* look at my legs when they're showing is when he's in love with someone else...or he prefers male companions. Oh dear. I hadn't thought of that. You don't think that's it, do you? I mean, wouldn't that be simply *too* depressing?"

Tarla squinted at her friend. "What are you talking about?"

Robin sighed. "He seems very gentle and soft-spoken for a man. If he prefers men, that could explain why I haven't been able to get through to him."

"Wait a minute," Tarla said holding up one finger. "Who do you think prefers men?"

"Geoffrey. Who did you think I was talking about? Higgs?"

Tarla chuckled at the face Robin made. "No. I'm sorry. I guess I was only giving you half my attention."

"That's all right. I'm not making any sense anyway. This waiting is driving me nuts."

"Me too," Tarla admitted. "I can't help but wonder where they are and if they're safe, or in trouble, or—" She wouldn't say her worst fear aloud.

Logan opened one eye a crack to peek at the candle in the lantern. Judging by the short stub left to be burned away, he guessed it was nearly dawn. He was proud of this team. No one had moved or made a sound in hours. Unfortunately it had all been a waste of effort. Somehow the caretakers figured out what they were up to and chose to ignore them. He hated to think what that meant.

A lifetime of imprisonment. Of course, he'd been facing that anyway, and the farm was considerably more pleasant than Leavenworth would have been.

Being drugged and having no defenses. He had to admit, the time he'd spent with Tarla while both their defenses were down was like a taste of heaven. It was only after their minds cleared and they both remembered that he wasn't good enough for her, that he was sorry he'd been given that taste. At least with the drug in his system, he didn't feel the ache in his chest.

All in all, he wasn't sure which was worse—remaining on the farm and becoming one of the puppet-people, with Tarla, or returning to his own dismal world without her. It wasn't so confusing when he put it that way.

"Okay, everybody," he said, stretching his arms and legs. "There's no sense putting in more time here. They didn't fall for it."

A harmony of groans accompanied the unbending of stiff bodies.

"Damn!" Gianni muttered. "I think I need some medical treatment for real now. How do you think they knew?"

Logan shook his head. "For all we know, they could have heard us planning it. The main problem is, we have no idea how closely we're being watched. But it was worth a try. And we'll keep on trying till we get out of here." The sad faces around him brightened a little from his attempted pep-talk, but it was hard to sound optimistic when he didn't believe a word he was saying.

As he had estimated, the sun was just topping the horizon when they exited the barn. In a matter of seconds, they were surrounded by people who were relieved to see them unharmed and anxious for a full report. However, the relief was quickly buried beneath the news that the mission had been a complete failure.

Geoffrey took advantage of the gathering to tell everyone that they could resume eating but should continue to avoid the water. If they felt at all unusual after eating, they were to notify Tarla immediately.

The hungry crowd practically tripped over each other to get to the kitchen. Refortified, there was barely a complaint uttered when Geoffrey gave out the day's chore assignments. Though he knew they all needed to get some sleep, he requested a meeting with Logan's team, Tarla and Robin. He had ordered Higgs not to share his story with anyone else yet, but knowing the temptation would probably be too great for him, he asked Higgs to join them as well.

Geoffrey waited until all the other teams departed then gathered his group under one of the large shade trees near the big house. As soon as they were settled, he asked Logan to open the discussion.

"Actually," Logan said, "you heard all there was to report when we came out of the barn. Everyone was in place. I heard the hissing sound and pretended to fall asleep. We waited as planned but nothing happened. They had to have known we were up to something."

"There is another possibility," Higgs said. He paused for Geoffrey to acknowledge him before continuing. "They might have come for you and you may have attacked but they overpowered you then replaced your memories with what they wanted you to remember, which was, that nothing happened. They might have that much power."

Logan rolled his eyes. "Look, Higgs, I've had just about—"

"Hold off on that," Geoffrey said quickly. "I think you need to hear something first." He still wasn't entirely convinced that Higgs's tale was true but he also wasn't convinced otherwise. "Go ahead, Higgs, tell them what happened. But, please, try to stick to the basic facts without your assumptions. I'd like everyone else's opinion without being influenced by your superior knowledge of extraterrestrials." As he had hoped, Higgs took that as a compliment and proceeded to give a fairly concise report that was only slightly more enhanced than the story he'd told Tarla and Robin. If nothing else, he provided a much needed boost to the team's spirits.

Gianni laughed the loudest. "Right! Out of all the men stranded here, she picked you to teach her about sex!"

"You were lucky it wasn't a giant lizard who came for a few lessons," Lee taunted.

"If you were so damn good," another prodded, "how come she didn't abduct you and take you home in her spaceship?"

"Oh, sure," Higgs whined. "You can all laugh but you wouldn't think it was so funny if you were the one forced to strip and play stud-horse to the creature from the black lagoon."

Geoffrey cleared his throat to stop the not-so-good-natured teasing. "That's enough everyone. I can vouch for the fact that Higgs was near hysteria when he came to my tent. *Something* happened to him out there and, considering the fact that we're sitting under a green sky it's certainly possible that he was used, or abused, by a woman from outside the farm." He covered his mouth with his hand but couldn't quite conceal his smile. "I do apologize, Higgs. I am trying to believe your story but you must see how difficult it is to imagine. All the residents we've talked to claim they've never *seen* anyone from the other side of the wall, let alone be assaulted by one."

Higgs opened his mouth to reply but Tarla cut him off.

"Okay," Tarla said. "No matter how hard it is to imagine, this is all we've got. I've been thinking about it for hours and I keep coming back to one thing. This woman warned Higgs not to drink the water. By tonight, if everyone is feeling even more clearheaded than last night, we should know whether the warning had basis. If so, we have to consider what else she said."

"Yeah! And you know what that was?" Higgs asked in a challenging tone. "She's coming back for me. She'll make me do it again. And she threatened to turn me into dust if I didn't have something new to show her. Maybe you should all come and watch. Then you'll see that I didn't make any of this up!"

"That's it!" Gianni exclaimed, fighting a grin. "We'll all go watch Higgs perform and when he's got the alien blinded by lust, we grab her. Maybe if we threaten never to let her use Higgs's body again, she'll take us to her leader."

Everyone burst into another round of off-color

joking but Geoffrey put a stop to it by saying, "It could work. If Higgs distracted her sufficiently, we might be able to capture her."

"A hostage?" Logan asked, still looking somewhat amused.

"Have you got a better idea?" Tarla countered then was immediately sorry she had, for it brought his attention to her. As much as she wanted to lower her gaze, she didn't allow herself to be such a coward. Finally, he was the one who looked away to speak to Geoffrey.

"The only other thing that's come to me would be for one man to go into the tack room with a mask of some kind to prevent him from inhaling the gas. We could stage another fight and have the loser appear to have a broken nose or something, like Wilkes's jaw. That way the mask wouldn't be noticed for what it really was."

"They have too much power," Higgs declared. "I didn't stand a chance and I was only facing one of them."

Logan ignored him. The differences between Higgs and himself weren't worth wasting breath on. He kept his eyes on the major until the man was obliged to make a decision.

"We'll try to capture the woman first," Geoffrey said after a few more seconds of silent deliberation. "If that fails, then I'll consider sending in one man, but only as a last resort."

Contrary to the old adage, keeping their hands busy for the remainder of the day did not make the time go faster. At sundown, Tarla and the other nurses took a poll of everyone's mental condition. They were bored with the menial tasks and anxious for action. No one could be described as *relaxed*.

On a personal basis, she could attest to the fact that

in spite of numerous glances passing between her and
Logan, neither was overcome by desire. Her defenses
were firmly in place, and apparently his indifference
was as well. The only emotion she was suffering from
was   lingering   bewilderment…and   some
disappointment.

Geoffrey's team gathered together without his
having to call them.

Tarla made her report first. "I don't think there's
any question about it. The only thing we have all
avoided is the water and everyone is behaving
normally."

"If, by normal," Logan added, "you mean Higgs is
so antsy he's making my skin itch and Wilkes is
preparing to go ten more rounds with Lee Tang, then I
agree. The drug, or whatever it is, must be in the
water."

Geoffrey   nodded.   "Of   course,   this   is   only
supposition, but, if we hadn't stopped drinking the
water yesterday, I believe we would all be totally
passive by now."

"Just like the puppet-people," Logan said.

Robin made a face. "We'd probably be bedding
down now, perfectly content to sleep until it was time
to work again. *Yuk*! What a horrible thought."

"Agreed," Geoffrey said. "We would have given up
on any escape attempt and our caretakers would still
expect that, which gives us the advantage of surprise."

Logan agreed. "It's probably also safe to assume
that they'll be lowering their guard once they're
certain their drug has taken effect."

"Which means, we need to act the way they expect
us to," Geoffrey stated. "Slow-moving, little or no
conversation, early to bed, early to rise. This meeting
is to be the last of its kind. We'll have to be extremely
discreet from now on."

Higgs couldn't stay silent another moment. "If you capture the woman tonight, none of that may be necessary. I could tell she was somebody important. Used to giving orders, you know. They'll probably agree to anything we want to get her back."

"Are you still willing to go through with this?" Geoffrey asked Higgs.

"I'll do whatever I have to," he replied seriously, despite several snickers from the others.

"Then, unless anyone has thought of an alternative," Geoffrey concluded, "we go with the hostage plan." He waited a few seconds, but no one spoke up. "That's it then. We all retire to our tents except Higgs, who will be patrolling the area as he did last night. There's even less moonlight tonight and heavier cloud cover which will help some, but that field is still wide open. It's going to be very difficult to sneak up on her without her seeing us."

Logan offered his advice. "The clothes we have are all light colors, but the blankets are dark. If we're lying on the ground, covered by the blankets, we should be fairly well camouflaged. At midnight, my team will crawl out of their tents, hidden under blankets and position themselves in a horseshoe around the spot where Higgs is to have his rendezvous. Once he gets her good and distracted...preferably naked and disarmed...we'll close up the ends of the horseshoe and move in."

"What about weapons for us?" Alicia asked.

"No weapons," Geoffrey said. "Take ropes to tie her up, but I don't want to risk any accidents that might reduce our bargaining power."

Logan went over the timing and each person's positioning and movements. "Any questions?"

"Should I give some kind of signal when I see her coming?" Higgs asked. His unintentional pun earned another round of chuckles and, once he got the joke, he laughed with them. "I'm serious," he protested in vain. "I could whistle to let you know she's approaching then I can say something appropriate when it's a good time to move in, like…*now.*"

"It works for me," Lee said with a grin and everyone else agreed.

Gianni gave Higgs a pat on the shoulder. "Even if you imagined this whole thing, I appreciate you giving me something to laugh about."

Geoffrey shook hands with each member of Logan's team wished them luck then they each straggled off to their own tents to try to get a few hours' sleep before beginning another vigil.

At the appointed hour, Logan's team stealthily slipped out of their tents and started creeping toward the field. Higgs had to keep reminding himself to walk slowly and ignore the dark mounds slithering their way across the ground. As he meandered repeatedly along the same patrol path he had set for himself the night before, he kept his gaze focused on the spot where he had first noticed the woman in the field.

What if she doesn't come back? He would never live it down. *Why couldn't she have chosen someone else, like McKay or Wilkes?* No one would have laughed at them. *What if she does show up and he can't get it up?* It was one thing for a couple of guys to share the same whore in front of each other but this was different. *Geez!* He was going to have to do it in front of the whole squad!

He did a quick check of his male anatomy to make sure it hadn't disappeared altogether. He had to forget about how many people were watching and counting on him to make good. He decided his best bet was to call up one of his favorite fantasies and concentrate on that.

Keeping his attention on the field, he pictured two gorgeous lingerie models driving along in a terrible thunderstorm. Suddenly, their car stalls out, right in front of his house. Since his parents are out of town, he's the only one home. By the time the two girls knock on his door to ask for help, they're both soaked, their thin tee-shirts clinging to their perfect, perky, and braless breasts.

As his mind automatically replayed the part of the fantasy where they exchange their wet clothes for towels and proceed to show him their appreciation, he felt his body quickening. If Parisia came—oops, *when* Parisia came for her next lesson, he would simply close his eyes and pretend she was one of his stranded models.

Despite his positive attitude, however, when another hour passed and she hadn't shown up, all his worries resurfaced. He glanced up at the black sky and wondered if he was going to get rained on now as well. As he passed near one of the mounds on the ground, it spoke to him.

"*Psst!* Higgs. Isn't it about time for wonder woman to show up for her date?"

Higgs was about to shoot back a smart reply when he saw a figure in the distance. He walked a few steps more until he was fairly sure it was her. Puckering his lips to make the promised announcement of her approach, he realized he hadn't been told what tune to whistle. The only song that came to his mind was "The Star-Spangled Banner," and that seemed a little disrespectful. Telling himself that what he was about to do was in fact his patriotic duty, he licked his lips and whistled the opening bars of the national anthem.

Holding on to the mental picture of his two wet models, he prepared himself to confront the enemy.

CHAPTER 10

"Nice to see you again, Parisia," he said when she was close enough for him to confirm her identity. "I didn't drink any water, like you said. What's in it anyway? Some kind of tranquilizer?"

"Something like that," Nadia answered brusquely. She had been dying for this hour to arrive all day and she had no intention of wasting one more second than necessary on foolish conversation. She was more than ready to get on with it but she remembered the procedure from the previous night and knew he required certain actions before he could deliver what she needed. "You may ask your question after and I will answer, as I did last night...*if* I find your performance satisfactory."

"Oh, I think you'll be satisfied with what I'm going to show you. And I have a big surprise for you at the end."

There was something different about him tonight, Nadia noticed. He seemed more sure of himself, even smiling at her with a hint of mischief. The pulse between her legs throbbed a bit stronger as she anticipated what he may have planned for her. Her fingers grasped the neck closure of her caftan.

"Wait," he said, taking her hands in his and lowering them to her sides. "Part of what I have to show you is the undressing."

Nadia had been undressed by Fulton a thousand times and couldn't imagine how it could be done differently but she was willing to give the Earth man a chance to surprise her. "Go on."

Her first surprise was that he didn't immediately remove her caftan. Instead, he ran his hands through her hair, over her face, and down her clothed body. He continued to stroke her in that manner as his mouth pressed to hers—*kissing*, he had called it. Shortly after his tongue began its interesting little dance in her mouth, she felt the urge to touch him back in the same ways and was rewarded with an approving murmur from him.

The removal of their clothing took place an inch at a time, and more touching and kissing accompanied the gradual exposure of naked, tingling flesh. The law against men touching women in her world was fundamental to their way of life. And yet, Nadia couldn't help but wonder why women would deny themselves this delicious entertainment. How could they believe something that felt this good was detrimental?

As Ray Higgs's mouth closed over her nipple, concern over the other women's beliefs fled her mind. She only knew that nothing had ever been as exciting as what this man was doing to her and she didn't care if she was the only female in her world who knew about it.

So caught up in a whirlpool of sensation, she noticed, but didn't care why he tossed her caftan far from where she was standing. All that mattered was that he lowered her to the grass and was rubbing his nude body against hers. She parted her legs for his entrance but received her second surprise instead. As he buried his face in her womanpiece, she squealed with shocked delight. The notion streaked through her brain that she could teach this trick to Fulton, then, in the next instant, only one thought remained. *More*.

She was lost to the desperate hunger he aroused, fed and aroused again. She climaxed several times and yet she still felt the clawing need to have his manpiece ramming into her body.

She heard herself cry out to him, begging and pleading in a way no woman of Heart would ever demean herself and finally, *thankfully*, he gave her what she demanded.

"*Now!*" he shouted.

"*Yes!*" she cried back. "*Now! Now! Now!*" The explosive release hurled her to the very edge of consciousness, where her weightless body spun out of control in a sea of darkness. As she floated back to awareness on wave after wave of pleasure, she felt the man abruptly shift his position so that he was straddling her hips and pressing her shoulders to the ground in the most peculiar fashion.

All of a sudden, her hands were yanked over her head, her legs shoved together, her wrists and ankles bound so quickly, she was immobilized before she was fully alert.

"What is the meaning of this?" she screeched indignantly. "Release me this instant!" She glared up at the man she had mistakenly assumed was under her control then realized too late they were no longer alone.

"Ride's over, sweetheart," Higgs said with a grin. "Time to pay up."

"Okay, Higgs," Logan said. "We'll take it from here." As Higgs rose to his feet, Logan's gaze dropped to his sex, which hadn't yet gotten the message that the game had been cut a few seconds short. He shared a look of amazement with the others as they realized the little man was *not* built proportionately all over.

Some of those looks turned to envy as Alicia and Lee stepped forward to assist the hero into his clothes then offered to escort him back to his tent…with Sergeant McKay's permission. Logan gave it but told them to first let the major know they had their hostage.

As they saluted and walked away smiling, Logan thought the last three days held more surprises than the previous three years. With a shake of his head, he got back to the business at hand. "Gianni, check her clothes for that weapon Higgs mentioned."

"You have no right to take what is mine!" she squawked. "I *order* you to release me! You will all be severely punished for this impertinence!"

Logan decided they would be better off with their eardrums left intact and promptly rectified the problem. He pulled off his shirt, twisted it into one long band and, covering her mouth, tied the makeshift muffler behind her head. Her first reaction was incensed shock but as she checked out his bare chest, her nostrils flared as if catching an intriguing scent and a predatory gleam filled her eyes. She was clearly considering taking him on for dessert. He hoped all of her kind weren't as hungry for men as she was or he was going to have one hell of a time convincing his team to fight for their freedom.

His gaze shot to Gianni to see what was taking him so long and caught the man staring at the woman with his mouth open. Despite her bindings, she was managing to move her thighs and hips to relay her message of sexual need loud and clear. "Gianni!"

Gianni's attention jerked back to the robe in his hands. He pulled two objects out of a pocket and passed them to Logan.

No longer doubting Higgs's claims about anything, Logan deduced that either the cigar-shaped thing or the thin metal square thing was a weapon. He turned them in his hands, but carefully avoided touching anything that looked like a button or trigger. "Cover her up…before any of you catch whatever she's got. Don't untie her though, just wrap her up in that thing."

It took several men to handle that order but she was soon trussed up like a large black sausage.

"Well," Logan said. "I think it's safe to assume she doesn't have any of those super mental powers Higgs warned us about." Standing at the woman's feet, he asked her, "How is it that you were going to punish us?" Her eyes were filled with loathing. He pointed the flat box toward her chest. "With this?" No reaction. "Or this?"

The second he raised the silver cigar, her eyes squeezed shut in expectation of something bad. "Very good. Of course, I don't know how to use this thing but I'll bet if I pushed this little slide up and down or pressed one of these buttons, I'd figure it out eventually." She definitely didn't want him to do that. "So, what do you say? Would you like to be cooperative or shall we play trial and error?"

Her narrowed eyes shot out lethal threats but she appeared willing to hear more, so he explained. "Cooperative is where we take the muffle off your mouth but you talk only to answer our questions. And you *do* answer our questions…*truthfully*…or we move on to door number two."

Before she could indicate her choice, Geoffrey, Tarla and Robin arrived. "You haven't missed much,"

Logan said to Geoffrey. "Higgs exaggerated a little about her size and powers but everything else is pretty much the way he described."

Geoffrey took a moment to appraise the bundled-up female on the ground and went with a friendly tone. "Hello, I am Geoffrey Cookson, of the United States, Planet Earth. Higgs said your name is Parisia, that your people are human like us and that we're in an alternate dimension, on a mirror planet called Heart. Is that correct?"

She tried to say something that only came out as muffled noise, glared at Logan, then mumbled again.

"It sounds like she wants to talk to you, Geoffrey," Logan said. "Must be that British accent of yours. Okay, lady, you've got one chance to play nice. If you behave and answer our questions, you might get home in one piece."

Her eyes widened at his implication that she might *not* get home again then she slowly nodded her agreement to his terms. Logan retrieved his shirt and helped her into a sitting position.

Nadia's mind worked frantically to come up with a means of escape. She had to get back before dawn, at which time someone might witness her passage through the barrier. If her little excursion were discovered, she would be chastised and humiliated, her plans for the future irreparably damaged. She understood Earth women had no power over their men, so she couldn't depend on them to assist her.

Looking from one man to the other, she had the feeling that the blonde man could be manipulated, whereas the scarred man exuded too much hostility to be of use to her. Directing her response to Geoffrey Cookson, she said, "Ray Higgs spoke the truth."

Geoffrey hunkered down to her level and smiled. "We mean you no harm. We only want information."

Nadia smiled back and spoke in a tone meant to sound cooperative. "I will tell you whatever you wish to know, but only if you treat me in a civilized manner. Untie me, allow me to dress and return my property to me."

Geoffrey ignored her order. "If we are truly on another planet, how did we get here?"

She guessed he might be more pliable if his peers were not observing him so closely. "I prefer to speak only to you. Send the others away."

Geoffrey glanced at Logan and noted his disapproval of that idea. "If you wish to be left alone with one man, it will be him," he told her, pointing at Logan. "And I assure you he's not nearly as *patient* as I am."

She might have given it a try but the minutes were ticking by and she had no more time to waste. She emitted a loud sigh of disgust. "I should have known it was impossible for men to behave in a civilized manner. What is it you wish to know?"

Geoffrey began his list of questions by repeating his first one. "How did we get here?"

Since she had no idea how extensive his scientific knowledge was, she decided to stick as close to the truth as possible, rather than try to fabricate answers and risk being tripped up in a lie.

"You came through a gateway. As far as we can tell, there is a magnetic field that flows between the northeastern hemisphere of Earth and the northwestern hemisphere of Heart. Apparently, the magnetic pull goes only one way, from your world to ours, and it only causes a problem when there are violent, electrical storms in the fields on both worlds at the same time. When that happens, a gateway opens and whatever or whoever is in the eye of the Earth storm is pulled through. Fortunately, the precise conditions required for such an incident have been rare."

"It sounds like Higgs was right about that Dragon's Triangle business after all," Logan said to Geoffrey. "But how did we land here in one piece?"

Nadia waited for Geoffrey Cookson to indicate that she should answer the other's question. "Once you were through the gateway, your pilot regained sufficient control to land your craft."

"Why doesn't anyone remember that?" Tarla asked.

Nadia assessed the woman who spoke without the man's permission to interrupt. Perhaps she had some power after all. "A near-term memory depleter. We find it is best to keep our existence as secret as possible. May I ask you a question now?"

Tarla looked to Geoffrey and received his approval. "All right."

"Why do you allow these barbarians to abuse one of your own kind? Do you have no control over them at all?"

Tarla wasn't certain which question was more surprising—that this woman considered them sisters of some sort or that she assumed the men could be controlled. "As second in command, I fully endorsed the actions of our men. By imprisoning us here, it is *you* who have abused *us*."

Nadia arched an eyebrow. "Release me and I will make arrangements for all the women here to be freed. You would have happy lives, unburdened by the demands of any man."

Geoffrey brought the interrogation back on track. "Higgs said your men are impotent. Is it your people's intention to use us as breeding stock?"

Nadia laughed aloud. "Introduce your primitive genes into our society? What a ridiculous notion! Our men's bodies provide the sperm necessary for reproduction without the barbaric act of copulation."

Logan snickered. "You didn't seem to find it so disgusting a few minutes ago."

"If you don't need us for reproduction," Geoffrey countered, "what was the purpose of your visits?"

Nadia paused to form a credible answer. "I needed to experience this physical contact for a scientific experiment I am conducting."

"Why didn't you use one of your own men?" Logan asked.

"Contact between men and women on Heart is unacceptable."

"Hold everything," Robin interjected. "I'm beginning to get a very interesting picture here. A minute ago you offered to free the women to get yourself out of here but not the men. And you keep referring to men as though they're some inferior species. Is it possible that your men are not only impotent, they're slaves?"

Nadia eyed her with curiosity. This one sounded as though she found the idea of keeping men as slaves quite attractive. "Slavery is against the law. Our men are servants."

"Hot damn!" Robin said with a laugh. "Talk about an upside-down world. Green sky, blue grass and women in charge."

"Heart is much safer than your world," Nadia said, "where men wage wars and fight one another in their own homes. We have no such violence here."

"How do you know Earth is like that?" Geoffrey asked.

She shrugged. "We question crossovers when they first arrive, before the memory depletion."

"Are your people all forced to drink the water? Is that how you keep them so peaceful?" Logan asked.

Her eyes narrowed warily. "Higgs told you about

the water?"

"Of course," Geoffrey said. "But we had already guessed that we were being tranquilized by something."

"I see. You should have all been fully assimilated by tonight. No previous crossovers ever figured it out in time." Panic turned her stomach as she realized that her warning to Ray Higgs made her responsible for this uprising. The sexual pleasure she had discovered wasn't worth the price she might yet have to pay. How could she have known that Earth men could be so devious? No wonder her people kept them medicated.

She glanced at the western horizon and noted a hint of the approaching dawn. "Please. I have answered your questions. Allow me to leave now. I have important duties to attend to this morning."

"I regret any inconvenience," Geoffrey replied, dropping his friendly tone. "But you've barely begun to answer our questions. You claim your world is peaceful but surely someone must break a law from time to time. What sort of enforcement agencies do you have? Police? Militia?"

Nadia frowned. She wasn't familiar with those terms but she understood the meaning. "Laws are enacted and enforced by Parliament."

"And who heads up Parliament?" Geoffrey asked.

"The Imperial Prefect, Par—" She abruptly recalled her lie about her identity. "Nadia of Hinac is the ruler of all the provinces on Heart."

"What is your position?"

She hesitated again. As she feared, one lie was leading to another and starting to get complicated. "I am Parisia, Representative of Acameir."

"Would the Imperial Prefect have the power to free all of us?"

"Not alone. The majority of Parliament would have to agree to it and that would never happen."

"Nevertheless," Geoffrey said, "We would like to meet with your ruler."

Nadia gaped at him in shock. "That's impossible! Even if you were freed from this commune, no man may speak to her other than her personal servant."

Logan frowned at her skeptically. "Then you'll have to come with us and make the proper introductions."

She gasped. "*Never.* I couldn't do that. No Earth person is permitted beyond the barrier."

"That's why you're going to be our escort," Logan told her.

"No! I refuse to assist you. I…I will remain here in the commune rather than betray my people."

Geoffrey brought her attention back to him and spoke with feigned innocent curiosity. "You said none of us are permitted beyond the barrier. What if someone did get through? Are there guards around the wall?"

Nadia smirked. "That would be an unnecessary use of womanpower. No one can penetrate the barrier from this side, and even if someone did, their action would be picked up on the monitors."

"And after that?" Geoffrey asked then saw that she didn't understand. "If someone broke through, how would that person be stopped?"

Nadia opened her mouth to reply but nothing, not even a lie, came to her. Since no one had ever managed to escape from the commune, she was not aware of any procedures to deal with it. "That information is confidential. I do not have access to it."

Logan took one threatening step closer. "Tell me something you do know, lady. If it's impossible to penetrate the barrier from this side, how did you get out of here last night?"

Her gaze dropped to the control box in his hand before she could stop herself. She tried to hide her mistake with a cough but he wasn't fooled.

"This?" he asked, holding up the box. "Would you like to be nice and explain how to use it?" She only glared at him. "No problem. I'm sure we can figure it out. Geoffrey?" He handed him the box. "This should be a piece of cake for an engineer."

Nadia's inner panic was nearing the surface. "You must not fool with the controller. Improper use could have disastrous results."

Geoffrey turned the box over in his hand and studied the four red buttons and the numbered dial. "It would be better if you instructed me—"

"*Never!* I have answered your questions but I will not help you invade my home. I have made my decision—I will remain here in the commune."

Tarla knelt down beside the woman and spoke softly. "Parisia, my name is Tarla. You wouldn't want to remain here anymore than we do. You said slavery is forbidden and yet we are being held captive and required to work in the fields to provide food for you. Surely you must see how wrong that is."

"We don't need the food," Nadia replied defensively. "The farm is merely the best means to keep the Earth men busy and self-sufficient."

Tarla cocked her head thoughtfully. "Busy? As in, busy hands are happy hands? Is that why they're still farming and cooking by century-old methods? To keep busy?"

Nadia was duly impressed by this woman's deductive reasoning. She definitely showed signs of intelligence. "Precisely. Their days are so filled with mundane chores that they couldn't possibly get into mischief."

"And the more modern bathroom facilities?"

"Hmmph! We would never leave sanitation up to men."

"One more question," Geoffrey said. "How closely are we being observed?"

Nadia gave him a sly smile. "Closely enough."

"Are we being watched now, out here?" Tarla asked. When the woman didn't respond, she reminded her, "Your freedom depends on your cooperation. We wish to know how much your people are aware of what we say and do."

Nadia thought about it for a moment then decided the truth could not make things any worse than they already were and it might just help. "There is a sky monitor that views the entire farm from a distance. The cloud cover tonight has probably obscured the picture."

"And inside the buildings?"

"Only the barn is monitored for sight and sound."

Tarla nodded thoughtfully. "So, when someone goes into the tack room with a medical problem, they are seen and heard by someone. Correct?" She quickly glanced at Logan then back to their captive.

"At the moment, there are observation techs on duty around the clock, though that is not usually necessary. Your avoidance of the antidote has caused a number of inconveniences," Nadia said with obvious annoyance.

Logan motioned Geoffrey aside and Tarla and Robin followed, leaving the rest of the team to guard their captive. As soon as they were out of the woman's hearing, Logan said, "My guess is, she's told the truth for the most part but either something she said is a lie or she's holding back an important bit of information."

"Agreed," Geoffrey said. "For one thing, she said the magnetic pull only goes one way but polarity can be reversed. If we got here, we should be able to get back."

"Why would she lie about that?" Tarla asked.

Geoffrey shrugged. "Maybe her people just want to keep their world secret, so they don't allow anyone to go back to Earth to talk about it."

"I'm not so sure," Tarla said. "I had the feeling she was stating facts as she knows them. If there is a way back, she may not be important enough to have that information. But that makes me wonder about something else. We haven't heard a single story about anyone from outside the farm coming to visit before. Why now, and why would she be the one given permission to make contact?"

"Maybe she didn't have permission," Logan murmured, then realized what had been bothering him. "That's it! She's here illegally. I'd bet on it. She was dying to get back one minute, then willing to stay forever the next. I'd say she definitely did not want her ruler finding out she was here. Now all we have to do is figure out how to use that to get what we want."

Robin was first with a suggestion. "We could promise to release her after she got us out of here and directed us to where we could find that imperial person."

Logan added, "If she's telling the truth about there being no police or guards, we could probably take over the capitol or palace, or whatever it is, before they knew what was happening."

"And what if she wasn't telling the truth?" Geoffrey asked. "If they were able to get us off the plane and corral us here without us having any memory of it, they could do it all over again. We'd be right back where we started. No, I think we need to stick to the original plan and use her as a hostage to negotiate our release. Perhaps if we prove that we can behave in a civilized manner, they might be willing to deal fairly. Any aggressive action on our part will only serve to confirm that we are the primitives she called us."

"I agree," Tarla said. "There's only one part of the plan I think you need to reconsider. From what Parisia said, there's no way her ruler will negotiate with a man, no matter how passively he behaves. Our representative should be a woman."

Logan knew she meant herself and his immediate impulse was to refuse to let her take such a risk. A heartbeat later he conceded that he had no right to do that and he remained silent.

"Are you volunteering?" Geoffrey asked Tarla.

"Yes, sir."

"Same here," Robin said. "She can't go alone."

Geoffrey shared a look of resignation with Logan. "I don't like it but you're right. It will be the two of you, plus Lee and Alicia, just in case you need to defend yourselves. You may as well get started right now. We'll take care of stowing our guest out of sight."

While Geoffrey and Tarla went over the plan and the terms she would request, Logan tried to think of one good reason Tarla shouldn't go or why he should but nothing logical came to him. All that remained was to wish her luck, as if she were any other soldier going off on a dangerous mission.

You might never see her again. Tell her.

But Logan knew there was nothing he could say that she wanted to hear. "Good luck," he finally said, giving Tarla and Robin each a curt nod then returned to his prisoner as they walked away.

Tarla told herself she was imagining things. Logan hadn't looked at her in any special way. He hadn't been about to say something then changed his mind. It was just tension and the dark playing tricks on her eyes.

"Do you suppose Alicia and Lee are finished tucking in sweet little Ray by now?" Robin asked, grinning and wiggling her eyebrows suggestively.

Tarla made a face. "Let's just hope they all know the meaning of discretion. The last thing we need now is for Wilkes to find out the ladies preferred Higgs over him."

"Oooh. Not a pretty picture. But speaking of discretion…" Robin pointed at three figures huddled together in front of a tent. As they walked closer, she could tell it was the trio they had just been discussing. Their approach was instantly noticed.

"What's going on?" Lee asked Tarla.

"The four of us are going into the tack room and try to negotiate our release. I think we should have a brief strategy meeting before we go in."

"You got it," Lee said then turned Ray's face to hers and gave him a quick kiss on the mouth. "Sleep tight, baby."

Alicia waited for him to look up at her. "We'll catch you later, love. Behave yourself till we get back." She lowered her head to deliver a considerably longer kiss than he'd gotten from Lee.

On the way to the barn, neither Tarla nor Robin asked and neither Lee nor Alicia offered comments. Instead Tarla summarized what they'd learned after the other two women left with Higgs. "There's no way of knowing if Parisia was being honest or if she's even typical of her people. The best we can do is assume she was somewhat truthful and stay on our toes."

"In other words, we're going to play it by ear," Robin said with a laugh.

Tarla smiled back. "Right. And try to let me do most of the talking so they get the impression I have some control over my people."

Robin saluted crisply. "Yes, sir. You're the boss-lady."

"That's what I want them to think. Otherwise, I'm not sure they'll believe I have the power to negotiate. So, no matter what I say, even if it sounds outrageous, back me up. You can argue with me later." She met each of the women's eyes and knew she could count on them. "Ready?"

They all nodded and wished each other luck before entering the barn. Robin lit the candle lantern by the door and led the way into the tack room. Once they were all inside, Tarla threw the bolt on the door and spoke the words she and Geoffrey had decided on.

"I am Captain Tarla Yan of the United States of America, Planet Earth. We have captured one of your people, Parisia, Representative of Acameir. We wish to open negotiations regarding her release."

CHAPTER 11

Simone felt like pulling her hair out in frustration. Didn't these Earth people ever sleep? She had purposely requested a change to the night shift in hopes that there would be less activity in the commune…which translated to fewer decisions for her to make.

Not that there was any real decision to make here. This was an emergency and emergencies required one to follow the proper procedures regardless of loyalties. She just wanted to stall for a while in hopes that her co-worker, Orleander, would return early from her break and then *she* could handle the situation. To protect herself, she paused the recorder so that the delay would not be evident.

Nadia would do flips down the halls of Parliament if she heard that Parisia had ventured into the commune and gotten caught. Advisor Iris, on the other hand, would be extremely grateful to anyone who helped cover up a potential security leak about the Imperial Prefect. Simone couldn't imagine why Parisia would have taken such a risk but she was certain the reason must be of world-shattering proportions.

Five minutes passed, yet the four women in the transfer room had not magically vanished from her monitor, nor had Orleander returned. Simone knew she had to act.

She was about to call Advisor Iris when a solution occurred. She didn't have to tell Nadia anything. All she had to do was get her to come to Observation and *just happen* to witness the situation for herself.

Simone dashed to the door and scanned the corridor to make sure Orleander was nowhere in sight then placed a call to Nadia.

A very groggy Fulton answered on the sixth ring.

"This is an emergency," Simone stated. "I need to speak with Nadia immediately."

"May I tell her who is calling?"

"No, you may not. But rest assured, she will appreciate being awakened after I speak to her."

"All right," Fulton said nervously. Nearly two minutes went by before he was back on the line. "I'm sorry. Nadia is not here."

"Not there? That's ridiculous. If you are saying that merely to avoid leaving your warm bed…"

"I swear," Fulton whined, hearing the implied threat. "I've looked everywhere, even outside. She's not here."

Simone would have questioned him further but the sound of footsteps warned her that time was up. "If she comes in, tell her to go to Observation. Speak to no one but her about this call, or she will be very displeased with you." Without waiting for his reply, she disconnected from him and called Advisor Iris. The woman answered at the same moment Orleander walked in. Simone gave her a frantic signal to join her at the monitor as she spoke to Iris.

"We have another emergency in the commune, madam."

"Oh my. I'll be there within the hour—"

"I don't believe this should wait," Simone interrupted. "If you'll turn on your monitor, I'll transmit from here."

"One moment then."

While Simone waited for the Advisor to go to her monitor, she backed up the recording to the point when the four women entered the transfer room. Fortunately, she was fast enough with the controls to prevent Orleander from suspecting anything unusual.

"Go ahead," Iris said with a yawn. All remnants of fatigue fled from her voice, however, when the young woman on the screen issued her short statement. "She lies," Iris said, more to herself than Simone. "It will take me but a moment to refute her claim." She took a calming breath to organize her thoughts. "As of right now, Observation is under security quarantine. No one is to enter or leave without my express permission and neither of you is to communicate with anyone but me. Is that understood?"

"Yes, ma'am," Simone said quickly.

"Yes ma'am," Orleander repeated. "Should we put the women to sleep?"

Iris studied the frozen images on her monitor. Their stances were defensive but courage was evident in each face. They could be dangerous. "Yes, but leave them in the transfer room for now. Advisor Iris out."

With the touch of one key she disconnected from Simone. By pressing a few more, she brought up the view of the Observation Room from the concealed scanner to confirm that Simone and Orleander were the only ones there and that they were following her instructions. She thanked the suns that she had doubled the tech staff for she truly did not trust Simone.

Once she was certain the situation was temporarily

put on hold, she placed a call to Parisia's private line.

"Hello?"

It sounded like Parisia but Iris had to be certain. "Security precautions please." In the blink of an eye, she had a visual of Parisia on her monitor then the palm of the Prefect's hand was flattened on the screen. Iris's computer verified that it was indeed the Imperial Prefect but she and Parisia had devised one other fail-safe. She asked, "What happened on the twelfth day of the sixth month twenty-four years ago?"

Parisia moved her hand away from the screen. That question had made her smile when they'd chosen it. Now, knowing that it signified a critical security breach, it filled her with anxiety. "My daughter, Brianne, cut her first tooth."

Iris gave an audible sigh of relief. "I apologize for disturbing you but we have a problem." She relayed as much as she knew so far and what actions had been taken. "Obviously, they have not captured you but somehow they know your name. What makes it doubly confusing is that the woman referred to you as a representative rather than the Imperial Prefect."

"There's something else that's not quite right," Parisia said, rubbing her eyes. "From what we know of these people, doesn't it seem rather odd that they would choose *women*, rather than men, to confront us?"

Iris nodded slowly. She had been too concerned about Parisia to fully analyze the situation. "It does seem unlikely that they would send women to negotiate with captors. Unless they knew something about the structure of our society."

"It can only mean one thing, Iris. They *have* captured one of our people and convinced that person to reveal certain information about us. But who? And how?"

"I will have the four women taken to the sanatorium and isolated. If you'll meet me there, we can question them together."

Nadia glared at the silly girls who had been assigned to guard her. She had tried being friendly, demanding and threatening. She had offered every bribe she could think of to entice them to help her escape. Obviously, the scarred man had chosen them to guard her knowing they were immovable.

At least she had been allowed to dress properly and, though her hands and feet were still bound, she was somewhat more comfortable. She laid on the cot and turned toward the side of the tent. There had to be a way to save herself. Escape appeared unlikely for the moment but she was certain that eventually an opportunity would avail itself. If she couldn't get the controller back, she could always go through the transfer room. If her timing was right, Simone would be the tech on duty and she could be convinced to keep a secret…for the right reward.

She recalled Simone telling her she would be working nights now and it was already nearing dawn. The best thing to do was pretend to be docile long enough for her guards to give her a little freedom, then by nightfall she could make her break.

But what if the men who captured her figured out how to use the controller in the meantime? What if they escaped from the commune and told someone about her presence? It wouldn't be long before her absence was connected with the escape in spite of her using Parisia's name.

She laughed at the route her thoughts had taken. Earth men didn't have the intelligence to analyze the controller or manage a successful escape. There was no real reason to fret. Just in case, however, she started to create a credible excuse for why she had ventured into the commune.

A short while later, she was satisfied that she was prepared for every possibility and allowed herself to go to sleep.

Logan flopped onto his stomach and punched his pillow one more time. Years in the service had accustomed him to grabbing an hour of sleep whenever and wherever he could. He was an ace at shutting out distractions and ignoring uncomfortable surroundings to get the most out of a catnap.

So why was he having so much trouble taking advantage of the rest time he'd been granted and badly needed?

He knew the answer, he just didn't like admitting it, even to himself. His quixotic instincts had him wanting to protect Tarla regardless of the fact that she didn't want his protection and probably didn't need it.

As long as he had kept her classified as an unattainable fantasy, thoughts of her never kept him from sleeping. But now, after having held her, touched her, *tasted* her and discovered exactly how she looked when she was filled with wanting him, the reality and the fantasy were all mixed together.

He couldn't help but wonder what it might have been like if he and Tarla had met before—His thought stopped there. Before what? Before he was born maybe? There had never been a time in this life when he would have belonged in the same world as Tarla.

What if she didn't come back? What if the people on the other side of the wall decided to hold onto her and the other women and leave Parisia here? He shifted to his side to consider that possibility. He doubted that would happen, but if it did, he felt certain either Geoffrey would figure out how to use the device that got Parisia through the wall or Parisia herself would eventually break down and help them escape.

One way or the other, Logan was betting their present circumstances would soon be changing. He just wished he had a crystal ball to see whether that change would be for better or for worse. The only thing he knew for certain was that even life in paradise would be torture if Tarla was within reach, yet untouchable. And as long as she believed he was a low-life, murdering, drug-smuggling traitor, she would remain untouchable.

Of course, he could always tell her the truth, but since there was no one here to back up his story, why waste the breath? It would be his word against everyone else's—just like it had been at his court martial.

Tarla, Robin, Lee and Alicia awoke on the carpeted floor of a very large unfurnished room. There were no windows, only a closed door in the wall across from them. Tarla rose and walked toward it but was stopped halfway there by an invisible barrier.

"Well," she said turning back to the others, "I don't know if we've made progress or not. We've gone from a walled-in farm to a cell."

Robin stood up and stretched. "I wonder how long we were out. I feel like I had a really good night's sleep."

"That's how Logan and Wilkes described their experiences too," Tarla reminded her. "But in actuality, they were only gone a few hours. At least we didn't wake up still in the tack room. Hopefully this means they're going to talk to us."

No sooner were the words out of her mouth than the

door opened and two women dressed in long white robes entered. Lee and Alicia were on their feet in an instant.

One of their visitors appeared to be middle-aged and was so pale and slender, it seemed as though a light breeze would blow her away. Tarla thought she looked friendly but troubled. The other was shorter, plumper and much older. Her worried frown appeared to be a fixed expression.

"Good day," the younger woman said with a near-smile. "We understand that you wish to speak with us."

Tarla took a step forward and repeated her earlier statement. "I am Captain Tarla Yan of the United States of America. We have captured one of your people, Parisia, Representative of Acameir. We wish to open negotiations regarding her release."

"That is most intriguing, particularly since I am Parisia of Acameir, and my title is not representative but Imperial Prefect of Heart. This is my Domestic Affairs Advisor, Iris of Mergany."

Tarla had been mentally prepared for the unexpected but she'd hoped to get past the introductions before feeling bewildered. "The woman we are holding hostage claims that *she* is Parisia and that Nadia of Hinac is Imperial Prefect."

"Nadia?" the older woman asked skeptically. "What does this woman look like?"

Tarla shot a glance at Robin. Someone was lying but who? "She is tall, full-figured, has very long black hair and a rather large nose."

The two women exchanged whispers then the Advisor said to Tarla, "Your description matches that of the woman we know as Nadia but it is difficult for us to believe you have captured her. Tell us how this happened."

Tarla straightened her shoulders, met the older woman's penetrating gaze then related the facts as if she were delivering a report to a superior officer. She could tell her straightforward delivery was appreciated but the content of her report was beyond belief for the Heart leaders.

"Impossible," the woman who claimed to be the real Parisia murmured. "That is too much, even for Nadia."

"I have no reason to lie to you," Tarla protested. "And how else would I have learned the names Parisia and Nadia, or known about the gateway, the drug in the water, or that your planet is called Heart?"

"We are not accusing you of lying about having captured one of our women," Parisia said, "but the circumstances are simply too unlikely. Our entire society has been structured to prevent the sort of male aggression you have described. It is impossible to believe that one of our women would not only permit, but *welcome* an invasion of her body."

"All I can tell you is she said she was conducting an experiment and it was not for breeding purposes."

As the pair whispered to one another again, Tarla had the distinct impression they might not want Parisia/Nadia back. She remembered how that woman had tried to play on their sisterhood and thought that angle was worth a try here. "Excuse me?" She waited until she had their full attention. "Surely you wouldn't consider leaving one of your own among all those primitive men."

"What is it you wish in exchange for her freedom?" Iris asked.

"It's very simple," Tarla replied. "Send us all home."

"That may sound simple to you," Parisia said with a sigh. "But it is a request we could not fill no matter how desperate we were to make a trade."

Tarla had anticipated that response. "We know you have something called a near-term memory depleter. You could use that on us so that we'd have no recollection of Heart at all."

Parisia shook her head. "I'm afraid you misunderstood. We can't send you back because we don't know how."

"How can that be? You're able to heal critically ill people and build invisible force fields, yet you can't figure out how to make the gateway work in reverse?"

"It's never been considered a priority."

"Well it damn well should be," Robin interjected, unable to remain silent a moment longer. "How would you like to be stranded a zillion miles away from your home, turned into zombies and treated like lab rats?"

Tarla held up a hand to stop her from continuing. It was important that these women thought of them as equals, and she was fairly sure the way to accomplish that was through intellectual rather than emotional channels. "If you truly do not have the ability to send us home, at least release us from the farm and give us access to your technology. We have men and women with a wide variety of talents and skills. Given the chance, we may be able to solve the problem for ourselves. Besides that, we need a more stimulating life than what you had planned for us. We don't know what your society is like but it has to be closer to what we're used to than the farm."

"Anything else?" Parisia asked.

Tarla ran down her checklist. "There may be some minor details as we go along but there's only one more major request. No more drugs or using any other methods you have to control or alter our behavior. We want our freedom in every way. Our hostage said you are human, so you must know how important individual freedom is. We're asking no more of you than we believe you would ask of us if the situation were reversed."

Parisia slowly nodded. "This is a very grave matter. One that I must discuss with others before taking any action. I cannot make you any promises but I assure you that I empathize with your position and will try to come up with an acceptable compromise for everyone concerned. It may be some time before I am able to meet with you again, so I will have you moved to a more comfortable room to wait. Your cooperation and patience will be appreciated."

Parisia and Iris weren't gone more than ten minutes when Iris returned. "Come along," she said, holding the door open.

Tarla stepped forward but the invisible barrier stopped her progress.

"Oh my, forgive me," Iris said, then took something out of her pocket. It looked like the small box that had been taken from their hostage. "If you will all stand back and off to the side, I'll have this out of your way in a moment."

They did as she directed, then watched her point the box at the center of the barrier. A white beam shot out from the box and with two sweeps of her arm, she drew a large "X" across the wall then put the device back in her pocket. "You can pass through now."

Since she couldn't see any change with her eyes, Tarla tested the space in front of her with her hand to confirm that the barrier really had disappeared then motioned for the others to follow. Iris led them down one corridor then another, with barely a glance behind her.

Tarla was a little surprised that they had gained so much trust so quickly. It was almost as if…"Advisor Iris? May I ask you a question?"

"Certainly."

Tarla ordered herself to block the multitude of questions lined up in her mind and focus on just one with her intuitive ability amped to its highest level. "Are you telepathic?"

Iris raised her eyebrows. "No. Why do you ask?"

"You don't seem at all afraid of us now. I thought perhaps you'd read my mind to know that you're safe and we wouldn't attempt an escape."

Iris angled her head at Tarla. "I'm not telepathic, nor are any of our citizens that I know of. But my intuition is usually quite good and it says, despite your willingness to commit violence, you are all intelligent, logical women. Harming me or attempting an escape would not serve any purpose at this time. Therefore, I'm perfectly safe with you at the moment. Here we are." She opened a door and waved them inside. "Full illumination please." Immediately the room was flooded with light.

"Very nice," Robin said, scanning the large room. "We finally found civilization."

Tarla smiled as she took in the red, white, and blue color scheme. The furnishings were all combinations of geometric-shaped cushions and pieces of what appeared to be stone but were practically weightless. Apparently they could all be mixed and matched to serve different functions. Iris pointed out the bathroom then slid back a panel on one wall to reveal a kitchenette.

"Lighting and temperature are voice activated. If you are hungry or thirsty, the cooler and cabinets are stocked with a variety of items. If you wish to heat something, place the entire tray or container inside the laser oven." She opened a door to demonstrate. "The unit will automatically read the instructions and cook it accordingly."

Iris closed up the kitchenette and moved across the room to a low table surrounded by cushions. "This room is normally used as a waiting area for family or friends of a patient. It is equipped with an entertainment center for your distraction." She touched the edge of the table and a directory listing of options appeared on its surface. "It is touch sensitive and self-explanatory. For instance, if you would like to hear some music…"

She passed her finger over that word and the room was suddenly filled with the sounds of a symphony orchestra. The tabletop now offered a means of changing the volume, tone and musical selection. Iris gave a quick demonstration of how to use those features then touched the edge of the tabletop again to turn the system off.

"It is capable of running as many as a dozen programs simultaneously, though I've never figured out why anyone would want to do that."

"I have another question, if you don't mind," Tarla said. Iris nodded her willingness to listen. "We were told that when a person from Earth lands here, he is interviewed and that is how you know so much about our planet."

"That is correct."

Tarla took a breath and forced herself to speak as though she wasn't personally concerned about the answer to her question. "Were we each interviewed then?"

Iris met her gaze steadily. "No. There were too many of you and not enough trained interrogators. Besides, a good number of your group required medical attention. That was the first priority."

"But as I understand it, even if you had interviewed us, we would have no recollection of it because of your memory depleter."

"Also correct," Iris replied evenly. "But, as I said, we did not conduct the standard interviews...and I have no reason to prevaricate about that."

Tarla stared into the older woman's eyes and decided she had told the truth. Relief flooded through her. If she needed to reveal her secret, she wanted it to be on her own terms. Thinking of her Innerworld ring, she asked, "What happened to all of our belongings?"

Iris angled her head. "Your weapons were destroyed, if that's what you are curious about."

Tarla couldn't think of any way to find out what she really wanted to know without asking directly. "I...*we* were wondering about more personal items, like family photos and jewelry."

Iris walked to the door and opened it. "I am sorry to say, everything was discarded since it was assumed you would not have need for such items again. As Parisia advised, it may be a while before we can get back to you regarding your demands, so please be patient and make yourselves comfortable." A second later, she was gone.

Lee went to the door and tried to turn the knob. "It's locked."

"So much for trusting us not to make an escape," Robin said with a laugh. "But at least they're no longer trying to bore us to death. Anybody else curious about what they call entertainment?"

Tarla shut out the other women's voices and turned her focus toward what was bothering her about the room. It only took a quick scan of the colorful space. There were no windows or timepieces. Not knowing whether one hour or one day had passed since they'd entered the tack room, added to her already tense state.

She was a little envious of Robin. She was free to enjoy the moment since she had complete faith that

Tarla would take care of any strategic problem that arose and Lee and Alicia would take care of any physical threat. Determined to take advantage of the calm, regardless of how long it lasted, she joined the group at the entertainment center.

"What do you think *Fictionvision* is?" Robin asked.

"Let's find out," Alicia said and touched that word on the directory. That list of options was replaced by only two words: *Comedy* and *Drama*.

Lee chose comedy and a list of alphabetical titles and running times began slowly scrolling along the tabletop. "Your turn, Tarla. You pick one."

Tarla squinted at the flow of printed words. Finally she just closed her eyes and lowered her finger to the table.

They all leaned forward to see her selection.

"*Mother Knows Best*?" Robin read with a laugh. "This should be ripe."

Before anyone else could comment, the title appeared in script on the blank wall in front of where they were seated.

"Lights out, please," Lee requested to the ceiling, then grinned when her order was obeyed.

Without the lights, Tarla could see that the images were three-dimensional and completely surrounded them. It looked as though they were sitting in the living room of the show.

Despite the bits of information Nadia had given them about her society, the program still came as a bit of a surprise. The comedy aspect seemed to be at the expense of the bumbling houseman who meant well but managed to screw everything up so badly that only the wise, long-suffering heroine could straighten it all out when she came home from work.

"Do you think this is really how they live here?" Robin asked.

Tarla drummed her fingers on the table and accidentally shut off the program. "Lights," she directed. "I think we'd have to consider it based in fact, but fictionalized and exaggerated to be entertaining."

"That show was more pathetic than entertaining," Lee said with a grimace.

"To us, maybe," Tarla said. "But their culture obviously differs from ours. I don't know if Iris did it on purpose or not, but she's handed us a way to get some insight about their society. A little while ago, we were dealing blind. With this, we might be able to learn enough about our opponents to get everything we need to know." She was satisfied to see the nods of agreement from the others. "As of this moment, ladies, school is in session. Let's begin with the news of the day."

Nadia had said Heart was peaceful and the news seemed to back that up. It contained primarily positive rather than negative news. There were no reports from war zones or famine-stricken countries, no homicides or hijackings, no arrests of drug lords or deaths of innocent bystanders because of a shoot-out in a park.

What was in abundance was statistics—how many tons of corn had been produced at how much profit for such-and-such corporation, percentage comparisons of utility usages on this date over the past twenty years to reflect an improvement of efficiency level, numbers of patients admitted to sanatoriums and for what diseases. Minute details of progress made on a health research study of some microscopic bacteria was the lead story of the day.

In the field of science, there was evidence that FTL/faster-than-light travel had been developed in a certain distant galaxy by beings known as Faxons.

In sports, the Pajanese team was leading the Blue

League in the free-style dance competition and Litay was the forerunner of the Red League. It looked like the finals were shaping up to be the most exciting in ten decades of tournament dancing.

The closing story of the day was apparently meant to be a big shocker. A woman confessed to having taught her son to read. She was sentenced to six months of extreme ostracism, during which time the child would be placed in a foster home where he would undergo a series of memory depletion sessions.

Robin was the first to speak, "Talk about a matriarchal culture!"

"Did you notice, there wasn't a single man involved in that whole broadcast?" Alicia added.

"Obviously," Tarla said, "Nadia was telling some truths. This is definitely a female-dominant society. We should be able to use that to our advantage."

Lee stood up and went to the kitchenette. "However, other than the fact that men aren't equals, these women seem to have a pretty solid and peaceful handle on things. I'm going to try one of these meals," she said pulling a tray out of the cooler. "Anybody else want anything?"

They all decided to have something to eat and drink then returned to the entertainment center. Tarla was disappointed that there were no educational offerings for them to study the history of the planet. She would have liked to have known how it could be so much like Earth yet evolved so differently.

"Let's try a drama next," she suggested.

Simply by watching a few programs, they were able to draw some conclusions about life on Heart.

In every instance, regardless of the story line, men were scarcely seen. And when they were portrayed, they were always servants, meekly carrying out the orders of a female. Women ran the government and businesses, constructed buildings and traveled to other planets. Robotic technology took care of any job that might require excessive strength or dirtying one's hands. Men cooked, cleaned, did laundry, took care of the children, and generally did as they were told. On the other hand, despite their political, economic and social power, the women of Heart highly valued their feminine gentility.

A vision popped into Tarla's head of Logan wearing an apron, holding a baby on one hip, while stirring the contents of a pot on a stove. She couldn't quite hold the image though. It was too ludicrous to contemplate. There probably wasn't enough of that strange drug on all of Heart to totally domesticate a man like Logan.

"I can't figure out the politics," Lee said after they'd all seen enough. "It sounds like capitalism, socialism, democracy and imperialism all got blended into one system. But if the whole planet is at peace, it must work."

Alicia hugged her knees to her chest. "These women obviously respect power. Not brute force, but the mental kind. I think they probably do a lot of bargaining and scheming behind the scenes. I'd say power and politics are what keeps their world turning."

"And production," added Tarla. "There seems to be a lot of importance placed on progress, productivity and efficiency."

"You know," Robin said. "It all makes sense if you consider the one thing that was missing from all those programs—male-female relationships. There wasn't even a hint of friendship, let alone love or lust. These women have turned their men into eunuchs who are happy to take care of all the aggravating, time-consuming tasks that have kept the majority of our women too tired or busy to compete in the political, business or scientific arenas for centuries. Hell, we might have had a woman president a hundred years ago, if no one ever fell in love and put being a wife and mother before her career."

"It sounds reasonable on the surface," Alicia said, with a thoughtful frown. "But knowing what it feels like to fall in love or be held in a man's arms, I don't think many women would be willing to give up the physical companionship for a more efficient world."

"Which brings us to our hostage," Tarla stated. "I think we can assume that she wasn't supposed to trespass onto the farm, and from the shocked expressions on Parisia's and Iris's faces, I'd say if she was conducting an experiment, it was strictly personal."

Robin made a face. "It sounds like our bargaining ticket isn't worth a ride on a merry-go-round. They'd probably just as soon leave her on the farm rather than let her infect the rest of their society with her unusual interest in men."

"I'm afraid you're right," Tarla said. "Maybe that's why the Domestic Affairs Advisor brought us here, to figure out on our own how weak our bargaining chip was. If we want our freedom, we're going to have to come up with something to offer them that they need but don't already have. The problem is, I have no idea what that could be."

CHAPTER 12

Brianne knocked lightly on Parisia's bedroom door. "Mother? It's four o'clock. Parliament will be convening in two hours. Are you awake?"

"Yes, dear," Parisia replied. "Come in."

Brianne entered, expecting to see her mother resting on her bed but instead, found her sitting at the window.

"I have such a lovely view of the city from this tower. Sometimes I get too busy to appreciate it."

Brianne heard the unusual note of melancholy. Taking a seat, Brianne touched her mother's hand. "Are you feeling all right? Did you get any sleep?"

Parisia blinked at her as though she only now realized she had company. Giving her daughter a soft smile, she said, "I'm well. And I may have gotten something better than sleep—an idea."

"Oh? For which problem?"

That made Parisia laugh. "It might be a way of solving two at once. Or create an even bigger one. I'm afraid I was sitting here brooding about how much I would miss the little extras I've come to take for granted if I was no longer Prefect."

"That's a particularly odd thing to say considering the fact that your greatest opponent will probably never have the chance to hinder you again."

Parisia shifted toward Brianne. "You heard something?"

Brianne shook her head. "Nothing worth waking you for. Nadia's houseman confirmed that she has been missing since sometime last night. She has also been paged throughout the imperial city, and no one has seen or heard from her. Iris is satisfied that the Earth woman has told the truth. They have captured Nadia. Who else would have had the nerve to give your name as hers and hers as the Imperial Prefect?"

"If we could prove what they said she did with that Earth man, I don't think anyone would find fault with me for leaving her in the commune. Has the technician had any luck with the recording made by the sky monitor?"

"I don't believe so. The cloud cover was extremely thick last night."

"Last night, yes, but what about the night before? They said she was there the previous night as well." Brianne was already across the room calling Iris as Parisia completed her thought. "The only way I can permanently censure Nadia is with irrefutable, shocking proof. Otherwise, she's liable to concoct some tale that will put doubts in certain minds, as she has in the past."

As Brianne completed her call to Iris, her bright smile lifted Parisia's spirits. "Iris was a step ahead of you this time, Mother. She just finished viewing a segment of the prior night's sky recording. She said the close-up is very grainy but there's no question about it being Nadia behaving most improperly with an Earth man. Apparently the techs were so busy watching the group in the transfer room, they missed the activity outside.

"To quote her, *if you have the courage to show that film to Parliament, not only will Nadia lose every supporter she ever had, they will agree to anything you propose afterward.*"

Parisia's smile now matched her daughter's. "Then I'll just have to gather up my courage, because what I'm going to propose would be best presented to a Parliament that was already in a state of shock."

"Mother! Just what is this idea of yours?"

"First ask Delbert to bring me a snack and cup of tea while I bathe." As she headed for the bathroom and Brianne went to the door, she said, "Oh, yes, and a freshly pressed special appearance gown. The gold one, I think. I'll explain my plan while I get ready. I can't believe I was sitting there feeling sorry for myself. Remember this, Brianne. Every so often things need to be stirred up to keep everyone on their toes, no matter how frightening the change might seem."

Brianne didn't care what the shocking plan was, she would back it wholeheartedly if it meant seeing her mother happy. Just now Parisia looked as she had years ago—full of energy and spirit, anxious to do battle on the floor of Parliament.

She was halfway down two flights of winding stairs when she saw Delbert coming up, carrying a tray. On it was a silver tea service, two china cups and a plate of sandwich triangles. "You've been reading Mother's mind again, Delbert." She smiled to let him know she was teasing as she walked back up the stairs with him. "She just asked me to have you bring her a snack and tea. She also requested—"

"A freshly pressed gown," Delbert finished for her. "Her gold one is already hanging in her dressing room."

Brianne laughed. "You really do know what she wants before she does, don't you?"

Delbert lowered his eyes shyly. "We've been together a very long time...and Parisia has always been just a bit predictable. Do you require any assistance? Jason is helping the chef at the moment, but I'm sure he could be—"

"No, no. It's not necessary to interrupt him. I'm going to Parliament exactly as I am. No one will notice me with the show Mother and Iris have planned."

If he had suggested one of the other housemen, she might have accepted the offer, but she never felt completely comfortable about being served by her twin brother. Had they been born to anyone other than the Imperial Prefect, it would never have been a problem. When Jason turned twenty, he would have been put into service in another household. As the Prefect's son, however, he was in the awkward position of being too exalted to work for a lesser family.

The Imperial Prefect had the exclusive option to terminate a pregnancy if she learned that a male had been conceived. Parisia would have aborted if it had been a singular conception. With a female twin, however, her decision had not been so simple.

She had encountered a series of problems in her attempt to conceive an heiress and the doctor had warned her that she might never conceive again. Knowing there would be difficulties in the years ahead for her son, she chose to bear the non-identical twins in order to have a daughter to carry on the family line.

Parisia was coming out of her bath wrapped in a warm robe as Brianne and Delbert reentered the suite. "He anticipated you, as usual," Brianne said as she and her mother both sat by the table where Delbert placed the tea tray.

"Would you like me to do your hair while you have your tea?" he asked Parisia while pouring her favorite brew.

She smiled up at him affectionately. "That would be very nice, thank you. Something to make me look very serious, I think."

Brianne wondered if she would ever find a houseman as perfect for her as Delbert was for Parisia. He was extremely bright and pleasant looking for a man, and not at all clumsy as so many of them tended to be, which were the reasons Parisia had chosen him to begin with, both as a servant and sire for her offspring.

Actually, Brianne thought she'd be happy just to find a servant that could style hair as well as Delbert. It was his exceptional skill and eye for beauty that had earned him the very rare privilege of touching Parisia and her daughter. Of course, it was only their hair he could touch and he had to ask permission first. Otherwise, he always remembered to keep a respectable distance from them both.

Delbert was the only man Brianne had ever communicated with, even as a child. Parisia had used his sperm to fertilize her egg then kept him on as caretaker after the twins were born. Parisia never had reason to replace him in all the years since.

Though Brianne understood the reason, she still felt sad when she recalled the day she had become a woman and Delbert had no longer been permitted to treat her as a child. From that day forward, physical contact between them had been prohibited. It was upsetting at first, especially that day she fell and hurt her knee. She had cried for him to pick her up and give her a hug to make it feel better. He had been hurt that day too, but the law had to be obeyed—especially in the home of the Imperial Prefect.

The separation was much harder with Jason. She supposed it was because they were twins and bound in a different way than most brothers and sisters. They both had a difficult time remembering the no-touching rule, until finally Jason was threatened with banishment. Rather than be parted from his family entirely, he and Brianne both worked harder to adjust to the new rules. To help him along, his antidote dosage had been temporarily increased as well.

"Brianne?" Parisia said softly. "You look quite distressed. You mustn't be. I will admit that my proposal is radical but with Nadia out of the way…"

As Parisia began to spell out her plan, Brianne shook off the confusion she always felt when she thought too long or too hard about Delbert or Jason. She was the daughter of the Imperial Prefect of Heart, which meant if there was no major opposition, she would be the next Imperial Prefect. It was not good to question traditions that formed the foundation of their society. Her role was to see that those traditions were carried on in order to ensure domestic peace and tranquility throughout the world.

With part of her mind lagging in the past, she thought perhaps she had misunderstood what her mother was suggesting and asked her to repeat what she had just said. When she realized she hadn't misunderstood at all, she was filled with unease. It seemed extremely ironic that while she had been thinking of carrying on age-old traditions to assure world peace, the Imperial Prefect was planning on breaking a few primary laws…for the same reason.

Tarla saw the rows of cots, the men with bandaged wounds, the IV bottles and bare light bulbs. It's not real, she told herself. It's only a dream. You can make it go away if you really try.

She was sick to death of war, the senseless maiming and killing. How naïve she had been to think that because she'd worked as an emergency room nurse, she could tolerate the sights and sounds of an army hospital unit. For each soldier she nursed back to health, another died. Soon one young man's face blended in with the next and the next, and there were times when she had to look at the chart to remember whether this was Bill or Troy or a new patient just arrived. Had he lost a leg or a hand? Or was this another drug overdose?

But there was one name she didn't forget. One face that stayed with her whether she wanted it to or not. She saw him there now, lying on his cot with his eyes closed, pretending to be asleep so she wouldn't bother him. But she was too smart for that ploy. He *was* going to talk to her today if she had to drag words out of his mouth.

As she did several times a day, she checked his pulse, took his temperature and listened to his lungs, chatting to him all the while as though she expected him to respond. Suddenly he opened his eyes and looked at her, and he didn't need to speak aloud.

He adored her. He worshiped her. He needed her to love him and need him in return. She had never known a man whose loneliness matched her own, and yet, without a word she knew he felt it too. "Logan," she whispered, and bent to kiss his lips.

Somehow she was now beside him then beneath him and they were on a bed of straw.

"I love you," he murmured as his hands and mouth aroused a hunger that had her trembling. She felt him against her, hard and ready to join their bodies together. But as she lay there, breathlessly awaiting the moment, Gianni and Higgs appeared in their white gloves and MP helmets and lifted his body off hers.

Tarla watched them escort him away, his wrists cuffed and his ankles shackled. "But he said he loves me," she cried. "He couldn't have done any of the things you're accusing him of. I know. Do you hear me? I know it's not true!" Gianni looked back at her and laughed.

The real sound of laughter pierced the dreamy veil and brought Tarla abruptly awake. She immediately realized that the giggles were coming from Robin and Lee and had nothing to do with her, but her heart still pounded from imagined desperation.

"Oops," Robin said when she noticed Tarla sitting upright. "Sorry about that."

Tarla waved away her apology. "It's okay. I'm surprised I fell asleep."

"We all did," Robin said with a shrug. "There's coffee if you need some."

Tarla knew she needed something but she wasn't sure exactly what. A flash of sexual need from her dream teased her drowsy mind and she promptly swept it away. But there was a piece she couldn't ignore so easily. She actually *did* know Logan was innocent. But what good would it do to defend him? They weren't even on Earth any more. And her conviction didn't come from evidence anyone would accept anyway.

Except Logan. Because he knows the truth. And might appreciate having someone else know it as well, no matter how she came to know it.

By promising herself to examine that thought at a later, more appropriate time, she was able to focus on the present.

"You'd think they'd at least send us a message to let us know what's going on," Tarla stated to the room in general. "This waiting without knowing how long it's been is driving me crazy."

"Now that you're up, do you mind if we watch another program?" Robin asked.

"No, but how about the news first?"

Robin turned on the entertainment center and selected the news. The weather report was followed by the same sports news they'd heard before. Tarla was about to tell Robin to switch it when the picture changed to the Imperial Prefect and her Domestic Affairs Advisor exiting a room and being surrounded by reporters.

"Why did you call an emergency session of Parliament, Madam Prefect?" one reporter called out.

"What took all night to decide?" asked another.

"Why was the media excluded?"

Iris raised a hand and the crowd held their breath. "We apologize for any inconveniences or hurt feelings. A situation of utmost delicacy has occurred and, until all the parties involved have agreed on the actions to be taken, it will have to remain confidential."

"Until when?"

"Your constituents have a right to know what this *delicate* situation is!"

Parisia spoke in Iris's ear. She was clearly insisting her Advisor make another statement, much to that woman's disapproval. After another exchange, Iris straightened her shoulders and stepped forward. "Parisia will answer all your questions at an open media conference at three o'clock this afternoon in the Grand Hall. She respectfully requests that you do not browbeat any other members of Parliament until then. They have had a long night also and have been sworn to confidentiality."

Robin said, "That's got to be about us, right?"

"Sh-sh-sh," Tarla sounded as the picture switched back to the commentator.

"That was just moments ago and, as you heard, we have to wait six more hours to find out what all the secrecy is about. For some educated guesses from women around the nation, we go now to our roving reporters…"

"Six more hours," Tarla muttered. "Assuming they keep similar time to us, that makes it about nine in the morning. Good heavens! We've already been gone more than a day."

"Can you imagine what everyone back on the farm is thinking?" Alicia asked. "They must be—"

The front door opened and Parisia and Iris entered. Robin turned off the entertainment center and they all rose expectantly.

"We apologize for the delay," Parisia said. "It was quite…complicated. Please be seated. We have several matters to discuss with you."

They all sat, the Heart women on one side of the table, the Earth women on the other, but no one tried to pretend they were at ease. The tension in the room was too thick to cut with polite greetings and pleasant smiles and neither faction bothered to make the effort.

Tarla understood that in a bargaining situation, whoever talks first usually loses. She wondered if the person who first said that had ever tried to sit quietly while his or her freedom was on the line. Thankfully, Iris didn't abide by that theory.

"Yesterday we introduced ourselves to you but we did not insist you reciprocate. As a show of respect, we invite you to use our birth names, Iris and Parisia and, in return, it would be helpful to know something about each of you. We are aware that you were all involved in a violent confrontation—a war—before you came here. We'd be interested in knowing what your contributions were in that conflict."

"I'm Tarla. I'm a trauma nurse. I was a captain in the Army, which makes me the senior ranking officer of the women stranded here."

"Robin. I'm a mech/tech, uh, mechanic and technician. I can repair anything with an engine in it, with or without a computer."

"Alicia, helicopter pilot. But I'm qualified to fly other craft too."

"Lee. I was in the infantry during the war, but back home I own a martial arts school."

Parisia wrinkled her brow. "That phrase is not familiar. What sort of art is taught at your school?"

"The art of self-defense, strong mind, strong body."

Parisia's eyes widened. "Were you one of the women who had the violent encounter with two men the first night?"

Lee grinned and pointed at Alicia. "She was the other one."

"Amazing," Parisia murmured, shaking her head. "We realize you must be quite anxious to begin negotiations and I assure you we have a proposition that should interest you. However, it will be much easier to work out details if we each understand a little more about the other's background and philosophy."

For quite a while she and Iris asked questions which mainly focused on Earth's recent war, what the women's specific duties were, how it began and how it ended. Tarla supplied most of the general answers, with the other women offering personal details when requested.

When Iris and Parisia were satisfied with what they'd learned about the war, they took turns describing their culture and how it had taken a different direction from Earth's. Though Tarla and her team had gleaned a good deal of information from the

Fictionvision programs, they listened attentively, particularly when Iris related the legend of the Velids' attack on Heart and subsequent transfer of power from men to women.

"No one is certain about what actually happened or whether men were ever really in control. All recorded history begins centuries after the women enslaved the remaining men. The legend has survived primarily as a reminder of why men must not be allowed to exercise their natural urges. Based on what you've told us about this last war on Earth, we have acted wisely."

Tarla felt as though she should come to the defense of her planet but the facts were against her. "Nevertheless, Earth is our home. We wish to return to our families and friends."

Robin sat forward. "And our men may have some terrible characteristics but we prefer them that way to what your *antidote* turns them into. Obviously, at least one of your women thought the same way."

Parisia blushed and cleared her throat. "With regard to your captive, we have confirmed everything you claimed, except that she is Nadia, not Parisia. What she did was not sanctioned by Parliament, nor would it ever be. It has been decided that her punishment will be to remain in the commune for five years, at which time her case will be reviewed. Thus, we have no wish to bargain for her release."

Tarla's heart stopped and started again with a lurch. It was exactly what they had feared. She made herself keep breathing while she waited to hear what sort of decision had been made about them.

"However," Parisia said after giving her words time to sink in, "we wish to bargain for your services instead."

The four Earth women shared surprised glances.

They had thought the game was over when it had barely begun.

"Iris related the positive aspects of our society. We are quite proud to boast of thousands of years of peaceful, nonviolent existence. But one of the reasons this has been possible is because we have no enemies in our solar system. No one has forced us to defend our world.

"Recently it has come to our attention that faster-than-light travel has been developed on other planets, making it possible for beings from distant galaxies to visit us one day. We would like to believe they would come in peace, to exchange ideas or establish trade. But that would be dangerously naïve of us."

Iris picked up the narrative from there. "Parisia has just spent most of the night convincing Parliament that we can no longer assume that we are safe in our peaceful system and that we need to be prepared in the event of an alien attack."

"That sounds reasonable," Tarla said.

"To you perhaps," Parisia replied. "But this is a radical idea here. You see, we have no army, no defense system, no weapons of any kind. It will take vast sums of money to implement a plan of any sort and there is no budget allocation for such. Without being able to see an immediate threat, several members of Parliament are strongly against diverting funds from ongoing projects."

"This is where we have you to thank," Iris interjected. "The loudest opponents to Parisia's defense proposal—as we anticipated—were Nadia's supporters. Once they were shown proof of what she had done, they were only too happy to withdraw their support of her and back Parisia."

Tarla thought she heard an opening to start bargaining, but she couldn't be sure. It seemed too easy. "I'm glad to hear that our efforts weren't completely wasted."

Iris's wrinkled face relaxed into a near smile. "And now you are wondering if it was enough to trade for your freedom."

Tarla was relieved to hear that they were finally getting to the crux of this discussion.

"Very simply, the answer is no," Parisia stated before Tarla could confirm Iris's supposition. "However, I told you we have a proposition and, in a moment, you will understand why we took such a circuitous route to get to it. Our lack of a defense system and weaponry is only part of our problem. Even with Parliament approving the funds needed, we still lack something vital to our defense—the attitude necessary to commit violence.

"Our people abhor physical aggression. There's not a single person on this planet who has ever purposely harmed another sentient being. Of course, there is the possibility that the proper attitude could be attained by certain select individuals…in time. Unfortunately, we may not have that time."

"I thought you said there was no immediate threat," Tarla said when Parisia paused for more than a moment.

Parisia and Iris shared an apprehensive glance. It was becoming quite clear to Tarla that the Advisor was the more cautious of the two and, though they seemed to be in accord most of the time, Parisia occasionally ignored Iris's advice to play it safe.

This time Parisia hedged. "There is no impending danger that we are certain of. Just an unsubstantiated rumor. If it turns out to be true, we must be prepared. If it is false, it would still be wise to have a defense system in place against a possible threat at some later date.

"As I was saying, none of the citizens of Heart have the necessary attitude to implement a viable defense plan in the near future. You, on the other hand, have lived with violence all your lives and have very recent experience with a deadly confrontation on a planetary scale. Thus you have an ability that we wish to utilize.

"In summary, we are asking you to create a defense system which would encompass everything from plans and strategy to weaponry and implementation. It is our hope that while you are doing that, we will find volunteers within our society willing to carry out your plans. Training those women for their new duties would also fall under your jurisdiction."

If Tarla had been given a hundred chances to guess what Parisia had been leading to, she would never have come up with the right conclusion. "As much as we would like to make a deal here, I'm afraid you've overestimated our capabilities. We're not experts at waging war. We've merely learned how to survive in a violent world."

"Which is more than we know how to do," Parisia countered. "In some ways, our technology has advanced far beyond yours but with instruction we believe you could comprehend it. You would simply have to determine ways to redirect the use of that technology for our defense. The four of you have most of the basic expertise needed—leadership, mechanical and navigational ability, and the proper attitude for defense. I assume the other six women have worthy skills that could be contributed as well."

Tarla sighed. "It's not—"

"Wait," Iris said, holding up her hand to stop Tarla's protest. "First hear what we are offering. In exchange for creating and implementing a defense system, your women will be given complete freedom in our society. After your work for us is done, we will allow any of your people—women and men—to return to Earth if you still wish to do so at that time."

"So you *do* know how to do it!" Tarla exclaimed. "You lied?"

Iris shrugged.

"But Nadia said the magnetic pull went only one way."

Parisia arched an eyebrow. "Nadia also told you her name was Parisia."

"Will you give us a moment, please?" Tarla stood and motioned for Robin, Lee and Alicia to follow her to the kitchenette for a whispered conference. She was hoping one of the others had some alternative ideas, but they were as bewildered as she was by the unexpected proposition.

None of them believed they were capable of doing what was being asked of them. It was possible that Parisia could stretch out their duties indefinitely just by saying the defense system was not yet finished to their satisfaction. They had no reason to trust Parisia or Iris about anything.

But they *had* offered to send them home to earth.

With nothing better to offer, they seemed to have no choice but to accept and negotiate for the best terms possible.

Tarla waited several tense seconds after they were reseated to present their counter-offer. "We will *attempt* to create a defense system, but you must free *all* the Earth people on the farm immediately. No more antidotes for women or men. And finally we wish to set a specific time period for our return to Earth—upon completion of the defense system or six months from today, whichever comes sooner."

Parisia and Iris reflected little surprise at the demands. In fact, they didn't even need a private conversation for Parisia to give their reply. "Six months is unreasonable. Remember, we will need you to train our volunteers after the system is in place. One year, *and* you put in at least six full days every week during that time. Next, we will agree not to medicate your women, but under no circumstances will we release the Earth men from the commune, with or without the antidote."

"That's understandable," Tarla said with a nod, having been certain that was what they would say about the men. "Considering the structure of your society and the personalities of some of the men in our group, I can see how it could present a number of difficulties if they were all released at one time. On the other hand, there are men in the commune whose expertise far outweighs our own. It would be foolish not to take advantage of their talents and skills. Allow half of our men to leave the farm, drug-free, and you'll have a better defense system than anything we could create alone and it will be in place in half the time."

This time Parisia and Iris did need a private conference, and it took several minutes before they agreed on the next concession.

After they returned to the group, Parisia said, "Releasing even one unmedicated Earth male among Heart women is an incredible risk that we would prefer not to take. And yet, we understand that committing violence and waging war are deeds more suited to men. Therefore, we have a final compromise to offer, but it will have to be a completely confidential one. If you do not agree, you will be returned to the commune and we will not have further discussions with any of you."

Tarla frowned but nodded her understanding.

"We propose that you choose ten men, and only ten, whose skills would be most helpful in completing this project. Each of the ten women may keep one of those men with her in the residence we will provide. She will be held responsible for his behavior. To outsiders it must appear that the men are your servants and that you are all abiding by our laws governing contact between the genders. Also, the men must behave as though they are taking the required antidote.

"If anyone suspects that the laws are being broken, our deal will be automatically negated. Naturally, Iris will review everything you need to know in advance of your integration. Do you accept these terms?"

Tarla summarized the deal as it now stood, then asked Robin, Lee and Alicia if they had questions or were ready to decide. Reluctantly, all four voted to accept.

"It's better than returning to the farm and vegetating for a century while waiting to die," Robin said with a sigh.

"We'll do it," Tarla told Parisia in a much more confident tone than she felt. The problems they would have to overcome were mindboggling—not the least of which was selecting the ten men to be freed and pairing them up with the women.

CHAPTER 13

By keeping her soft underbelly flat on the floor and all fifty of her legs curled tightly against the hard black shell of her back, Yeoman Ugmish assumed the most proper pose of respect as she slithered quietly into her superior's niche. She waited until he twisted the top half of his segmented body toward her and rubbed his antennae together.

"Was the mission a sssuccesss?" Commander Xytoc hissed through the narrow space between his two front fangs.

She twitched her antennae once in response, careful not to raise her head until he gave her permission to do so.

"You may rise and ssspeak."

Ugmish unfurled her legs and lifted her body off the ground. He was still half a length higher than she stood at full elevation. His hooded black eyes dared her to give him bad news, causing both of her stomachs to churn even though her report was positive.

"Special Envoy TM7 has returned from Faxona. The mission was a success. The plans for the FTL transport have already been delivered to research for analysis."

"Excccellent. Tell them I will expect a preliminary timetable for retrofitting it to our ships by firssst sssunrise."

"Yes, sir," Ugmish replied, knowing she would bear the brunt of the analysts' tantrums when they heard that deadline. The commander might have used the word *preliminary*, but he would hold them to whatever estimate they gave, and unfortunately, he always demanded answers in half the time needed to supply realistic ones.

"Return to me after you've delivered that message, I may have need of you."

With an obedient bow, she slithered back out of the niche as quickly as possible.

Not for the first time, Xytoc congratulated himself on having found a yeoman who was as efficient at her duties as she was accommodating to his personal needs.

He stretched and scratched his lower belly with a pair of his hind legs. FTL travel! He had been skeptical when he first heard of its development. It was almost too fortuitous to be believed.

He should not have doubted the predictions of Master Stargazer Po, who had told him that he was the one who would lead the Velids into the final battle against their deadliest enemies.

The portion of his brain that housed the memories of his ancestors seemed to burn a bit brighter as he contemplated the glorious victory awaiting him. The fires of vengeance had been kept alive through the many generations passed by preserving those old memories.

Xytoc called them forth now to inflame his purpose and fortify his commitment.

It had begun as a mission, to seek out other life forms and study them to increase their understanding of the universe. That mission was to be ongoing, generation after generation, as the Velid ship made its way through myriad galaxies, exchanging information. Reports were transmitted back to their home planet after each encounter.

The first disaster had occurred in the Templar System, when they landed on a small, unnamed planet inhabited by a primitive life form that had yet to learn how to build shelters or farm for sustenance. They were frighteningly ugly specimens of a race who utilized only the rear two of their four legs for movement. They lacked even the barest skills needed for universal communication. The creatures were terrified by the visitors and went into hiding. Two Velids tracked them down to try to make them understand that they had come in peace. For their efforts, they were captured and stoned to death.

Many generations later, the Velid expedition found another, more advanced planet inhabited by the same four-limbed species. The beings were known as humanoids and the planet was called Heart. Recalling the Templar beings' negative reaction to the Velids' natural appearance, they morphed their outer appearance to match the natives' bodies, thinking it would put the Heartlings at ease. That time the entire landing crew was killed, without provocation, and the shuttle destroyed.

It was clear that the grotesque species had an innate, lethal hatred of the Velid race, regardless of which shape they took. The humanoids had to be stopped before their civilization progressed to space travel and threatened the Velids in their own galaxy. Prior to the remaining Velids departing from Heart's solar system, the mother ship repaid the humans with total extermination.

As an added precaution, they buried a sonic emitter beneath the planet's surface. Its job was to send out an intermittent beacon to warn others of their kind of potential danger.

From that point on, the purpose of the expedition had altered from academic studies to searching for and annihilating all humanoids. Most recently, the battalion of exterminators had returned to the Templar System and eradicated every hint of civilization on the small planet where the first vicious attack had occurred.

Because of the development of FTL transport, information was suddenly being traded on an intergalactic scale in incredibly short periods of time. The Velids now knew there had been a sufficient number of survivors on Heart to repopulate the planet and that those beings had since mastered space travel. Believing that it was only a matter of time before their enemies successfully launched an attack against the Velids, Xytoc was convinced that they had to strike first in order to survive.

The only way to do that, however, was to move the fleet across the galaxy at such speed that the attack would be a complete surprise. And for that, they needed to retrofit their ships with the latest technology. Thus he had sent Envoy TM7 to steal the plans for the FTL transport from the Faxons. Using the Velid metamorphic ability to duplicate any living organism, the envoy's mission had hardly been a challenge.

If the stars were on their side, the sonic emitter was still functioning and could be used to guarantee the accuracy of their navigation despite the hyperspeed.

Xytoc considered Po's exact prediction. He had said it would be the final battle. That had to mean it would mark the end of the entire humanoid race, because the Velids would not give up until there was not a single cell of that species left alive. Their deadliest enemies could only refer to the humanoids of Heart.

The facts gleaned about Heart also included that it was ruled by females who were completely peaceful, had no military and no protection from outside invasion. Though Xytoc trusted the information to be accurate, it did not change his mind about the necessity to eradicate the race. The females currently in power may be non-aggressive, but they were capable of bearing offspring who were genocidal.

Despite Po's prediction and the indication that Heart had no defenses, Xytoc still wanted to do everything possible to ensure an overwhelming victory. He intended to recall every battalion immediately. When he departed for Heart, it would be with a massive show of strength. Every ship would be converted to FTL and every able-bodied Velid would be drafted to increase the size of the attack force to a hundred times what it was.

He would make certain that the name Xytoc went down in history as the most brilliant, fierce commander of all time—the Velid who exterminated the last humanoid in the universe!

CHAPTER 14

Simone's brain was clicking away faster than she could assimilate all the gossip. The entire imperial city buzzed with suppositions, rumors and facts. The problem was in deciding which tidbit fell into which category.

The general consensus was that Nadia must have suffered a mental collapse. A small pocket of women believed she never had been a hundred percent normal. An even smaller number, like Simone, found it very hard to believe that Nadia, with her eyes focused on the imperial throne, would do something so blatantly risky, as well as *illegal*.

This group privately whispered their doubts to one another. They were of the mind that Parisia might have orchestrated the entire fiasco, including fabricating the supposed recorded evidence, in order to get Nadia out of the way.

Had Nadia been present at the special Parliament meeting, Simone was positive Parisia never would have convinced them to go along with the radical changes she proposed. Nor would Parliament have been convinced to approve a revised budget so that trillions could be diverted to something as useless as a defense system.

Heart had no enemies. More than likely the funds would be secretly redirected into some personal account of Parisia's or her daughter, Brianne's. And what better way to hide the misdirection than to use women from Earth, who wouldn't know what was being done and couldn't care?

Simone could not stand by and do nothing for five years until Nadia *might* be allowed to reenter society. She had to come up with a plan that would accomplish all her objectives. One, speak to Nadia to confirm that she had been unjustly incarcerated. Two, free her and prove to Parliament that Parisia had lied. This of course, would result in Nadia's position being elevated, possibly even to Imperial Prefect. And third, make sure Nadia felt eternally indebted to Simone.

She knew the third goal might automatically be achieved by the first two, but she would probably have to share the credit with other helpful supporters. Another idea formed that would bind herself to Nadia in a more personal way.

It took a few calls and promised favors but she pulled it off with a minimum of difficulty. Nadia's relatives were tremendously relieved to so easily settle several potential legal complications. Simone's generous offer was accepted before the gossip died down and heads cleared.

By the end of the day, Simone would move out of her mother's home and into Nadia's to keep it maintained in good condition until the owner returned. She also accepted responsibility for Fulton's employment contract and temporary guardianship of the underage offspring, Chloe. It was thought to be a very kindhearted gesture from Nadia's former best friend, especially since her family was so anxious to disassociate themselves from their relative and her criminal behavior.

Simone didn't tell anyone, not even the other women who were committed to helping Nadia get reinstated, but there was another reason why she was intent on carrying out the first step of the plan. She had an important, *private* question for Nadia.

If Parisia did not lie, and the visual recording Simone heard about truly existed, then Nadia had knowledge of something no one else did—what it was like to be touched by an unmedicated man.

Had Simone not witnessed the episode in the transfer room between the Earth man and woman and seen the woman's blissful expression, she would not have had a single question about Nadia's innocence. She had always been told no woman in her right mind would welcome a man's touch, and Nadia was not insane, so she wouldn't have *acted improperly* with an Earth male.

Unless she had seen what Simone had and couldn't erase the images from her mind.

Unless she also wondered if an enormous lie had been perpetrated for centuries to maintain the power of one family.

Satisfied that she had set her plan in motion, and the details would work out along the way, she placed a call to Fulton to let him know she would be moving in and reassure him and Chloe they needn't worry about being taken care of.

"I promise you, everything will be fine," she told him sweetly. "And you mustn't concern yourself with learning new routines or duties to please me. Whatever you normally did for Nadia will be perfectly acceptable to me."

Tarla hadn't expected to see anyone when they

exited the tack room. After all, a little over two days had passed since they'd gone in to request an audience with their caretakers. So it was quite a surprise when they opened the bolted door and saw Willy jumping to his feet.

He shook each woman's hand and happily welcomed them back. "Everybody's been so worried!"

"I hope you haven't been in here waiting for us all this time," Robin said.

"Actually, we've been taking shifts. Parisia tried to escape through here twice. Someone's guarding the outside door too."

"She's not Parisia," Tarla said. "But that's the least important thing we've learned."

"I hope that means you were allowed to remember where you've been and what happened to you."

"Yes," Tarla said, nodding. "And we have good news and not so good news. But we'd better give it to Major Cookson first."

They found Geoffrey in the big house helping with lunch preparations. Tarla instantly noticed how his handsome face was creased with worry and fatigue and that his usually neat blond hair looked as though he hadn't combed it all day. Geoffrey was so relieved to see the women and hear they had returned with a proposition, he kissed each one on both cheeks and returned Robin's exuberant hug.

"Thank heavens you're back!" he exclaimed with a very un-British burst of emotion. "I thought we were going to have to force Logan to start drinking the water again to calm him down."

Tarla's surprised expression made him laugh. "Don't tell him I said that. He's spent the last two days denying that he was concerned. As eager as I am to hear what happened, I'm going to ask you to hold off for a few more minutes so that Logan can hear it at the same time. Everyone should be coming in for lunch any moment."

Tarla agreed, though she was anxious to get started. "If I might make a suggestion, we should go somewhere private for this debriefing. A lot of people aren't going to like it."

Geoffrey's smile faded. "That sounds rather ominous."

Before Tarla could give him any reassurance, the first group of laborers came in from the field. Everyone was excited about the women's safe return, but no matter how much pleading or cajoling they did, Tarla wouldn't reveal any details yet.

As soon as Logan arrived, a lunch tray was shoved into his hand and Geoffrey and the women whisked him off to a shaded spot some distance from the big house.

Tarla considered what Geoffrey had said about Logan's being worried. Either he had been grossly exaggerating or Logan was extremely good at hiding his feelings. He barely reacted to their return.

Though Tarla delivered most of their report, Robin, Lee and Alicia supplied some details and independent opinions throughout.

"I wish it were a better deal for more of the men," Tarla said in an apologetic tone when she'd covered everything.

Geoffrey shook his head. "You did better than we expected." He glanced at Logan for affirmation. "When you were gone so long, we weren't at all certain you'd be able to return. Or if you were, that you wouldn't have any memory of what had happened."

"We were waiting one more day," Logan said. "Then we were going to march through the barrier."

"Does that mean you figured out how to use that little box?" Robin asked Geoffrey.

"Yes. It was really quite simple. But we didn't want to cause a disturbance if you were making positive progress, which, apparently, you were."

Tarla felt obliged to be modest about their accomplishment, but he stopped her.

"None of that now. You've negotiated an agreement that will result in everyone's being returned home eventually. What we need to concentrate on next is selecting the ten men. Any suggestions?"

Tarla was ready for that question. "We discussed this and decided there's no way to be fair about it, like with a random drawing. The most logical plan would be to make a list of every man's expertise and former career and choose by skills and qualifications that would correlate with the end goal."

Robin continued, "Once the ten men are chosen they should be paired up with women who have experience in the same field if possible. Men don't have the freedom of movement women do over there, so it would be unseemly for a man to be servant to one woman but spend time with another."

"However," Alicia said, "we request one consideration that has nothing to do with skills. We may have to live with these men for as long as a year. We'd appreciate the opportunity to reject someone as a roommate if we are completely incompatible."

Geoffrey thought their selection plan was reasonable. He said, "If you get the other women to help, you should be able to interview every man before they return to their chores."

"What about the others?" Logan asked. "Some of the men who were here before us might be of use. Hans told me he was a scientist. That could help."

"Possibly," Tarla said. "But only if the effects of

taking the drug over a long period of time can be reversed. We don't know that, so I'd hate to risk it when we can only bring ten men with us."

"Agreed," Geoffrey stated. "Let's get to it."

The other six women were quickly gathered and given a brief overview of the situation. There would be plenty of time for in-depth explanations later. The individual interviews took less time than the selection process. A few men were immediately chosen for the A list, those who would obviously be beneficial to the project. A lot more were placed in the B group, those who had usable skills or knowledge but were not unique in their ability.

When the list of candidates was narrowed down to twenty-two, Geoffrey and Logan excused themselves to let the women make the final selections by compatibility. Both their names were on the A list since Geoffrey was a strategist, as well as an engineer, and, besides his leadership ability, Logan was a weapons expert, experienced instructor and veteran wartime soldier.

Once the men left, the women felt free to eliminate a few qualified men, such as Wilkes, because of personality or personal habits.

To no one's great surprise, Ray Higgs turned out to be a computer hacker besides being an expert on science fiction and alien worlds, both of which put him on the A list. There was a brief dispute as to whether Alicia or Lee would claim him, but finally he was paired with Kara, who had majored in computer science before changing to nursing.

The other man on the A list from the start was their pilot, Nathan Boswell. Alicia was his obvious best partner.

Robin's argument that a mechanic and an engineer were perfectly matched earned her the right to choose

Geoffrey.

Though all the nurses had been required to take extensive math and science courses, Sunny and Trish had excelled in those subjects. They were paired with Edward smith, the flight navigator and Jeremy Fleischer, the copilot, who had been working on his doctorate in nuclear physics prior to being drafted.

Darcy, who had been the office manager for a successful group of doctors, prided herself on her efficiency and organizational ability. It seemed appropriate for her to team up with Hal Becket, whose background was business and accounting, since a budget had to be strictly adhered to.

From the balance of the list, they selected three other men—Thomas Jefferson/T.J. Jones, Greg Oliver and Kevin Atchinson. Like Logan they were career soldiers, trained in weapons, experienced at fighting enemies, both seen and unseen, accustomed to following orders and familiar with bloodshed. They shared those qualifications with a lot of other men, but the remaining women chose them for a variety of personal reasons.

Tarla didn't need to use her intuition to see what was coming. One by one the women rejected Logan as a roommate and chose one of the others. Though he had done nothing negative the last few days, his criminal record and dangerous aura were simply too problematic to overcome. T.J. was another hard case, a young black man with a cocky attitude, but Lee felt she could handle and, possibly, offer him some much needed direction. Then Mandy and Charlene opted for Greg and Kevin, strictly based on attraction.

That left Logan.

And Tarla.

At dinner, the ten men were asked to join the women for a meeting in the barn. Tarla repeated everything previously told to Geoffrey and Logan before announcing how everyone was to be paired off. Throughout her speech and the subsequent questions and answers, Logan's gaze stayed fixed on her. Without looking at him, she had no doubt that he had already guessed who he would be living with for the next year.

"How did you know?" Tarla asked after the pairs were named and she caught the smirk on his face.

"Simple deduction. Being such a nice girl, you would have let everyone else pick first, and none of them would want to live with me. You don't either, but you had no choice."

"It isn't that—"

"Don't bother," he murmured, cutting off her attempt to deny the truth of his words. "I'm like the fat kid in the neighborhood. Always the last one to get picked in a game, but at least I still get to play. Don't worry. You're perfectly safe with me. I only assault and murder men...not women. And as long as no one's pumping me full of drugs, I can promise to keep my hands off you. I assume you can make the same guarantee to me."

Tarla had a smart retort in mind but she didn't get the chance to deliver it.

"Now comes the hard part," Geoffrey declared after each pair had shared a few words. "We have to tell everyone else what's going on and convince them to be patient while we fulfill our part of the bargain. I'm placing Gianni in charge of keeping the peace. He can choose whoever he wants to help him."

"What about Nadia?" Tarla asked. "Willy said she tried to escape while we were gone."

"That's right," Geoffrey replied. "But she's no longer our hostage. She's a prisoner on this farm. It's up to her people to keep her here now, not us.

However, I'll take the control box with me just to make sure no one, including her, can leave too easily."

As predicted, there were a lot of unhappy men after they heard the details of the agreement. Naturally, Wilkes and his pals were the loudest and nastiest. But even they didn't match the fury that erupted from Nadia when she read the formal decree from Parisia that sentenced her to five years in the commune. It was decided to keep her restrained until she calmed down, or at least until the group of twenty left the farm.

Gianni understood he had quite a job ahead of him but he believed he and a few others could manage, especially since the major was leaving Nadia's paralyzer in his possession. Nevertheless, he considered telling everyone it was safe to go back to drinking the water again.

Parisia and Iris had set the rendezvous for midnight and had given Tarla a brooch with a timepiece in it. They thought it would be best to get the Earth people settled in when the least number of residents would take notice.

By the last hour of the day, most of the hostilities and envy died down and farewells were said. The couples took nothing into the tack room with them other than the clothes they were wearing, since they had been told everything would be provided. Moments after they all filed into the tack room and bolted the door, the back wall opened.

"Welcome back," Parisia said to Tarla with a pleasant smile. On her right stood Iris with her fixed expression of worry, on her left was a younger, slightly taller version of herself. Behind them was a long, empty hallway. "Let's go to a more spacious area for our introductions." The Heart women turned and led the group down the hallway to a vacant room that appeared to be the one they had awakened in before.

The first thing Tarla noticed after they entered the room was that Parisia and Iris kept their gazes away from the men, but the other young woman kept sneaking peeks at them. She appeared to be both curious and fearful.

Parisia introduced herself and Iris first. "And this is my First Aide, Brianne, who also happens to be my daughter. She has volunteered to act as liaison and advisor for your group so that your integration will be as smooth as possible. Tarla, if you'd be so kind as to provide each person's field of expertise with your introductions, it would be appreciated."

Tarla ran through the roster, embellishing the men's capabilities to justify their questionable presence. From the relieved looks on the Heart women's faces, her additional effort had been sorely needed.

"Thank you, Tarla," Parisia said. "We're pleased you have agreed to help us. The first order of business is to get you settled in your new accommodations. You'll be in a temporary-stay facility close to the Imperial Palace and Parliament. Normally it is filled with visiting dignitaries, but an entire delegation returned to their home province yesterday after the special meeting of Parliament. Among the units they vacated were six one-bedroom and two two-bedroom apartments, which Brianne immediately leased for your group. Conveniently, there is a large meeting room on the top floor that has also been leased for your work area."

Logan leaned down and murmured into Tarla's ear, "Six plus four equals ten bedrooms. Where are the servants' quarters?"

Iris's nostrils flared as she inhaled sharply. Looking

only at Tarla, she said, "Your houseman will be forgiven this time but be certain he and the others are aware of our laws in the future." Though she kept her gaze on Tarla, she summarized the most important rules for the men to obey without question. "A man never speaks unless spoken to first by a woman, nor does he look directly at any part of her form. A man never makes physical contact with a woman, no matter how slight. There should always be a minimum of one arm's length between a man and a woman, unless he is in the process of performing a requested service."

"Do we have to walk two steps behind them too?" T.J. asked sarcastically.

Lee swiftly pinched a muscle at the base of his neck, making him wince in pain. "Not so funny anymore, is it, wise-ass? Get this through your thick macho heads, boys. This is no joke. You ever want to see blue sky again, you play along the way we've been told. If that means you bite your tongue and walk two steps behind us, you do it. Got it?" She waited for a jerky nod from T.J. before she released him. To Parisia and Iris, she said, "I sincerely apologize for the impertinence of my stupid houseman. He'll improve quickly, I promise you."

Tarla thought Brianne's eyes were going to pop out of her head for a moment, but she got her shock under control when her mother started to speak again.

"With regard to the apartments, even though you may be somewhat crowded, we felt it was better to have you all in one confined area rather than scattered throughout the city. As it is, people will be watching you every chance they get for a while. It would be in everyone's best interest not to give them too many opportunities to find fault.

"There's a shuttle waiting to take you to the facility.

Brianne will escort you and fill you in on the essentials along the way. We wish you good luck and good night." Parisia and Iris left the room and headed in one direction, as Brianne led the group in another.

Tarla sensed the woman's anxiety. Moving up beside Brianne, she murmured, "There's nothing to worry about. We train easily and hardly ever bite our caretakers."

Brianne's eyes opened wide again before realizing Tarla was teasing her. "This is not the sort of thing I'm usually required to do," she said in a confidential tone. "I'm a little nervous."

"Then you must be able to imagine how we feel."

Those were apparently the right words to say, for Brianne cleared her throat and found the confidence to begin her task a moment later. "As Parisia said, I will be your liaison for the duration. We must insist that you limit your contact with other residents of the city as much as possible."

She stopped the group at the foot of a wide escalator that spiraled upward. "Please watch your balance. These stairs are moving rather swiftly." Brianne stepped on and turned to face the others. When the last man had boarded, she continued, "Your apartments have been stocked with some food and other supplies. Accounts will be established for each woman to purchase goods as needed, including clothing. The entertainment center in each apartment comes equipped with a manager, which can be used to purchase items you require and have them delivered.

"It is our custom to have our housemen go to the market every few days to personally select fresh food, but I was told Earth men are not always skilled in the culinary arts. If that is the case, prepared meals can be ordered for delivery as well. I have been told that your civilization has developed considerably beyond what we provide for those in the commune, but if you have any questions at all, I will be readily available to assist."

By the time they reached the top of the escalator, Tarla estimated they'd gone up at least forty floors. From the last stair they stepped onto a moving walkway. This carried them outside onto a rooftop, which appeared to be a parking lot, though none of the vehicles sitting between the parallel lines were familiar.

Each object looked somewhat like a child's bubble pipe with the stem and bowl sitting on the pavement and a big bubble emerging from the bowl. There were a range of sizes and colors and the bubbles seemed to have been blown in a variety of formations, including an enormous oblong one that turned out to be the shuttle Parisia had mentioned.

Glowing lights lured Tarla to the half-wall at the edge of the roof. Between the artificial illumination and the clear, star-filled sky, she got her first glimpse of the imperial city. A network of narrow silver ribbons wound between and over skyscrapers, which were formed like cylinders, spheres, corkscrews and pyramids. Most of them appeared to be constructed of reflective metal, colored in a rainbow of pastel shades.

A closer look revealed that a few of the bubble pipe objects were zipping along the ribbons. "How do they move?" Tarla asked Brianne with open fascination.

"A system of magnets. It's quiet and completely energy-efficient." Brianne pointed to her right. "You see the building over there, with the golden dome and towers at each corner? That's the Imperial Palace."

"Wow! It looks like the Taj Mahal," Robin said with open admiration.

Brianne directed their gazes to the aqua cylinder next to the palace, which was nearly as high as the structure they were on. "That's Parliament. Your residences are in the section of smaller buildings behind that."

Tarla scanned the faces around her and knew the others were stricken with the same awe she was. Even Logan was unable to maintain his bored expression as he took in the amazing panorama.

"Shall we go?" Brianne asked, clearly pleased that they were impressed by her home.

As they boarded the shuttle, Brianne advised the men that they were required to sit in the rear of the vehicle with at least one row of vacant seats between them and the women in the front.

For the trip down the side of the building, the forward portion of the shuttle raised so the passengers ' seats remained level. Brianne had the conductor take them on a tour of the vicinity so they would have an idea of how to get around. She pointed out the marketplace, shuttle stops, grooming and fitness salons and so on. The swift, silent ride didn't last nearly long enough for Tarla, who undoubtedly felt more *at home* than any of the others, but she reasoned she'd have plenty of time in the coming months to explore every inch of the beautiful city.

The building they were taken to was a salmon-hued, five-story pentagon with a garden courtyard in the center. For expedience, Brianne took the entire group into one apartment to demonstrate anything they might not be familiar with. She was clearly ill at ease as she pointed out how the various pieces in the living room could be rearranged to create beds for the men, repeatedly apologizing about there not being enough private rooms for everyone.

Rather than assign specific pairs to the various apartments, she pointed out where the available units were located and left it to the women to choose.

Kara and Darcy, and Trish and Mandy, resolved part of the decision-making by offering to share the two two-bedroom apartments on the ground floor. Tarla and Robin selected the two units on the top floor by the conference room and the others took the ones in between.

Brianne handed each woman her personal access key, saying, "I believe it would be wisest for everyone to get some rest and use this first day to get acquainted with your new environment. Tomorrow I will come by and show you the workroom we've prepared for you. As mentioned, I am the official liaison for the group and will be continuously available to provide assistance or guidance. But I will request one favor."

She handed Tarla a small red box with one black button on top. "I would prefer you be my primary contact. If everyone else would go through you, it would be much more efficient. And if I'm not present when you need me, just press this button and we'll be able to speak to each other."

As soon as Tarla agreed, they all bid each other good night and went their separate ways.

Tarla had avoided thinking too deeply about the new arrangements, but once the door to her apartment closed and she and Logan were alone in a relatively small space, she could no longer avoid it.

While she stood in the middle of the main room trying to decide how to begin, Logan went about rearranging the furnishings to create a bed for himself.

"We should probably talk about this," she said as he moved around her.

"Are you giving me permission to speak?" he asked without looking at her.

"Don't you dare pull an attitude with me! I didn't make the rules here."

"No, you didn't make them, but you have to abide by them, same as me. The way I figure it, our best bet is to follow their laws to the letter, even when we're in here alone. That way it becomes habit and we're less apt to make a mistake in public. I intend to give that order to all the men."

"*You* intend to give the order?" she asked with a challenging air. "The first habit you'd better adopt is that *you* don't give orders to anyone anymore."

He glared at her for several seconds then turned away. "You're absolutely right. From here on, you're the chief of this operation."

She clucked her tongue and rolled her eyes. As he walked past her to get another cube, she touched his arm to stop him. "Logan, please—"

"No touching," he said sharply, jerking away. "It's against the law."

Despite the fact that the excuse for his attitude sounded logical, Tarla knew he was purposely being more of an ass than necessary. She was positive he resented the role reversal and planned to take his bad mood out on her, even though he knew it wasn't her fault. Well, two could play that game.

"Fine," she said, sticking her nose up in the air. "As of right now, we are no longer Captain Tarla Yan and Sergeant Logan McKay of Earth. *I* am Supreme Commander of the Armed Forces of Heart, and *you* are my lowly houseman." She snapped her fingers at him. "Run me a bath, turn down my bed and make me a cup of herbal tea to help me sleep."

Logan gnashed his teeth but he nodded and headed for the bathroom. Insisting they obey Heart's laws when they were alone had been the only thing he could think of to keep a rein on his sanity. The mere thought of her taking a bath and going to bed a few feet away from him made his skin itch.

As long as she abided by the arm's-length rule and remained annoyed with him, he figured he could hold the ache in his chest to a dull throbbing. If she insisted on touching him and being nice, there was no telling how long it would be before he was making a fool of himself again.

Tarla frowned as she followed him into the bedroom. The fact that the only access to the bathroom was through there would present problems between any two people who weren't naturally close. She and Logan were going to have to sit down and work things out very soon, but she was probably going to have to tweak his nose a few more times before he'd start being reasonable.

The bathroom was only one obstacle. They were facing as much as a year of cohabitation and it would go a lot easier if they didn't try to do it as enemies. They both needed to ignore their previous incidents of intimacy and behave like roommates who happen to be sharing living space through necessity. They didn't need to become best friends, but they did need to be able to get along with each other.

While he was in the bathroom, she inspected the contents of the clothes closet and bureau drawers. Brianne had said the apartments would be stocked with a few items. The key word had been *few*. There were four plain caftans hanging on the rack—two aqua and two pink. The pink were considerably wider and longer. She took out a smaller one and laid it on the bed. Most of the drawers were empty, but one had two pairs of large pink boxer shorts in it, and another had two sets of aqua chemises and tap-style underpants. Obviously, the first order of business upon awakening was going to be a shopping spree with the manager.

The scowl on Logan's face when he came out of the

bathroom and she showed him the clothing selection was more explicit than a thousand curse words, but he still managed to hold his tongue.

"I'll have my tea while I bathe," she said in a regal tone, then went to keep an eye on the water level in the tub while he marched off to the kitchen. She was pleasantly surprised to discover that he had added perfumed bubbles to the water, set out a fluffy towel and washcloth, and formed a head rest with another towel rolled like a log. Perhaps having him as a personal servant wasn't going to be all that hard.

When he brought in her tea and set it on the ledge of the tub, she was firmly set in her queenly mode. "That will be all for now. But I'm sure I'll be famished when I wake up, so plan on preparing a full meal."

On his way out, he mumbled, "You sure you don't want me to scrub the scales off your back, *madam*?"

Tarla smiled. He couldn't possibly keep up the subservient act for long. She estimated that he'd either explode or be ready to negotiate a truce within twenty-four hours.

CHAPTER 15

A quarter of the time Tarla had set for Logan to detonate flew by while she slept more soundly than she had in a very long time. The unmistakable smell of sautéing onions and garlic seduced her out of a pleasant dream that dissolved without a trace of recollection.

She slipped out of bed, made a quick visit to the bathroom and put on the aqua caftan. Thinking Logan might need to use the bathroom while she was asleep, she had tried sleeping in the caftan for modesty's sake, but her legs had immediately gotten twisted in the yards of material. The satiny chemise and pants were not as prudish, but they were much more comfortable.

Following her nose, she found Logan at the stove with his back to her, stirring something in a frying pan. He was wearing only the loose-fitting slacks from the farm, obviously having decided against the pink caftan. The pants were hanging dangerously low on his hips and she had the most wicked urge to give them a yank the rest of the way.

There was probably some law in this culture against

a man going shirtless, especially a man built like Logan. She thought it best not to mention it though, lest he think she was bothered by his display of muscles.

"Something smells wonderful," she said mainly to alert him to her presence. When he didn't turn around, she tried again. "I see you didn't waste any time learning your way around the kitchen." Still no response. "Logan! Do I really have to order you to talk to me?"

He turned to get a jar out of the cabinet and was momentarily surprised to see her standing in the doorway. Removing two small discs from his ears, he asked, "Did you say something?"

She came closer to look at the little circles of plastic he had set on the counter.

"They're sound remotes for the entertainment center. I was listening to the news." He went back to stirring a strange-looking green concoction in the pan.

"What are you making that smells so good?" She couldn't help but notice that each time she came near, he took a step away. He really was carrying this a bit too far, she thought.

"Breakfast. You requested a full meal but you weren't specific. I hope this will do. I think it's supposed to be like an omelet."

"You think?"

He almost smiled. "They don't eat eggs here, or animal meat either. They seem to be strict vegans."

"How did you figure that out?"

"I just did what any new houseman on the block would do. I went next door and met our neighbor."

"Logan, you didn't! We were told to limit our contact with the natives."

He shrugged. "It was a choice between asking one of those natives for help or starving to death. Don't worry. Vance, the houseman, was the only one home and he took pity on me. Showed me how to dig recipes out of the manager and gave me some basic instructions. You'd like him—Oh, I almost forgot. No fraternizing between sexes." He scooped the hot, fluffy mixture onto two plates and placed one on the table where there was already a glass of juice, napkin and flatware.

She sat down and waited for him to bring the other plate to the table. Instead he began eating at the counter. That's when she realized he had set only one place at the table. "This is ridiculous. Come over here and sit down."

"A man is not supposed to sit at the same table with—"

"Stop it!"

"—a woman." He ate another forkful of food.

"All right. But a houseman has to obey his mistress's orders, and I order you to sit here and eat with me...at every meal."

With exaggerated slowness he carried his breakfast to the opposite side of the table from where she was sitting.

"Now what are you doing?" she demanded.

"Practicing. Remember, we men are supposed to look drugged. That was the other reason I wanted to make friends with Vance. I'm studying him."

At least that made sense, she thought. "That reminds me, you don't have to worry about what you eat or drink here. Men are given their antidote in a concentrated dosage once a month." She took a taste of her food. "This is very good...whatever it is. Sort of a quiche-omelet-soufflé. It's hard to believe there are no eggs in it though."

As they both ate, she tried to keep her eyes downcast as he was doing, but her gaze kept creeping across the table. Again she was uncomfortably aware of how her familiarity with the male physique did not immunize her against the effect Logan's body had on her senses. "Did you, uh, spill something on your shirt?"

He glanced down at his chest, as though he'd forgotten it was bare. "No. I just hand washed it and it hasn't dried yet."

"You could have put on the pink caftan. I bet you'd be darling in it." She was satisfied to get a sneering glance from him. At least he'd looked her in the eye for a second. "We both need clothing. Let's go see what the manager has to offer."

When she tried to clear her place, he growled at her, so she left him alone to clean up the kitchen. Surely by the end of the day he'd stop being so unreasonable about strictly obeying the laws when they were alone. She would simply have to push a little harder to make him see the silliness of it.

While she waited for him to join her in the main room, she decided to let some sunlight in. As Brianne had instructed, she said, "Shutters open."

Instantly what had appeared to be a solid wall folded back, accordion-style, to reveal the city outside. Tarla had to touch the wall of clear glass to assure herself that a barrier was actually there. One side of the floor-to-ceiling window opened onto a balcony that ran the entire length of the apartment.

"*Logan!* Come here, quick!"

He was at her side on the balcony in a flash, the urgency in her voice overriding his intentions to keep his movements at a snail's pace.

"Look. There's still no second sun today. Why do you think that is?"

Relief that she was fine rushed through him. Fortunately, she was too intent on the view to notice his concern or relief. "I thought Geoffrey's idea about it being an orbiting moon sounded reasonable."

"Remind me to ask Brianne."

"Yes, ma'am."

She ignored his sarcastic tone and took a deep breath as she continued to admire the view of the city. "After the conditions on the farm, would you have ever thought this was on the other side of the wall? I thought it looked incredible at night, but now it's…it's…I can't even think of a good word. I hadn't realized how badly I missed home."

"Home? Since when did Baltimore ever look like this?" He wondered at the dot of dark pink that appeared on her cheekbones.

"Uh, yes, home. You know, a, uh, city, as opposed to the Manchurian front lines." She quickly turned her face back to the view. "I wonder if Robin and the others have taken a look outside yet."

He didn't think she needed a response. Besides, all his concentration was focused on remaining at arm's length from her, when what he was dying to do was wrap her in his arms and absorb every last drop of pleasure she was experiencing.

"I know we probably should stay inside, but I can't do it. We've got to take a walk after we do our shopping. Okay?" She turned and raised her gaze to his.

With tremendous effort he made himself look at the view. "It isn't right to ask my permission to do something. Remember that."

"I was *not* asking your permission. I was asking you if you'd—Oh, never mind." For a moment she'd forgotten they weren't two friends who could take a walk and enjoy the sights together. "Let's just go get our purchase order in before it's too late to have it delivered."

It took only a few minutes on the manager's purchasing network to learn that men had the option of wearing simply-styled caftans or the two piece outfits they'd worn on the farm. There was only a choice of pastel colors, probably more to be pleasing to the mistress's eye, and weight of material for warmth. The women's wardrobe selection was expanded to include a variety of embellishments, such as appliques and trims. However, the basic item was still a caftan, which Tarla found to be unwieldy. She wondered if she could get away with wearing a small-sized man's pants outfit. Perhaps later, after they were no longer a curiosity to Heart's natives, she could afford to be a little eccentric.

Though Logan had done a fine job making breakfast using ingredients on hand, they agreed that they should also order some prepared meals. A trip to the public marketplace would also be best put off for a later date.

Delivery of their purchases was scheduled for early that evening.

Tarla barely had a chance to think about her next diversion when her door chime sounded. She started to get up but Logan barked at her.

"Sit!"

She bristled at his using a one-word command as though she were his trained dog. As he opened the door however, Tarla could see how right he had been to insist on playing butler—two unknown women were standing in the doorway. Their shocked gasps and expressions of dismay when they noticed his naked, hairy chest had Tarla up and improvising in a heartbeat.

"You foolish man!" she scolded, mimicking the mistress from the *Mother Knows Best* show. "When I told you one of your duties was to answer the door, I did not mean you should stop in the middle of dressing to do it! Don't you have any common sense at all? Now go back to the other room and put your robe on before I'm forced to punish you."

Logan's head had remained bowed through her tirade, but as he slowly moved away from her, he let her see his gritted teeth. She knew she'd gone a bit overboard but he deserved that for snarling at her.

"Please excuse him," Tarla said to the women. "He's very new to his position."

The embarrassed flush on their faces began to fade as the younger of the two said, "Yes, of course. We understand. In fact that is why we're here. We heard quite a few new people moved in during the night and we wanted to be the first to welcome you and offer any assistance you might need."

Beneath the gracious words, Tarla clearly heard the voice of a very snoopy female who wanted to be the first with fresh gossip to share. "Please come in," she replied just as graciously and waved them into the room. "I'm Tarla."

Again the younger visitor spoke. "And I'm Reva. This is my mother, Syracuse. We're temporarily staying on the first floor while some work is being done on our home."

Tarla observed the rather elegant way they seated themselves and arranged their caftans, and attempted to imitate them. "May I offer you a cup of tea?"

"That would be very nice," Reva said.

"Logan!" Tarla called toward the bedroom. "What is taking you so long? Come out here and attend to my guests."

As he sluggishly dragged himself into the room wearing the pink caftan, Tarla had to cover her mouth and pretend to be coughing to smother the giggles. He looked positively hilarious...and as dangerous as a man can look in a long pink robe.

"My, my," Syracuse said. "That cough is an unhealthy symptom. You must make a visit to the sanatorium as soon as possible."

"I could show you the way," Reva offered brightly.

Tarla cleared her throat and avoided looking at Logan again. "Thank you. I don't think it's anything to fuss about, but I'll let you know if it gets worse. Logan, my guests and I would like some tea. Let's see if you can manage that without burning yourself or breaking anything."

She could practically feel the frustration spewing from him, but the satisfied expressions on her visitors' faces confirmed that they were both behaving in an acceptable manner. She had no doubt however, Logan's shirtless debut would be talked about for days.

"However will you manage with only the one bed and bath?" Reva asked. "This size unit is usually leased out to women visiting without a servant."

Tarla sighed as if she was terribly put out by the arrangement. "It was the only thing available on such short notice, and as you can imagine, it's going to be difficult enough training him without having to deal with a lack of privacy." She sighed loudly again. "But we'll all manage somehow."

Reva and Syracuse were as practiced at posing veiled questions as an Innerworld tracker, but Tarla felt fairly certain she wasn't saying or doing anything that might jeopardize their situation. Thankfully, Logan remained out of sight most of the time, for she couldn't look at him in that get-up and keep a straight face.

Also, very thankfully, the interrogation session was interrupted by more visitors.

"Logan!" Tarla called again. "Don't pretend you

didn't hear the door, you lazy man."

Logan shuffled from the bedroom to the door. The only thing he did swiftly was put his finger to his lips as soon as he saw that it was Robin and Geoffrey.

As required, Geoffrey entered several feet behind Robin. His head was obediently bowed and he was wearing the same pink caftan as Logan. For some reason though, Tarla didn't think he looked nearly as funny as Logan.

Tarla introduced her guests to Robin and was vastly relieved when Reva and her mother said they had to leave—probably to spread the tale of having seen the primitives at close range.

"Whew!" Robin said with a heavy exhale as she flopped down on a cushion. "We came over here to escape the two that descended on us. I guess we really are going to have to be on our toes every minute."

Logan's smirk at Tarla shouted *I told you so*, without having to say it aloud.

She was humble enough to admit that his assertion hadn't been entirely ridiculous. "Logan suggested we practice acceptable behavior by never acting as we normally would, even in private, but I really don't think that's necessary."

"I agree with Logan," Geoffrey said so quickly that he had to have been thinking the same thing for a while.

"You do?" Robin asked with a pout.

"Yes, I do," he replied seriously. "Consider how those women who came to visit us reacted to your being in pants."

Robin made a face and explained to Tarla and Logan. "I didn't think I was committing a crime, but apparently the hospital scrubs we wore on the farm are only appropriate for men in the city. We're supposed to stick with these circus tents." She pulled the aqua caftan away from her body to demonstrate her point. "It was strongly recommended that our men be instructed to wear their robes when they go outdoors, however. The pants are only for inside, private wear to make doing their chores easier. They don't approve of any clothing that might reveal the shape of the body for either men or women."

"Geez!" Tarla said, shaking her head. "What an upside-down, inside-out world this is."

"I don't wish to belittle your sense of frustration, Tarla," Geoffrey said with a frown. "But *we* are the ones being forced to wear pink nightgowns."

The giggle Tarla had previously suppressed threatened to bubble out again, until she caught a glimpse of the thunderclouds in Logan's eyes. Robin also managed to hold her amusement to a muffled snicker.

"I'm sorry," Tarla said. "It's not *that* funny. Maybe we should pay a visit to all of our people this afternoon and reinforce the seriousness of our situation."

Logan had been quietly brooding but he thought of a better way to handle it. "More than likely everyone else has also been visited, or will be soon, by nosy neighbors. Call them to come here so we can all share anything new we've picked up. Make sure you remind them what to wear and how to behave on their way. There's no telling how many busybodies are peeking through their windows."

Tarla noted that he wasn't having any trouble being his usual take-charge self in front of Geoffrey. She wasn't sure which way he annoyed her more— domineering or subservient. Following the instructions Brianne had given, she called the other apartments and summoned the group together.

As Logan had guessed, almost everyone had been

officially welcomed to the city by a *friendly* neighbor then pumped for information. Occasionally they had learned a tidbit in return. Logan was the only one who had dared to make contact with another houseman, but the others agreed that it might be useful to establish a friendship with another servant if the opportunity arose.

"Just remember one thing," Tarla warned sternly. "Under no circumstances can you risk revealing that you are not medicated or that you're performing any services different from theirs. The way the women checked us out, I think we should assume they'd try to get their servants to pass on anything they see or hear as well. Some of them may just be curious. But others may be opponents to Parisia's defense plan, looking for a reason to urge Parliament to reverse its decision. Without that plan we all go back to the farm indefinitely."

When the delivery woman arrived with Tarla's order, the group returned to their individual apartments to collect their deliveries as well. Geoffrey and Robin returned a short while later to share dinner with Tarla and Logan.

Much to both women's irritation, the men insisted on practicing their servant roles despite Tarla and Robin begging them to put it off for an hour. It seemed to Tarla that both men were more bent on aggravating their partners than becoming accustomed to the new rules.

By the time they'd finished eating and Logan and Geoffrey had everything cleaned up, Tarla retaliated.

"I want to take a walk around the block before it gets dark," she said to Robin. "Would you like to come?"

Robin shrugged. "Sure. Why not?"

Tarla turned to Logan and put on her regal air. "You

will accompany us…at the proper distance of course."

She saw Logan's jaw clench and waited for him to balk at having to parade outside in a robe. Then she'd have him! He couldn't play the servant only when it was *his* preference. Unfortunately, he deduced the same thing. Taking a deep breath, he went to the door and held it open for her.

Robin's slow smile showed she was on board with Tarla's plan. With a smirk and a crook of her finger, she ordered, "You too, Geoffrey."

Logan's continued stubbornness pushed Tarla into dragging out the walk much longer than she had originally intended, in spite of the fact that curious eyes observed their progress every step of the way. It was Robin who eventually took pity on Geoffrey and brought the walk to an end.

The moment Tarla and Logan were alone in the apartment, she knew she'd made a serious mistake. He was absolutely fuming! Her stomach squeezed into a knot of anxiety. How could she have forgotten how dangerous he was? He wasn't a kitten to tease with a piece of yarn. He was a full-grown panther.

And he was stalking her.

"Now, Logan," she said, trying to conceal her fear as she backed away from him, "it's your own fault. I mean, I probably went too far—"

"Probably?" His voice was eerily soft. *"Too far?* You paraded us halfway back to Earth."

She kept walking backward around the room, occasionally bumping into furniture, but he continued to track her. She had only wanted to push him into a compromise, but now she could see she'd pushed him way beyond that.

"If you would just be reasonable about this servant business when we're alone, I'd be reasonable about acting the mistress when we're in public. It makes me extremely uncomfortable to have you waiting on me. I understand the need for caution, but we also have to find a way to live together in this apartment without driving each other crazy."

"That is definitely not possible since you've already driven me way past crazy. You think you're uncomfortable? Look at me! *This* is uncomfortable!"

She obeyed his order to look at him without thinking of the consequences. A giggle escaped before she clamped her hand over her mouth.

"Go ahead, *mistress*, let it out. You've been strangling on it all day."

She sucked in her cheeks to hold back the smile. "I *am* sorry, Logan, *really, really*—"

"Way too late for sorry, angel. I want to hear you laugh. I want you to get every last giggle out of your system, before you wreck this whole operation by cracking up in public...or before I go completely nuts and turn you over my knee!"

She thought the predatory gleam in his eye seemed to glow a little brighter with the thought of spanking her. "Logan please, you're scaring me. I said I'm sorry—"

"And I said I want you to laugh. If you can't do it yourself, maybe I need to help you." He took a large step toward her but she escaped his grasp.

"Stop it!" Tarla ordered and sped up her retreat.

"I'll stop it when I hear you laughing," he countered, then picked up his own pace.

She evaded him for almost a whole minute as she circled the room and dodged between pieces of furniture. Suddenly his hands latched onto her caftan, bringing her to an abrupt halt and pulling her close. As she tried to get free again, his fingers wiggled in her sides. "Laugh, Tarla," he said, tickling her without mercy.

She squealed from the unexpected tickle and saw a victorious grin spread across his face instantly erasing all traces of aggression. It was such a relief to realize he had intended to tickle rather than humiliate her, she almost gave him the laughter he'd demanded. But her own stubborn streak kept her from giving in that easily. "You can't make me!" she declared.

He found an extremely vulnerable spot below her ribs that caused her to squeal again, yet she still managed to hold back a real laugh.

The more she squirmed in an attempt to escape, the more effort he put into tickling her. The struggle tilted them both off balance and they tumbled over a row of foam cubes and onto the floor in a tangle of legs and arms and yards of pink and aqua fabric.

That did it for Tarla. She burst out laughing and Logan joined her the next second.

"You broke the couch," she teased between chuckles and gasps for air.

"I can fix the couch. What are you going to do about my broken back?" He returned, managing to reduce his laughter to a crooked smile.

"No problem," she said as seriously as possible. "I'm a nurse. I can fix your back." With him sprawled half on top of her, she scraped her fingernails down his spine to give him a taste of his own medicine. His reflexive jerk gave her such satisfaction, she tried to extract a bit more revenge by tickling his sides as he had done with her. But that only caused him to pay her back again. As each tried to get the better of the other, they rolled across the floor, laughing too hard to really administer a good tickle.

"I give up! You win," Tarla finally said, fighting more for a deep breath of air than for her freedom. His body had hers pinned to the floor and, though he looked much too pleased with himself, she didn't have the strength to continue the mock battle.

"If I win, that means you lose, and you know what happens to losers?"

She cocked one eyebrow suspiciously.

"They have to pay off the winner," Logan informed her. "Now what payment should I demand?"

CHAPTER 16

Logan looked as though he was giving a great deal of thought to choosing her payoff.

"I won't make you go on any more walks in public," she offered quickly, before he could think of anything more difficult for her to forfeit.

He shook his head. "Not nearly enough."

"Umm, I won't talk to you like you're a complete imbecile in front of guests."

Now that she was no longer laughing or engaged in a tickling match, she began noticing other things—like how right his hard body felt covering hers and how she could feel the coarseness of the hair on his legs because their caftans were twisted above their knees. How he shifted to find a more comfortable position. How his lower body was changing shape where it was pressed to hers...

"Still not enough," he murmured as the expression on his face turned serious and his eyes darkened with desire.

There was something else she noticed—she was suddenly getting very warm...and incredibly, *abnormally* horny...and her nerves felt like they were on the outside of her body…almost as if—

No! That was completely impossible. Not here. Not after all this time. Not with a Terran.

Not with Logan!

She forced her gaze from his seductive eyes only to have his mouth capture her rising interest. If she was right about what was happening to her, there was nothing she could do to stop the inevitable burning desire, the mindless need.

But maybe she was wrong. Maybe the business of touching his mind had her imagination running amok. It might be nothing but stress…

Though Tarla couldn't verbalize her third concession to the winner, her eyes closed and her lips parted in preparation of giving him the prize she assumed he wanted.

His groan sounded more like one of resigned defeat than glorious victory, but before she could question it, his mouth came down hard on hers…*exactly as she needed*. Rather than the tender consideration he had shown her before, this kiss was filled with greedy passion.

Without being granted the time or ability to hypothesize further, her primitive instincts claimed full control of her response. She angled her head beneath his and drew his tongue deep into her mouth. There was no battle for superiority here, nor concerns about the past or future. No more analyzing if her body's reaction was more than lust. There was only the present and the explosive sensations he ignited within her.

It took only a slight maneuver to push the caftans above their waists, leaving only his cotton boxers and her satin pants as obstacles to their suddenly raging need. She parted her thighs and wrapped her legs around him, cradling his hips so that he was perfectly centered on her.

His mouth continued to devour hers and she returned his hunger in full. Their tongues stroked and licked, moving in and out to match the rhythm set by their lower bodies as they rubbed against each other, harder, faster, wanting more, but unable to stop the pleasure they were taking long enough to make it even better.

Moaning in frustration, she tightened her legs, bracing him hard against where she desperately needed him to rub, and was unexpectedly flung over the edge. Between her sharp movements and cry of relief, it was more than he could handle, and he too felt the uncontrollable burst of orgasmic relief.

He rolled them both onto their sides and held her close while they caught their breath.

Tarla's mind was enveloped in a silky fog while chords of pleasure continued to thrum through her body. She was aware of the internal heat slightly cooling, but the nerve endings all over her body were still twitching. She ordered herself not to be concerned…the symptoms were the normal result of a huge need to relieve stress combined with extended celibacy.

She was also slightly aware of another, separate, worrisome thought straining to the surface but she suppressed it as well. Whatever it was could wait a few more minutes while she enjoyed the exquisitely sensual moment.

Then all the worrisome thoughts were forgotten, for Logan's lips returned to hers, gentler now, the way she remember his other kisses. She felt herself floating and knew he had picked her up in his arms and was carrying her, but all her attention was focused on his incredible mouth and the way he could make a simple kiss say so much.

His lips barely left hers for more than a heartbeat or two, and yet he managed to remove their caftans and underwear, pull back the bed covers and lie down with her still nestled in his embrace.

Logan would have loved to simply stand beside the bed and memorize how his dark angel looked from head to toe, with no part of her concealed from him. Her eyes were closed, her face flushed with passion. He was afraid that if he ended the kiss to do as he wished, the lust-driven spell she was under would be broken. She'd awaken and realize who she was with and what she was doing. Her common sense would return and end his chance to live out one of his fantasies.

So he gave up one pleasure for another and determined to keep her in her current state of desire as long as possible. If he was very, very good, perhaps she could be tempted to repeat the experience occasionally. After one day, he knew his sanity could never stand a whole year of either a mistress-servant relationship or the casual roommate arrangement she was pushing for.

He had no delusions of convincing her that he loved her or of receiving her love in return. He was simply hoping for a cease-fire and whatever concessions he could seduce from her.

Though climaxing *with* her without being *inside* her had never been one of his fantasies—it had never even occurred to him that could happen at his age—the release did give him the patience he needed to carry out a new plan.

Straddling her closed thighs, his lips paid homage to every feature on her face, his teeth nibbled her ears, his hands leisurely stroked her neck, shoulders and arms, while occasionally, as if entirely by accident, he moved his chest so that his hair brushed lightly back and forth over her breasts. Only when she arched upward to increase the contact did he take her breasts in his hands and gently knead them.

Her moan told him that was almost but not quite what she wanted. He smiled against her mouth then kissed his way down her neck, across one shoulder and down to a nipple which had appreciatively puckered for him. Her abrupt intake of breath was his reward for closing his mouth and teeth around the peak and stroking it with his tongue. As his hands continued to massage the fullness of both breasts, he moved his mouth to her other nipple, until her attempts to gyrate her hips beneath his weight reminded him that she still had more peaks and valleys impatiently waiting to be explored.

Planting a trail of kisses over her abdomen, with a brief pause to flick his tongue in her navel, he led her to believe he would soon arrive at his ultimate destination. However, he had a detour in mind. As long as she remained willing to bear his lovemaking, he intended to taste every beautiful inch of her. But he thought it best to give her a preview of coming attractions to entice her to tolerate the delay.

Easing his way upward so his shaft was once again full and heavy against her stomach, he eased his way down her body again until he was knocking at her secret door. She was so bewitched by his touch that the slightest move on his part to change his position had her spreading her legs to accommodate him.

With his hands beneath her thighs he bent her legs toward her chest to expose her even more. The sight of her femininity glistening with the moisture of wanting him practically unmanned him, but he pulled himself together and carried on. "So beautiful," he whispered, unable to hold back all of what he was feeling.

He allowed her to hold him for the moment it took to guide him to her entrance then he moved her hands away and held them. As he slipped into her depths, he reclaimed her mouth for another long, deep kiss. With little more than the skillful rotation of his hips, he drove her to the brink once more.

Then he withdrew from her body.

Her breath caught in her throat and her eyes flew open. She didn't understand and she was too dazed to ask. Scraping his callused thumb over the tiny bud of nerves he had teased, he felt her shiver. "Patience," he whispered.

It was the mantra he had been saying over and over in his own mind, for it was becoming more difficult by the second to do what he intended. Leaving her body after finally learning the feel of it just took the number one spot on his list of hardest things he ever had to do. But keeping his plan in mind helped him accomplish it.

He crawled back far enough to be able to kiss her toes. When he'd caressed every part of one foot, he alternately kissed and licked a path up that leg, then repeated the slow procedure on the other. This time, however, he didn't stop at the top of her thigh.

He gave her warning of his next sweet torment by cupping his hand between her legs and lightly stroking the soft curls.

"*Logan*, please."

He had not thought it possible for her to make his name sound like a prayer, yet she did, and he could not help but comply.

She was wet and open as he slid two fingers slowly up and down over her sensitized flesh. He watched her clutch the pillow beneath her head and listened to her kitten cries grow stronger with each breath. When she began tilting her hips to meet his strokes, he quickened his efforts for several seconds then pinched her sensitive, extended flesh between his fingers.

She whimpered and trembled and sighed with immense satisfaction, but he wasn't finished with her. While the aftershocks of pleasure continued to hold her in thrall, those same two fingers that had so skillfully released her tension, delved deep inside her and pushed against the upper wall.

The shock of sensation jolted her so intensely that only the press of his mouth kept her hips on the bed. As his tongue rekindled her smoldering fire, his fingers scissored rapidly back and forth inside her. Within seconds she cried out again but the grip she had on his hair was anything but relaxed.

"*Please*, she gasped. I need you inside me. *Deep inside me!*" she added in a strained, barely audible voice. "You win. I lose. Okay? Stop torturing me!"

Logan's heart swelled. He'd done it. Seduced her to a point of her begging. Another part of his anatomy was uncomfortably swollen but denying his own pleasure was part of his plan to win her over. "I'm not trying to torture you," he said with a chuckle. "I'm just trying to please you…and show you—"

She wrapped a hand around his shaft and squeezed so hard he was stunned into silence. *"Stop talking!"* she demanded in a deep, unfamiliar voice. The next instant, with more strength than her petite body should have been able to muster, she flipped him onto his back, pinned his shoulders down with her hands and mounted his erection.

Logan might have been able to enjoy her aggressive behavior if he had ever seen any hint of it being possible…or if he didn't feel how dangerously hot her body suddenly was…*or see the whites of her eyes turn blood red.*

Only because he had held back so long did he

remain rigid enough for her to take what she wanted from him, but once she was finished and slumped into an unconscious heap on top of him, even his manhood lost interest in having a happy ending.

In all his fantasies about Tarla, she had never turned into an alien bent on sucking the life out of him.

"I want an explanation," Robin stated without preamble.

Geoffrey blinked the sleep out of his eyes and strained to focus on the woman standing over him with her fists planted on her hips. Even half asleep and in the dim light, he could tell she was furious with him. "I beg your pardon?"

"No, I will not pardon you. Not unless your explanation is completely believable."

Geoffrey pulled himself to a sitting position, careful to keep the sheet over his lower parts. When he'd opted to sleep in the nude, as he regularly did, he hadn't expected Robin to accost him in the middle of the night. "I will be most happy to explain whatever you'd like, but could it not wait until we've both had a bit more sleep?"

Robin huffed. "That's easy for you to say. *You* weren't laying here wide awake wondering whether you had bad breath or body odor!"

Geoffrey pinched the bridge of his nose and shook his head. He was fully awake now but she still made no sense. "I'm afraid you have me at a distinct disadvantage, Robin. Perhaps if we begin again and you explain what you want *me* to explain, we can solve your insomnia."

Robin huffed again and paced back and forth a few times before she could get it out. Even when she began to speak, however, she faced away, rather than look at him when he answered. "Do you prefer men? I mean, if you do, I'm fine with that, as long as I know it up front."

Geoffrey couldn't have been more stunned. He couldn't imagine what he'd done to cause her to question his sexual preference other than wearing a pink nightgown, and he hadn't been given a choice about that. However, he figured if he ever wanted to go back to sleep, he'd best answer her question. "No. I do not prefer men."

"Then what is it about me that you find so unattractive?"

Her second question proved he *could* be more stunned after all. "I...I don't find anything about you unattractive, Robin. You're...you're a lovely woman." Possibly the loveliest he'd ever encountered, he added to himself.

She whirled around at him and crossed her arms defensively. "Then why do you step away when I come near? Why do you avoid looking me in the eye? Why haven't you picked up on a single one of my obvious flirtations? And don't tell me it's because you're trying to fit in around here. You were doing your best to ignore me from the first minute we saw each other. I will admit that it's very self-centered of me, but I am not accustomed to being ignored by men. Usually it's the other way around. On the rare occasion when I choose *not* to ignore the man, I expect him to at least...show interest in return."

Geoffrey was finally following her train of thought, convoluted though it was. He had unintentionally bruised her feminine ego. By not drooling over her the way he was tempted to do, he'd become a challenge to her. Though he had wished her flirtations were based on a mutual attraction, he hadn't believed it possible. That would have been no less than a miracle in his mind. Now it was up to him to say something that would soothe her injured pride and spare him embarrassment at the same time.

He cleared his throat and chose a lead-in sentence. "I have a confession to make." Although he avoided looking at her, he sensed her coming to his side.

"A confession?" she asked, her tone of voice revealing her eagerness for an acceptable excuse.

He nodded. "I'm...I'm incredibly shy around women. Especially exceptionally beautiful women like yourself. I never know quite what to say or how to behave."

She sat next to him and smiled as he tried to make more space between them. "I really do make you nervous, don't I?" she asked sweetly. "I don't mean to. I just go after what I want. Really, there's no reason to be nervous," Robin assured him. "Unless you're a virgin. You're not, are you?"

Geoffrey was able to chuckle at that. "No, I am not a virgin either."

"Good. Then there really is nothing for you to be shy about with me. I have all the same parts as any other woman you've been with. And if there's anything you're not sure about, I'll be more than happy to help."

He cleared his throat again and tried another tack. "My being shy is not the only thing holding me back from...from acting on my attraction to you. I pride myself on being a gentleman, as old-fashioned as that may sound. A gentleman would never take advantage of a woman when her resistance was down, even if she thought she wanted him at the moment. To pursue you in any way while you are so vulnerable, would be akin to my seducing a grieving widow. Only a rogue would behave so unconscionably."

Robin narrowed her eyes at him. "Hold on one teeny second. Let me try to rephrase your explanation into plain English...I mean, American. You think this wacky situation we're in has made me a weak little girl whose mind is too mucked up to know the difference between being attracted to a man and needing a strong shoulder to lean on."

Geoffrey grimaced at her annoyed tone. "I merely said that you're vulnerable right now—"

"News flash, smartass. I was attracted to you the first time I saw you, *before* we boarded the plane. Not only did I think you were an absolutely gorgeous specimen, there was something about you—your aura maybe—who knows, but it made me want to find out more about you. If all I needed was a man to protect me from the unknown, do you honestly believe I would have picked *you* rather than Logan or T.J. or any of the other muscle-bound young apes in our group?"

Geoffrey didn't know whether he'd just been flattered, insulted or chastised, so he gave no reply whatsoever. It worried him that her arguments sounded logical. Despite his belief that this was all just a game to someone as attractive as Robin, he realized she had the power to force him to play if she remained determined to do so.

"Time's up, Geoffrey," Robin said, breaking into his imaginings. "You don't want to answer my question because you know I'm right and you're wrong, but you're not ready to admit it. So let's make a deal. You say you're attracted to me but don't want to take advantage because I'm vulnerable right now. Okay. How much time do you think needs to go by before I stop being vulnerable and start knowing my own mind?"

He could see where this was headed and tried to derail her. "A year."

"*Bzzt!* Wrong answer. Try a week. One has gone by

already. More than enough time to get over a shock."

"Not true. The current situation, with us sharing living quarters, is a brand new shock. Six months."

"One."

"Three," he said, combing his fingers through his hair in frustration. "Dammit, woman! I don't even know what I'm negotiating about any more."

"Two months," she said firmly. "I won't insist you give up this foolish chivalry for two months. But if I still want us to be more than roommates after that, you're mine to do whatever I want with."

Geoffrey shook his head and sighed. Since he was certain her interest in him could never last as long as two months, he agreed to her ultimatum.

"Good. Now there's just one more thing." Before he could avoid her, she twined her arms around his neck and pressed her mouth to his. He gently resisted for a moment, but she held tight until he was kissing her back. For a few more seconds she savored the intimacy, then she eased away. "I just thought you should have a taste of what you'd be enjoying tonight if you weren't such a perfect gentleman."

Before she went back into the bedroom, he asked, "You really didn't find any of the other men to your liking? I would think Logan—"

"Nope. You're the one. Besides, Logan's not available. He just doesn't know it yet."

She left him in the confused condition she'd intended and returned to her own bed, alone. She didn't feel badly that he'd negotiated her into a two-month period of neutrality. After a kiss that magical, he'd never be able to hold out that long.

Nadia shoved her breakfast aside. How could they expect her to eat this slop every day for the next five years? The least Parisia could have done was to send

Fulton over to prepare her meals and take care of her laundry!

Losing Fulton after putting so much time into his unique training made her punishment that much worse. She wondered who would hire him now, and whether his new employer would figure out how to bribe him for gossip about his previous mistress, even though it was strictly forbidden for housemen to discuss their past or present employers.

If others learned of the services she had required of him, she might have difficulty hiring any houseman in the future. Even if she managed to acquire someone suitable, she knew she would never again be able to take the risks she had before—not if she ever wanted to climb back up the political ladder.

And the only thing that was going to keep her spirits up for five years was the belief that it was possible for her to recapture lost ground one day.

She was no longer under guard and the restraints on her wrists and ankles had been removed, but what good did it do? She was still a prisoner in a primitive commune while the Earth women now had freedom in her world. Ray Higgs, the scarred man, and the pretty blond man were gone too. By eavesdropping she'd learned of the outrageous defense plan Parisia had pushed through Parliament. If only she had been there...

But she hadn't been and there was no use fretting over past mistakes. What she had to do now was figure out how to improve her present circumstances.

Escaping was not an option at the moment. The controller had gone with the pretty man and her earlier plan to get Simone to help her was no longer feasible. Not that anyone would stop her from going into the transfer room and pleading for assistance while Simone was on duty. It was just logical to assume that

Simone would never jeopardize her own future by aiding an ostracized citizen.

Actually, the only option she did have was which communal task she would perform in exchange for sustenance. As if it wasn't demeaning enough to have to manage without a servant, the earth cretins kept insisting she would have to do manual labor or she would not be permitted to eat. And it wasn't even decent food!

The mere thought of dealing with smelly four-legged beasts or dirtying her hands in the fields was completely repulsive to her. It was beyond her imagination to envision herself serving or cleaning up after men. The only chore she thought she might learn to tolerate was the preparation of food. At least that work was done indoors and required clean hands.

"Mornin', ma'am. Nadia, aint' it?"

Nadia looked up…and up. The man who had dared to approach appeared to be taller and broader across the shoulders than she was. His hair was blond, but cut so close to his scalp that he looked nearly bald.

"I'm Guy Wilkes," he said, as if she should be impressed, then sat next to her without asking permission.

She glared at him but it didn't seem to faze him in the least.

"Thought you might be needin' a friend about now." With a bold look on his face, he placed his hand over her knee.

Shocked at his impertinence, she bolted up from her seat. "How dare you touch me without permission?" she hissed. "I will report you to…to whomever has a semblance of authority in this deplorable place."

Wilkes laughed out loud and slapped his thigh. "I'll be goddamned! You really do think you're some sort of queen bee, don't you?"

She rose abruptly and started to walk away but he grabbed her robe and brought her up short. Sneering at him over her shoulder, she ordered, "Release me this instant, or I'll..."

"Or you'll *what*?" he challenged her right back. Standing up, he exchanged his hold on her robe for a fistful of black hair, tugging hard enough to make her eyes water. "If you think you can scare me like you did that wimp Higgs, you'd better think again, babe. In my world—which happens to be this here farm at the moment—men do the orderin', not broads. And that includes when, where and how we screw."

Nadia's heart pounded with fear. It was quite clear that this man was capable of hurting her very badly, but she had no idea why he would or what he wanted from her. She had no experience with physical force, other than the few times she had caused Fulton minor pain to keep him obedient. This man made her remember all the frightening things she'd heard about men while she was growing up. Not knowing what else to do, her gaze darted from side to side in search of someone to come to her rescue. However the elderly men working in the kitchen seemed completely oblivious to her plight.

"Don't bother lookin' to them for help. These old geezers can't move fast enough to get out of their own way, and everyone else is out doin' their chores already. But don't get the idea that the others would help even if they were still around. Let me tell you the score, plain and simple. There's a whole bunch of men on this farm who are both angry about bein' left behind and bored with havin' only five-fingered Mary for company. It don't matter how important you were where you come from. Here, you're just a horny broad who's already spread her legs for one of our kind, so you oughta be just as obligin' for everybody else."

She inhaled sharply. Though some of his expressions were unknown to her, his hand gestures had been adequately explicit. "I was conducting an experiment."

Wilkes smirked. "Yeah, right, babe. You just stick to that story if it makes you feel better. As a matter of fact, I have a little experiment you can help me with right now."

"I have no intention of helping you with anything!" She tried to pull out of this grasp, but he only held on tighter.

"Listen up, bitch. Every man here heard how you ordered that pint-sized Higgs to give it to you, and I'm not the only one who thinks you should try a real man on for size. Now, before this situation gets really messy, I figger somebody oughta take control of it."

She angled her head at him. The word control caught her attention. "And I suppose that *somebody* is you?"

"None other," he answered with a cocky grin. "I have a business proposition for you, but I don't want anyone to overhear it. Let's go to my tent."

A business proposition, like control, was something she could understand, even if his methods and other terminology were unfamiliar. Thinking she had a chance of coming out ahead in this encounter after all, her self-confidence returned. Straightening her shoulders and lifting her chin, she demanded, "Remove your hand from my person, then I will allow you to accompany me to your tent for a discussion." He released her hair but she could see he didn't like giving her even that slight advantage.

Wilkes had been right about everyone being gone. There wasn't a man in sight between the big house and his tent. At the last moment something warned Nadia not to go inside with him. "No one can hear you now," she said, stopping in front of the tent. "What is your proposition?"

He motioned for her to enter. "Inside first. I don't want to take the chance of anyone seein' us talkin' either. Your people could be watchin'."

That seemed unlikely since everyone was supposed to be at their work stations, but Nadia decided she was better off doing as he suggested rather than risk angering him again. Since the tent wasn't high enough for her to stand erect, she sat on one of the costs while he closed the tent flap and lit a lamp. Her patience and confidence were both fading quickly, but her curiosity kept her from walking out on him.

Without warning Wilkes turned and backhanded her cheek. She cried out more from shock than pain. When she tried to get up and away, he hit her again, this time so hard she fell back onto the cot. A scream welled up in her throat but before it erupted, his hand closed over her mouth.

"Not a sound," he growled and viciously squeezed her cheeks while he straddled her body to hold her in place. "Rule number one, you keep your goddamned mouth shut 'cept when I tell you otherwise. I'm the boss here and the sooner you understand that, the faster we can get down to business. What you just felt were nothin' but love pats compared to what you'll feel if you don't behave. Got it?"

With her cheeks throbbing and his greater weight holding her down, she did the only logical thing she could—she nodded in understanding.

"Good bitch. Rule number two, you don't go nowhere or do nothin' without me. From now on we're Siamese twins. Got it?"

She nodded again. With a sinking sensation she now realized the reality of the brutal male was even worse than the stories she'd been taught.

But Ray Higgs hadn't been cruel, or even aggressive. And the pretty man had seemed quite rational. Perhaps one of the other men left behind would be willing to protect her—She tossed that thought out. None of the others she'd seen looked nearly as strong or mean as Guy Wilkes. She had to accept the fact that she was completely at his mercy— for the moment.

Wilkes released her cheeks and stared down at her, as if daring her to speak without his permission. After a few seconds he seemed satisfied with her obedience and said, "Here's the deal. You gotta work to eat around here. Now I figger, you bein' the only pussy around here oughta be worth a hell of a lot. 'Specially one who likes gettin' fucked as much as you do. If you keep givin' it away though, it ain't gonna be worth nothin'."

She thought she comprehended what he was saying, but his speech was so peculiar, she couldn't be certain. Rather than question him, however, she held her tongue and hoped she'd catch on as he continued.

"Instead of you doin' chores like the men, you'll provide them with your personal, one-of-a-kind service and they'll make sure you get all your needs taken care of. 'Course, you gotta have somebody plenty smart and strong to manage your business for you and make sure you're protected against anybody tryin' to steal the goods without payin', and I just happen to be sick of wastin' my talents pickin' fruit and milkin' cows. You got the picture now, babe?"

She could hardly believe her ears. She had been fretting over what chore she could tolerate in exchange for food and, though she found Guy Wilkes to be as repugnant as a man could be, he had come up with an option she hadn't thought of. Thinking of how enjoyable her experiences with Ray Higgs had been, she smiled up at the man who thought he was so smart.

He grinned back at her. "Rule number three, no lyin' here like a dead fish. No matter who you're with, you act like you're lovin' every minute of it, just like you did with Higgs. And just to be sure you do, I'll be right here watchin' you every minute you're workin'. Got it?"

She gave him another nod as she felt a twinge of anticipation in her lower abdomen. The thought of him observing while another man pleasured her was strangely exciting. Even better than watching herself with Fulton in the bathroom mirror. She wondered if the image had a similar effect on Guy Wilkes. The answer to that came the next instant.

"Time to show your boss what a good little worker you're gonna be," he said and tore open the front of her robe. Letting out a soft whistle of appreciation at the sight of her breasts, he groped and kneaded them in his big, meaty hands. "The boys are gonna love these tits, babe."

Feeling a surge of power at his male weakness, she made the mistake of letting him see it in her eyes. He immediately repaid her by giving her nipples a harsh, twisting pinch. *"Ow,"* she whimpered before recalling his order not to speak, and he quickly pinched her again.

"That was just a taste of how it can be between us. You obey the rules…" He bent down and sucked one of her nipples into his mouth, teasing her with his tongue and teeth until she moaned for him. Then he abruptly bit into her flesh. "Or you can fight me and get hurt. It's your choice, babe."

She massaged her bruised breast with one hand while wiping the moisture from her eyes with the other. When he rose to his knees and shoved his pants down below his partially swollen manpiece, she was no longer certain this was going to be better than dealing with smelly four-legged beasts.

"Now use that mouth of yours the way it's supposed to be used," he told her with an ugly sneer on his face.

She obeyed his command, but what followed wasn't anything like it had been with Ray Higgs, or even Fulton. Obviously the ultimate pleasure could only be achieved when she was the one giving the orders.

Simone stretched luxuriantly and moved her arms and legs over the satin sheets on Nadia's big bed. She mentally congratulated herself once again on having made such an excellent move.

Nadia's unusual tastes had proven to be an unexpected bonus. Simone knew she was supposed to disapprove of the lavish bathroom with its mirrored wall, the rich foods Fulton served and the satin sheets. But the truth was, she found it all very stimulating to her senses, as well as her thought processes.

There was only one thing that truly shocked her, and even that had turned out to be delightful. When Fulton had offered to prepare a bath for her, she certainly hadn't expected to find him waiting to attend her in the nude. Nor could she possibly have guessed the extent of his assistance. When he had asked her about her wishes, she had simply told him to do whatever he normally did for Nadia. Once she got over the initial embarrassment of being disrobed by him, she quickly overcame the shock of being touched as well. Wanting to learn everything there was to know about Nadia and recalling the scene she had witnessed in the transfer room, Simone decided to allow Fulton total freedom and soon made some amazing discoveries!

She stretched again and ran her hands over her body, touching and stroking places where she had never lingered before. That sort of contact was considered sinful and ultimately harmful to one's mental health. Perhaps there was a good deal of truth to that. Giving in to the physical pleasure that could be derived from such touches had certainly caused problems for Nadia.

But Simone now knew there were also lies mixed in with the truth. And Nadia had been ostracized rather than be allowed to reveal the real truth about what it was like to be touched by a man.

The more Simone thought about it, the more convinced she was that Nadia had a valid reason for trespassing into the Earth commune. It made sense to Simone that before Nadia could challenge age-old laws and traditions, she would need to do more research. Unable to conduct that research among her own people, she must have decided it was worth the risk to use Earth men.

Simone had not been able to learn all the details, but apparently the Earth women had been instrumental in exposing Nadia's misdeeds. She wondered if they were also responsible for convincing Parisia that Heart needed their assistance in developing a defense system.

There was clearly something very strange going on about that too, but Simone wasn't well enough connected with Parisia's advisors to get to the bottom of it. Nadia had had plenty of strong allies, but without her to speak for them, they had all backed off rather than defy Parisia and chance the same future as Nadia.

As much as Simone would have liked to be the courageous woman to oppose Parisia's defense plan and challenge Heart's traditional laws, she knew she didn't have Nadia's strength of character or commanding personality. Besides, she had been playing both sides for so long, it could be hard to convince people that she had finally made a choice.

For many years she hadn't been sure which side would provide her with the best future. More recently she had been leaning toward Nadia for a number of reasons. For one, Nadia's political opinions suited her better than Parisia's. More important however, Parisia and Brianne's inner circle was firmly fixed and nearly impenetrable. Nadia's court was still flexible. Though Simone didn't think she herself had sufficient leadership qualities, she did believe she'd enjoy being the leader's Domestic Affairs Advisor. The mere thought of possessing the same power now held by Iris gave Simone a shiver of excitement.

She continued to mull over what facts she had with those she had to guess at. Considering every possibility along with her personal goals, she eventually came to a conclusion.

She had to come up with a plan to help Nadia escape. Then, together, they would challenge Parisia for the imperial throne.

CHAPTER 17

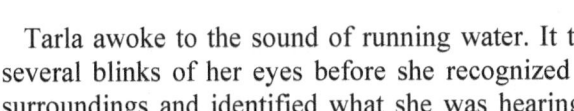

Tarla awoke to the sound of running water. It took several blinks of her eyes before she recognized her surroundings and identified what she was hearing as the bathroom shower. Once total awareness set in, she closed her eyes again.

In an instant, the events of the previous evening flashed through her mind. There was absolutely no question of whose fault everything was.

Hers. He certainly hadn't forced himself on her. In fact, she was fairly sure that at one point, she forced herself on him. She was also quite positive that she wasn't drugged in any way.

Unless a flood of hormones produced due to a biological anomaly within her body could be called being drugged.

Would Logan believe that, without her explaining everything about who she was? She didn't think so. She could only hope he'd assume she'd surrendered to her desire for him. Realistically, the chances of his accepting that were nearly as low.

There was the very slim possibility that the gripping fever was a one-time thing...brought on by stress or the alien environment.

First of all, she was at least a decade past the age when the Noronian mating fever should have been triggered by her soul's mate.

Secondly, the fever should only be triggered by another Noronian.

But Romulus's fever was triggered by Aster, a Terran who simply had a mere trace of Noronian ancestry.

Thirdly, both people experience the symptoms simultaneously.

Not in the case of Aster and Romulus. It had been determined that her symptoms were delayed due to her not being pure Noronian.

And finally, the two people are supposed to feel the magnetic pull between them at first sight. She and Logan could barely tolerate each other.

But her initial reaction to him was that there was something different about Logan, something very special.

Could he have felt it also, without understanding what it meant? Could that have been why he'd told her he loved her so quickly?

If that were the case...

Tarla's analysis was cut off as the bathroom door opened and, through the steam, Tarla saw Logan toweling dry his hair. Her breath quickened at the sight of his incredible body. She forgave herself for that reaction, acknowledging that she wouldn't be much of a woman if she didn't appreciate the beauty of his masculine form. That in itself wasn't definitive proof that they were soulmates.

She tried not to think about what that body felt like pressed against hers. Her hands still remembered the texture of his skin, his hair, the hardness of his muscles. Her lips were still tender from his kisses.

The true test was yet to come. Would the fever rise again without provocation?

Logan stepped out of the bathroom with the same sort of apprehension he'd often had upon approaching enemy territory—tense, anxious, afraid but going forward anyway. He saw the way Tarla was watching him, as though she had never wanted a man as much as him and, before last night, his heart would have soared. But this morning, that look struck fear in his gut.

He also noticed how comfortable she seemed with the sheet barely covering her hips. Yesterday, had he seen her like that, he would have been across the room in a heartbeat. But not this morning. Not after what he'd seen. If he needed more proof it was right in front of him. The Tarla he knew, the *real* Tarla would have had that sheet tucked up around her chin...if not completely over her head.

She smiled softly up at him and patted the bed. "We need to talk."

He eyed the spot she was patting and remembered how that hand had painfully clamped around his shaft with the power of a vise. "I, uh, think we need to just get going. Remember, work starts today and we need to have some breakfast." To prove his point, he hurriedly sorted through the boxes of clothing that had been delivered yesterday, chose a caftan for her and one of the pants sets for himself. Since the conference room was on the same floor as their apartment, he assumed that attire would be acceptable.

She narrowed her eyes at him. "And I think today will go a lot more smoothly if you and I aren't trying to avoid each other."

Logan recalled his naive idea that if he serviced her well enough, she'd be anxious to share her bed with him again in the future. It had never occurred to him that he wouldn't *want* to repeat the service.

"Do I have to command you?" Tarla said with a smirk. "I thought last night got us past playing the mistress-servant thing in private."

Without meeting her gaze, Logan quickly dressed and headed for the kitchen. She was right behind him, wrapped in the sheet a few seconds later.

"What's going on, Logan? Are you angry with me? Did I fall asleep before you were finished? I realize I may have come on a little stronger than—"

"A *little* stronger?" Logan barked back at her. "I've got bruises to prove that's an understatement. You want to know what's going on with me? I'll be glad to share my feelings with Tarla...if she's still in there. Or did I finally meet the real Tarla? The one who's obviously a freaking *alien*!"

Tarla's mouth opened and shut twice before she could speak aloud. "You know? How? Robin doesn't even know."

Logan started to respond then just shook his head in disbelief and started pulling things out to make breakfast.

"Logan," Tarla pleaded as she reached for his arm.

He jerked away before she could make contact.

This certainly wasn't the way she imagined this conversation would go but now it was imperative she give him a believable explanation quickly, before they were expected to appear in the conference room.

"Please sit down, Logan." Her gentle voice only got her a snort. He obviously thought she was dangerous, so she used the most authoritative tone she was capable of. "I will explain and you *will* listen. If you find it impossible to accept what I have to say, you will at least keep it to yourself and behave normally in front of the others. If you cannot do that, I will...let's just say I have ways of forcing you to comply."

He tried staring her down and using his lethal glare against her, but a moment later he sat down at the kitchen table.

"Very good," Tarla said. "Now, tell me how you know I'm an alien, and a *freaking* one at that."

He sighed, ran his fingers through his hair and shifted on the chair before he finally spoke. "I didn't really know for sure. Until you confirmed it. I just thought maybe your mind was taken over by one of the sex-craved Heart women, like Nadia. Or that you were some sort of shapeshifter pretending to be Tarla Yan."

"I suppose we should thank Higgs for those imaginative possibilities. But I still want to know why you thought I wasn't the same Tarla you've known."

He took another moment to respond then shrugged submissively. "First clue? You wanted sex. With me. Not just accepting, like you were when we were in the tack room. You were hungry for it. And then there was your super-human strength. And your body temperature went so high I felt like I was handling burning coals. But the worst was how your eyes changed. The whites turned blood red. It just kept getting worse until you had the big-O with me deep inside you. I think those were pretty good clues.

"But you should know, if you were trying to use my sperm to breed, I didn't come. And it would be a waste of your time to try again. I had a vasectomy years ago."

For the moment, Tarla dismissed his nonsense about using him to breed. She could barely breathe after hearing the details of what she'd done. Her memory of those final minutes was completely clouded. "And then I passed out," she murmured. "I assume the symptoms all went away seconds later."

He frowned. "Yeah, completely. What do you mean

symptoms?"

Tarla finally sat down across from him. She really had no choice but to tell him everything. "Please understand, my position prohibits me from sharing the truth with any Outerworld Terran, which is what you are to me, but considering where we are, I don't suppose the regulations are applicable anymore."

A half hour later, she had managed to give him a very condensed version of her life story, including the most important facts about Innerworld. She also told him a little about the Noronian mating fever, saying it might have been the cause of her disturbing symptoms, without revealing that it could mean they were soulmates. She would hold that back until she was absolutely certain.

Logan remained quiet throughout, not asking a single question. Unfortunately, she had the feeling he hadn't heard most of what she'd told him.

"Do you believe me?" Tarla asked.

He shrugged. "What's it matter? There's no way to prove or disprove anything you have to say."

"There might be a way," she said reluctantly. "But you'd have to trust me."

He arched one eyebrow. "Seriously? Okay, let's say I trust you. What's your proof?"

"Remember your migraine and the massage I gave you?" She got another brow arch for that stupid question. "When I pressed your temples with my fingers, I accidentally touched your mind. I didn't mean to, and I locked most of it away without prying, I swear. But I saw you being beaten by men of your unit and I suddenly knew you were innocent!"

His eyes narrowed dangerously. "You can crawl around inside my head anytime you want? And I can't even tell you're doing it? *That's* proof that you're a good alien instead of an evil one?"

"Oh no, no, no!" she said quickly. "I'm trying to tell you that if I can do that and know the truth about you, I can open the path the other way and let you look around in my mind. That way you'll know—"

"*Screw that!*" Logan spat out and lurched up from the table. "I don't want to know what's inside that head of yours. And I definitely don't want any more *touching* from you…for any reason!"

Too upset to eat, Tarla left Logan in the kitchen while she headed for the bathroom to get ready for their first day at work. A half hour later, she was physically, if not emotionally, ready to go.

"Is there anything you'd like to ask me before we walk out this door?" Tarla asked. When he just looked away, she said, "Fine. Hate me. Distrust me. Whatever. Just keep our problems locked inside this apartment. If the others know we aren't coping, this whole thing could fall apart. And we could end up back on the farm with no memory of anything better."

They barely had a few minutes to exchange greetings with the others before Parisia, Brianne and Iris arrived.

"I hope you are all comfortably settled into your apartments," Parisia said pleasantly. "Because we are most anxious to begin. I thought we should take this morning to orient you, commencing with a history lesson so that you might understand our sudden need for a defense system. However, I must first ask you each to take an oath of confidentiality. We believe it would be extremely detrimental to our cause if certain people learned every detail of what we are doing here."

As soon as the group of Earthlings agreed to maintain total secrecy, Parisia launched into the legend about the early days of Heart and led up to the recent rumors about the Velids once again being on the warpath.

Iris delivered the second speech. "From our previous conversations, it is clear that Heart's technology has progressed beyond Earth's, but is not as advanced as some other civilizations we have encountered. For instance, we are able to travel through space, but not at faster-than-light speed, nor are our ships equipped with weaponry of any kind. Our scientists have learned to harness the energy of the sun and the power of laserlight, and have discovered how to utilize magnetic energy in a variety of ways, such as transportation and health care."

Iris explained that the specifics about their technology and that of other cultures could be accessed through the computers in the room. Brianne would remain with them at all times to guide them through the data systems and supply any other assistance they might need.

Tarla got the distinct impression that Brianne would also be staying with them in the role of watchdog.

Iris concluded her segment with a statement that everyone was relieved to hear. "We do not expect you to singlehandedly build weapons or convert our spacecraft into vehicles of war. If you formulate a viable plan based on the technology available, we will provide you with the means and staff to create it."

Tarla felt Logan staring at her and, with little more than a glance in his direction, guessed at what he was thinking. Again, she politely raised her hand before speaking. "As you are aware, our men are more familiar with waging war than we women are. With all due respect to your laws and traditions, it would be much more efficient if you would allow the men to address questions to you directly."

Parisia and Iris glanced at each other, then Parisia said, "Of course. That would be reasonable under the circumstances. As long as they remember to resume a submissive nature outside of this room."

For several hours, both the men and women of Earth posed questions and Parisia and Iris took turns answering as well as they could. Regarding information they didn't know, Brianne made notes to help them research it later.

One thing was very clear. The Heart men couldn't, and the Heart women wouldn't, perform any violent or aggressive act, even in defense of their homes. If an enemy was coming, it would have to be dealt with before it had a chance to land on the planet, and in such a way that a woman would not be expected to do much more than push a button to activate an automated system.

When all the basics had been covered, Parisia made a suggestion that raised Tarla's spirits. "Since several of you are nurses, I believe you might find our advancements in health care interesting. I could take you on a tour of the sanatorium this afternoon. I'm afraid the men will not be able to accompany us, however. While we're at the sanatorium, my son, Jason, will be taking the men on a trip to the market and other places they should become familiar with."

Around midday, Jason arrived with a cold lunch for everyone. As custom dictated, he was introduced to the men, but not the women.

Robin whispered in Tarla's ear. "Now *that* is a crime against nature!"

She didn't need to say more for Tarla to understand. Jason was in his early twenties and so attractive, he could be called beautiful. His long dark hair was tied back, showing off a handsome face and jade-green eyes. Unfortunately, the vivid color failed to mask the blank expression in those eyes. Though he seemed to be built tall and extremely thin, he kept his head bowed and his shoulders sloped, giving himself a shorter, more rounded appearance. How could a mother do that to her own son?

Tarla's gaze moved toward Parisia but it was Brianne who caught her attention. That young woman's eyes were filled with compassion as she watched her brother unpack the lunches he had brought. Was it possible that not every Heart woman thought men should be drugged into passivity?

After lunch, the group split to go on their separate tours, with plans to return to the workroom in two hours. Though Robin, Alicia and Lee weren't nurses, they were still highly impressed with the sanatorium.

While they walked through the facility, Parisia told them about the progress their medical experts had made over the years. "Our doctors perfected the laserlight to repair broken bones or torn tissues about a century ago, but it wasn't until they began experimenting with magnetia—a fusion of magnetic and crystal energy—that they discovered how to speed up the healing process. The human body may be mostly water, but it contains metallic substances as well. When the body is injured, those elements are thrown out of balance. With magnetia, they can be properly readjusted."

"One of our men was brought here with a migraine headache," Tarla said. "How was his pain relieved?"

Parisia smiled. "That was a combination of magnetia and medication. A headache is caused by an imbalance of the chemical makeup of the brain, which in turn, disturbs the metallic properties."

Because of Norona's laws banning interference with Terran culture and natural progression, Tarla was not permitted to reveal any of the advanced medical technology or methods used in Innerworld. Suddenly she realized how this strange adventure could have enormously beneficial results for Outerworlders without her personally breaking any Noronian laws.

"Would it be possible for us to observe and study some of these procedures?" she asked. "If we could take this information back to Earth, it could revolutionize health care overnight."

Parisia and Iris exchanged another of their non-verbal communications before Parisia answered. When she did, Tarla sensed she was saying something very different from what she was thinking.

"Of course," Parisia replied. "As long as it doesn't take away from time you should be spending on our plan."

Tarla was more than satisfied with that. Not only would they be doing something constructive in their leisure time, it would provide her with a place to go in the evening in case Logan continued to see her only as a *freaking alien.*

Logan's muscles were beginning to feel the strain of purposely restricted movement, as he and the other men imitated Jason's slow progress through the marketplace. He vowed to begin doing calisthenics each night in the privacy of the apartment just to burn off all the energy being trapped inside his body. It might even help him deal with the pent-up tension Tarla caused, he thought, though he didn't really believe anything could accomplish that feat.

Jason was quietly and boringly explaining how to select the best potatoes for mashing, when Logan lost control of his patience. A quick glance at the others in his group let him know he wasn't the only one being driven over the edge. As soon as they moved out of earshot of the female vegetable merchant, he said, "We've seen more than enough, Jason. Let's go back."

It was somewhat easier to pretend to be drugged once they knew they would soon be able to act normally again. The moment they were inside the workroom, the men groaned and stretched and teased each other on their performances. Their joking was a natural outlet for the pressure of the last hour in public and continued for several minutes.

Then, at the same instant, Logan and Geoffrey noted Jason's wide-eyed, bewildered stare, and realized the enormity of the mistake they had just made. They had completely forgotten that the act had to be kept up at all times.

Geoffrey loudly cleared his throat and moved his eyes to remind the others that Jason was watching them. But it was already too late. "I hope you will pardon that display, Jason," he said. "I'm afraid we still have a ways to go to be perfectly behaved Heart men, like you."

Jason's brow wrinkled slightly. "I remember...laughing...with Brianne." The thoughtful frown relaxed into a complacent smile again. "Brianne and I are twins. We were permitted to socialize with each other when we were children."

"How lucky for you," Logan muttered sarcastically.

"Yes, it was," Jason replied with absolute sincerity. "No other Imperial Prefect has ever had a male child. I have caused complications."

T.J. snorted. "Somebody 'round here oughta cause—"

"*T.J.!*" Geoffrey said, cutting him off. The young man rolled his eyes and slumped down onto a chair with his arms crossed. Geoffrey made himself a mental note to have Tarla or Robin speak to Lee about loosening the reins on her roommate a bit before he exploded.

"What kind of complications?" Logan asked, not

certain why he wanted to know yet sensing it could be important. When Jason blinked and angled his head at him, Logan realized his train of thought had been derailed by T.J.'s aggressive behavior. Because of his own experience with the drug, he had no problem empathizing with Jason's lack of focus. "You said that your being a male has caused complications."

Jason nodded. "Yes, it has."

Logan reminded himself to practice his patience and spoke to Jason as if he were a little child. "What kind of complications?"

"Employment. As the Imperial Prefect's son, I cannot work in a lesser household. I try to assist in the palace kitchen, but I do not seem to be of much help. I could be Brianne's personal servant but she insists my waiting on her makes her uncomfortable."

Logan recalled Tarla's similar claim, but as a Heart-born woman, Brianne shouldn't have been bothered by her brother serving her. "You said you used to socialize with your sister. When did that stop?"

Jason frowned and squinted with the effort it took to remember. "When she became a woman. Then it was no longer proper for us to play children's games."

Geoffrey was looking at Logan curiously and Logan gave him a brief hand signal to let him continue. "Are you given some kind of antidote once a month?"

"Of course. All men must take their antidote on schedule. We could become very ill without it."

"Do you remember when you got your first dose?" Logan prodded.

Jason rubbed his temples, as if all this thinking was making his head hurt. "It was...I think it was...also after Brianne became a woman."

Logan turned to Geoffrey. "You know, we could probably use a young man to help around here, running the household errands we won't have time for, fixing lunches, that sort of thing."

"And *you* know we aren't supposed to fraternize with the natives," Geoffrey countered. "What's on your mind?"

Logan shrugged. "I'm not sure yet. An experiment, maybe. Or a little insurance." Or a soft spot for the underdog, he added to himself. "I'll figure it out as we go along."

"All right, but have Tarla put in the request so you don't ruffle feathers more than necessary."

Logan turned his attention back to Jason. "What do you say, Jason? Would you be willing to help us out with our project?"

"I would very much like to work here with you," the young man replied shyly.

"We'll see what we can do, kid," Logan said with a wink. "Before we're finished, we might even find a way to solve your complications permanently."

At the end of the sanatorium tour, Parisia requested a few minutes alone with Tarla.

"I have something to give you," Parisia said after taking Tarla into an empty office. "But I do not wish for either Iris or Brianne to hear of it."

Tarla agreed to keep her secret and Parisia extracted a small wooden box out of her caftan pocket. She carefully raised the hinged lid and handed it to Tarla.

Inside the little box was a quantity of tiny, balls of yellow gel. She picked one out and rolled it between her fingers. She gave Parisia a questioning look and noted that the woman's usually ivory face and throat were flushed.

"I hope you do not think it too indelicate of me but I don't know of a better way to handle this. Since your men are unmedicated and circumstances require that you reside in pairs as woman and servant, it has occurred to me that you may not be able to control their, uh, biological urges indefinitely. If one of the men should force his, uh, attentions on a woman, and that mating resulted in her becoming with child, it would be most difficult to explain.

"Rather than risk such a problem, I would appreciate it if you would divide these pills up among your women. If they take one on the first day of each menstrual cycle, they will be rendered infertile for the remainder of the month."

"Birth control pills?" Tarla asked in amazement. "Why on Earth would you—I thought your men couldn't…"

Parisia held up a hand to stop her. "They can't. These are given to our female house pets to prevent accidental conception." She smiled at the disbelieving look Tarla gave her. "Don't worry. I assure you they are completely safe and effective for human females as well."

After what happened between her and Logan last night, she certainly couldn't promise that none of the couples in her group would engage in sex for the next year, so she pocketed the box and assured Parisia that she would take care of it.

The remainder of the day was spent with Brianne demonstrating how to work with the data systems and interpret the universal and planetary maps.

At the first opportunity, Logan had Tarla request Jason's assistance. Though Tarla agreed to make the request, she doubted that Brianne would allow it. Thus, it was quite a surprise when she went along with the idea after no more than a momentary consideration. In fact, it was Brianne who came up with an acceptable justification for his presence. As her personal servant, it would not be unusual for Jason to accompany her back and forth between the palace and the workroom then stay with her throughout each day in case she had need of him.

Before Brianne and Jason departed, Logan managed to get Jason off to the side for a private conversation.

"Your sister seems happy about you spending time with us," Logan said.

"Yes. I am also and I promise to serve well."

Logan saw Jason's expression change to thoughtfulness and asked, "Do you have a question?"

Jason nodded slowly. "I do not fully understand who I am to serve."

Logan considered his answer before he spoke it. He was treading on dangerous ground, yet he was convinced the risk could be worth it. "As of this minute, I'm your employer."

Massaging his temples, the younger man said, "But you are a man. Men are servants, not employers."

"That's right," Logan assured him. "But this is an unusual situation. We're helping your sister and mother with a very big complication, so the usual rules can be broken."

Jason's frown vanished.

"Now, the first order I'm going to give you has to be a secret between us. You can't even tell Brianne. Do you understand?" He waited for Jason to give him another slow nod. "When are you due to take your antidote again?"

Jason closed his eyes for a second then said, "Soon, I think."

"Okay. I don't want you to take it while you're working for me. If you show any sign of illness, I'll make sure you get what you need."

Jason's eyes grew wide and he whispered, "But that's against the law."

Logan patted his shoulder. "Remember what I said.

In order to help Brianne and Parisia, we have to break some of the rules. The question is, can you avoid taking the antidote without anyone finding out except me? Maybe pretend to take it then throw it out?"

"I suppose," Jason said reluctantly.

But will you remember this conversation ten minutes from now, Logan wondered. He figured he'd have to remind the kid at the end of every day until he found out what date his antidote was regularly administered.

Both Geoffrey and Tarla had asked what he had in mind, and he had hedged. The truth was, he wasn't all that sure of the answer to that himself. He just couldn't stop thinking about Duncan and Hans and all the rest of the men who had been fermenting on the farm for decades.

Through Jason, he hoped to discover whether or not the effects of the antidote would wear off in time. If so, it might be possible for those men to resume normal lives and return to Earth with everyone else.

Besides that, he couldn't help but hurt for that poor kid who had never even had the chance to feel what it was like to be a man. Maybe when the time came, he'd give Jason his seat on the plane for the return trip to Earth, and he'd stay here as Brianne's houseman. Compared to the sentence awaiting him at Leavenworth, the Imperial Palace was looking pretty good.

CHAPTER 18

"A *delay*?" Commander Xytoc shouted at the quivering scientist. "I will not tolerate any delays. You will complete your work according to ssschedule, or you will be sssquashed!"

The senior scientist crept a bit closer to the exit before attempting to explain again. "It is not our fault, sir. The plans for the FTL unit call for an element that we do not have on this planet. It is impossible to complete production without it."

"Where *can* thisss element be found?"

The scientist's antennae twitched nervously. "The closest planet is in the Aries system."

"*Aries*!" Xytoc roared. "It would take nearly a thousand sssunrises to get there and back. *No!* I will not wait that much longer when we are ssso clossse to total victory. You are a sssscientist! Jussstify your position. Find a sssubssstitute for the element. Sssynthesssize it. I do not care how you do it, but our troops *will* be taking off in shipsss capable of FTL no later than ninety sssunrises from today. Disssmisssed!"

The scientist slithered away as quickly as possible,

content that he had gained an additional thirty sunrises to complete his task. He was already working on a synthetic for the missing element. It had a slightly unstable quality to it, but it should work well enough to satisfy the commander and keep himself and his team from being squashed.

He was just glad he didn't have to be on any of those ships when they departed for Heart!

CHAPTER 19

Gianni noted that the line in front of Nadia's tent that night was a lot shorter than it had been the first week she went into business. When he first realized what was going on, he'd felt obligated to have a talk with both Wilkes and Nadia, mainly to verify that the woman was a willing participant. Based on her responses and previous behavior with Higgs, he was convinced that the arrangement was acceptable to her.

Gianni wondered what he would have done to keep the peace if Wilkes hadn't become her pimp. It kept two potential troublemakers busy, while pacifying an entire troop of restless men. Capitalizing on Nadia's sexual appetite was working so well, Gianni had taken advantage of her services himself last week, but this week, he just didn't feel the need.

The first few days after the advance team went beyond the wall, griping and speculating could be heard from sunup to sundown. Hardly anyone mentioned it any more. For the most part, the men had all settled into a routine of working all day, playing cards with a deck they'd made up or visiting Nadia in the evening, then sleeping until it was time to go back to work.

Most of the men, Gianni included, found that having one glass of the sparkling water with dinner was the equivalent of a cold beer. It was relaxing without scrambling their brains and it helped to make the long, boring days a little easier to get through, knowing there was something pleasant waiting for them back in the big house.

"That's it then," Geoffrey declared. "Everyone agrees this is the plan we're going to suggest." He received a chorus of endorsements then addressed Tarla. "Are you prepared to present it as is?"

"Absolutely," she said without hesitation. "It's fairly straightforward. I shouldn't have any problem answering any questions about it."

"Shall I call my mother and Iris?" Brianne asked her.

Tarla glanced at Geoffrey and Logan and noted their nods. "Yes. We're ready."

As Brianne made the call, Tarla pondered over the progress made during their first two weeks on the job. Though the team was made up of a wide range of talented men and women, they had all had plenty of doubts as to whether any of those talents would be of use in performing the monumental task they'd been given. Partly because they'd worked around the clock every day, only taking breaks to eat and get some sleep, their doubts had been groundless.

Kara's and Ray's computer expertise smoothed the way through the research stage, and Ray had a bottomless reserve of science fiction stories from which to draw ideas.

Jeremy's, Trish's and Sunny's backgrounds in math, general science and physics came in handy for translating Heart's technology into language the others could understand, while Geoffrey and Robin used their engineering and mechanical skills to come up with ways to apply it.

Alicia, Nathan and Edward applied their navigational knowledge to interpreting the maps and star charts.

As expected, Logan, T.J., Greg, Kevin and Lee concentrated on defense strategies and ideas for weapons using Heart's existing technology.

Hal's and Darcy's business acumen was temporarily on hold, but they knew they would be needed for more than brainstorming as soon as the plan was approved and set into motion.

Mandy and Charlene had little to contribute to the war effort, other than acting as sounding boards for everyone else. Therefore, they used the bulk of their time studying the medical data banks in hopes of returning to Earth with a wealth of valuable information.

Tarla managed to subtly offer suggestions, using her greater knowledge of advanced technology and defense, without anyone but Logan guessing how she might know those things. He didn't give her secret away, but she felt his derision every time she spoke.

Generally, progress had also been made in personal areas, each couple gradually drifting into compatible relationships of one kind or another.

After a rough start, T.J. eventually accepted Lee Tang in a maternal role. Alicia, Darcy, and Sunny had settled into comfortable friendships with their roommates, while Trish's, Mandy's, and Charlene's partnerships showed hints of progressing beyond that. Shy little Kara had Ray acting like an adolescent with his first attack of puppy love, much to everyone's amusement.

Robin and Geoffrey were spending so much time

brainstorming together, they often finished each other's sentences. Geoffrey had not yet given in to Robin's urging that he share her bed, but Tarla could tell he didn't have much resistance left in him.

Robin had told her what his main excuse was and, though it was quite admirable, Tarla's intuition insisted there was more to it than he was admitting. If Robin could find out what his real excuse was, Tarla was certain there could be a happily ever after in their future.

Only she and Logan had failed to find a workable solution to the dilemma of living together. She let her gaze land on him for a moment, but as soon as he noticed, she looked away, just as he did when she caught him watching her. Their tasks didn't require that they work side by side like Geoffrey and Robin, so it was not difficult to avoid each other.

At the end of each day, it was usually late enough to simply retire to their separate corners. And if it wasn't, Tarla visited one of the others until they ordered her to go home.

Robin, of course, honed right in on the problem and told her to lock herself and Logan in the bedroom and stay there until they either had sex or killed each other.

They had gotten so good at avoiding contact with one another, they were able to get ready for work each morning and go to bed each evening without spending more than a few seconds in the same room together. Tarla had been convinced that, in time, she wouldn't have to *think* about avoiding him, that it was bound to become routine sooner or later.

To her extreme relief, she hadn't had another episode of hormonal insanity, which allowed her to believe that whatever *had* happened to her, it was *not* the Noronian mating fever and Logan was *not* her soulmate.

So why, fourteen days and nights since they'd had their fateful encounter, did her stomach still flutter when he walked by? And why did it still hurt so badly that he believed she was a freak whose mere touch was poison to him?

To further mess with her mind, with each passing day, she saw more about him to admire. He was intelligent and reasonable, a strong leader when he had to be and a gentle persuader at other times. Everyone in the group looked up to him with respect and trust. No one seemed to remember the court martial or his chains, and they didn't even have the advantage of *knowing* he was innocent.

It was clear she'd made a serious error in letting him know about how she'd touched his mind. Perhaps if she'd explained how doing that accidentally would be possible if they were soulmates, but since that didn't seem to be the case...

She forced herself to think of someone else—Brianne and Jason. It had taken less time than she'd imagined for Brianne to stop being flustered when one of the men forgot the rules and addressed her directly or accidentally made physical contact.

Jason had literally become Logan's shadow. He was always ready to perform any service requested of him but he would look to Logan before going ahead. The most interesting thing about Jason was that lately he seemed to be standing a little taller than he had at first. Tarla thought perhaps he was watching Logan so closely that he was beginning to mimic him.

Parisia's and Iris's arrival ended Tarla's ponderings. The time had come for the Earthlings to prove their worth.

"The plan itself is fairly simple," Tarla began as

soon as everyone was situated. "And from what we've researched, all the technology required to implement it exists already. Since Heart has no ground forces willing to combat an enemy face-to-face, and we assume that it would be difficult to find enough volunteers to pilot a large force of armed aircraft, there is only one solution.

"Using the same principles that went into constructing the invisible wall around the farm, a shield could be created to envelop the entire planet. Instead of simply being a barrier, however, the magnetic energy would be strengthened to the point where it would repel anything attempting to penetrate it. In other words, if an enemy ship tried to break through, it would rebound and destroy or cripple itself in the process. If they tried to fire a projectory, it would boomerang back to the ship that launched it. Thus, an attacking force could destroy its own fleet without anyone from Heart having to do a thing."

"That sounds quite logical but what about a friendly visitor?" Parisia asked.

Tarla gave Geoffrey a glance. He had said that would be the first question. "Any approaching ship would be picked up on monitors in a continuously staffed space traffic control tower. The visitor would have to identify themselves and their purpose, and deactivate any weapons systems before being granted entrance. To enforce that, a squadron of ships assigned to constantly patrol the air space inside the shield would be equipped with several devices.

"One, a controller, similar to the one you use to create an opening or repair a weakness in the barrier wall, only on a larger scale. Second, a weapons detection system to scan the visiting ship to make sure they are unarmed or at least deactivated.

"And third, a laser cannon capable of destroying a

large ship if it became necessary. The main reason for this is, we have to assume that an enemy could develop a controller like you have and be able to create an opening in the barrier themselves, in which case it would be the patrol ship's responsibility to stop them before they reached the planet's surface."

Parisia and Iris murmured to each other for a few seconds, then Iris responded for them both. "What you have proposed is so simple, it is somewhat embarrassing that we had not thought of it ourselves, but as we have explained, defense has never been a priority on Heart. There is only one part of the plan that we can immediately foresee as a problem, and you pinpointed it in your opening statement. It could be nearly impossible to recruit pilots for the squadron of patrol ships who would not only have to be trained, but be willing to perform a lethal act."

Tarla nodded her understanding. "Yes, we took that into consideration, and came up with a suggestion. We have already agreed to stay and work for you for as long as a year, although the system we've proposed shouldn't take half that time to install.

"All of these men, and most of our women, are willing to take on the task of patrolling the barrier while you search for trainees to replace them. The rest of the women would supervise the monitoring station. We strongly recommend that you release the remaining men from the commune and allow them to serve as pilots as well. That would give you over a hundred patrol pilots in all, enough to provide uninterrupted surveillance of the entire planet."

Parisia and Iris were clearly disturbed by the idea of having even more free, unmedicated Earth men to deal with. After a little more whispering, Parisia said, "We will consider it, but only if we fail to find enough volunteers ourselves."

Tarla expected that reaction. "Then we have another suggestion we'd like you to consider. If you fail to recruit a hundred women to be trained as pilots, perhaps you need to adjust your laws so that some of your men—"

"Stars above!" Iris exclaimed. "Don't even say it aloud. We have pushed Parliament to the very limits of their tolerance with this defense plan. They would never agree to something that would erode the very foundation of our society."

Tarla had anticipated that as well. "Then we strongly recommend you begin the search among your women immediately. Our agreement was for no longer than one year. When that time is up, we expect you to hold to your part of the bargain and send us back to Earth, whether your defense system is firmly in place or not."

For some time, Parisia and Iris asked more specific questions which, in several cases, had to be answered by others in the group. It was eventually agreed that the Earth women should be on hand when Parisia presents the plan to Parliament the next afternoon, in the event she has difficulty with a question.

Between the concern that the plan would not be approved and the anxiety attached to the women's having to appear before Parliament, the next twenty-four hours dragged by under a cloud of nervous tension. When it was time for them to go, the men decided to wait together in Logan's apartment.

The men's companionship was strained as the first hour melted into a second and a third. By the time they'd finished dinner, they were behaving like trapped animals.

"I gotta get outta here!" T.J. declared and headed for the door. "I'm goin' for a walk."

"Hold it," Logan said, moving quickly to block his

path. "You can't go storming out of here to burn off energy. Somebody could see you acting very *un-*servant-like, and this is definitely not the time to rouse suspicions. Do some pushups instead. Besides, Lee would be very disappointed if you weren't around to hear their news when she gets back."

"Screw her," T.J. said, not really meaning it. In a huff, he marched across the room and out onto the balcony, but his outburst had served to release some of the tension in the apartment.

The moon and stars were shining in a black sky when the women finally returned. The men held their collective breath as the women filed solemnly into the apartment and closed the door behind them.

"The plan was approved with an enormous budget," Tarla announced quietly, and pandemonium erupted the next instant. Squeals, laughter and congratulations were accompanied by hugs and kisses all around. In the midst of the celebrating crowd, Tarla found herself facing Logan, the only one she hadn't hugged. They stood there, staring at each other for several seconds before Logan made a move to walk away.

On impulse, Tarla reached out and caught his arm to stop him. "This is ridiculous," she said and held up her arms to give him a hug too. He responded so slowly, she wondered if time had been somehow slowed down. But then his arms circled her waist and hers went around his neck, and their bodies eased together.

Tarla's eyes drifted shut as they each tightened their hold on the other. "I'm so sorry I hurt you," she whispered. She felt him exhale heavily against her ear and held him even closer. She had no idea how long they were like that before she realized that the room had become silent.

"It sure is getting late," Robin said in a louder than

normal voice. "We'd all better get to bed so we'll be ready to start on phase two tomorrow."

From the expressions on all their faces, Tarla could see that no one was thinking about sleep but they understood that it was time to leave Logan and Tarla alone. At the last moment, Robin pointed to the bedroom and hand-gestured as if she were locking a door. Tarla wrinkled her nose at her and shooed her away.

There is a large gap between knowing something is going to happen and taking the first step toward it, but Tarla managed to take that step. She walked to the doorway of the bedroom and, with a cock of her head, said simply, "In."

He entered but tensed when he saw her close and lock the door. "What's going on?"

"I'm locking you in with me."

Arching one eyebrow, he spoke sarcastically. "You may not have noticed, but the latch is on this side. I could walk out whenever I want."

"It's symbolic," she said, then watched his other eyebrow rise to match the first. "Robin ordered me to lock us in here until we either had sex or killed each other."

Instead of accepting her subtle invitation to sweep her onto the bed for a few hours of unbridled passion, Logan backed away and crossed his arms defensively. "And what if I'd rather not do either?"

Her heart stopped and started again. "How about talking? Would you at least be willing to try that again?"

He paced back and forth a few times before agreeing. "Okay, but we leave this room."

"No."

"No?"

"That's right. This room is where the current

problem between us started. So, this room has to be where it ends."

He frowned, paced and finally leaned against the locked door. "Okay, but no touching, just talking."

"Agreed. Now, since my earlier explanation only made things worse and you don't want me to touch you so you can read my mind, why don't you ask questions and I'll answer."

Logan sighed and crossed his arms. "Okay. Are you human or something else?"

"Humanoid, like everyone else here, only my DNA would show subtle differences because I'm of the Noronian race."

"Where's Norona?"

"A different galaxy from Earth. It can be reached by ship in about two weeks."

He angled his head, looking very skeptical. "How'd you end up being an Army nurse if you're from another planet?"

"Did you really not hear any of what I told you before?" She wanted to get to the important parts, but she ordered herself to be patient. She apologized and again related the highlights of the safe but unfulfilling life in Innerworld that led to her becoming an Outerworld emissary. This time he had a few questions, which she answered as concisely as possible.

"Now tell me about the Noronian mating fever."

He changed the subject so abruptly, she was caught off guard and her cheeks flushed instantly.

"You said you'd answer all my questions," Logan reminded her with a frown.

"Yes, of course. I'm, uh, just trying to figure out the best place to start since it's what made you believe I was a freak."

For the first time, he pushed himself away from the

wall and uncrossed his arms. "Why not start with the truth about what causes it?" He sat on the armless chair on the opposite side of the room from the bed.

Tarla realized he was suddenly comfortable but she had no idea why. "It's a natural part of maturing," she said hedging.

"It didn't look natural to me. What aren't you telling me?"

The way he was looking at her now warned that her answer—her truthful answer—was the only thing that would keep her out of hot water. "When it's time for a Noronian to...to take a mate, the symptoms can become quite extreme, especially if the, uh, treatment is put off for a time."

"I gather *the treatment* is full intercourse, not just having a climax."

"That's right," she said, half-smiling over his quick grasp.

"So, let's say Wilkes had been here instead of me, would you have assaulted him?"

"Gawd no!" she blurted out too quickly. "Even crazed with fever, I'd have to have some attraction!"

An eyebrow raised again. "Geoffrey then. Would you have ordered him to go *deep inside you*?"

Tarla felt her cheeks get hot and couldn't come up with a lie fast enough.

"I see. So, you're saying that not just any warm body can deliver...*the treatment*. But what I don't understand is how you choose your doctor?"

He was making her so nervous, her scalp was beginning to itch. Without thinking it through, she said, "We don't *choose*. It's fate. When our soul's mate appears, we just *know* and when we're of age, the fever is triggered and having intercourse with the mate cools it down but the only permanent cure is to be joined."

"I see," he said again. "Does that mean I'm your soulmate?"

She shook her head in denial. "Don't be ridiculous. You can't be. You're not Noronian. And anyway, I'm pretty sure it was a one-time thing. It's been two weeks without another episode. Besides, I'm well past the time when it should have happened."

"But what if it wasn't just a one-time thing? What if it happens again?"

She swiped at the nervous perspiration beading on her upper lip. "If it does, I'll check in with Heart's medical staff. I'm sure they'd be able to help."

He smirked. "Couldn't you just come to me?"

"Don't worry. I got the message. You hate me and never want me to touch you again."

"I don't hate you," he said quietly.

Tarla was suddenly unable to stand still. She needed air. Her thoughts flew to the shower and the possibility of being drenched in cold water. *Oh dear god no, not now.* She started for the bedroom door but Logan was across the room in a heartbeat.

The instant he closed his hand over her shoulder, he felt the heat. He didn't have a few days to digest everything she'd told him. He didn't even have a few hours to decide how he felt about her lies and deception. A battle had been raging between his head and his heart for two weeks without a decision, and now he only had seconds to turn her away or help cool her down.

"I don't hate you," he repeated and turned her around. Her eyes had not yet filled with blood but she was obviously very uncomfortable. He waited for her expression to change from panic to surrender then picked her up and carried her to the bed.

She tried to speak but he quickly pressed his lips to hers. "Hush. I've got this," he said with a hint of a grin. Seconds later, he had removed their clothes and was kneeling between her thighs. He'd already discovered what she liked and, since he had been unable to shut out the sensual memories despite his freak-out, he would have loved to do a repeat of that night, but this was clearly not the time to be selfish.

She was already very wet and when he stroked her, and when she trembled and whimpered of wanting him, his body surged in sexual response. He understood that foreplay was not what she needed at the moment.

Without further delay, he thrust his shaft deep into her body and let her take the lead after that. He held his own pleasure back until she'd had enough to start cooling down, then he allowed himself to discover what it felt like to truly be with Tarla. *His* Tarla.

Tarla had no idea how long she'd been asleep but she felt rested. She also felt Logan's body pressed against her own. At least this time she'd stayed conscious long enough to make sure he was somewhat satisfied also.

He said he didn't hate her. But he didn't repeat his earlier claims of loving her. Now that she had no doubt that he was the trigger to her fever and that, no matter how improbable it was, he was the man meant to be her other half, she wondered what she could do to renew his trust and bring those thoughts of love back to life.

It wasn't supposed to be this hard. Then again, nothing about her life had ever seemed easy.

What she did know was that no other man's body had ever seemed so familiar, so right, so perfectly fitted to her own.

She also had considerable experience with pleasing a man. That had to be something she could use to work out all their differences. She shifted onto her side to get a peek at him while he slept and couldn't resist placing a soft kiss on his parted lips. Without opening his eyes, he kissed her back, just as lightly. She added a little pressure to the next kiss and he smiled against her closed mouth.

His hand found her hip, eased around to cup her bottom then eased up her side, over one breast and up her throat to her cheek. "You're cool," he murmured.

"Mmm-hmm. Thanks to you."

He moved his hand back to her breast and kneaded it but she moved his hand away. "Go back to sleep," she whispered. "I've got this."

He chuckled and, to show his willingness to fully cooperate, placed both his hands behind his head.

She gave him one more peck on the mouth then let her tongue draw a trail down the side of his neck to a nipple. As she drew it into her mouth with a gentle suck, she felt his chest muscles contract. Three times they'd been intimate and every time, he'd focused on giving her what she needed. He was overdue to have the favor returned.

Her hands and mouth explored his broad shoulders, his muscled chest and abdomen, pleased to note that she hadn't needed to caress his manhood to have it standing at attention for her. Not wanting to be unappreciative, her fingers roamed lower, down between his thighs until they were teasing the soft man flesh there. He opened his legs to give her freer access and she repositioned herself between them.

Logan had managed to keep his eyes closed until she wrapped one hand firmly around his erection while simultaneously rolling his sacs in the other. But when she also closed her mouth over the tip and tongued his opening, his eyes squeezed shut again.

Using every skill she'd ever learned to keep a man

on the verge of climax as long as possible, Tarla played with Logan until she heard the words she awaited.

"Tarla, please!"

She intended to use her mouth to take him through his orgasm but he grasped her shoulders and pulled her upward. "Not like that. I need to be inside you. *Deep* inside you."

She barely had a chance to straddle his hips before he *was* inside her, thrusting, pumping, rolling them to their sides, lying on top of her, pulling out then frantically entering her again from behind, pulling out, turning her onto her back then pushing into her core once again.

The low, growling sounds he was uttering mirrored her own animal need. She hung on the precipice of her own release, instinctively knowing they would only be able to make it to the other side together. She could tell he needed something desperately, yet it was out of his reach. All she could do was cling to him and share her strength.

Suddenly she understood what was happening, knew she couldn't stop it, knew if they didn't give in, one or both of them could lose their minds.

"Logan," she forced out breathlessly. "Hear me. You need to try to calm down. I love you. I have from the moment I saw you." He couldn't stop the motion of his lower body but her words combined with his willpower calmed him considerably. "I'm sorry I doubted your feelings. I need to know if you still love me."

His voice was barely a muffled groan but he managed to say, *"Yes...still...always."*

Hoping he was too distracted to stop her, she brought his fingers to her temples and pressed her fingers to both of his. *Then you'll have to forgive me for what I'm about to do,* she thought directly into his mind.

In a heartbeat, the room was filled with a loud humming sound, the temperature rose abruptly and a coil of golden light swirled around and around their joined bodies, until they were completely immersed in the light.

A moment later they experienced a climax more powerful and more satisfying than either could ever have on their own. Tarla knew this climax, feeling her own and Logan's at the same time, was that of a joined couple.

Expecting Logan to be upset enough without being bombarded by the reality of having their two minds joined, Tarla erected a strong mental block between them. She sat up and waited for him to catch his breath.

"What the hell was that?" Logan muttered, rubbing his forehead. It took him a moment to prop himself up next to her.

"First let me assure you, I only did what I did to save you."

"I know that. Wait, how do I know that?"

"I can answer that in a minute," Tarla said, quickly trying to sort through everything she had to tell him. "Remember how I said you couldn't be my soulmate because you weren't Noronian?"

"Vaguely."

"Well, I believe I may have been mistaken. You see, a long, long time ago, when Noronians first went to Earth, some of them took Terran lovers and had children. That made it possible for a little Noronian DNA to show up in their descendants, even thousands of years later. Based on what just happened, I'd say you're one of those descendants."

He smirked then chuckled. "You're saying I'm part

alien?"

"Looks that way. But then, to be honest, I've always thought of you and all Terrans as aliens."

He started to retort then changed his mind. "Go on."

"If we were on Earth I could take you to Innerworld now that we're joined and they could test you to be certain." His look of bewilderment wasn't lessening. "What just happened, shouldn't have. Not without you experiencing the fever and not without the full ceremonial rituals. The only thing I can imagine is that none of the usual rules applied because of us being on this mirror planet."

Logan sat up straighter and took a deep breath. "You've used the word *joined* before. I'm ready now. Explain."

"It's how the soulmates reconnect and become as one."

"You mean in the spiritual sense?"

"And emotional." She paused. "And mental. I have a block in place to protect you. But whenever you're ready I can remove it."

Logan rubbed the bridge of his nose. "That thing you did, with the fingers against the temples, that was you opening our minds to each other? If you remove the block, I'll know everything you do and vice versa?"

He seemed to be taking the news much better than she'd expected. "Exactly. And feel what I feel and vice versa. Understand, even with the block in place, you may discover you already know some things you didn't before, like how I had to do what I did to save you. Also, if you'd prefer, I can teach you how to create the block."

"And what about the fever?"

She smiled. "All done. Joining is the permanent cure."

"Good to know," he said in a sarcastic tone then stood and headed for the bathroom. "We better get moving."

Tarla had imagined sharing the shower with him this morning but the force with which he slammed the door was far from a sexy invitation. Obviously he wasn't taking the news so well after all. She might have been worried except for one thing—he had admitted he still loved her. She just had to prove how much better being in love was when it went both ways.

"Good God!" Robin muttered as soon as she saw Tarla in the workroom. "You're positively glowing."

Tarla smiled and winked at her. "I took your advice."

"Oo-o-o," Robin sounded, wiggling her eyebrows. "Just tell me two things—did you get any sleep at all last night and is he as hard as he looks?"

"Yes and yes. Now hush before he realizes we're talking about him. Let's just say he hasn't quite given in to my charms yet."

Robin smirked. "He's a man! His automatic assumption would be that we're talking about him. The only question he'd have is how you rated him."

Tarla glanced over at him and looked away when his gaze snared hers. He was very angry. "I think he knows the answer to that too."

"Well, that tears it!" Robin said. "The hell with the agreement. I'm just going to have to tie Geoffrey up and force myself on him, that's all there is to it."

Tarla laughed aloud at the impossibility of Robin forcing herself on Geoffrey. "I have another idea. It's obvious to everyone that you're mad about each other, even if he keeps denying it. The two of you have gotten very close in impersonal ways. Why not get him talking about his background, you know, family, childhood, old girlfriends. You could start it by talking about your own experiences. Somewhere along the line you might dig out the real reason he's putting you off."

"You mean, play psychiatrist instead of seductress?" She considered it for an instant then concluded, "I guess I could try, but that doesn't sound like me."

CHAPTER 20

All her life Tarla had dreamed of the day she would encounter her soul's mate, what his kiss would be like, how different life would be once she was joined with her other half. At no point had she imagined it to be a hellish state of being tolerated.

Two more weeks had passed since she and Logan were joined and yet they were little more than roommates. He had insisted he didn't blame her and that he understood she hadn't had a choice. They were no longer avoiding each other, but they certainly weren't enjoying each other's company either. If she asked him a question, he politely answered, but the only actual conversation focused on the project. She had decided to let him work out their new relationship in his head, without pushing him to talk about it. He had all the facts he needed. He knew she loved him. She was positive he still loved her…underneath several layers of stubbornness and resentment.

She was living with the sexiest man on the planet without getting sex. Enough of being understanding, she decided. Somehow, someway, tonight the stalemate would end!

After dinner that night, she asked him to come into the bedroom to help with a sticking drawer. As soon as he entered, she closed and locked the door.

He gave her a bored look. "What do you think you're doing now?"

"I want sex."

His eyes widened. "I thought you said joining took care of the fever."

"That's right. I didn't say I *needed* sex. I said I *want* it. And since you're my mate, no one else would be able to satisfy me. I gave you two weeks to sulk and get past the terrible, shocking thing that happened to you. Poor Logan, forced to be bonded for eternity with a woman you find so repulsive you can barely look at her let alone touch her."

"You're being ridiculous."

"Poor Logan, his dream of finding the perfect little Terran wife, getting married and living happily ever after in the suburbs, all gone...because of an evil alien who forced herself on him and robbed him of his dream."

He headed for the door but she got in front of him and poked him in the chest. "No! You are not allowed to ignore me any longer. I had dreams too you know. And they didn't include ending up on a mixed-up world, living with a man I love with all my heart and mind, knowing he wishes he'd never met me." Suddenly the truth of her words cut away the patient façade she'd been hiding behind and the tears welled up in her eyes before she could regain control.

"I'm sorry. This was obviously a mistake." She reached for the door lock but Logan covered her hand with his and held it.

"You are so wrong."

She sniffed. "About what?"

"I wasn't sulking. I was...thinking."

"It looked like sulking."

"If I'd been sulking, I would have looked like this." He stuck out his lower lip.

She almost smiled. "So what were you thinking so hard about?"

"Mostly I was trying to figure out who to blame."

"And did you figure it out?"

"Not really. My life's been a string of getting the short end or being in the wrong place at the wrong time. It got so that's all I ever expected. I had fallen in love with a beautiful, sweet woman who made me think of the home in the suburbs and happily ever after—that was you by the way—and I screwed that up. Then I was on my way to life imprisonment. In a way, that was my fault too. But, no matter how much thinking I've been doing, I don't see how my brain being permanently tied to yours could be my fault."

In the middle of all those words, she heard the ones to use against him. "Are you admitting that you had wished for a happily ever after with me specifically?"

He frowned. "Yes, I guess so."

"And you don't find me repulsive?" He smirked at her. "It sounds to me like the negativity that followed you around before we were brought here got reversed. You have your freedom, more or less, you're in a beautiful world, with an important job, people who respect you and you are permanently bonded to the woman you claim to love. It sounds like you should be happy, not sulking."

"I wasn't—Okay, maybe a little. But I would have preferred it to be my idea. I felt like I didn't have a choice."

"If the joining hadn't happened like that, and we'd been able to have a more normal sort of courtship, do you think you might have asked me to marry you, Terran-style?"

He raised her hand to his lips and kissed her knuckles. "Maybe."

"Then let's pretend the joining hasn't happened yet. I'll keep our minds separated as long as you'd like. Forever, if you wish. And whenever you're ready, you'll do the asking. We could even get married for real when we get back if that would make you more comfortable."

"Hmmm. You're very logical for a female."

She poked his chest again, but this time it was with a smile. "I could report you to Iris for that. So? Are we good now?"

He kissed her hand again. "We're good."

"Then may I please have sex now?"

His jaw dropped and he laughed. "I thought you were kidding."

"Don't worry. Since I did the asking, I'll do all the work." She used her poking finger to back him up to the armless chair then tugged his shirt over his head. Her fingers combed through the hair on his chest as she kissed and nibbled one aroused little peak then the other. While her mouth kept him distracted, she loosened the waistband of his pants and eased them and his shorts down to his ankles.

The strength of his erection was visible proof of how she made him feel, but she wanted much more after what he'd put her through the past two weeks. She wanted him to be really sorry he'd waited so long to give in to the inevitable.

Kissing her way down his abdomen, she knelt to help him out of his shoes and clothing. In that position, her hands learned the shape of the hard muscles of his calves and thighs, then moved up to squeeze his well-formed buttocks and lick his taut stomach. She softly blew her warm breath along his arousal, making him twitch in response before she touched him with her hands.

Wanting to bring him as close to the edge as possible, she teased him with her tongue and teeth until his fingers tangled in her hair to still her head. She knew what he wanted and gave it to him...for a few seconds. But as soon as he began moving rhythmically within her mouth, she backed away and stood up.

He swayed a little after her untimely departure and tried to bring her closer, but she pushed him down onto the chair behind him and stepped back.

With a seductive smile, she slowly opened the closures on her caftan. "Now, Logan, you know I'm not going to make it that easy. Not after how crazy you've made me. Besides, between the drugs and the fever, you've never been with the *real* Tarla." She let her robe and chemise slide off her shoulders and down to her waist, baring her breasts to his gaze.

"I know you watch me sometimes when you think I'm not looking. The next time you do that, I want you to see this." Her hands cupped her breasts, lifting and kneading them as she watched him curl his hands into fists. "See how thoughtful I am? I'm saving you the trouble of preparing me for your entry."

Her hands pushed the caftan to the floor then shimmied out of her chemise and underpants. Her fingers grazed over her belly to the nest of black curls below. She parted her legs so he could clearly see how she stroked herself and how very damp she was already.

After a few seconds, she stopped and opened her eyes. "It's not the same as when you touch me, Logan." She closed the distance between them, put her arms around his neck and tongue-kissed him for several long seconds before saying, "I would very much like to have sex with you now."

In one swift movement, he cupped her bottom and settled her on his shaft with her legs straddling his lap and the chair, while delivering an eating kiss that left no doubt that he planned to use her at least as much as she intended to use him. She felt the tip of his shaft pressed against her core and moaned her need into his mouth. She rode him slowly and rhythmically then faster and harder as his kisses ravaged her mouth and encouraged her not to hold anything back.

It felt as though his hands were everywhere at once, gliding over her hair, her face, her breasts, back and hips, feeding her desire while tempting her to make the pleasure last, it was impossible to hold off the rampaging flood of sensation that took possession of both her body and her mind. She felt and heard Logan succumb to his climax within a second of her own and realized she had lowered the block between their minds and feelings.

"It's okay," Logan whispered next to her ear. "I'm still not ready for you to be in my head twenty-four/seven, but during sex, well, I definitely get that part. In fact..." He rose, holding her in place, and moved to the bed. "I can't wait to do it again."

Barely giving her a moment to catch her breath, his body was again arousing hers, demanding she stay with him in that other world where nothing mattered but giving and taking pleasure. Without another thought, she turned the next round over to him.

Despite Robin's best efforts to follow Tarla's advice, Geoffrey thwarted her at every turn. She suspected that he saw right through her attempts to steer their relationship onto more personal ground, but then subtlety never had been one of her strong traits. As the days of their second month together turned into weeks, she accepted the fact that he was going to hold out until the last minute of the postponement he had agreed to.

But the morning of that day had finally dawned. Anticipation had Robin bouncing out of bed with more energy than usual, but she determined not to say a word to Geoffrey until they were alone in their apartment that night. There was no sense warning him in advance and giving him all day to think up another excuse to put her off.

Seeing how happy Tarla was hadn't improve Robin's frustration level during her waiting time. The glow she had noticed in Tarla's eyes after she and Logan finally solved their problems was now obvious to everyone. The two of them openly shared glances across the room that were so meaningful, it was almost as though they could read each other's thoughts.

Another mysterious thing she didn't understand was what was going on between Logan and Jason. Being a connoisseur of handsome men, Robin couldn't help but be aware of the changes in the young man regardless of how innocuous he was most of the time.

When he had first shown up, Jason was very much like the old men on the farm. Now, two months later, his eyes seemed more focused. He was able to follow conversations even when several people were talking at once. She even thought he appeared more confident, though that could be because Logan kept reminding him to stand up straight and raise his chin and look him in the eye when they spoke to each other.

These things could have been her imagination but the change in his physical appearance was definitely real. He'd put on enough pounds that it was noticeable. Rather than the extra weight making him soft and pudgy like other Heart men though, it seemed to be having the opposite effect on Jason, almost as if he were working out. Overall, he just looked more masculine.

Robin had asked Tarla about all the private conversations she saw Logan and Jason having, but she said that, other than saying that he liked the kid, Logan was being very secretive about it.

Fortunately, their project was keeping everyone too busy to fret over any little things for long. With the backing of Parliament and the extravagant budget, Parisia had been able to assign all the technical staff needed to carry out the details of the plan. A factory was turned over to them and prepared for the new work that would be accomplished there—making weapons and converting passenger craft to patrol ships.

Once the actual labor began, the team of Earthlings were able to concentrate on learning how to fly the aircraft and developing the operating systems for the space traffic control tower. Mastering the lessons needed to pilot the ships turned out to be easier than driving a car. Nevertheless, Tarla, Kara, Mandy and Charlene elected to remain closer to the ground in tower supervision assignments.

The only real obstacle they had encountered so far was Parisia's hedging about bringing the rest of the men over from the farm. She kept insisting that the search for volunteers among their women was proceeding, and they might not need to do anything that could upset Parliament when they were being so cooperative.

As Geoffrey served Robin her breakfast, she had to bite her tongue half a dozen times so as not to alert him about what day it was. Once they got to work at the factory, she actually managed to forget about it herself for several minutes at a time. She even forced herself to sit still through an unusually long dinner with Kara and Ray without revealing how anxious she was to go home.

However, when Kara yawned without trying to hide it, Robin could have kissed her for finally giving them an excuse to leave.

"Oh, Kara, I'm sorry. We're keeping you up," she said, looking as if she just realized the time. "Come on, Geoff. Time to toddle off, mate."

She was mentally congratulating herself on being an academy award class actress as they entered their apartment. Certain he was still unaware of what day it was, she vacillated between saying a few words to ease into the fact that she hadn't changed her mind about wanting a closer relationship with him or simply tackling him to the floor.

She was about to go for the tackle, when he practically ran to the bathroom. Thinking he was ill, she went to the closed door and knocked. "Geoff? Are you all right?"

"I'm fine. Just thought I'd take a shower before bed."

Robin smiled. He usually took his shower in the morning. Maybe he knew what day it was after all and was planning to surprise *her*. Quickly she retrieved the gold ribbon she had put away for this moment, then stripped off her clothes. After tying the ribbon around her neck with a pretty bow, she checked her image in the mirror and decided against greeting him so blatantly. Finally, she remained nude with the gold ribbon, but got on the bed with the sheet covering her from the waist down.

With thoughts of the night ahead filling her mind, she was ready to go back to the idea of tackling him by the time he finally emerged from the bathroom. She expected him to laugh, or be surprised or at least join her on the bed. She did not expect him to take one brief look at her, groan, and cover his eyes as if he couldn't bear the sight of her.

"Oh, my God," she whispered as reality crashed in on her. Tarla had been right about him not giving her his true reason for not wanting to consummate their relationship. She just had never considered the possibility that he found her unappealing. She yanked off the silly tie and buried her face in the pillow so she wouldn't have to watch him walk out of the room. Before she could stop it, a frustrated wail escaped her.

She felt his hand on her shoulder but refused to raise her head. The last thing she wanted was his pity.

"Aah, Robin, please don't cry," he murmured, stroking her hair.

"I'm not crying. Just humiliated," she stuttered into the pillow. "I feel like a complete ass!" She felt his weight on the mattress beside her.

"If there's an arse in this room, it's me, not you."

She shook her head. "Don't try to be nice. That's been the problem all along. If you had just come right out and said you really had no interest in me—"

"No interest?" He turned her onto her back and made her look up at him. "I'm on fire day and night from wanting you."

She sniffled and swiped at a tear trickling down her cheek. "I don't understand."

He caught another tear with his finger and wiped it away. "No, I wouldn't expect you to. As you once said, you go after what you want. You'd never let something pass you by for fear that it might cause more pain than pleasure."

"Will you please speak American?"

He gave her a shy smile. "My experience with beautiful women taught me that they are fickle creatures. You being the most beautiful woman I have ever seen, I was certain your interest in me was fleeting at best. Though I couldn't avoid you completely, I thought if we at least didn't go to bed together, I could stop myself from falling in love with you, thus preventing a broken heart."

"That is one of the dumbest things I have ever heard," she said with a grimace.

"Dumb and utterly futile. I fell in love with you anyway."

Robin's eyes filled with moisture all over again as he took her into his arms. "Well, it's about time you wretched man, because I've been in love with you forever."

As his lips met hers in the kiss that would mark the beginning of their life together, she only regretted that she hadn't tried bursting into tears two months ago.

Fulton massaged his temples to ease the discomfort in his head. He didn't want to think about what he had just heard, but it wouldn't go away. He liked working for Simone. She never scolded him or made him hurt inside the way Nadia did. She never threatened to stop him from seeing Chloe. He had felt good since Nadia left and Simone came to stay.

But what he had just heard could change that. Simone and four women who had visited her before were making plans to bring Nadia home. The mere thought of having to go back to serving her made Fulton's head hurt worse.

He had heard Nadia had done something bad and that the Imperial Prefect had punished her. Though he didn't know what Nadia had done, he did understand that she was supposed to stay away and that Simone and her friends did not agree with the punishment. They were also very upset about something called Parisia's defense plan and thought they could stop it by freeing Nadia.

Simone was now his employer, but the Imperial Prefect was hers. It was bad to do something against the wishes of one's employer. So, Simone must be planning something bad. If she succeeded, Nadia would be back, and he *knew* that was bad.

He felt as though he should do something about it, but what? The law forbade him from approaching any woman other than his employer.

Certain the thoughts that were making his head hurt would soon go away by themselves, Fulton distracted himself by washing the dishes from Simone's meeting.

He realized how important this matter was when he hadn't forgotten about it by the next morning. Fulton's head felt a little better when he awoke, but upsetting dreams had kept him from getting a good night's sleep. *Nadia was back.* Tormenting. Scolding. Frightening and petting him. There had to be a way to stop the dream from coming true.

Later that day, while he was at the marketplace, he saw Jason, the Imperial Prefect's son, and an idea occurred to him. Nadia had always hated it when he tried to make a decision on his own, but Simone had praised him when he had something ready for her before she asked for it. Good or bad, he had to tell somebody what he heard, and if Jason would listen, he could possibly pass it on to his sister. And then Fulton's head would stop hurting completely.

He barely got his information out when Jason grasped his arm and started pulling him away from the marketplace.

"Can't you move a little faster?" Jason asked in the kind of impatient tone that Nadia usually used.

Fulton pushed himself but he was already feeling a little dizzy from trying to keep up. There was

something curious about Jason's behavior, but
confusion over their destination took precedence in
his brain. He obediently followed Jason to a big room
on the top floor of a residence. There, four men and
two women were seated around a table with Brianne
of Acameir. They had papers in front of them, as if
they were having a meeting.

*But men were not permitted to sit at the same table
with women.*

Jason left Fulton by the door while he went over and
whispered something to a man with dark hair.
Fulton's confusion turned to shock when that man
looked directly at Brianne and suggested she hear
what their visitor had to say. He tensed, waiting to see
what horrible punishment she would deliver to that
man, but all she did was rise and walk beside him and
Jason.

Jason introduced Fulton to Logan then Brianne put
him at ease again by addressing him. "You have
permission to speak in front of me."

Fulton kept his head bowed as he related what
information he had retained. "My employer, Simone,
has met with four women in her residence many
times." He paused to glance at Jason for reassurance.

"Tell them what you told me," Jason said. "What do
they talk about when they meet?"

"I do not usually listen," he said for Brianne's
benefit. "But sometimes they speak loudly. About the
Imperial Prefect and Brianne. And…and Nadia."

Jason gave him a prompt to continue. "You heard
them talking last night…"

Fulton looked at him curiously. There was definitely
something different about him but he could not tell
what it was. His gaze moved to the man called Logan.
There was also something very unusual about him.

"*Fulton*," Jason prodded. "Last night."

"Yes. Last night they were making plans to bring Nadia back home."

Brianne gasped. "That's ludicrous. They wouldn't dare."

Logan frowned at her and said, "Is it possible for this man to lie?"

Fulton felt Brianne staring at him and tried to make himself disappear.

"No," she replied. "It must be true. Did you hear how they planned to do this?"

Fulton nodded. "One of the women, Olympia, had a box she called a controller."

After a few seconds, Jason had to give him another push. "Now tell them what you heard them say they will do after they bring Nadia back."

Fulton swallowed nervously. This was the part that had made Jason grab his arm. He prepared himself for another strange reaction. "They are going to go to the Imperial Palace while Parisia, Brianne and Iris are asleep. They plan to take them away and Nadia will be made the Imperial Prefect."

"They speak treason!" Brianne exclaimed. "I must warn my mother and Iris immediately."

"Call and have them come here," Logan said. "Maybe we can help." He turned back to Fulton. "Did they say when they were planning to act?"

Fulton frowned. "I...I don't know. But I think it was soon." They made him promise not to repeat any of what he had told them, or let Simone know he had revealed her plans. Then, much to his relief, they allowed him to leave before the Imperial Prefect and her Advisor arrived.

"How did Parisia and Iris take the news?" Tarla asked Logan as they cleaned up the dinner dishes together.

"They were shocked right out of their perfect manners. Apparently, Nadia's been a pain in the ass for years but no one ever attempted to overthrow the government before."

"So, is Parisia going to take these women into custody or what?"

Logan drained the soapy water from the sink. "She can't. Fulton isn't permitted to testify against a woman. Besides that, Iris thought Nadia and her friends needed to be caught in the act to prove to everyone that they really are traitors."

That word hung in the air between them but neither voiced their thoughts. Dealing with Logan's frame-up was a matter for a future time. "How does she intend to do that?" she asked. "Or should I say, what plan did *you* come up with?"

Logan gave her a modest smile. "Fulton is supposed to let Jason know if he hears anything else but we can't depend on him. Because a few doubts keep popping up about the validity of the video of Nadia and Higgs, Iris doesn't want to simply rely on recordings made by a camera. She's decided they need impartial human witnesses to put a stop to the gossip once and for all. Parisia is assigning a group of women to secretly watch the barrier around the clock. She told them she heard a rumor that some Earth men are planning an escape.

"The instant anyone from the farm is seen coming through, the message will be passed along a string of observers, all the way to the palace. These women will be instructed not to interfere with the escapees' progress and also to prevent anyone else in the area from getting in the way.

"Our ten men, Alicia, and Lee will be waiting for them inside the palace, where Iris is going to make sure there are reliable witnesses to whatever happens."

"But how will you know when to expect them?"

"We won't, unfortunately. We'll just have to set it up and wait."

Tarla narrowed her brows. "Beginning…"

"In two hours," he finished for her.

"Until…"

He met her worried gaze and warmth seeped into his heart. "Until it's over."

"But that could be days…or weeks." She took a step closer and let her eyes tell him what she was thinking.

With a sexy smile, he eased her into his embrace. "True. It's impossible to tell how long I'll have to stay at the palace."

Wrapping her arms around his neck, she murmured, "Then I'd say we'd better make the most of the next two hours."

"My thought exactly," he whispered, as he picked her up in his arms and carried her to the bedroom.

Three days later, Tarla could barely concentrate on her work. Excuses for visiting the palace kept disrupting her sensible thoughts. She hadn't expected to miss Logan so much in such a short time.

Being in the apartment without him was more nerve-wracking than when she and Logan had been trying to avoid each other. She missed seeing him across the kitchen table, watching him shave, sharing the shower with him, waking up in his arms. Somehow, in the hours since he'd accepted his *bondage* to her, she'd become addicted to his presence. When he was near, she felt secure, protected, cherished and desired, all at the same time. When he wasn't, she felt…*alone*.

She hoped the day would come when he felt comfortable with her in his head all the time but for now, she had to be content with sharing their feelings only when they were making love.

At one o'clock in the morning, Simone and her small band of daring rescuers donned their black, hooded capes. They had purposely chosen a cloudy, moonless night, and didn't want to take any chances of being spotted or identified ahead of time.

Olympia carried the controller that would get them through the barrier, and they each had a canister of paralyzer spray in case they should encounter any of the savage Earth men along the way.

As Simone had assumed, all the men had retired by the time the women entered the commune. Since she had studied the recordings made by the sky monitor, she had little difficulty locating Nadia's tent.

Also from the recordings, she knew there was usually a man in the tent with her, so she thought it best to get Nadia to come outside to talk. "Nadia," Simone whispered into the dark tent. "Are you in there? It's Simone." When she heard no response, she poked her head inside.

Suddenly she was grabbed and held immobile by a powerful arm across her waist and a hand around her throat. All she could manage was a squeak of warning to the others but they were too terrified to run.

Olympia was the only one who thought to use her spray. As she pointed the canister above Simone's head, however, Nadia exclaimed, "Stop! Guy, please let her go, she's a friend."

Simone felt the clamp on her throat loosen, but the monster bracing her against his huge body didn't release her as Nadia had ordered.

"First we find out why she's here," he said in a chilling voice. "Then I'll decide whether to let her go. Get your ass outside with the rest of them so I can see what's going on."

Simone could not believe her eyes as Nadia practically jumped to obey his command. Since when did anyone—least of all a man—order Nadia to do anything?

Once he'd hauled her outside as well, the big man gave another order. "Everybody give Nadia your weapons and anything else you brought with you. And let me see some faces." When they hesitated, his fingers circled Simone's throat again and tightened painfully enough to cause her to whimper. "Do as I say or I break this one's neck."

That threat got him what he wanted and he ended his choke hold. Without letting her move away, he pulled back Simone's hood and gave her hair a hard tug to make her look around toward him. "Hmmm. I'm glad to see not all Heart's women are ugly cows like Nadia."

Simone's shock at his impertinence was surpassed by Nadia's failure to do anything but bow her head in shame.

"Now, explain," he said simply and gave Simone's hair another yank so she'd know he was speaking to her.

The slight pain didn't bother her nearly as much as the way he combed his fingers through her curls and stroked her neck when she began to speak. "We have come to bring Nadia back and put her on the throne." With the man scaring her half to death, the speech she had planned didn't come out as intelligently as she'd intended.

Simone told of how many women were suspicious of the recording Parisia had used against Nadia and how they disapproved of the new defense plan but were afraid they would be exiled like Nadia if they spoke out against it. There were also serious concerns about the Earth women and men who had been freed among the more civilized Heart residents.

And finally, taking care that only Nadia would understand what she referred to, Simone said, "To protect your interests while you were gone, I moved into your home, took temporary custody of Chloe and maintained Fulton's employment. He is quite a devoted and *well-trained* servant. I found his assistance with my personal toilette particularly...*stimulating*."

Nadia's one eyebrow arched in comprehension. "Am I to understand that you approve of the way I trained him?"

"Absolutely. And I think there are other women who should be told—"

"Enough!" Guy growled. "I don't give a damn about how you train those sissies you call men. I want to hear how you figured on putting Nadia on a throne."

Simone had to fight the fear he instilled in her. "I...*we* thought that a direct takeover would be most effective. It would never be expected and, if we got Parisia, Brianne, and Iris out of the way entirely, we could fabricate a story about them fleeing the planet with the imperial treasury. At the same time, Nadia could explain how she was unjustly accused, creating a mood of sympathy and support for her as the new Prefect. We were hoping Nadia would have some ideas of her own to add once we got here."

Nadia's gaze scanned the expectant faces before speaking. "This is the best idea I can offer. Go home. Continue to talk privately to other women about your concerns until the number of our supporters grows. Then, in five years when I am released, the transition of power will occur as smoothly as the sun rises each morning."

"Five years?" Simone asked incredulously. "We

were hoping you would come back with us now."

Nadia shook her head. "The risks are too great. You must be more patient."

"Hold it," Guy said, finally releasing his grip on Simone and turning her to face him. "Are we talking a real throne and palace and servants? Crown jewels? Stuff like that?"

"Of course," Simone replied, trying to smooth the wrinkles he'd made in her caftan. "The Imperial Prefect has enormous wealth."

"And power?" he asked.

She grimaced at his ignorance. "She rules the entire planet of Heart."

Guy rubbed his jaw thoughtfully and paced back and forth a few times. "Are the Earth people in the palace?"

"No, but they are all housed in a residential complex a short distance away," Simone answered.

"What kind of resistance were you expecting between here and the palace?"

Simone frowned and shook her head. "I do not understand."

"Who might try to stop you? Police? Security?"

"We have no need for human security on Heart. Everything is monitored and recorded by computer. On a night such as this, however, it is too dark and cloudy for the sky monitors to pick up a clear picture. No one saw us coming here. It will be the same going back."

"Damn!" Guy exclaimed, slapping his thigh. "It's almost too easy. Okay. Here's what we're going to do. I got at least a dozen men who'll follow me if I tell 'em to. That should wipe out any risk. First we grab the broads you talked about and stash 'em back here. Then we take out our own people to make sure they don't make waves neither. Sounds like we could all be sittin' pretty in about twenty-four hours!"

Nadia grasped his arm. "Guy, please listen to me. This is not wise."

Without a pause, he backhanded her cheek. "Shut your mouth, bitch. I'm gonna make you a queen."

CHAPTER 21

"Heads up," Logan said, shaking Geoffrey's shoulder. "We're about to have visitors." Between the two of them, they had their group awake and alert in a matter of seconds. Using the wrist communicator Iris had given him, he notified her next. According to plan, she took care of getting the impartial witnesses, plus Parisia, Brianne and herself, into the specially constructed space off the enormous foyer, where they would be safe from danger while still able to observe the proceedings.

As Logan had instructed, dim lights remained on throughout the palace at all times so that an intruder would not be able to slip by unnoticed.

Logan counted heads to make sure every one of his people were present. "Okay. It looks like our waiting has finally paid off. About two hours ago, I got a report from observer two that five hooded figures disrupted the barrier and entered the commune. Just now those five came back out, but they brought a hell of a lot more than Nadia out with them. Apparently some of our men decided they'd had enough of farming."

"How many?" Geoffrey asked.

Before Logan could answer, his communicator beeped. "Go ahead," he said into the tiny speaker.

"Um, this is observer seven," a woman said in a clearly flustered tone. She and the others had been warned that a man could answer, but that didn't make it acceptable. "A large number of suspicious looking people just walked by my post. Most of them were men, but I'm sure there were several women also."

"How many altogether?"

"Um, they were moving too fast to count but I would estimate fifteen to twenty."

"Good work. Out." Pressing the button to end the communication, he said, "That's about the same number the first observer guessed. Higgs, do those two locations help any?"

Higgs showed him the map he was holding. He had already marked the third and seventh posts.

Logan took one quick glance and with his finger drew a line down one street and across another to the palace. "Since they aren't expecting a reception, they probably won't bother to make any detours. The only question is which way they'll come in. They aren't carrying ladders, and we've made sure there's nothing on the grounds to help them scale the walls, so we can probably go with our original assumption."

There were twenty ground floor entrances, all of which were securely locked except the kitchen. Brianne had told them everyone knew that door was often left unlocked for deliveries. Thus, unless Simone managed to get hold of the palace keys, they would probably head for the kitchen entrance. To get to the tower where the imperial suites were located from the kitchen, the would-be revolutionaries had to pass through the foyer.

The furnishings had previously been arranged to

provide hiding places for the Earthlings lying in wait, so that the intruders would not be aware of the trap until they were all within the foyer.

Logan received four more reports in quick succession which confirmed that Simone was indeed leading her group directly to the kitchen door.

"That's it," Logan said. "T.J. and Lee—go on to the kitchen, just like we planned. As soon as the last one's inside, you follow them at a distance and block any attempted retreat. Greg and Alicia—up the stairs to the first landing just in case someone makes it that far.

"Everybody remember what we promised. If at all possible, avoid physical violence. We're being watched and recorded, and it would help Parisia a lot if we appeared to be civilized. Make sure your laser pistols are set for extended stun. No higher, no lower. You've all had plenty of practice with these new weapons, so I don't expect to see any of you getting caught in crossfire."

Geoffrey gave them their final instruction. "We still don't know for certain, but since it is possible that they are armed with paralyzer spray, put your masks on and keep them on until you are advised that the air is safe to breathe. Good luck."

They quickly shook hands all around, donned their masks, and went to their assigned positions. Logan's communicator beeped one more time with a report from an observer just outside the kitchen door then he turned off the sound. They had repeatedly timed the walk from the kitchen to the foyer so that they would know approximately when to expect the uninvited guests, but counting off the passing seconds only served to increase the anticipation.

Finally, a short figure tiptoed into the room, followed by several taller ones. The men and women in hiding had been ordered not to reveal themselves until they heard T.J. whistle, which would mean the last rebel was inside the foyer.

Logan was beginning to wonder if the observers had all been wrong about the number of people involved, when T.J. gave the awaited signal.

Before Simone's group had a chance to analyze the sound, Logan's team opened fire. Streaks of silent light zapped one bewildered intruder after another, instantly stealing their consciousness. As they dropped to the floor, some of those who had been shielded attempted to use the paralyzer spray, but it was no match against the laser pistols.

The entire confrontation was finished in less than a minute.

By the time Tarla awoke that morning, every household in the city was buzzing about the failed coup. As soon as she heard on the news that it had happened hours before, and yet Logan had not come home, she was seized by panic. Immediately she tried to reach Brianne but no one at the palace was accepting calls. She then contacted the other seven women to make sure they'd heard also. Thoughts of their men being injured sent them racing to the sanatorium.

They were told a number of people had been confined there during the night, but none were the men they sought. At least they were able to confirm that the incident at the palace did not result in any fatalities.

Though the women had been advised not to go to the palace previously, they were too worried to care about protocol.

As it turned out, there was so much activity in and around that building, they had to work at getting attention. Eventually, they were led up a long flight of stairs that ascended to Parisia's tower suite.

Tarla's fear was replaced by annoyance the moment she entered the parlor. The group of men and women she'd been so worried about were enjoying a leisurely breakfast. The men all rose to their feet as soon as they saw who their visitors were.

Robin's temper exploded the quickest but the others were right behind her. "Why didn't you call to let us know you were all right?"

"Do you have any idea how upset we were?"

"We went to the sanatorium, thinking you could have been hurt!"

Parisia stood and held out her hands. "Ladies, please forgive me. Your friends are not at fault. I am. Another crisis arose as they were about to leave and I detained them again. We did make an attempt to contact each of you, but you must have already left your apartments."

The women had to accept Parisia's gracious apology and explanation, though there was still a good deal of tension reverberating through the room.

Tarla walked over to Logan with her heart pounding against her ribs. The sight of him standing there, unhurt and looking like he missed her as much as she missed him, melted away any irritation. She knew Parisia and Iris would not approve, but she couldn't wait another second to touch him. Her need was mirrored in his eyes, but they both restrained it and limited the contact to discreetly holding one another's hand and sitting side by side on a sofa.

The others followed their lead and Parisia and Iris pretended not to notice the forbidden behavior. On the other hand, Brianne had spent so much time with the Earthlings she was no longer shocked by all the touching that went on between the sexes.

"Ladies, please have some breakfast," Parisia said,

"while we bring you up to date. Logan, perhaps it would be best if you related the events that led up to the capture of our dissidents."

Tarla thought he sounded terribly tired while he stated the highlights of what happened during the night. She squeezed his hand, passed a little of her energy over to him and he gave her a grateful smile.

Logan brought his report to an end as quickly as he could. "Once they were all unconscious, we were able to identify them. It wasn't much of a surprise to see that the men were Wilkes and twelve of his pals. What *is* a surprise is, why so few? Why didn't more of the men break out if they had a chance?"

Geoffrey gave a possible answer. "We hope it was because Gianni was able to convince them not to cause trouble, but we're not so sure that makes sense. Parisia has given us permission to go into the commune when we leave here and check on the men who stayed behind."

"We were told at the sanatorium that a number of people had been confined there," Tarla said to Parisia. "Have you decided what you're going to do about them?"

She nodded. "They are being heavily medicated at this time. In a week or so, once they are sufficiently reoriented, they will all be exiled to the Earth commune for a period of no less than twenty years. Our people are working on a new means of administering future doses of the antidote that will not be avoidable, as the water was."

Tarla didn't like the sound of that, not as long as there were still innocent Earth men in that commune who could be affected as well. There had to be a way to protect them.

"I am not certain there is an adequate way to express our appreciation for what you did for my family," Parisia said. "Without your help, I doubt we could have prevented a disaster."

"Just make sure you include Fulton and Jason in that appreciation," Logan reminded her. "Without them, you wouldn't have been warned ahead of time."

"Yes, of course," Parisia agreed. "We intend to reward them with some special privileges."

"Lucky them," Logan muttered under his breath, and Tarla squeezed his hand again.

Parisia frowned. "As I was saying, we are extremely grateful for everything you have done on our behalf, but I'm afraid we must ask you for even more." She paused and gave Iris a slight nod.

Though her face remained passive, Iris's nervousness showed as she cleared her throat, straightened her spine, rearranged her caftan and clasped her hands together on her lap. After a few more seconds of hesitation, she said, "Parisia mentioned another crisis that arose this morning. The news we received would have been horrendous at any time but, for it to come in the aftermath of the attempted takeover seems almost too much to bear."

It took her another moment to organize her thoughts. "We are a neutral planet, unaffiliated with any universal organization. However, the United Planetary Association sends us reports and advisories that might be of interest or import to us. Usually, by the time we receive something, it is relatively old news. That was not the case this morning.

"A courier arrived an hour ago from UPA on a ship equipped with faster-than-light capability. His orders were to personally deliver a confidential letter from the UPA President to Parisia. Allow me to preface what the letter stated by saying that sufficient proof and details were provided to remove any doubts as to the authenticity of the information gathered by UPA agents."

She paused again and shared a look of grave concern with Parisia. "This is the crux of the matter. The rumors about the Velids that we heard a few months ago have now been substantiated. They do exist and they are intent on destroying the human race. It has also been confirmed that the humanoid population on at least four known planets was completely annihilated by the Velids. To make a catastrophic situation worse, there is evidence that they have acquired plans for an FTL transport, which means distance will no longer be an obstacle to their goals."

"How much time do we have?" Logan asked, jumping directly to the bottom line.

Parisia sighed. "As Logan has already concluded, the Velids may already be on their way to Heart. The UPA sources could not uncover any specific timetable. They were only able to warn us of impending danger."

"The good news," Geoffrey said, "is that we're almost ready for them. Weapons development and ship conversion is nearly completed. The barrier is ready for final testing, the space traffic control tower is operational and strategies have been worked out to combat a wide range of eventualities."

Logan wasn't as confident. "There's still one big piece missing. We have yet to start training the additional pilots needed to patrol the barrier."

Parisia and Iris exchanged another one of their looks before Parisia responded. "We thought we had more time and didn't need to force the recruitment so soon."

"Have you found anyone willing to train?" asked Tarla.

Parisia's cheeks flushed a little as she admitted,

"No, not yet."

"Then there is only one solution, as distasteful as it seems to you," Tarla declared. "After discounting those involved in the attempted takeover, there are still eighty-four able-bodied men with wartime experience inside the commune. They could be trained in a matter of weeks, and with them, you wouldn't be taking the chance they might panic when the time came to act, the way some of your women might."

Brianne spoke up for the first time since the women had sat down. "I agree with Tarla," she told her mother. "We have no other realistic choice. Parliament will endorse anything you suggest right now. But to keep the situation under control, perhaps the additional men could be housed in the flight center outside of the city where they would be training."

Parisia murmured a few words to Iris, who then gave a reluctant nod and asked, "Tarla, do you think those men would agree to remain isolated and stay away from the women in the city if we freed them?"

"The only men who could not be trusted to cooperate are the ones in your sanatorium right now. I believe the rest of them will agree to anything that would save their lives and eventually get them back home. Logan? Geoffrey? What do you think?"

"We definitely need them," Geoffrey said.

Logan added, "If anyone causes a problem after he's released, he'll immediately be sent back to the farm. That should be threat enough to keep them in line."

As Brianne had pointed out, they had no other choice. Since time had suddenly become of great importance, Parisia had Brianne escort their twenty guests to the transfer room and into the commune immediately.

They did not have long to wait before all the men

began gathering in the big house for lunch. Expecting something close to a surprise homecoming celebration, it was bewildering when their presence was barely noticed…until Tarla caught sight of Gianni and several other of their men across the room, getting themselves water directly from the hand pump. "Logan, look over there, at Gianni."

"Oh, no," he groaned as soon as he spotted the man. "That's why so few men broke out with Wilkes. They've been drinking the water."

"What are we going to do now?"

"Exactly what we came to do—take them back with us."

Tarla wrinkled her forehead. "But if they've been consuming the antidote for any length of time, their aggressive natures have been neutralized and their reflexes are probably shot."

Logan leaned closer and murmured, "The effect of the drug is reversible, even after years of taking it." He waited to see if she could figure out how he knew that.

Realization brightened her eyes. "Jason?"

"Right," he answered with some pride. "He was given regular doses for more than ten years, but in only two months without it—"

"He's starting to look and behave more like a healthy human male," Tarla said, finishing his sentence. "So, *that's* what you've been up to with him! I should have guessed. Is that why you didn't want to let me into your head?"

He shrugged. "I may have one or two other secrets."

She rose up on her tiptoes and kissed his cheek. "You're a good man, Logan McKay. Of course, Parisia would probably exile you if she found out."

"True, but so far, Jason's been careful to behave the way she'd expect him to when he's around her. I'm only surprised that she hasn't noticed any change in his appearance."

Tarla shrugged. "Maybe she has and doesn't disapprove as strongly as she's supposed to."

He arched an eyebrow at her. "Hmmm. Let's just deal with one problem at a time."

Much to everyone's relief, the men who had been left behind on the farm had not become total puppet people. Aware of the drug, most of them had limited the amount of water drunk each day. They were clearheaded enough to understand that they were being freed, while sufficiently relaxed to follow any orders they were given.

With Brianne's help, the slightly tranquilized men were efficiently herded through the transfer room and onto shuttles that took them straight to the flight center. It was decided that someone had to stay and babysit the newcomers until their minds cleared enough for them to comprehend what was going on. Geoffrey, Robin, T.J., and Lee volunteered to take the first shift, while Brianne made arrangements for beds, food and other necessary supplies to be delivered. Everyone else was finally free to go home and catch up on their sleep.

In spite of all the things they could have discussed on the way back to their residence, Tarla and Logan made the trip in silence. She assumed exhaustion had him too tired to talk. For her, it was a matter of having too many things to say. Her assumption about his state of fatigue was proven wrong the moment they were inside their apartment.

She was about to ask if he'd like something to eat or drink when he abruptly pulled her against him and his mouth stole the words right out of hers. She didn't need to be privy to his thoughts to know that this kiss told of long nights of unsatisfied need for her.

Unlike the gentle, beautiful way he usually made love to her, what he was doing to her now was closer to the primitive assaults of their pre-joining encounters. He was completely out of control as his tongue stabbed at hers and his fingers tore at the closures on her caftan.

And she couldn't have loved it more.

She hadn't even known how desperate she had been to feel his hands on her breasts until they were there, molding her flesh and feeding the runaway fire his kisses had ignited. He was behaving like an uncivilized animal, and it was exactly what she needed to release her pent-up frustration.

Her fingers tangled in his hair to force him to hold still for a return attack on his mouth. There would be time for leisurely lovemaking later. With no further preliminaries, she yanked open his pants and pushed them over his hips while his hands were just as hurriedly lifting her caftan and underslip and disposing of her panties.

She gasped once as his body roughly pinned hers up against the wall and made her feel the raw power of his desire. But she brought him inside and used him with a savagery that belied her smaller size.

She lowered the mental block and hungrily seized everything he had to give her.

He welcomed the blending of their minds and devoured all she had to give him.

And the explosive release of their combined physical and emotional selves left them trembling in its wake.

Wordlessly, Logan carried her to the bathroom where they shared a shower that was much more arousing than cleansing. When they finally made it to the bed, they were again frantic to join their bodies in an attempt to make up for lost time. Their second frenzied coupling finally allowed them to fall asleep in each other's arms.

Tarla awoke with the realization that she hadn't raised the mental block before they fell asleep. She knew he would understand but she'd made him a promise to allow him as much privacy as possible, so she quickly rebuilt the shield between them.

Careful not to wake him, she quietly got out of bed and put on the satiny blue underslip she'd discarded so hastily a few hours before. Stepping out on the balcony for some fresh air, she took in what had become one of her favorite views—the city at night. Somehow it was both visually stimulating and emotionally calming. It exuded the sense of security she'd taken for granted in Innerworld and never felt on Outerworld.

From what they'd heard today however, this was no longer a safe haven. Unless she and her people successfully performed the tasks requested of them, the entire population of Heart could be decimated at any moment.

As terrifying as that possibility was, that wasn't what had awakened her. It was Logan's memories, the ones she had locked away months ago. They had all been freed while she slept with the block removed. But she didn't want to know all those things because of the joining. She wanted him to tell her about his life. She needed him to *want* to share his story with her…even if she knew all of it already.

She sensed a movement behind her a moment before Logan wrapped his arms around her and kissed her bare shoulder. Leaning back against his solid chest, she sighed with the contentment she always felt when he held her like this.

"I reached for you and you weren't there," he

whispered into her ear.

She folded her arms over his. "Sorry. I couldn't sleep."

"Worried?"

"Yes." She took a deep breath and asked the question that had been on her mind for days. "Assuming we've done a good job and we will all survive whatever is about to happen here, do you want to go back to Earth?" She felt his heartbeat quicken as she waited for his answer.

"I'm not sure. It's not like I have a lot of choices. I go back and end up serving a life sentence at Leavenworth. I stay here, and I could be turned into a house pet for somebody like Nadia."

"We could appeal the conviction."

Logan snorted. "Not much chance of that. For every crime I was accused of, there were at least two witnesses who swore I was guilty, and half of them were officers. An appeal would be a waste of time."

"But you're innocent," Tarla countered.

"I know *you* know that," he murmured and kissed the top of her head. "But the *way* you know it isn't exactly admissible in court...at least not in...Outerworld."

"Well then, we could live in Innerworld or relocate to Norona. As my mate, you are welcome wherever I am."

"Good to know I have so many choices," he said with a hint of bitterness.

She turned in his arms. "Are you going to start sulking again?"

He chuckled and kissed her nose. "I don't sulk. Sorry. Sometimes I forget that I'm no longer trapped in a world specially designed to torture me."

"I'll forgive you if you tell me all about your life before we ended up here."

He gave her a curious look and turned her around in his arms again. "You know all there was."

"Humor me. For just a little while, pretend our minds aren't open books. *Tell* me about your life."

"Geez," Logan whispered and hugged her tightly. "You are a pushy little thing." With a bit more prodding, Logan related the bleakness of his childhood and his inability to walk away from an underdog in need of help...and his belief that no woman as incredible as her would ever want to be his wife.

She turned around and placed her hands on the sides of his face. "Close your eyes and take a deep slow breath." As he exhaled she drew his head down for a tender kiss. "There. I just put a big pink bubble around all those awful memories. You don't ever have to relive them. Now tell me about the men who beat you into confessing."

The horror of the days that led up to the trumped-up court martial came flooding back and it took him a minute to comply. "As usual, everything would have been just fine if I'd minded my own business, but I was never very good at that. Just about everyone in the company knew about the drug smuggling ring and suspected there was some spying going on too. It didn't take much for me to find out that my captain and a number of others in our unit were involved, but I needed some solid evidence before I could turn them in.

"One day I saw the captain taking a young Chinese boy into his tent and thought if I got close enough, I might hear something important. Instead, I wound up stopping him from raping the kid at knife point."

Tarla's sharp intake of breath caused him to pause before going on. "I didn't kill him. When the boy ran out, the guy turned the knife on me. We fought. He lost. But he was still very much alive when I went for help. Somebody—I never figured out who—cut his throat before I got back."

"Could it have been the boy?" Tarla asked.

He shrugged. "Maybe, or one of the man's partners who decided to take advantage of an opportunity to be rid of him. I might have been able to save myself from being brought up on a murder charge, if I hadn't opened my mouth about my suspicions to the wrong major. I was locked up so tight after that, it was a week before I found out all the charges being brought against me. Apparently, the whole network was about to be exposed and they needed a scapegoat, fast. I had conveniently offered myself up to them and they didn't waste a second accepting."

"But I heard you pled guilty on all charges. Why didn't you defend yourself?"

He let out a dry laugh. "That's where the scene you saw comes in. I tried to deny everything. And got beaten nearly to death for it. I was informed in no uncertain terms that I could plead guilty and accept a prison sentence with a remote chance of parole someday...or die right there, branded a traitor."

Again she turned around and kissed his pain away. "I love you, Logan. Even if I'd never touched your mind, I would know you were innocent just by watching you all these months. You are a totally unique, wonderful, caring, brilliant man, and everyone here knows it."

He dipped his head to kiss her again, but she touched her fingers to his lips. "Wait. I'm not finished. I started this conversation for a reason and got a little sidetracked. I understand the odds, but I wanted you to know that, even if you decide to go back to Earth, we're a team now. Forever. As long as I'm with you, I'd be happy to help appeal your case, then have two children and a dog and live in a pretty little house with a big yard in a small town."

He kissed her quickly, before she could stop him again. "Not fair. You got that right out of one my fantasies about you. If you're going to make all the decisions, we may as well stay here on Heart." His grin assured her that he was teasing. "But the truth is, I think I'd like Innerworld. Maybe they could change my appearance and train me to become an emissary like you."

She studied his eyes. "Possible. The emissary part I mean, not the makeover. I love you just the way you are."

He grinned. "Even the scars?"

"Maybe they could go, but only because they are reminders of times you don't need to think about any more."

He was about to kiss her again but stepped back. Looking very serious, he closed his eyes for a few seconds. Then he smiled and kissed her again. "I have to admit. That was a pretty cool trick. I haven't actually forgotten any of it, but it's like there was a big chunk of heavy rock inside my chest and now it's gone. How did you do that?"

She smiled. "One of the positive side effects of joining is that we can ease the other's pain. But I only helped. Remember, you're to blame for everything."

He rolled his eyes skyward. "Anyway, it reminds me of what I wanted to talk to you about today. I know you've been as careful as possible to keep the mental block up between us."

"Please don't be upset," she said quickly, guessing what he was going to say. "I was so tired, I just forgot—"

He pressed a finger to her lips. "I know. And now I realize it's got to be hard for you to keep it up all the time. I just wanted you to know I really appreciate it and maybe one of these days—"

She stopped him with the same touch. "I'm just happy you're willing to be open while we're making love. I'd hate to have to use any of my focus for something so mundane."

He ran his hand down her back and gave her bottom a squeeze. "I do love the way you focus."

"I'm very glad to hear that, "she murmured sliding a hand down his body. "Because I'm feeling a powerful need to focus again right now."

Like any devoted Heart man, he was happy to grant her wish.

CHAPTER 22

Tarla looked around the busy space traffic control room with a great deal of pride. She could hardly believe how quickly the last six weeks had flown by. Earth and Heart people alike sent up grateful prayers for every day that passed without any sign of an attack force.

The group of dissidents had been peacefully exiled to the commune after time-release capsules of the antidote were surgically implanted in their brains. Even if they never touched the water, the drug would be periodically dumped into their systems for a full year. By that time, the medics hoped to have perfected a more permanent, behavior-altering solution.

Gianni and the other men staying at the flight center were completely back to normal by their third week off the antidote and had been flying practice missions on a daily basis.

A few problems had shown up when the barrier was first formed, but the last series of tests had gone perfectly.

Though no one had thought it could be done in such a short time span, Heart's new defense system had been fully functional for a week now. A few Heart women had even volunteered for control tower assignments once they were assured their jobs would be non-violent.

Aside from all the activity associated with protecting the planet, another unusual sight had captured everyone's attention. For the first time in recorded history, the second sun had appeared two weeks ago and, instead of vanishing again within a day or two, it had risen every day since. Fortunately, not one crossover had shown up during that time, but it was still odd.

"Tarla?" Charlene called from her monitor station. "Could you come take a look at this?"

Tarla hurried over to her and squinted at the spot of static in the upper left corner of the screen. She touched several keys that should have either cleared the reception or told her what the problem was, but the computer insisted all systems were in good working order. "Kara? Mandy? Are you having any problems?"

"Yeah," Mandy said. "I've got the same snow in the opposite corner."

"Mine's at the top," Kara added.

Tarla went from one station to another checking the monitors for each sector of space then sat back down at her own place. Flickering spots were somewhere at the edge of every monitor.

It took nearly a full minute of intent staring at the screen before she realized the static was expanding and very slowly moving toward the center of the screen. She needed only a microsecond after that to guess what that meant. "Lord help us. Those are ships! There must be thousands of them closing in on the planet from all sides."

She ordered herself to be calm. Everyone else would react however she did. Taking a deep breath, she stood and faced everyone in the room. "All right. No one panic. Remember, they can't get through the barrier, they can only weaken it if they repeatedly hit the same spot. It's our job to notify our pilots of the hit locations so they can repair the spot before it gets hit again.

"Zoli, contact the flight center and get the rest of the pilots up in the air immediately, then sound the general alarm. The rest of you know what your jobs are. You did great during the training exercises, and I know you'll be even better under real pressure. Good luck."

Satisfied that her voice hadn't cracked through her prep speech, she sat back down, opened the channel to the ten pilots in her sector, and reported the situation.

"They're still some distance away, and definitely not using FTL at the moment. The computer is estimating that you should have a visual of them on your screens within an hour. We've already begun transmitting our request that they identify themselves on the universal frequency, but no response yet."

"Are you okay?" Logan asked over the com, his voice filled with concern.

"I'd be better if you were here." She felt him smiling for her in spite of the deadly threat heading right for him.

"I'll be back before you have a chance to miss me."

"I love you."

"I love you too, angel."

"Hey guys," Robin's voice chirped in. "None of that mushy stuff. I'm nervous enough."

"You, my dear, are never nervous," Geoffrey said in a teasing tone. "You thrive on this kind of excitement and you know it."

A chorus of laughter filled Tarla's ears. "Robin's right everybody. No more chatter. This is the real thing."

Just as the computer had called it, the first visual sightings of vessels were reported an hour later. The giant wall screen that had shown nothing but empty space was now filled with the views from each of the hundred patrol ships. The massive fleet of approaching vessels was possibly the most terrifying thing Tarla had ever seen, but she suppressed her fear to keep the rest of the women in the control room calm.

"They still haven't identified themselves or attempted to contact us in any other way," Tarla said over the open channel. "We have to assume we will soon be under attack. Stand by."

She felt her heart pounding as she counted off the seconds to impact.

Suddenly the wall screen displayed a series of fiery bursts as the front line of invaders crashed into the invisible barrier. The control room simultaneously reverberated with incoming reports and outgoing repair orders.

Like everyone else, Tarla correlated locations of hits with pilot positions as quickly as she could. "Logan, 42.2 lat, 26 and 26.5 long. Robin, 44.1 lat, 25.2 and 25.3 long." For nearly fifteen minutes, the explosions occurred at a faster rate than the barrier could be refortified. Then as abruptly as they had begun, they ceased.

When the smoke cleared, there was only a fraction of the original number of enemy ships left intact, but it was still a lot more than Heart had protecting it.

"They're going to try firing now," Logan declared. "Get ready for round two."

Tarla held her breath and punched in the code that

would reverse the polarity of the magnetic field in the barrier. This was the only part Geoffrey had been truly concerned about. Without knowledge of the enemies' weapons, they couldn't be entirely certain that the polarity reversal would do the trick.

The room was completely silent as the women watched every vessel on the screen fire what looked like torpedoes directly at them. Exactly as Geoffrey had intended, the torpedoes ricocheted off the field and went soaring back to their sources with lethal accuracy.

This time, when the smoke cleared, there wasn't a single, whole ship left in sight.

"Withdraw!" Commander Xytoc shouted as soon as he heard the dying screams come to an end. How could a planet of weak, human females destroy nearly every ship in his fleet in a matter of minutes? They weren't supposed to have any defense system! He would see someone squashed for feeding him such misinformation!

There must have been something wrong with the ships themselves, he concluded a moment later. After all, this was supposed to be a surprise attack, but the FTL power had died well before they'd reached their destination, giving the enemy far too much warning of their approach. The scientists would be the first to pay for their error.

Thank the stars for the sonic emitter hidden on the planet eons ago. When the FTL failed, the navigational system was corrupted. Drawing on ancient memories, he had sent out a search signal for the emitter and received a response. The emission was weak but still functioned well enough to guide them into the proper quadrant.

The invasion that he had been convinced would

fulfill Master Po's prediction had turned out to be a disaster. Thus, there must still be another battle in his future. He considered the five ships he had held back from the attack fleet. They didn't amount to much, but it was enough to begin rebuilding his army. In time, he would return. In time, the humanoids *and* this planet would cease to exist.

Meanwhile, he intended to learn everything there was to know about this enemy before striking again. Fortunately the Velid ability to morph into whatever being they saw was the perfect tool to accomplish that goal. He didn't need an army for that phase.

All he needed were a few soldiers hiding in plain sight.

Celebrations were carried on in every nation of Heart for weeks, despite the fact that the citizens learned that *men* had been primarily responsible for their salvation. It had been an overwhelming victory without a single weapon being fired by anyone on Heart. The Earth crossovers were now heroes and heroines, and the media dubbed them "The Guardians."

Eventually the excitement dwindled and the time came to discuss the future with Parisia. A meeting was set up with her, Iris, Brianne and the original twenty members of the defense team.

"There is no question about your having more than fulfilled your part of our bargain," Parisia said. "But we would like to make you a new offer. We need you here on Heart. Surely you can understand that. If you would agree to remain here, in the positions of Guardians, we would make sure your lives were rewarding and comfortable.

"We believe if we acted quickly, we could even find mates for each of your men. A few women have acknowledged their willingness to live with one of Heart's heroes and make certain adjustments rather than learn how to be a heroine themselves."

"What about the other Earth men on the farm?" Logan asked.

Parisia was surprised by his question. "I suppose they could be brought over as well, but they have been taking the antidote for many years. They may only be capable of servitude at this point."

Tarla glanced at Logan and gave him a discreet wink, then said, "Your offer is very kind and we do see your need. We'll discuss it amongst ourselves and present it to the other men, but I seriously doubt if there will be more than a handful of people interested in staying. Going home is all anyone's talked about since the battle."

Parisia closed her eyes for a moment and appeared to be in some discomfort. Iris touched her hand and Parisia composed herself again. "I am very sorry that so many are looking forward to returning to Earth. I truly wish you could."

"What do you mean?" Tarla asked warily. "Don't you intend to hold to your part of the bargain after everything we did for you?"

Parisia's expression was deeply troubled as she slowly shook her head. "It is not a matter of intention. We do not possess the technology to send you back."

"But you said you did!"

"How dare you!"

"You manipulative bitches!"

Iris clapped her hands to stop the insults before the Earth group decided to up their verbal abuse to a physical attack. "*Enough!* No lies were told! We merely promised to allow you to return. We never said we knew how to do it. You came to that conclusion on your own."

Before any of the Earth group could shake off their bewilderment, Parisia made another promise. "I will assign a team of our scientists to devote their full time to the problem, commencing tomorrow."

Iris added, "We have made one observation that could be of use."

Everyone gave her their attention.

"The appearance of the second sun is sporadic and does not always precede a crossover event, so it would seem to have no connection. However, without exception, whenever a crossover occurs, there is *always* a second sun."

Geoffrey shrugged. "We were told that when we first arrived, though the source was hardly reliable. I suppose it could be relevant. But I will insist our people work with your scientific team to be certain progress is being made."

Parisia nodded in agreement.

"And you offered to free the men," Tarla reminded her.

"Yes, I will. Except for those involved in the attempted takeover."

"And you will permit them to choose mates?" Geoffrey asked.

"If they choose willing women," Iris amended. "Details will have to be worked out to everyone's satisfaction."

Logan still looked skeptical. "Freedom from the farm won't mean much if we have to behave as servants."

Parisia paused a moment before responding. "Earth men will be granted the special status of Guardians and protection of our planet will be their responsibility. They will not be medicated in any way as long as they obey our laws."

They spent the rest of the day discussing ways to

best integrate the Earth men into Heart society with the least amount of disruption, but the problems facing them were too numerous to solve in a single day.

Before Parisia left, she called Tarla aside. "There is another deception I must confess to." She put her hand in her pocket and brought out a tiny velvet bag. Discreetly passing it to Tarla, she explained, "I have had this since you arrived. Because it was determined to be a device rather than jewelry, I decided to hold onto it. I don't know if it is of any use to you here, but I thought you might still like to have it back."

Tarla's eyes widened when she peeked inside the bag and saw her Innerworld ring. She had to fight the urge to give the delicate woman a huge hug of gratitude. Instead, she slipped the bag into her own pocket and respectfully bowed her head.

That evening, after Logan and Tarla were finally alone, he asked, "Disappointed?"

"Of course. I'm disappointed that Parisia tricked us. I guess I can't blame her though. In this case, the end truly justified the means. I'm also disappointed that I can't take you to Innerworld yet, but I have faith that wherever we are, it's where we're supposed to be." She wrapped her arms around his waist and rested her head on his chest.

Logan knew exactly what she meant. After all the lonely years, he'd finally found the place where he belonged—in Tarla's arms.

And it was time he showed her how much her love truly meant to him. He took her hands from his waist and guided her to the cube couch. "Sit. *Please.*"

She eyed him curiously but sat down.

He paced back and forth twice before explaining. "I've given this a lot of thought and I've finally made a decision. Once in a while when I wake up in the morning the mental block between us is down. I recognize what it is now and I don't get freaked out, but it's really hard to deal with. I mean, I can't think of any one thing because there's so much mess in my brain."

When he saw the worried expression on Tarla's face, he quickened his speech. "But there was also this unbelievably good feeling because I could feel you inside me...and I loved that part. You once said you could teach me how to put the block up myself. Can you also teach me to manage having two brains at the same time?"

Her broad smile and head bobbing assured him she could. But when she started to rise, he held up a finger. "Stay." Only because he said it with a grin did she let the order stand.

"And if you teach me to put the block up will I be able to keep a secret from you?"

Skipping over what his speech implied, she asked, "What kind of secrets?"

"Secrets like this one." He took a small box out of his pocket and knelt down at her feet. "I know you believe we are already joined as one, but you know that wasn't the way I wanted a commitment from you. Maybe I'm a little old-fashioned, but I still believe two people being bonded for life should be a little more romantic. So here goes.

"Tarla Yan, I love you with all my heart, my body and my mind and I want to spend the rest of forever with you by my side *and* in my head. I'm ready to accept all the things that go along with us being joined according to your customs, but I would consider myself the luckiest man on Earth, Heart and every other planet in the universe, if you would accept the Terran custom of being my wife. Will you marry me?" He opened the box and showed her a small ring made of Heart's reflective, pink metal.

Tears welled up in Tarla's eyes and she was suddenly so choked up, she couldn't utter a sound.

Logan swiped a teardrop from her cheek with his thumb. "I actually need an answer for this to work. Unless you'd rather I tickle it out of you."

With a squeal, she launched herself toward him with such force they both landed on the floor. "*Yes!* Yes, yes, yes, yes, yes, I will marry you, Logan McKay." She held out her left hand and he slid the ring on her finger.

She hugged him so tight, he tickled her ribs to get her to loosen her hold.

"Are you certain about the mind-melding?" she asked as seriously as she could manage under the circumstances.

"Absolutely."

She sat up, suddenly filled with energy. "We could get started right now if you'd like."

He rose, pulled her to her feet then picked her up. "Tomorrow will be soon enough. We have much more important things on our agenda for the rest of tonight, like carrying you over the threshold and consummating our marriage and having a honeymoon."

As he closed and locked the bedroom door behind them, she was more than willing to do things the Terran way.

EPILOGUE

Innerworld, Terra Date 2059 A.D.

Roman Locke ordered himself to relax, unclench his jaws and open his fists.

Drek! He was a grown man. The two-year apprenticeship he'd just completed certified him as a tracker who could take on solitary assignments. So why did a request for a meeting with his parents make him feel like a little boy waiting for permission to go play?

Yes, they were the Co-Governors of Norona's most important colony. But here, in the home where he'd grown up, they were still just Mother and Father. Yet, he couldn't help but wonder if they were keeping him waiting to remind him of their ability to control his future, regardless of his maturity.

Fairly certain they'd requested this meeting to discuss his potential career choices and, knowing they couldn't possibly want him heading in the direction he'd already chosen, he had his valid arguments ready to present.

"Sorry to keep you waiting, darling," Aster said as she rushed into the sitting room and kissed her son on the forehead.

Romulus gave his son's hand a brief but firm shake. "Have you had dinner yet?"

"Actually, I thought you just wanted to talk for a few minutes, so I made plans. What's going on?"

"Pretty much what we predicted. Outerworld is in chaos, so naturally we have to make daily adjustments in schedules. The Outerworld treaties were signed nearly a year ago but there are still plenty of skirmishes and disagreements over boundaries. Our emissaries are on constant alert—"

"And they are doing an incredible job of keeping us posted," Aster continued. "But there are simply not enough of them to be at all the hot spots all the time."

"What about the one who used to work for you?" Roman asked.

Romulus's expression darkened. "Tarla Yan. Not only was she my assistant, she was a very good friend. They never found a trace of the aircraft she was on. It's still a complete mystery." He sighed and shook his head. "She was an exceptional emissary and extremely courageous. Right now we could use at least a hundred more like her, instead we were just informed of transfer requests from four more emissaries in key positions. None of them had signed on for hazardous duty."

Aster glanced at Romulus then said, "There's also talk of the Americas undergoing a major political realignment to balance out the China Compromise. It could be the answer but we really need more eyes and ears to make sure we have the opportunity to intercede if it becomes necessary."

Despite the Noronian laws regarding non-interference with the Terran culture, Roman was aware of several instances when interference had been necessary to save the planet. One of those instances had involved his parents.

He saw the two of them share another glance and knew they were having a telepathic conversation, made possible by their joining. His sister, Shara, was able to read minds and send silent suggestions to whomever she wished. But he'd never developed any telepathic or other exceptional mental abilities.

"Your mother has suggested that we are unnerving you and I should get to the point. Have you given thought to which career path you'd like to follow?"

Roman had expected at least another half-hour discussion of public matters before getting to the private one he was dreading. "Of course. I've given several paths serious consideration."

"Was being an Outerworld emissary one of them?" Aster asked bluntly.

Roman's eyes widened with surprise. *Did they already know?* He did a quick mental scramble to deliver his convincing points. "I know you were hoping I'd get on an administrative track, but—"

Romulus interrupted him with a wave of his hand. "Understand, we both would be thrilled if you chose to follow any path that kept you nearby. But as Governors, we must always consider what is best for Norona."

Aster smiled, albeit somewhat shakily. "We've been told how skilled and creative you are and, obviously, no one knows better than we do how exceptional you are in a number of other ways." She sighed and directed the conversation back to her mate.

"What we were thinking, if it's acceptable to you, is to appoint you as a *transient* emissary in Outerworld. It's a bit unusual but considering the current shortage it seems to be a reasonable solution. Rather than be assigned to a specific station with an established cover, you could be moved to wherever an observer was needed most. Obviously, your unique abilities would be a major advantage in those situations."

Roman could hardly believe his ears! They had just offered him exactly what he wanted without his having to deliver a word of his prepared argument. Suddenly he realized this was far too easy. "You knew, didn't you?"

His father shrugged; his mother smiled and said, "Of course. All you've ever wanted to do was be like Falcon and we knew we couldn't force you to hide your, uh, *unique abilities* forever. Though you might not believe it, your father and I can be very logical at times, especially where your happiness is concerned."

Roman rose and gave them both warm hugs that left no doubt about how happy he was. Not only was he going to be an Outerworld emissary, he was being given permission to use his special talents in his work.

Finally, after years of existing in the shadow of his politically powerful parents, Roman Locke was free to start living life on his own terms. Acknowledging how hard this was for them however, he made a silent promise to repay them by solving the mystery of Tarla Yan's disappearance.

Turn the page for an

excerpt from

ROMAN

Innerworld Affairs Series
Book Six

Marilyn Campbell

Roman stared at the door to Erin's townhouse as though the answer to his dilemma were written across it. Since the last light had been turned off an hour ago, he had no doubt she was asleep by now. He could slip in, locate the cryptocube and be gone without leaving a trace of his visit. If she happened to wake up, she still wouldn't know he was there as long as he maintained his invisible mode.

Or would she?

He had already detected that she sensed *something* every time he had gotten close to her. And his tracker training kept telling him she was more than simply an intuitive Terran female. Then again, he found her so appealing, there was the possibility that he was subconsciously doing something to attract her attention.

He imagined his trainer, Falcon, frowning with disapproval and he stopped wasting time. The next second he switched from invisible to incorporeal long enough to pass through the wooden door into Erin's unlit foyer. It was times like this when he wished he had Falcon's gift of night-vision, or even his sister's telepathic abilities, but he had to work with the one unique gift he had.

As soon as his eyes adjusted to the near-darkness, Roman quickly scanned the entire downstairs, not really expecting to find the cube so easily. As he started up the stairs, he heard muffled cursing then the sounds of rushing water. He grinned. This was even better than her being asleep. At the doorway to the master bedroom, he hesitated a moment to make sure she was taking a shower.

As soon as he stepped inside her room, his gaze was caught by the rumpled sheets on the large bed. Then he noticed the distinct scent of sexual activity. He had seen her go into the house alone and hadn't considered the possibility of her having a partner waiting for her. The professional part of his brain both scolded him for the oversight and acknowledged how her being distracted, along with the noise of the shower, would give him an advantage in his search. Unfortunately, the only things of interest he discovered were a recently-used, electronic phallus on her nightstand and a collection of sexual aids in the drawer. Though the search for the cube turned out to be futile, the personal part of his brain demanded he hang around to see what sort of individual earned Erin's intimate attentions.

Roman held his breath as she came out of the bathroom dripping wet and stood in front of the air conditioning vent. He could make out the curves of her silhouette and confirm that no one else had shared the shower with her.

She was alone after all...and obviously very, very hot.

Hands behind her head, she raised the mass of tangled hair and turned around to let the air cool her neck and back. He ordered himself to leave immediately. Not only was he invading her privacy, the shadowed vision before him was as erotic as anything he'd ever seen in full light.

He started to turn away, but then her arms moved and he could tell she was running her hands down her body, caressing her breasts and skimming down her stomach. She moaned softly and he knew without clearly seeing what part of her she had just stroked. His sex swelled in response and he failed to withhold a sharp intake of breath.

Instantly Erin's eyes opened wide and she yanked a sheet off the bed. *"Who the hell are you? How'd you get in here?"*

Roman's head was filled with possible responses but two thoughts took precedence. His unexpected arousal had made him fully visible to her. And her eyes were glowing…just like Falcon's.

"You don't need to hurt me. Just tell me what you want."

He noted that once the sheet was wrapped around her, she was able to speak in her normally calm, confident voice. Her experience as a profiler had kicked the panic right out the window.

"I would never hurt you, Erin," he said sincerely. "You are far too important. I do apologize for the intrusion. I only came to retrieve something that belongs to me."

"Don't move," she ordered flatly and kept her golden gaze fixed on him as she turned on a lamp. In a heartbeat she reached beneath the mattress and had a hand gun pointed at him.

Roman considered dramatically pushing aside the edges of his longcoat to show off his two holstered laser pistols. Instead, he sighed and made himself invisible.

"What the—" She jerked her head from side to side.

As soon as he snatched the gun from her hands, it disappeared also.

"Where are you? How did you do that?"

Retreating to a spot beyond her reach, he replied, "If you promise not to point any more weapons at me, I will explain."

She huffed and arranged the sheet more securely around her. "Fine. But I want to see who's talking to me."

Roman became visible, took off his cowboy hat and gave her his friendliest smile. "Howdy, ma'am. The name's Roman Locke and I'm a Texas Ranger Specialist—"

"Hold it right there." She glided slowly toward him, wrinkling her nose while sniffing the air. When she was within inches of him, she gasped. "It's *you!*" Backing away too quickly, she tripped on the sheet and landed at his feet.

Rather than helping her up, he sat down. "It appears I'm not the only one in this room with a secret identity."

"That's ridiculous," she retorted with a smirk. "My identity is public knowledge. Which reminds me, you called me Erin but I'm sure we've never met. I also realize you're the one who's been stalking me. And now I know why I could never see you!"

"But you recognized my scent, right?"

"I admit to a keen sense of smell."

"You also have exceptional night vision. I saw the reflective glow in your eyes."

She let out another huff then clucked her tongue. "How is it that *you* broke into my house but *I'm* the one being interrogated?"

"It's okay, Erin. My trainer is half Felan. Are you empathic as well?"

"I have no idea what you're talking about. Or why

I'm sitting here, wearing only a sheet, while a maniacal cowboy holds me hostage in my own bedroom." She swiped perspiration off her upper lip. "And why the hell is it so damn hot in here?" She tried to rise but he grasped her hand and she went completely still.

He should never have touched her. The heat radiating from her body was nearly impossible to block but the bewilderment in her eyes kept him from melting into it. She began rocking back and forth, her breathing altered to short pants and her hands clenched into fists between her thighs. "You really don't understand, do you?"

"*No!* I don't understand any of this. Not you or your intoxicating smell or your disappearing act or why my eyes glow. But most of all I don't understand why the hell I've turned into some damn alley cat in heat!"

Roman almost managed to hide the smile he was feeling. With the lightest touch of his finger under her chin, he got her to meet his gaze. "Well, ma'am, I do believe I can help you with *all* of that."

ROMAN

available in print and ebook

THE
INNERWORLD AFFAIRS
SERIES

Romulus
Falcon
Gallant
Gabriel
Logan
Roman

MARILYN CAMPBELL has been published in the genres of suspense, erotic thrillers, futuristic, time-travel, paranormal, erotic and lighthearted contemporary romances, non-fiction metaphysical works and has had a screenplay produced. A true thrill-junkie, she has jumped out of an airplane, raced around the Indy 500 track, driven solo throughout the United States and believes a great roller coaster ride can cure whatever ails her. She currently resides in Massachusetts with her daughter and their four-legged companions, Milk-Dud and Sweetie.